THE
DORCHESTER
FIVE

PETER MANUS

DIVERSIONBOOKS

Also by Peter Manus

Fickle

Diversion Books
A Division of Diversion Publishing Corp.
443 Park Avenue South, Suite 1008
New York, New York 10016
www.DiversionBooks.com

For more information, email info@diversionbooks.com

First Diversion Books edition August 2017.
Print ISBN: 978-1-63576-165-8
eBook ISBN: 978-1-62681-714-2

To Deb, my voice of reason, and Kathryn, a beautiful reader.

PROLOGUE

I am Nightingale—

What follows is the story of a boy who was driving around Boston in his brother's auto when a lady came out into the street. He hit her. She died on the spot.

Before her death, the lady had been one of the church grannies you see everywhere in Dorchester, Roxbury, and the like, this particular granny being of the brittle, skin-and-bone variety, with the half-rim spectacles and the humped back and the little phrases like "praise be" and "Lord willin'" spat out like cusswords at the tail end of whatever else she may say. Her name was Hepsibah Oleander Tidwell, called Oleander by those who adored her, which, once she was dead, included just about every black person in Dorchester and certainly every black politician on Beacon Hill. One stands up for one's own—la fidélité du clan—I find no fault in that. At the time the boy hit her, this Oleander was dressed in her "best"—a bright yellow suit trimmed in white piping, plus gloves and a double row of beads round her neck that such ladies favor. Also a hat with netting across the rim. She was carrying a shiny handbag in one hand and her Bible in the other—the bag flew off, but she held onto that Bible. No doubt she realized in that instant that she would be passing from swaying and singing about the Blessed One to meeting the very Guy face to face. She got hit across from St. Brigid's, the side entrance with the spiked gate. You could see it all quite well in the video they played at the trial, regardless of the jiggling. This was some years ago, before every cell had vid, but a guy had one out and caught much of the action.

The boy's car was one of the ancient bugs, a '97 punch buggy to be precise, faded aqua in color, an unnoticeable thing—not a car you would imagine could kill someone. It looked like the old lady rolled over the hood, her weight mostly on a shoulder, and when she disappeared it was head first, feet following, to land on the side of her face. This, as it happened, transected her spinal cord at the base of the skull above the fifth cervical vertebra, resulting in spinal shock and, as I mentioned above, instant death. The kid did not know much, but he must have known that he had, in fact, just killed that old lady.

The kid's name was Jake Rodney Culligan. We will call him Jakey. He was, in truth, a bit stoned at the time of the accident, or so his people concluded when talking about it later, as it was his habit when he was driving his brother's car to dip into the ashtray and smoke the nub of any joint he might happen upon. Ashtray roach belonged to the person behind the wheel—such was Jakey's ethical code. As a result, he may not have had much of his wits about him, and this explains why he panicked and tried to get away after he hit the old lady.

And this, then, would be when the guys surrounded his car and started beating on it. Of course Jakey locked the doors and would not get out. I mean, we are all aware of what your average street mob will do when presented with a righteous excuse to beat up some punk, are we not? Plus it was a hot summer day, long into the afternoon, and everyone was just hanging around looking for a reason to get mean. L'ennui tue—the boredom kills—oui? So you know that if they could have got at him, they would have murdered Jakey Culligan on the spot for thinking he could get away with a hit-and-run on the neighborhood granny. That is a fact, and all the neighborhood morons hanging around watching would have cheered, and in fact did cheer, right into the camera, too, as the event grew nastier.

So all these angry guys yelled at Jakey and kicked at the windows of the VW and rocked it so that the tires lifted from the street. He tried to call his brother on his cell, but he could not reach him. As it happens, his brother was in the process of stealing some thirty cases of Jameson whiskey from a truck in Arlington Heights. This was a random, "just-happy-to-be-there" felony, not material to this story except that big brother Dylan had his cell muted. Jakey left a voice message in which he sounded quite desperate. Unfortunately, he dropped the "n-bomb," perhaps twice—something the lawyers enjoyed playing endlessly during the trial, although it was of little relevance, as no one outside the car could possibly have heard him. Perhaps they were intimating that Jakey hit the old lady because she was black—such rubbish. Of course, his language is not to be excused, but I would like to know who wouldn't lose it under such circumstances, particularly when a bit high and talking to his own blood? Also, I could add that in the video, although the guys beating on the car were not of one particular race or another, you do see one very dark fellow up on the hood of the VW, screaming as if crazed and kicking at the windshield with both feet, and inexcusable words do come to the mind uninvited. The truth is that the hideous words entered the thoughts of every man in that courtroom, white and dark alike. This I know, for I was there, and I observed this.

After the angry mob tipped the VW, the fuel line breached and the car went up in flames—actually, just a touch of flames, but a great deal of thick, yellow smoke. The kid inside smacked his head and passed out while the morons cheered. You do not see Jakey hit his head in the video, but that is what the doctor said. On the stand, she said there had been physical trauma resulting in a subdural hematoma followed by prolonged hypoxia. This meant that Jakey was brain damaged with severe burns to over fifty percent of his body. Who could doubt this, looking across the courtroom at him sitting there?

So now we have reached the end of Jakey Culligan's story... almost. But this unfortunate man-child is not the primary subject of this memoir. This is the story of the righteous mob—or at least the five men who got charged—the "Dorchester Five," in what we might call the "media-speak." These guys got off with slaps on the wrist for what they did to Jakey Culligan, while he got shuffled off to live out his existence at his ma's house on Fifth Street in Southie. Here, we must admit, Jakey's life was not altogether glum. After all, he had three prepared meals per day, which arrived in a van, sealed in plastic, piping hot.

He had daily massages and whirlpool baths, light-resistance weight training, and long, aimless wheelchair walks in the windy harborside park. He also had the very best in home entertainment systems and amassed a huge library of favorite films that he would watch over and over, never tiring—grand horror classics, such as Faces of Death, Dr. Giggles, Tokyo Gore Police, Ichi the Killer, Twisted Sisters, The Midnight Meat Train, House of 1000 Corpses, Nekromantik, Man Bites Dog, Slaughtered Vomit Dolls, Strange Circus, *and many, many more. And so this brain-damaged and disfigured fellow lived out his life in peaceful coexistence with his loving ma, who was most often passed out snoring on the couch, or else hanging out on the front steps with a case of Labatts and a couple of the other neighborhood lushes, smoking the countless Pall Malls (and bitching about how the container flats from the docks roar by non-stop, which they did not used to do back in the day, but the pols, oh how those fucks will screw the good folks of Southie every time!).*

Still, this is an inspirational story, because after eight years, when Jakey finally died quite young (a near inevitability given his condition), someone—patient, wary, and wily, like all predators—set about settling the score with the guys responsible for Jakey having lost out on the life full of hope and chance and lust and rage that every young waster craves and deserves. So in a way it is an art piece, much like a film from Jakey's own collection, this tale of five killings.

All that, yes, but now I must cut the pies. This is labor that requires undivided concentration, as the servings must be uniform in size, for otherwise our charges may grow disgruntled. Perhaps dangerous. Well, we know how guys can get when they believe themselves to have been unjustly slighted, do we not? One thousand peanut butter creme pies—eight identical wedges each. And so we maintain order, we bearers of the blade. One delicate, dedicated slash at a time.

Très sincèrement,
Nightingale

ONE

I am Nightingale—

Elliot enters The Underground and pauses to observe the vast, low-slung space held up by bulging pillars. The room has been fitted out with a scattering of scarred pub tables and a thirty-foot bar, manned by bullish men in vests and white sleeves who splash out drinks with more grace than their physiques might suggest. The place is jammed with guys in ties and ladies in slacks, all fresh off work and roaring with gaiety as they gulp at cocktails and poke their thumbs at their cells.

Elliot feels a little self-conscious, I notice, a little old—it's new for him, this question about his stamina. Still, as he descends into the throng, I sense the corners of his lips twitching and catch a ghost of a dimple, creasing his cheek. Ah, yes, Elliot knows the game. He is a womanizer—*un coureur de jupons*—by instinct. Indeed, he is here to meet me, although he has not yet realized this.

He knocks a few shoulders, just for kicks, glad that he made the last-minute decision to drop in. It is energizing to know that people are out, second wind in full tilt, on a weeknight, looking to score. It revives his faith in the human animal.

He is thinking this when a blonde in the crowd twirls about, giggling madly. She is one of the drones from his firm's trust department, common and buck-toothed but decidedly arousing. She spots him and her hand goes up, fingers twiddling. Then she hesitates as her mind clicks in on the fact that he might not know her, or at least might not choose to acknowledge her while out. A man hovers behind her, presumably the lothario who got her spinning on her heel. The man is young like she is, with a weak chin and a double-breasted glen plaid suit, of all the getups. His eyes bead in on Elliot even as he laughs forcedly, as if to remind the girl of his presence. Elliot remembers that she has a little-girl name—Patsy? Dee-Dee? He makes his way over; he is tall with a solid build, and although he is always studiously polite, it is other men who give way. The girl's eyes harden with interest.

"How are you?" he asks casually. Elliot has never used a clever line on a girl; the idea does not appeal to him.

"Mr. Becker," she says, still sober enough to smother the "fancy meeting you here" that wants to bubble out. "Penny. From the trust department?" Her accent allows him to capture her entire life growing up: the oily stink of the airport in her nostrils, brutal father, sadsack mother, slew of gum-cracking girlfriends, and the growing conviction that maybe she had it in her to sleep her way toward something better. The tip of her tongue rubs the rims of her freshly lasered pearlies.

He starts a meaningless conversation, at the same time dropping his gaze to her chest, just for a millisecond, just a flutter of his eyelids as if reacting to a mote of dust, but enough to signal her that, even if he had not placed her on sight or known she was alive before this moment, he is interested in bedding her tonight. She sips, her eyes locked on his as she nods along with whatever he is saying, her body taut, game for whatever he has in mind. He knows that she is checking out the grooves that score his forehead and the grey that laces his sideburns and that she approves of these signs of maturity because they mean that, unlike men her own age, he will not care whether she admires his foreplay. He will not want her to sit waiting for the call he will not make tomorrow. He will bed her, slowly and competently, and then allow her to go home and snatch a few hours of sleep without feeling like a whore for being satisfied with exactly that. He glances over her shoulder at the other man, reminding her.

"Oh," she says sweetly, making as if to step to one side, but barely. "This is Todd. Todd, Mr. Becker." She does not explain.

The younger man tries to prove something or other with a crushing handshake. Elliot had thought that this feint at machismo had gone out of style, but maybe it's back. Todd's palm is soggy from his beer bottle. He barks out whatever his last name is and then something else. The name of his firm, perhaps? Why the hell would Elliot want to know that?

"What are you drinking?" Elliot says pleasantly. "May I get you one?" He includes both of them in the offer. The girl is clearly thrown—should they not be sending Todd off on this errand? But she hangs in there, lifting her nearly full glass to her chin and rolling her eyes like marbles. Todd, likewise, displays his bottle, his wet-lipped smile smug.

Feeling pleasantly detached, Elliot makes his way toward the bar, where he jockeys for position. He is scanning the top-shelf options when, finally, he spots me. Actually, it is more that he spots a bit of leopard print and one grey eye, rather tired, and a pair of decidedly down-turned lips painted a bleary shade of mauve with a dark mole just off to one side, all of these slivers of womanhood fractured in the mirrors that form the backdrop of the bar. He ducks his head, squinting, pressing hard against the man to his right and automatically placing a placating hand on the guy's shoulder. He spots me again! I am sitting six or seven stools from where he stands. My ashy hair shields my face. The leopard print belongs to a gauzy scarf that wraps around my neck and trails down my back. He can barely make out more than the melancholy lips and the mole, but those are the parts of me he wants to see again.

He shakes his head as a bartender makes eye contact, then maneuvers his way over to me. Other bodies pass between us, but by the time he gets to me he has seen what there is to see—a woman with elbows on the bar and rounded back, wearing some sort of quilted suit, a skirt and buttoned-to-the-high-collar jacket in grey suede that attempts to double for work and after-work and thus more or less fails at both. My pumps are leopard print, matching the scarf. As he slides into the narrow space beside me, I turn and he smells the odor of freshly smoked cigarette, and suddenly he wants one even though it's been years.

"I don't mean to crowd you," he apologizes.

"Think nothing of it."

He notes my voice, low and unaffected. My glance, too, is indifferent. It occurs to him that my face, aside from the bee-stung lips, is not interesting, although I am sexually appealing nevertheless. My dangling earrings gleam from within my thick, colorless hair.

He says, "But don't you know me?"

I glance sideways.

"I'm sure we know one another," he says.

"I do not think so," I say without enthusiasm. He catches a slight accent—something nasal about my vowels.

"I'm quite certain," Elliot says, casting his mind back. "I never forget a face."

"Let me guess," I say. "I am Joan of Arc. And from the moment you saw me you pictured me nude and tied to a stake."

He jerks his head back, then laughs spontaneously. In part, he is impressed that a woman as unanimated as I would pop off a remark that cheeky. "Please don't misunderstand," he explains. "I really do know you from somewhere. Were you ever…?"

"Unlikely," I interrupt. I allow him the tiniest flicker of my eyebrow. "I don't travel much," I say in acquiescence. Then I meet his gaze. "Now is your chance."

He frowns innocently. "My chance at what?"

"At getting what it is you are here for."

He smiles, charmed. "And what, pray tell, am I here for?"

I tip my forehead toward the bar. "A drink, I would have supposed."

Elliot looks around; sure enough, the bartender is handy. He orders a whiskey and throws a thumb in my direction. "And another of whatever my friend here is drinking."

"I am just leaving," I say. "Settle up?" The bartender nods and turns away.

"Look, don't run off on account of me," Elliot says. "You don't want to talk, I can collect my drink and move along. I'm a very good boy like that."

He watches me shell some bills off a roll I have half-extracted from an evening bag. My nails are lacquered a dark purple, like my lips, with the tips left unvarnished and the edges cut flat across in the European fashion. The makeup on my eyelids is a violet-grey, and rather laid on. The mole just off my mouth might be a decal. It occurs to him that people may snicker behind my back—the office character, dwelling in a time warp. He watches me thumb the bills, catching them smoothly between two fingers and extracting them without disturbing the roll. How does he know me? He senses that his sketchy memory of me has to do with himself, and thus it interests him greatly.

"I am quite sure that you are brilliant at taking the hints," I assure him. I drop my bills on the bar and snap my bag. "In fact, I am sure that you are brilliant at all things you do." I swivel past him. "Nevertheless, at the moment I need a smoke."

"A smoke?" he repeats stupidly.

I shrug. "Not nearly my greatest vice."

"Heartening to know," he banters back. "And where do you commit this particular sin?"

"There is a designated area." I raise my chin for a moment, indicating the ceiling. "On thirty-two. A roof patio." I pause as if struck by this. "One trifles with one's mortality under the stars. *La destinée,* eh?" I smile, fleetingly, for the first time.

Elliot smiles back, encouraged, but he is not the one to blunder back into the ring at a flicker of the crimson muleta, and as I drop from my stool, he eases round to face the bar. His whiskey has arrived. It is chilly, the old-fashioned cubes melded together. He raises his glass and sees me in the mirror. I am looking back at him, my expression bemused. He turns.

"Maybe I can handle one more after all. Are you still buying?"

"What's it going to be?"

"An Irish coffee. Make it a double, won't you? It will be chilly up there."

When Elliot turns with the steaming glass, I am walking off, glancing over my shoulder at him, the smile still playing on my lips. Beyond me, he spots the trust department girl eyeing him expectantly, her dog-in-heat still at heel. He smiles and winks across the expanse. On her part, she spies the two drinks in his hands, sticks out her skinny little tongue, then turns her attention to the lucky lad who has earned her affection for the evening.

Unburdened by the idea that he may have inflicted some momentary wound, Elliot turns back to his new conquest. But I have disappeared. He scans the crowd, moving forward with his elbows out to protect his drinks, and happens to go eye-to-eye with a wolf wearing an ascot and a suit with a tight silhouette. The man palms his hair and looks away sharply, as men will do when they are caught displaying curiosity in another male. Elliot, without formulating a thought, follows the man's gaze in time to catch a glimpse of leopard print gauze as I exit through the doors to the hotel lobby. Elliot sees no reason to abandon the chase.

Out in the lobby, he is momentarily conscious of the fact that he is toting a couple of alcoholic beverages and, strictly speaking, ought to be waylaid for a polite scolding. But he is not the type minions take on. So he strides across the busy carpet, comfortable in his eight-hundred-dollar pinstripe. He scores an empty elevator and rides straight up, all paranoia squelched by his image in the antique-mirrored doors. Death is near, but he does not sense this. The Irish coffee vibrates, sending its acid aroma up to his nostrils.

On the thirty-second floor of the Hampstead Arms, an emergency spotlight aims a cone of light down at a stark circle of flowered carpet in front of the elevator. Otherwise the place is black. Elliot steps off. The doors thump behind him. To his left, a pair of massive doors—a ballroom, no doubt. To his right, a door is open, vague light oozing from beyond. I am calling him, you see, though his ears hear nothing.

Elliot saunters through to a small room, its bar stripped to the shelves. City lights do not quite pierce the windows, creating a murky half-glow that causes the draped tables to shimmer. At the far end, the French doors are ajar. Elliot can discern a terrace, one or two wrought-iron tables with stools arranged around them. A glass ashtray glimmers in the night, a yellow spark playing above it. Yes, he has found me, tapping at my precious cigarette. I turn away as he steps onto the patio.

"Is that my Irish, then?" I ask over my shoulder.

He crosses the tiles, feeling the night breeze riffle his hair. It is chilly, as I forewarned. He leans a palm against the stone railing, careful to keep his clothes from touching it, sips his whiskey and surveys the city. It is not a particularly scenic venue. Tremont Street looks gridlocked; he can hear the distant honks and, fleetingly, an angry voice that disappears into the air exactly as it reaches him. Still, there is something erotic about the scene. A hidden den of eros above the cruel, cold city—that manner of tripe.

I gesture with the cigarette. He shakes his head.

"I'm Elliot, by the way." He offers his hand.

I touch his palm with icy fingers. "Florrie," I say.

The name means nothing to him. Still, I pronounce it with my vague lilt and am more attractive to him for doing so. He watches as I expel smoke from my mouth; it rolls forth in splashy clots, evaporating before it can douse my chest.

"You've lost your scarf," he observes.

I gesture with my coffee. He spots it, tangled among the flourishes of the stone cornice that trims the edge of another level of the roof, down a story from where we stand. "You would not mind retrieving it?" I ask.

He snorts. "Then you blow me and we'll call it an evening."

I jerk my head as if to toss the smoke I exhale over my shoulder. "You're on."

He laughs, liking me for not shying away from his schoolboy humor. "Afraid I'm not that hungry for it," he says amicably.

"A shame. There was a time when you would have risked life

15

and limb for some lipstick round your manhood, eh?" I pause to duck my head and light myself a fresh cigarette. I fail twice, my lighter sending harmless spatters of sparks into the breeze.

"May I?"

I look up at him, then pass over lighter and cigarette. He rolls the cigarette between his lips, enjoying the feeling, then cups his palm and defies the wind by firing it up on his first try. He passes it back to me, ignoring the fact that I touch his hand with mine a little longer than necessary during the exchange.

"You are the—how do we call it—the self-made man," I say.

"What makes you think that?"

"A man does not carry himself like you do when it is family money, and so…"

He interrupts with a sharp laugh. "I strike you as having crept in through the kitchen?"

I answer logically. "You carry yourself as if you have had the opportunity to discover your capabilities. You are cavalier, and you have earned it."

He smiles. "Never thought of a supercilious attitude as something a person rates."

"Mmm, but it is," I say assuredly. "So tell me, Elliot, what made you who you are? I do not mean your life story. I mean…" I circle a hand, "the big break. The event you knew would jumpstart your career, propel you to where you are today."

He thinks, studying the city windows beyond me, then bringing his gaze down to my eyes. When he speaks, his tone is even and casual. "You're working," he says simply.

I am taken aback—so this is how he interprets my dead-on Jeanne Moreau! After a moment, I recover. "We are all working for something, Elliot, are we not?"

He gestures back at the hotel, equally pleasant. "What, do you have some sort of arrangement with the hotel detective?"

"I've learned my way around," I say opaquely, turning to gaze at the city.

He snaps a finger. "The guy watching when you left the bar.

Has a lot of styling going on, maybe a goatee and some sort of neck scarf. That the house dick?"

I murmur noncommittally. In truth, I have no idea who he is talking about.

He chuckles. "Never realized a stuffy joint like this would allow hookers. But I guess men who stay in nine-hundred-dollar rooms have the same needs as anyone."

"Men are men," I agree. "Look, Elliot, I can assure you that I meant you no insult—*pas du tout*. I merely came across an attractive man who looked like he could use some company."

He is irked by my trade patter, but lets it slide as he realizes that in fact he is not wholly uninterested. In any event, he is all the more curious about where he'd set eyes on me before. Had I been on the arm of one of his partners at a function? Elliot is not a man who has natural allies. Blackmail of an informal nature is certainly in his line.

I sigh. "I will leave you to your thoughts," I say, easing my weight off the wall.

"You asked about my big break," he says into the night sky.

I pause. "I did."

"Probably less long ago than you'd think. Spent the first decade of my law career kicking around as appointed counsel to lowlifes I wouldn't have recognized the day after I got them their plea. Graduated to rich chumps and their controlled substances. This case marked the end of all that. Got in on something big, used the opportunity, and haven't looked back since."

"Intriguing." I slip back to my former position. "What sort of case was this?"

"Assault trial," he says. He glances at me. "I was hoping for attempted murder at the time, but it turned out even better as it was. Heard of the Dorchester Five?"

"I have read that name, certainly, but it was quite recently."

"Yeah, you're talking about the drive-by shooting down by Savin Hill," he says. "Con just out of Walpole took a bullet in the skull, maybe six weeks ago. Terence D'Amante was one of the

Five, so the local stations revived the old story. Personally, I barely remembered the man's name until I read it in the papers, and I sure as hell didn't realize he'd been inside all these years. World's better off with him dead, frankly. Guy was an animal."

"But the Dorchester Five case itself," I steer him gently.

"Short version: eight years ago some schmuck ran over the neighborhood saint and then tried to blow the scene. Crowd turned, car tipped and burned. Mess all around."

"I remember now," I say in a low, distant voice. "Those men were local heroes."

He scoffs. "You flip a car with someone inside, don't expect a parade. You should have seen this kid. One of his ears gone, half his face a molten mess. Like out of *Friday the 13th*."

"*Nightmare on Elm Street*," I correct him automatically. "Freddy Krueger resembles the burn victim. In *Friday the 13th*, Jason wears a hockey mask." I may be circling in on my first kill—a delicate proposition indeed—but horror was Jakey's personal ballad.

"Right," he says, not caring. "Anyway, at trial, we played some vids of the kid from a couple weeks before he hit the old bird. Happy as a pup, lip-synching to his favorite bubblegum pop with his shirt off. What was that song—'Numa Numa' something—had the tune bopping around in my skull for the duration of the trial."

"'Dragostea Din Tei,'" I say. "The Moldovian hit from some years back." A favorite of Jakey's. I hum a few bars of the chorus.

Elliot smiles. He has always been charmed by a woman singing. "Point was to display this so-called hit-and-run killer as nothing like the charred wreck sitting in that courtroom. Something like that happens to a kid, intentional or not, someone's got to pay."

I nod, smoking. "But the Dorchester Five walked. So who, then, paid?"

He takes my cigarette from me and has a drag. "Fuel line manufacturer."

I try to look thoughtful. "I suppose the fuel line ruptured, causing the car to go up in flames and burn this poor fellow?"

He snorts a laugh. "No car should need to withstand being

bounced around by a bunch of dumb bastards, but you better believe that those pasty engineers in their short-sleeved dress shirts, trying to explain solder reflex and shock delays in open court, looked guilty as hell."

He drags on my cigarette and then pinches it, sending it pinwheeling into the night. This is a trick from his past—he realizes that he is flirting. Elliot Becker, Esquire is considering doing the deed with a high-priced hooker! And she's French, by God!

"So the Five walked because you maneuvered it so this company took the blame," I say.

He grants my summation. "More or less covers it."

"Which of the Five did you represent? Not Terence D'Amante, I gather?"

"Oh, I didn't represent any of the baddies. I stood for the vegetable," he says.

My voice fails me as I tamp down a flame of rage in my chest, but delicately, only to a point. Rage will be useful, quite soon. "By this you mean the victim?"

"What victim? Originally they charged the punk, too, while he's still in intensive care getting skin grafts. Those charges got dropped, but it wasn't because he hadn't broken any laws. Anyway, not the point. Point is, I saw the story when it broke and went directly to the mother. Bushwhacked through the clueless horde choking the streets of Southie, sat her down and told her about the money I could get them for handicap ramps, fancy wheelchairs, a life supply of pharmaceuticals, a healthy stipend for mother and son to live off, and—for the kicker—in every room, the latest in surround sound entertainment systems. Lady sees her life change—retired from whatever hapless job she's been dragging her fanny through these decades, parked in front of her favorite dramas on her new Naugahyde lounger, day in and day out for the rest of her sorry days. I talk about lifetime care packages, home health aides, someone to cook and clean and walk the mutt. By the time the old bag's heard me out, she's practically wetting herself.

One of her boys has finally come through for her—what were the odds of that?"

I smirk at his dead-on depiction of Jakey's ma. "I do not see, though, how this could translate into your big break. Would the community respect you, representing the injured driver as you did, when you allowed the defendants to walk?"

He laughs. "Litigation's not about winning. It's about tucking something nasty into the past. Trust me, I was the big swinging dick on the deal, and they all—I mean everyone involved—owed me a major debt. Talking about the DA, the defendants, the kid's family, the mayor's office. Lady, the governor was rolled up in a corner with his thumb up his ass. This was a race riot waiting to ignite, and Boston knows how long it takes that stench to clear. Elliot Becker figured the way to allow the proud neighborhood dudes to walk and the Irish proles to retire in style. And sister, at eight years out, Elliot Becker hasn't seen the end of the thank yous."

"All of this just by pinning the blame on the fuel line manufacturer?"

He flashes a boyish smile and gives me a wink. "Let's just call that the public story—a necessary element, but not what I'd call the crux of the victory." He seems about to continue talking out at the stars, but then he feels my hand as I slide it between his legs from behind. I caress the material of his trousers.

"Uh, you mind telling me what you're up to?" he says casually.

"I was wondering if your favorite war story had put you in the mood," I say. I press gently with my fingertips. "Well, well."

He glances over his shoulder and into my eyes.

"Just out of curiosity, how much do you go for?" he asks.

"I…start at two hundred," I say, feeling my way.

"For?"

I purse my lips. "Why, for these."

He laughs in genuine disbelief. "How much does all of you go for?"

"Oh, you get all of me in a blow," I assure him. "But a lay

is four hundred, and a combination—including the back door—runs up to five, depending on circumstances."

"The package deal," he says in an ironic tone. He turns to face me and shines me his killer smile. "And why would I pay," he says, "for what I can get for free?"

"You pay for talent," I say, then glance over his shoulder. "I offer myself free of all charges tonight, however, if you retrieve my favorite scarf."

He turns to the streak of leopard print silk, still straining to escape, then drooping as if with exhaustion. "Sorry, sweets. I may be a ballsy attorney but roof hopping's not my shtick."

I realize, then and there, that my need to pay homage has caused me to miscalculate. Naturally, my plan was to push him as he leaned out for my scarf. But this is not to be. I selected too high a roof, too precarious a reach. I calm myself. Jeanne Moreau would not panic. I must improvise, and to stall I back off while unzipping my skirt, then drop it to my feet and step out of it. Next I unbutton my jacket and let that fall behind me. I am wearing a silvery shell. I whisk it up over my head. I am braless and he takes in my breasts—two brown swollen wounds on a chest that is young and taut as a child's. Then I free my hair from the blouse, and my arms come down. I am all woman again, my breasts small but fleshy. My tummy settles, soft, round, the navel deep. I drop to a stool and peel off my hose. I am—how do you say it?—natural, unshorn, and as I stand, he feels himself go fully erect. It has been years since this has happened so spontaneously. He is half-stunned.

I cast a warning eye. "Payment first. Then I take care of you like never again."

He flips his wallet over to me in a gesture. I catch it and remove some bills, all while meeting his gaze. "Jacket, please," I say. He shucks it with a graceful shrug and passes it to me. I tuck his wallet in the breast pocket and drape it over one of the iron chairs. "The rest is up to you," I say, gesturing at his clothed physique.

For a moment, he hesitates. He is aware of the danger of being recorded these days and is also vaguely conscious that the whole episode—me, the terrace, the scarf—smacks of the playact. What he is not sure about, however, is whether he gives a damn. He has a sudden craving for risk that makes him almost desperate at the prospect that he might come to his senses and leave without having coupled with me. Playing it safe would surely be a suicide of sorts. And what would it mean if I were, in fact, setting him up, if he were exposed as having gotten a little kinky on a hotel terrace? Some sort of sanction from the stiffs at his firm? Roger Coburn openly despises him, but where would they stand if their biggest rainmaker were to walk? Fact is, maybe he could use a bit of a scandal. Fact is, he might enjoy one.

"So?" I have tucked his money into my purse and tossed it aside.

Slowly, he loosens his tie, although once he starts he begins to get a sense of what it will be like to have me servicing him in this gritty little oasis under the stars, and he finds himself accelerating. I approach and run my hands down his body. He glances down at the polished rises of his sculpted chest, his rock-hard waistline. He can see why I push my hands against him, understands why I am short of breath. Or so he imagines. I smile as he draws me in. When he presses a hand to my hair and moves to kiss me, however, I twist my head hard.

"Don't…waste our time," I say in a tone he cannot quite read.

He looks into my eyes for a long moment, almost recognizing me. My hair is a wig; that is clear. I back away, seeing his expression. A name comes into his mind, then flees just as quickly. It is this mercurial name—N…something—that will make everything clear.

"Come." I back into a shadowed corner of the terrace and lean against the brick half-wall, spreading my arms. "Like so," I instruct. "Then I will give you the thrill of your life."

He approaches. "I'm kind of seasoned for a first-time thrill, you know," he says.

"Ah, but this one will end all thrills," I say assuredly. "I promise."

He snorts, amused. "Spread my arms?" he says. His mood for sex is draining; he has actually begun to worry about some docs he needs to review for a Monday noon drop-dead on a merger. He leans back as I urge, against the cement railing, gripping it with his hands on the outside. He feels the grit of the pebbly stone, tiny fragments of it coming detached, sticking to his hands. "Like so?" he says. "And now you blow me to the moon, so to speak."

"Lean well back," I say. I stroke his torso, coaxing him to hoist his shoulders squarely over the top of the rail. "Relax the spine and let your head roll," I coo. "Breathe in the night air." I undo his trousers and lower them, along with his shorts, to beyond his knees. His veins pulse—oh, he is into it. My fingernails leave his buttocks and travel down until I am gently clutching each of his calves. He can feel my lips, my breath, as I hover.

He snaps a finger. "Do it, damn it," he mutters.

"Yes," I agree. "*C'est le temps.*"

I stand, clutching his legs, hoisting them up and then shoving his knees toward his face. For a moment, he is simply annoyed that I have exposed his anus—if that is my so-called thrill, it ends now. His exasperation lasts only seconds, for, as I continue to shove, it dawns on him that he is in danger of spilling over the rail in a backwards somersault. He has no thought at the moment about whether I intend this; he knows only that he must stop his current momentum. In fairness to him, he fights me less than he might, as he does not readily abandon his natural chivalry. He worries about hurting me, that is, and so he aims his efforts at the wall.

I shove harder, gasps of effort escaping me, and this is when it sinks in for Elliot that I am, in fact, trying to topple him to his death. The realization renews his focus as he clutches at the edge and then, by sheer luck, manages to catch my skull between his calves. His pants, still tangled round his ankles, make it impossible for me to break free. Gritting his teeth and hissing with effort, he tries to sit up, using me, his would-be killer, as the ballast that will tip his weight back to the safe side of the rail. His vision blurs from his effort, but he can see my face, distorted, clutched by his legs—his shrunken penis quivers between us as we lock eyes, each as determined as the other. The wig tumbles to one side as I twist my head, trying desperately to push his legs up and off me. He sees without really seeing my real hair; it is short, streaked, white-blonde. This means nothing to him, but at that moment a name flashes through his mind—*Nightingale*—and he knows that this is the key to my identity.

He is gaining, his strength superior, as I begin experiencing a pulsing in my ears that drowns out the world. I am passing out; his squeezing shins have cut off my oxygen. The realization that I have lost seizes my heart, and I deliver a final feeble shove even as I collapse to the deck. For a long moment I completely lose the world around me.

I open my eyes. I am alone, naked, dirty and bruised, lying twisted under the night sky. I remember, then, and jerk myself back defensively, but there is no half-mad Elliot there to yank me to my feet, bellowing the fear and fury out of himself as he beats me senseless for my attempt at murdering him. Elliot is nowhere. And, yes, I have the vague sensation of having heard someone running, just as I was coming to—I recall something odd about the footfall, a vaguely metallic clang—but it fades even as I hear it in my mind. I blink around at the empty terrace, not comprehending why he would run. I am near hysterics with disappointment. My first kill, a tragic screwup! *Putain!* Elliot will get the police, or worse, alert the others. I am over, a failure before I even got started.

But then, as I raise myself to my knees, I hear a swallowed gasp, like a child trying to stifle the giggles. I pull myself to my feet but see nothing. Panting, I peer over the railing wall. And there is Elliot. He is heels over head, literally, and gripping mightily, palms upward, fingers digging frantically into the underside of the wall's stone rim. I cannot see his face and likewise he cannot see me because the material of his undershorts spreads taut across his eyes like a blindfold. They are a beautiful shade of crimson and remain stretched between his calves although apparently his trousers have freed themselves and blown off to their own fate. No, I do not see

Elliot's face—I see only his taut buttocks, his straining arms, and his powerful fingers, trembling, holding on for one last moment.

I will never know whether, if I had had time, I would have attempted to save him or instead would have remained loyal to my cause. I prefer to think I would have "stuck to script," as we say, but who can know? As it is, he utters one piteous sob as he realizes that he must drop. Instinctively, I reach out and *fourrage* in his mind as he goes. And this is what I hear.

Falling, Elliot is not frightened—it is more adrenalin than fear that courses through him as his mind, realizing that this is the end, flares wide so as to expose to Elliot the entirety of his life, the homely, vital memories that exist just past the edges of consciousness. For these last moments his inner voice, along with his conscious thoughts, his sensory responses—all the layers shrill out in a cacophonous blast that is nevertheless strangely comprehensible. And so, although his entire descent takes less than fifteen seconds, this is ample time for Elliot to experience several vivid thoughts.

His first, which he dismisses as nonsensical, is that he had been right after all to have hesitated before dropping his trousers on that terrace because now here he is, living out the fool's nightmare of being pantless in public. Of course, it will be apparent to all that he was maneuvered into this condition with the promise of sex. In any event, he is confident that others will readily recognize him as a normal, red-blooded male in a predicament and not a pervert.

His second thought, a quick follow-up, is that his concern over what strangers will make of his nakedness tacitly accepts that the public will soon become aware of this episode, meaning that he is about to become a gruesome item for the headlines. Will the news titillate? He smothers the idea that he might be jeered. That is something Elliot simply will not accept.

His third thought as he hurtles through the sky, is about me. It occurs to him that he never did fully recognize me, although when my wig came dislodged he did place me, all in an incoherent flash, as somehow associated with the Dorchester Five. This, of course, indicates that I was not a passing psychotic out to lure any victim up to the roof, but that instead I was someone out for revenge against the key lawyer in a case that had impacted her personally. This idea gives him some slight comfort—an event like this, being tumbled off a roof by some sexed-up lunatic bitch, at least ought to be personal. Nobody wants to be a random victim.

And finally comes Elliot Becker's last coherent thought before impact—it is that he must tuck his body into a ball so as to protect his face. Broken bones, even a broken spine, is one thing, but a smashed face is not something any human being should live with. The idea of going through life with everyone avoiding looking at his face because it is too hideous to bear, the idea of living the rest of his life without ever meeting eyes with another human being, this would be true isolation, and the thought chills Elliot profoundly. And in this moment he realizes that he does, in fact, need to connect with others. He is not the ice-to-the-bone attorney he has always aspired to be. This realization means the world to him, although he never would have guessed as much, having consistently insisted, even to himself, that he needs no one and is proud of his cold independent character. It is a vast relief to know that it has all been a charade.

At this point Elliot is within twenty yards of the pavement, and his mind speeds up, registering only a skittering series of images, too quick to even be in color, like the old-fashioned photo kaleidoscope one might crank at a fair.

He sees his mother, holding him by the hair and slapping him across the face repeatedly for something as minor as leaving the cap off the toothpaste in their one bedroom tenement, her rough hands wet from mucking around in cabbage.

He sees his father's expression of anger and shame, the time he soiled himself when Elliot was visiting him in the hospice and the nurses had been too callous to wait until Elliot had departed, or perhaps they got a wicked pleasure out of exposing their wards' bodily frailties.

He sees silly Penny Dupris, sticking out her rolled tongue in mock playfulness, her eyes revealing her dismay at his having blown her off in favor of a more mature woman.

He sees his ex, sitting on the bed, her long hair witchlike, her look *defiant, although he had suspected that this was bravado, as she tells him that she had never once reached orgasm in the six years they have been partners.*

He sees a man, practically a child, but with a hideous face, his livid flesh layered and sewn like patches of pelt, some of them repulsively shiny as if without collagen, other bits purply-red with blood. The man is in a wheelchair. His eyes roll without seeing, or perhaps seeing quite well—who can tell? Another face skitters through Elliot's memory—and in that tiniest spark of time, for that atom of a moment, Elliot figures out who I am. Puzzle solved!

Elliot Becker hits the sidewalk, then, and is fortunate enough to die instantly.

I dress myself. I exit. I have had my first.

Très sincèrement,
Nightingale

TWO

Marina Papanikitas's Personal Journal

Yo, Zoey,

   5:57 a.m., and I am wired. First jumper tonight, and I'm thinking it may have shown. I do manage to clench the sphincter, and that's what truly counts for purposes of maintaining self-respect around the precinct. Been a long time, actually, since the last time I had to focus on keeping the thighs dry and the knees from going jackhammer on me. Caught me by surprise—like, woah, I still have remnants of human responses to blood and gore. Who'd a thunk?

   Even now, I shut my eyes, I see it. The corpse forms a kind of rumpled mound, spine snapped at the neck, knees crushed underneath, one arm off at an angle, splintered somewhere just south of the shoulder. He's partly dressed in your typical business attire, although somehow he managed to lose both trousers and shorts during his fall. Just not the guy's night. The naked rump is the highest point of his body—looms over the bloody parts of him, all lit up from the tripod UVs, its crest double-humped like some effed-up valentine. The drizzle gathers in his crack. Testes hang like a sack of moldy cotton. Death's got no dignity.

   Harry is somewhere behind me with the morgue guys. I catch a snatch of some story about a broad and a jackhammer. For a moment I'm bloody irritated at all the sexism I have to put up with. Then I remember that I'm the one who told Harry that joke, and the resentment gives way to a flicker of pride when they laugh loud. So I'm a little confused in my feminism—that news, Zoey?

The dead man's face is in profile against the sidewalk, eyes half-closed, mouth ripped at the corner, giving the false impression that he's got a sly smile going as he prepares to hit on me with some quip about the view up his ass. His nose sits flat against the cement, almost looks like the other half of his face is underneath the sidewalk, mirroring the part I'm looking at. That effect is offset by the spray of brains, fully intact teeth, and powdered skull that splays out around his half-face. Blood splatter reminds me of one of those jagged-edged comic book splats. "BAMF!" the caption would read. Did I ever tell you how as a kid I used to sneak into Nikos's comic stash? Always thought the Riddler presented the most intriguing psychosis—all that yearning to give himself away in cryptic scribbles. Guess the freak in me kind of felt for him.

I play my stinger's spot outward from the human remains. The blood is darker further from his head where it thins against the swirled sidewalk cement. Close to his head it's bright and pock-marked from the rain that's just starting to patter. Disturbs me the way fresh-spilt blood is so bright. I notice an eyeball, dented flat on one side, glued to the sidewalk. Some squiggly muscles cling to it. The other eye, the one still in its socket, gazes at the back end of its mate.

"So what do you know, Pop?" Harry greets me. Harry's always happy.

"Nice ass," I manage.

Snort from Harry. "Grab a handful. No one's lookin.'"

"Don't do man ass," I deadpan. "Thought you'd picked up on that."

"Ass is ass, Pop." Merry as a lark.

Harry's holding two coffees. "One of those mine?" I glance at him surreptitiously as he passes it, looking for some sign that he's struggling to keep dinner down. Nothing. Somehow his ability to handle the sight of a middle-aged man smashed on the pavement like so much pumpkin gets my own stomach where it needs to be.

But good for H.P. Always strikes me as funny the way other guys in the department refer to him as "Handsome Harry," because frankly he's not that good looking by my way of thinking. Guess guys tend to admire the brick house physique, thick neck, blunt head with the hair clipped so close it's like his whole skull's got a three-day stubble going on. Still recall the first time I laid eyes on him, my first thought is that the man is a walking, talking penis. Not in a bad way—just, you know, like a fact. Can't believe I'm only just getting around to telling you this, Zoey—guess you're right on about the "hole in our relationship" that this journal is supposed to patch. Anyway, girl, the Human Penis is who Harry's been ever since, just between me and me. Handy that his last name is Penders, allowing me to call him "H.P." without explaining. So Marina the Dyke gets her break into homicide, and they partner her up with the Human Penis. Yep, like you always say, Zoe, it's the little ironies that make life worth living. Old H.P. gets points, though, for those eyes—cold and blue as a winter sky.

"Sorry it took me," I say, sipping. "Forgot to avoid the construction on 93."

"Road work, night like this. Gotta feel for those guys."

"Yeah. Lucky for us we went in for this cushy gig."

I like the sting that the hot coffee gives my upper lip. Scalding or not, I can taste the cream and double sugar. H.P. knows what keeps his Pop chugging, that's for sure.

"So where'd our friend here come from?" I let my gaze move up the hotel. Around the first and second stories, the mortar is laid on in that purposely sloppy way so it gobs out from between the bricks like frosting. Second floor is capped with some fancy stone trim; above that the brickwork goes standard. Windowsills look like limestone. Probably a wonder of structural engineering in its day. Now it's a tourist charmer. Room rates undoubtedly dizzying.

I'm watching the drizzle falling at me, taking the glittering waves of it unblinking in my face, when suddenly I have one of my so-called psychic moments—plain as day I "see" this body dropping from the sky, a woman with cropped skunk-striped hair, red-violet dress in maybe velvet with a short skirt, matching gloves up her arms, stockings heavily patterned. Something flutters behind her, maybe a fringed wrap. She just falls, moving neither arms nor legs, like a bird that's been shot. She's alive, though—she stares ahead, calm, detached…gothic. I blink, and she disappears.

"Roof terrace."

I begin to see Harry as I come back to reality. He's scratching his neck. "What did you say?" I'm numb around my eyes—that's where the "vishies" always get me. I'm glad Harry isn't looking, although he turns his head even as I think that.

"That's where he took his fall," he says plainly. "Roof terrace off some party room."

I pull myself back to the moment. "Party get out of control?"

"No party. Deserted except for a couple of cocktail glasses."

"Prints?"

"Lipstick, too. Deep purple."

"And we know that was the spot how?"

"Guy's suit jacket, draped over a chair. Wallet intact, in his breast pocket."

"So we got an ID."

"We do. Elliot Becker, Esquire. Forty-nine years of age. Mass driver. Boston Athletic Club. Platinum Am Ex. Couple hundred in mixed bills. Couple of condoms."

I let my gaze begin the climb again, up to the hotel windows. "Optimist."

"Prepared," Harry concedes.

"What happened to his pants?"

"Tore off him during the fall. Someone found them hooked on a fire escape. Boxer shorts were up the alley a ways."

"Flashy undies?"

Harry snorts. "Red silk. Smooth fellow all around, I'm thinking."

I give the corpse a final glance. "Not so much, this end."

We ride up the freight elevator. Walls are draped in movers' quilts. "They doing a reno?" I ask while waiting for my handheld to kick in with a search result.

"Wedding," Harry says. "This weekend, or should I say tomorrow night at this point. Two hundred fifty guests on the thirty-second floor."

I watch Elliot Becker's law firm mug shot appear on my screen. "Tax. Trusts. Criminal. Guy was diverse," I say, handing the phone over for Harry to take a look. I watch the numbers above the door. "Let me guess," I say. "Thirty-second floor is where he jumped."

"Coincidence—or was he the groom?" Harry's always making "ball and chain" jokes. Used to grate on me before I got to know him. His wife's pregnant with their first, and he's walking on air. Claims not to know the sex, but he's lying.

"Look at that grin," I say about Becker. "This is the type who thinks he's God's gift to womankind. You can't lock a lover like that into a marriage."

Harry hands back my phone. "When's marriage ever got in a guy's way when he owes himself to womankind?"

"When has suicide?" I mumble.

"True enough," Harry agrees. "True enough."

Upstairs, we emerge into a backstairs alcove. Walls papered in gold stripes. Restrooms straight ahead, then an unmarked door with a push panel. I ease it inward and see the kitchen, everything unpolished metal, sterile, silent. Then I have one of my "premmies"—those tingles that don't quite blossom into vishies. This one is some muddled sensation about a bucket. I cross to yank the handle of the walk-in. A light goes on, and I run an eye around the empty shelves. The air carries that acrid odor of standing water. There's a plastic drum near the back, and I lean in, drawn to it, my fingers stretched to hold the door. It's empty except for a stainless steel ladle. None of this means anything, although it will in the future, as will the vishie of the gothic chick taking a dive. Never talk about my premmies or my vishies. Psychic cop—or maybe "spastic psychic" would be more accurate—equals crazy cop, even dangerous cop, to most people. You're my confidante and my shrink, Zoey. Just don't trust anyone else.

Harry crosses the ballroom, his reflection broken in the hundred windowpanes. His footsteps echo. Place is empty except for stacks of pink-cushioned chairs and tables with their legs folded, leaning against the walls. Table linens on the floor, sheathed in opaque plastic. Five piles of them, lain flat to avoid wrinkles. As I glance over, they turn into five bodies—five men, on their backs, naked and ready for autopsy. I look away before I can even discern the age or race of any corpse, not wanting details because details don't help. Never had vishies so on top of each other before tonight. It's giving me a bruiser of a headache.

"Across there is where he went over," Harry says. "Far wall."

I study the scene through the floor-length windows. There's a uniform outside, gazing at the surrounding buildings, smoking. If he notices us he gives no sign of it. The rain shifts, starts coming down with some muscle. The guy tosses his butt and hustles for cover.

"Who's that over there?"

"Malloy," he says.

"What's he doing dropping cigarettes around a crime scene?"

I'm just feeling bitchy due to the headache. Harry shrugs and walks away.

Out on the deck, I hunch against the cement rim and blink down at the lights below. There's some movement, a reflection shifting off the meat wagon's roof as someone backs up. The headlights catch the mist. Not much else. Wall is chest high on me. I squint at Harry, who's busy turning up his collar.

"Guy was, what, six foot one?" I talk loud to cut through the rattle of rain against tile.

"Got that from the pile of parts downstairs, did you?" he calls back.

"More or less. Big onions, big man."

"Huh. Good system. According to his license, Pop, he was six one."

"You're what, six two? This wall still would be pretty high for you to hop up onto."

"Meaning…" he leads me.

Malloy chimes in from behind us. "Meaning he didn't just hitch himself up to use it as a bench while he enjoyed his cocktail." Tension makes his voice thin. Guy's gunning for detective. Well, I know how that feels.

Harry doesn't turn. "Don't talk."

I take out the stinger and play the finger of yellow light along the wall's edge. "Rough."

"Be tough to get up there without some sort of chair to step from, even for a fit guy. Not unless he vaulted himself over."

Something catches my eye. "What the hell?" I squint through the rain at what looks like a diaphanous flag billowing from the tip of some plasterwork that trims another area of the roof.

Harry shines his flash at it. "Lady's scarf?"

Before we can even consider the prospect of trying to fetch it, a gust rips it free, and it swoops off, silent as smoke.

"Malloy," Harry says, watching the scarf disappear. "Got a job for you."

Malloy leaves. Don't know if he's excited at the prospect of galloping through the alleys after a piece of lady's headgear. In his shoes I would have been, but I'm dumb like that.

"So, listen," I say. "Were his pants ripped?"

"Sure. Right off the guy. You saw."

"No, I mean were they actually torn up."

Harry pauses. "What, you think he took them off?"

I shrug. "Took off his jacket. Lost his pants. Meanwhile his shoes are still on him. Makes me think he dropped trou before he took the fall."

Rainwater starts jetting out through a downspout in the corner, hitting the tiles with a smack. We stand there, watching whatever bits of evidence we might have scouted up eddying round the floor drain. Harry blinks through the rain at me; he knows I'm still in what we detectives call the bloodhound stage. It's my call, his silence says. That's Harry, Zoey, and that's why they paired him with the newbie.

Feeling the rain actually beginning to pool inside my jacket collar, I sigh and head for shelter. "We'll want to get over here pretty damn early if they're setting up for a wedding. That work for you?" Aware of what a twit I'm being, I still can't help myself.

"Sure enough," he says, totally straight. "Sure enough."

THREE

Marina Papanikitas's Personal Journal

LOVING the ginger echinacea, Zoey. What was your clue—my sneezing (I swear I tried not to wake you) or the sopping pile of clothes in the bathroom? People kept pausing by my desk all morning just to sniff the air near me—ever notice how a whiff of your home brew seems to get folks all flushed and breathy? Just might have a marketable aphrodisiac on our hands.

So, m'luv, back to "the sharing thing." My plans to play Sherlock at the Hampstead get pushed off till midday. Harry thinks we should hit the morgue for a gander at our vic sans the dramatic lighting, and I agree. Death doc pulls Harry aside for a little chat—they go back, and I'm still the new kid—but I'm plenty occupied marveling over how they've shoveled enough of Becker off the pavement to arrive at a near-recognizable jigsaw of a human. Can't handle more than a glimpse of the pulverized half of his head, myself, but when the menfolk huddle I hip the drawer just enough to ease Elliot's "face" out of sight. I find that cataloging my observations helps keep me lucid—stuff like the fact that Elliot manscaped. Elliot has decent—nay, excellent—abs. Elliot is missing a couple of fingernails and has some pebbly grime rubbed into the seams of his hands. Elliot has a mass of tiny, curved gouges on his thighs that seem out of place even amid the mashed knees and the pelvic bone piercing his flesh. Elliot has professionally manicured toenails, including the one with the tag.

"Partner's staving off a cold," Harry interrupts. Slaps my back and rubs. I think it's intended to keep me from fainting. Works. "Some storm last night, huh, Bernie?"

Bernie agrees. For a guy on the generous end of obese, he's a smoothie. Slides the unsightly body out of view. Shakes my hand gently as he peers at me over half-glasses. "Echinacea with ginger," he says soothingly. "The wife and I swear by it."

"Me and mine too," I say.

I wait until we're in the car. The area of Boston where the hospitals squat dwells under the curse of a permanent traffic snarl. I'm in no mood to jockey through the lane merges and blaring horns, so I'm glad to be shotgun. "What was so hush-hush back there?" I want to know.

"Doc knew Becker." Harry signals with his arm out the window like my grandpa used to. Weirdly, it works, and we swing into the traffic.

"Let me guess," I try. "To know Elliot was to love him not so much."

"True enough," Harry concedes. "Hence the 'just between us thieves' approach."

"Why? Is the good doctor afraid that he could get a colleague in trouble for sharing his suspicions, or is it more a matter of gossip being bad manners in front of the corpse?"

"Maybe a little of each. Apparently Becker took a do-it-your-self approach to home care plans for his clients. Most lawyers prefer the paint-by-number package—less chance for recriminations when the inevitable end occurs. The docs who sign off on some non-standard arrangement can be vulnerable as well. Nothing says litigious like a bereaved relative."

"So why take the risk?"

Harry shrugs. "Sometimes the patient insists. Sometimes there's a little kickback action. Some of these trust clients have a lot of cash to spray around, particularly when they sense the grim reaper penciling them into the date book."

I think about that. "Huh," I conclude.

Over at the Hampstead, the wedding crew is getting tetchy. It's not just that they want to deck the terrace with Chinese lanterns. They want the crime scene tape gone. I can see their point. Police yellow might be on the bridal palate, but the tale that goes with it, not so much.

The afternoon's breezy. Cinder skitters playfully across the terrace, newly power-washed by last night's downpour. I refuse to be discouraged. See, I got a thing in my head about the rim where Becker went over. Glimpsed something last night between the raindrops. Don't know what that something is, but I'm plenty curious. I flip out my trusty stinger—sky's glaringly bright, but the needle of light helps me train my eye. Takes a while, then I find what I'm after.

"Here we go," I say. "Notice Becker's fingers?"

Harry leans in to see, puts his hand over mine, cups it with his large fingers to keep the light steady. His hand's warm, even on a cool day. His calluses tickle my knuckles. It's not personal, an absent-minded gesture. He wouldn't have done it with another male, though.

"Grit in the seams," he says. "Same stuff as this. Mean something to you?"

"Maybe." I move along with the light, beaming it slowly along the outside of the wall, in the area just between the cement rim and the top line of bricks. I go about five feet, then double back. That's where I spot what I'm looking for: another indentation in the grainy cement—not really a gouge, but clearly a fresh, scratched disturbance. "See it?"

Harry peers over my shoulder. "That's a fingernail, stuck in the mortar."

I already got my tweezers out. "Snapped off below the skin line too." I bag it carefully. "That's going to match."

"Oh yeah," Harry agrees. "So where's it taking us, Pop?"

I step back to survey the wall. "Do something for me, H.P. Spread your hands along there, see if you can grip the rim in those two spots simultaneously."

He tries it. From across the way where the wedding crew is rolling tables around, it must look like I ordered Harry to position himself for a frisk. Harry's hands spread quite a bit farther apart than the gouges. He stands up, brushing at his tie knot.

"Huh," I say. "I'd have figured you and Elliot to be about the same span."

"Still, there's something going on there," Harry says. "What's the idea? Think Becker gripped the spot for a while, needing to talk himself into it, and then vaulted over? We know he did trusts. Maybe he swiped a bunch of assets. I hear it's popular."

"Works for me," I say slowly, making clear that it doesn't. I look off for inspiration as a couple of birds flit by. They disappear into the glare, reminding me of the scarf tangled in the roof molding. The truth clicks into place. "Do the reach again," I say. "This time face me."

"What, with my back to the thing?" Harry tries it, leaning his shoulders against the rim and stretching his arms. His legs are bent awkwardly, and he hitches himself up so that his back is arched, his shoulders extending well past the rounded edge, his arms spread. His coat falls back against the wall, his hands rest just wide of the two gouges Elliot made. I watch him think about this, his face staring up into the clouds. After a moment he raises his head.

"Guy was being blown," he says matter-of-factly. He tips his head at the stone cornice where the lady's scarf had been caught. "By her. Malloy better have that thing."

Riding down, Harry checks his watch. "Bartender's supposed to be in around now."

Elevator opens, and I'm greeted with the sight of an empty bar. Nothing less exciting than a nightspot stripped of its mood. A slushy noise, ice against metal, draws my eye to the far end of the bar, where a beefy guy stands from where he's been mucking around. He's overweight and balding, with a major swatch of freckles covering his pate and a spongy patch of white-grey chest hair frothing out where he hasn't buttoned his work shirt. Pre-tied bow tie dangles from his collar. Overall look: professional-grade weary. Somehow he's here instead of pulling pints somewhere in Yorkshire. He beads a watery eye on me as Harry and I cross the room, and I watch him peg me as clearly as if he'd said the L-word aloud. Doesn't mean much—most people pick it up and are perfectly cool with it, frankly. Harry and I don't sit.

"Thanks for agreeing to see us, Mr…"

"Donovan," he supplies. "Michael Francis. Go by McD."

"I like it," I say.

The barman checks a tap, which coughs air. "Long as you don't tell me you're lovin' it."

Harry snorts. "She don't get that, buddy. Eats twigs and berries exclusively."

He brushes off the patter. "I got a shift starts five this afternoon, so if you don't mind, I'd like to get through this." He slaps down the tap, letting the beer sputter forth. We watch it with him. He cocks it when the stuff starts gurgling out gold, moves to the next.

"Keep it quick, sure," I say agreeably. I flash a picture of Elliot, but the guy's apparently been forewarned and barely glances at it. "You served this gentleman last night?"

"Johnnie Walker, rocks. 9:30, maybe 9:35."

"How do you remember the time so well?"

He shrugs. "You do this job, you remember the shift. Paid cash. They got the receipts out back, you want the exact time."

"Just the one drink?"

"Yeah, plus the Irish. He didn't stick around for a second round."

"Irish whiskey?"

"Coffee. Double. Splash of Bailey's. Dash of cream."

"Johnnie Walker with an Irish chaser. I'll have to try that."

He eyes me like I'm dumb. "The Irish was for the lady."

"Ah," I say, happy to be educated. If I play it truly dense, I might ease him past the monosyllables. "You know this lady?"

He shrugs. "Seen her couple of times this past week or so. Comes in alone. Doesn't talk to no one except in passing."

"Was Johnnie Walker meeting her, you think? Or did he pick her up?"

McD wriggles a knuckle around his nostril, considering. "Neither one, you ask me."

"Oh? Not the pick-up type?"

McD lets beer slough into the drain below, considering. "Him or her?"

"Either," Harry says. Harry's less patient with witnesses.

McD slaps the cock closed, in his element. "Neither one of them was wearing a ring."

"You notice rings while serving a single round at the height of your shift?"

"Like I says, you do the job a while, you notice. No rings means they might want to settle up quick. You keep your eye out."

Harry chuckles. "Everyone's in a hurry to scratch the itch, huh?"

"Works both ways. Sometimes the lady wants to settle up to get away from some guy comin' on. Anyway, it wasn't just one round for her. She had a couple before the guy showed."

"Yeah? How long had she been there when Johnnie Walker homed in on her?"

He thinks. "Two vodka bitter lemons. But she nursed them. So I'm thinking an hour, maybe an hour and a quarter."

"Two drinks an hour?" Harry's surprised. "So she was waiting for someone."

McD moves his head back and forth like he can't decide. "You'd figure, but she didn't never look round or nothing. Just sat there sipping."

"Was it like that the other nights she was in? She just sat there, not looking for anyone?"

He nods. "Pretty much. She'd drink a couple, sometimes guys

would talk to her. Then she'd leave. Not all that unusual. It ain't only men who might need some air after work."

"Let's talk about her," Harry says. "Can you give us an approximate age?"

He thinks. "Kind of ageless," he says, gesturing artily.

I cut Harry off before he can respond. "Hey, everyone's got a couple of tells," I coax him. "Can I get a range? Twenties? Forties?"

He doesn't want to.

I push ahead. "Want to take a stab at height, eyes, hair color?"

Sigh. "Tallish, eyes maybe green, maybe grey or blue, hair kind of an ash-blonde."

I flash on my vishie—the falling goth chick. "What was her hairstyle?"

"Maybe chin length or a little longer. Heavy down into her eyes."

Didn't match up. I'm not disappointed for long, though.

"She had a thing over her head," he volunteers. "What do you call it—a kerchief."

I'm interested. "No kidding? Like for the rain?"

"No, no," he said. "More just for looks."

"Color? Pattern?"

"I want to say spots," he says.

"One lady's spotted scarf," Harry says to himself, writing.

"What about other characteristics?" I ask. "Anything strike you?"

"Not really," McD says. "Might have talked with an accent. Maybe French."

"Might have?"

"She was kind of a low talker. Low key all around."

"But Johnnie Walker noticed something."

"Seemed to. I go to serve him, he says no, then a minute later he's down the bar, ordering for himself and trying to buy her one. She don't want any, though. Then he comes back for an Irish, and I'm thinking it's for her. Could be wrong."

"Could be right, though," Harry says.

"Could be." McD pulls another tap. Harry makes a face at me.

"Sounds like a classic hook-up," I try. "So what was wrong with it, in your eyes?"

"I didn't say nothin' was wrong with it."

"But you're thinking it," I push him.

He hesitates. "Tell you the truth, she didn't seem like his type."

Harry circles a hand. "What type was she?"

McD sighs heavily. "I already said. Just some woman."

I get it. Becker had dressed stylishly and kept himself in shape. "She was dumpy?"

McD squints at the ceiling. "That'd be harsh. Lady wasn't bad. Foxy, actually, you take the time to look twice. Just saying…"

We wait, so he sighs and finishes his thought.

"I'm just saying that this Johnnie Walker was the kind of guy who, when he's hookin' up, he's looking to…" He fades out.

"…get something tight on his dick?" I finish for him.

He looks at Harry. "Some mouth this one's got on her, huh?" he says.

Harry smirks, like, all day.

FOUR

Marina Papanikitas's Personal Journal

Yo, Zoey,

So I bust ass to get home at a civilized hour, thinking maybe we do our daily catch-up the old-fashioned way—like over wine, maybe a candle. Not to be, not to be. You, I learn via kitchen table scribbles, are out shilling chanterelles and prawns till 2 a.m. In retaliation, m'luv, I am having myself a footbath and a huge glass of pinot noir before bed, laptop ablaze. Bunions at my tender age—believe it?

This afternoon was Elliot Becker's wake—or the law firm facsimile thereof, tossed by the partnership of Brown & Richardson, LLP. H.P. and I were there to sniff the air—got the personal invite from managing partner Roger Coburn, along with a warning that we were to "be discreet," which I took to mean no bulging holsters, dangling cuffs, or gum. Harry's read on Coburn was that the firm is kind of interested in having Becker's death pegged as a murder. Far better for a partner to be offed by a lunatic he creamed in court than go down as a jumper. Guess I'm enough of a cynic to catch why. Whether that means we'll get the cooperation we need from Coburn is a completely different matter.

Figured I could camouflage at a corporate do reasonably well, but whoever says women have fully infiltrated the field of law isn't talking about the places where serious money's being collected.

Circulating, I count maybe thirty-five females over the age of forty in a room of about two hundred, and most of those gals I peg as clients, judging from the liver spots and north shore drawls. Aiming to blend, I'd thrown on my midnight blue with the side pleats and rolled shawl collar—you know, Zoey, "the suit." Strung the freshwaters round my neck and aimed some concentrated heat at the mop. Turns out I'm way off. Today it's trim pants, fitted cotton shirts with the cropped tails flapping, and flats. Pearls are as yesterday as blue serge. The women around me I'm taking for lawyers are dangling solitaires at clavicle level and flashing selfies of At-Home-Dad with the Clomid twins. Gotta say, if I could have seen what was coming way back when, might have done the law school thing. I could use a dangling solitaire and some flapping shirttails. Not *quite* ready for the twins.

Space is big—must be three conference rooms long—and encased in plate glass on both exterior and interior walls. Stuffy, though. Too many people breathing one another's CO_2. Or maybe too much steam from the chafing dishes. People are actually eating and generally don't seem altogether somber in spite of the shindig's theme.

I poke my nose here and there with the idea of buttonholing Coburn, not for a real conversation but more to get an idea of how good a liar he is. Can't tell over the phone—not with a Brit, anyway. Everything's kind of going nowhere until I go eye-to-eye with a edgy type—one of those girls who stares at you with the whites of her eyes showing all around her irises. Probably rips through a hundred words a minute at a keyboard. Turns her back abruptly, but there's a *tête-à-tête* in our future.

H.P. gives me a poke. He's wearing a muted plaid sports jacket, like tweed, and a tie—bright green with old-fashioned bicycles on it. Got small, rimless glasses on his face. Weren't for the twenty-inch neck, he'd fit right in.

He smirks, aware that I'm pissed that my suit's gotten a little snug since last time I needed it. "They got those fancy fiddlehead things you and Zoey like so much," he says to be nice. "Don't be shy. Everyone's chowing."

"So I noticed," I say. "Any sad people down that way, or is it too much to hope for?"

"You kidding, Pop? Look at the size of this crowd. Gauge its net worth. Smell the slick sweat of Becker's rivals homing in on his trade. Good times, baby, good times."

"So you're saying it's nice to be missed, even if it's just because you made rain?"

"Best reason of all. Becker wasn't out to score a humanitarian award. Guy thrived on one-upmanship and not much else. He's grinning right now." Harry points downward to indicate the place where Becker's doing his grinning.

"Is that Coburn?" I say. "The thin one?"

We watch a tall, nondescript man with wet-combed hair and magnified eyes as he gooses his neck forward so as to appear to be giving his undivided attention to a small woman talking up at him. His suit's pale grey, his teeth bunched and yellow, just like a Brit's supposed to have. My eye wanders to the woman, following her long silver-brown braid, held in place with a decorative leather thong, then on down the drapey pants that don't quite mask the plump of her tush. The heels of her shoes are covered in some sort of raw hemp. When she turns a bit I see that she has thick bangs cut straight across, rag doll style. Her earrings are wood.

"Ten to one that's the ex," I say.

"Think so?" Harry is skeptical. "Kind of 'earth mom' for a guy who wore custom cashmere blends, wouldn't you say?"

"Just one reason they didn't last," I point out. "She's been out of town, at least according to her significant other. Foreign rights convention. Calls herself Bonnie McCloud now."

"Huh. Guess she wanted a name to go with her look."

"SO's name is Westerly, making McCloud her birth name. This is the real her."

"How'd Westerly come across?"

"Worried about how she'd take the news. Kept saying that he hoped she wouldn't find out while she was away from him."

"Very lovey-dovey."

"Seemed genuine, though."

"Well, she knows now. Want to mosey over, do a little girl-on-girl action?"

"Thought maybe you'd take her. She's in publishing—she'll love you in the specs."

"What's up?"

"Got someone else to talk to."

I catch the skinny woman hanging out in a crowd of secretaries. Most of them balance plates with swimmy bits of food on them, but she isn't eating and doesn't appear to be listening to the talk around her. I catch her eye, and she's instantly attentive. I raise two fingers to my lips and blow, then nudge my head at the exit. She blinks, then turns back to her friends.

The reception area is done up in a gaudy cherry burl as if to defy its modest proportions. Noise from the wake is audible but muted. A plump receptionist with molded too-black hair and a generous hand with the foundation stares blankly ahead, her lips moving faintly, and only when I'm right up to the desk do I catch that the soft grunts and chirps are her side of a chat she's having into her barely-there headset. Ignores me while she finishes her conversation, so I amuse myself by evaluating her cleavage, which could have been a wonder to behold maybe a quarter century back, but now resembles a heavily powdered old man's ass in a sling.

When she's ready, she greets me with more frost than I'd have figured I rated. London accent—hey, just like the boss man—but I don't have the ear to detect whether it's real. Ask about smoking, and she sends me down to the lobby.

Skinny Girl is there, arms crossed, not quite leaning against one of the pillars between the twenty-foot windows. It's bright and gusty out. Trash flitters about. Several anonymous people stand smoking, silent, staring at the harbor gulls. Almost makes you want to take it up, just for the excuse to steal a contemplative moment, couple of times a day. The girl hasn't bothered with her coat, and looks even thinner in the wind. Wearing a jumper over a black turtleneck, matching hose. Bunch of bright bangles up her arm. Cheap styling—just like the mags tell you.

"Thanks for coming down," I say. "Marina Papanikitas."

"Penny Dupris," she says.

"Penny, I'm a detective with the Boston Police." I go for my badge.

She waves it off. "I don't need to see it."

I smile, just to warm it up. "Shows that clearly, huh?"

Shakes her head, not smiling. "Not so much. I just got a couple in my family." She crinkles her eyes against a gust. "Not here in town, though. Up the Shore."

I tuck my badge away. "I'd offer you a cigarette, but..."

"That's okay, I don't smoke either. My mother died from emphysema."

"Sorry."

She shrugs it off. "We kept telling her to quit, but she didn't want to."

I let it drop. "So, Penny, I got the feeling upstairs that you might have something to tell me about Elliot Becker. Was I off?"

She lifts a hand to push back a veil of gossamer hairs that have escaped her ponytail to stream across her face. "Look, I don't want to start a thing about this," she says, "but I'm hearing a lot of junk. He wasn't drunk the other night. There's no way."

I nod. "How do you know, Penny?"

"Because I was with him."

I pause. "Okay."

She rolls her eyes and turns to look out at the distant harbor. "Not 'with him' with him. I just was there at The Underground, and we talked."

I notice how her fingers dig into her sleeves. More than the chill. "Were you Mr. Becker's secretary, Penny?"

She shakes her head. "I'm in the trust department. We monitor the firm's funds, make distributions, stuff like that."

"Sounds like a lot of responsibility."

Shakes her head. "It's just accounting. The lawyers oversee everything."

"Meaning Mr. Becker?"

"He was administrator for a bunch of trusts, so that's how I knew him. But only a little."

"I see." I decide to prod her and do it clumsily. "There haven't been any irregularities in Mr. Becker's handling of any trust funds, have there?"

She looks at me with her wide-open eyes, then away. "Look, all I'm trying to tell you that he wasn't drunk. I talked to him when he got there, and he barely stayed ten minutes. To tell you the truth, I think that the girls who spread around that he was drunk at the Christmas party last year were full of it. I've seen a lot of drunk, and I know drunk when I see it."

Not sure where to take it, I go along. "You know, there was nothing in the autopsy report about his blood alcohol level, but I'll be sure to make a note in the file about your having seen Becker shortly before his death, in case we get wind of this rumor you've been hearing."

She nods. "Well, that's all I got," she says. "It just bugs me that a dead man might go down with a bunch of gossip."

"Thanks," I say, then prod a little more. "Say, Penny, I'm wondering something."

She squints at me, holding her pesky hair back.

"This rumor about Mr. Becker getting drunk at Christmas. If it's not true, then where do you think that came from?"

She rolls her eyes. "Mr. Becker was the kind of guy who came on to women. Like he'd hold up mistletoe, or try to talk one of us into going into the pool with him at the summer outing. So people would say he was drunk when really he was just..." She lets it go.

"Being friendly?"

She snorts a dry laugh. "I was going to say 'hitting on you.'"

"You think he could get aggressive with women?"

She nods. "I do, actually. But I don't think he meant any

harm. I think he honestly thought it was flattering for him to show interest."

"Lot of guys think they're hot. Most don't try to bully the women at work into bed."

She shrugs. "I'm not saying he was a great guy. I'm just saying he didn't get drunk and topple off some terrace the other night."

"Did he try to pick you up the night he died, Penny?"

"I was with my fiancé, so he couldn't have been serious." She displays a diamond chip on a silver ring. "But, yeah, he came on to me. That's just the way he talked to women."

"Did it bother your fiancé?" I wonder momentarily if she'll think I'm going somewhere ridiculous with this, but she doesn't get defensive—must be the cops in the family.

"Todd thought it was hilarious."

"Say, Penny, you happen to see where Becker went after he talked with you?"

"To the bar."

"And after?"

"Not really. I waved at him at some point. The place was really packed."

"Was he with someone when you waved at him?"

"No, he was alone. I remember because I was a little concerned that he might come back, and Todd might start trying to be a comedian—like comparing how much they can each bench, that sort of thing. And whatever Mr. Becker was, he was also my boss, right?"

"I see. I ask because the bartender said that Becker bought a woman a drink."

She shakes her head, then stops. "Yes," she says. "He was holding two drinks. One was hot. I remember seeing the steam and being relieved because that wasn't what either me or Todd was drinking, so it couldn't have been a round for us."

"But you didn't see a woman near him?"

She squints her eyes, thinking.

I can't resist leading her. "Maybe closer to Becker's own age than his usual target?"

She tries, then sighs as she gives up. "All I remember is a lady in a wig. My mother wore a couple of wigs when she was going through chemo, so I notice them."

"Remember anything about this lady?"

She shrugs. "I remember thinking 'retro.'"

"Her clothes, you mean?"

"Look, I don't have the foggiest idea if she was with Mr. Becker."

I keep my eyes on hers. "I've found that people seem to have some sixth sense when details that seem random are going to turn out to be important."

"What, now I'm psychic?"

"If you want to call it that. We all are, to some degree." Not that I'm out to convince anyone, Zoey, but...

"If you say so," she says. "She had a scarf, like this." She mimes putting a scarf over her head and wrapping it tight around her neck. "See? Really dated."

"Like me." I glance down at my suit with a smile.

She takes me at face value. "No, not like you. You're just not keeping up. This lady was doing something vintage, but it wasn't a look anyone's doing right now, so it looked a little costumey." She sighs. "Does that make any sense?"

"Actually it does," I say. "So if you had to pick a year...?"

"Talking way back." Penny tilts her head. "Paris new wave?"

"Before my time," I point out, trying not to sound relieved. "Look, gut reaction—you think she was the one Becker bought the drink for?"

Penny shrugs and makes wide eyes. "All I can tell you is that I didn't see him again."

H.P. catches up with me at the precinct, sliding onto my desk jauntily while I'm tapping out some notes.

"What took you?"

"Good wake," he says. "Good conversation, good food, good people. Yourself?"

I give him the short version of my chat with Penny.

"I find that interesting," Harry says. "From the bartender, we get Becker as a smoothie. From someone of the opposite sex and a generation younger, guy's a lech."

"But a harmless one," I point out.

"That's not the kind of lech any guy wants to be," he points out. "You think he wouldn't catch on that the girls he's hitting on call him Becker the Pecker behind his back?"

I shrug, a tad guilty about my nickname for Harry. "Why keep it up, then?"

Harry takes off the gold-rimmed specs and tucks them in a pocket. "Every night when he gets home he looks in the mirror and can't believe he's swinging and missing. It's got to be the girls he just happens to be meeting. They're blind. So next time out, he does it again."

"It's a theory," I admit. "This Penny also seems to be harboring some suspicions about Becker's handling of his trusts, if you ask me, but she's not quite in touch with her thoughts on that yet. What did you get upstairs? Something better, I hope."

Harry pivots and makes his way to the coffee machine. "Tell you one thing," he says. "Roger Coburn wasn't crazy about Becker's methods. Apparently our guy was lazy on the law and very adept at the backroom deal. Not Coburn's style at all. Plus Becker would bring in whatever work he managed to corral, ignoring firm protocol, conflicts checks, all the red tape that Coburn assured me lawyers are not supposed to take lightly. I got the distinct sense that Coburn had been snooping around Becker's files to make sure the firm wasn't going to find itself liable for something the guy did. You want a cup of this?"

"I'm good," I say.

He puts the pot down and sprinkles some non-dairy creamer into his mug, then thoughtfully watches it dissolve. Not a chance in hell he's going to taste it.

"What are you thinking?" I say.

"I'm thinking that for all of his effort to play it close to the chest, Coburn can't hide that he's relieved that the guy's dead. When I remarked that it must be a shame to be losing the revenue Becker pulled in, Coburn looked puzzled. You know that funny way that the English look when they pull a puzzled expression?"

"No. Show me."

Harry ignores the invitation. "Coburn said that the firm's distribution system is one where the lawyers eat what they kill."

"This means...?"

"Means that if some big-money partner pulls his stakes and walks, or, you know, takes a dive off a building, the others don't suffer the loss the way they would if everyone's earnings went into a pot and then got redistributed. They don't pool, if you will."

I snort. "That's a crock. Money coming in is good, regardless of the system."

"True enough," Harry agrees. "But whether or not we buy what Coburn was peddling, it came off like he had been making the rounds behind closed doors, trying to rally support among his partners to give Becker the heave. It just felt like I was getting the choice tidbits of some well-rehearsed talking points on what Becker did and did not mean for the firm."

"Don't know much law, but you can't just bum-rush a partner. You gotta buy him out."

Harry raises a finger. "Ah, but it might be less costly if the guy's crossed the line a couple of times. Legal ethics is a big bugaboo these days, and Coburn's been taking notes on our boy Elliot. I know this. Some things they tell without telling, you know?"

"I'm familiar. You talk to the ex?"

"That I did, for a moment or two," he says. "Very sweet. Not altogether broken up over her ex's death, but there's some guilt there. She gave me her card. Maybe you'll be the one to get back to her—she's the liberal feminist type, so she'll like you."

"Where's the guilt coming from? She dump him?"

"She did, at that. Had an affair and everything."

I feel an eyebrow rise. "This is what 'very sweet women' are doing these days?"

He spreads his palms like I've stumped him. "You know I'm such a softie when it comes to your sex. That's why next time it's going to be you who talks to her."

"So what have we got?" I rest my chin on my knees. "I'm seeing a self-styled playboy, fast approaching fifty, who strikes out with the ladies, could soon be on the outs with his law partners, and has an ex who pities him. Cripes—maybe the guy did throw himself off a building."

"True enough," Harry says. "True, true, true enough."

FIVE

Marina Papanikitas's Personal Journal

Yo, Zoey, m'sweet,

I walk in to find a mass of wholesome goodness on the kitchen counter: bunch of powdery nuts, packet of dates aged to resemble so many shrunken heads. Hey, and in the sink some veiny weeds and two dinosaur eggs. Someone's been to the Asian market, my detective instinct tells me. Meaning someone is back at trying to pry open someone else's mind on what constitutes elegant eats? Well, bring it, babe. Appears, however, that you have rushed off in that "forgot the effing miso paste" style of yours. This is going to be odd, but I have grown accustomed to our non-speaking mode of keeping close. So, to the journal I go, even as I await your arrival.

Picked up a puppy at the precinct, by the way. Cop named Malloy, who for some reason craves my approval. Think I might have muttered "good job" or something when he found that leopard print scarf the other night—next to useless, of course, as evidence, although now I know the lady we're chasing wears a lot of scent—so now he keeps popping by with updates. Lab report on the drink Becker was having on that terrace before he took his fall—hey, guess what, it was whiskey. And guess what, the lipstick on the rim of the Irish coffee glass was a lady's. That sort of stuff. I just keep telling myself that not too very long ago, that was me.

The memory makes me tolerant—and super grateful to those who held their temper during my pre-homicide years.

On my way home, I drop in on Bonnie McCloud. Kind of on a whim—she's on my to-do list, but not my commute route—but when I call from the car, she picks up and says sure, so I hit the blinker on Broadway. Lives in a pocket of Rosindale meandering toward upscale. I claim the hydrant spot—cop's prerogative—and find her kneeling on the grey lawn with her back to me and her long skirt splayed, hair in a fat knot, poking bulbs into a bed. House is uber-gingerbread—carvey trim and crooked windows everywhere. Whimsical paint choices—talking orange, pink, yellow—my eyeballs spasm just looking at the place, even shrouded in evening light. Neighbors probably grouse, but the beige siding and chainlink most of them have gussied their places up with doesn't exactly score them style cred.

I tread up the walk, and Bonnie turns an ear, then stands, lifting a gloved hand to wipe at her nose with the back of her wrist, her eyebrows raised politely, but her eyes prepared to say she's not interested. Am I, like, somehow putting out a J.W. vibe these days?

I smile and pull out my badge, remind her that she met H.P. at the law firm.

"Sure, yeah, nice to meet you." She's got a young voice; talks kind of lispy, too. Pulls a gardening glove off to give me a firm finger squeeze. Cheeks and nose looking a little raw, but that's from the chill air and not weeping. "Mind if I finish this up while we talk?" She sticks a finger down into a brown paper bag and takes a peek. "I'm a little late getting them in this year, and I've got about twelve to go."

I seat myself on the steps as she kneels on her worn rubber pad. "Daffs?"

"Up the path. These are tulips. I do my dahlias in pots, and put them in come spring under the bay." She rests on her haunches and laughs at herself. "We like color."

I smile. "You wear it well."

She looks down at her alpaca sweater and patchwork skirt and shakes her head as if just realizing what she's got on. "It's more Dominic than me. He sees something he thinks he'd like me in, he buys it," she says apologetically. "And, like most men, he doesn't think in terms of outfits. But when he designs a book cover, I'll tell you, it sells." She resumes digging.

"How long you two been married?"

"We're not," she says simply.

"Oh. Your house or his—I mean if you don't mind my asking? I house-share, myself."

"Same. We bought it together about two years ago."

"Must be tricky, making a commitment after a divorce."

She sits back, one knee up under the skirt. "It's all tricky, is what I'm learning," she says. "We're thinking about tying the knot in January, though. Dominic's got an ex, too. Fortunately, she's in a relationship right now."

I watch her press a bulb down. "You think Elliot was unhappy about you and Dominic?"

"Elliot wasn't the jealous type. He wanted me to be happy." She resumes digging.

"Think he was unhappy, generally?"

"I'm pretty sure he was, but I don't think for a minute that he killed himself." She seems to frown upon hearing her own words. I can't see her face well. "Actually, I know he didn't."

"Got a reason you can put into words, or is it that you just know?"

She shakes her head and leans on the heel of her hand so as to deepen the hole. Her shoulders move with the work. "I don't have to consider it," she says. "Elliot and I were married for five years and divorced for seven. He had a lot of insecurities, but suicide wasn't in his vocabulary. Elliot was murdered. I got the feeling that your partner knew it when I met him, and my guess is that you know it too." She stops digging and looks up. "Don't worry, I don't expect you to answer that. I'm just saying that I'm relieved that you're going at it from that angle, because I know that's what it must have been."

"Any insights into why he might be up on that hotel roof terrace with someone?"

She sighs. "I can think of a couple of reasons, but my best guess is that he was there to get laid." She drops the trowel and sits back on her haunches, apparently having lost her taste for planting. "I don't mean to make him out like a pick-up artist, but that was his thing, and he was kind of proud of it. I don't think he grew up happy. When he got out of law school and put on a suit, suddenly women were very attracted to him. He ran with it."

"Why would a woman want to kill him, though?"

"I don't think any would, at least not because he'd dumped them. I mean, he played the field, but that wouldn't have been a surprise to anyone he was seeing. He was open about it."

"Surprised you, didn't it?"

She laughs sharply as she shakes the soil off her gloves. "It didn't, actually." Her eyes are bright in the dusk. "Guess that's why I let myself start up with Dominic."

"Good enough for the gander, that sort of thing?"

"Well, no." She scratches gently at her face, wary about the soil on her hands. "It was more that I realized that Elliot and I would eventually split. He wasn't a guy who was going to change, no matter what he might intend." She looks off, thinking, and I watch her squeeze her hand into a fist like she's trying to choke off a line of memory.

I change my tone. "So, look, you said you could think of a couple of reasons that Elliot might have been up there on that roof terrace. Like what, other than going there with a woman?"

She thinks. "Actually, I don't know what I meant by that. Just a turn of speech."

"Care to tease it out with me? I mean, I know we're just speculating, here, but psych games can be worthwhile. I've had some luck with them in the past."

Bonnie sits back, some of her tension subsiding. This is her kind of thing. H.P. was right to want me on her. "So…what are you asking me to do?"

I lean forward, elbows on knees. "Let's make up a story for Elliot going up to that roof terrace other than to be with a woman."

She plays with her hair. It's not right, she's thinking, but she wants to. And I don't seem like a typical flatfoot—I won't seize on whatever she says like it's an admission. And, of course, on some level it would be a relief if Elliot had not been killed by a spurned woman. Elliot was a dope, but she'd rather him to have died with some dignity.

Shutting up seems like the way to go, so I do that. She begins without prodding, but slowly, as if sorting her thoughts as she goes.

"Elliot was homophobic as the best of them, so all I can think is that he would be trying to work some deal. Elliot prided himself on his ability to work backroom deals."

"Why on the roof, though?"

She shakes her head but continues. "Maybe so as to not be overheard? He'd have liked the idea that he needed to take steps to protect the confidentiality of a deal he was concocting." She glances my way. "Ironically, he'd never shut up about one of his scores once he closed it."

"What kind of deals are we talking about? Legal stuff?"

"Yes, of course," she says, then pauses. "Well, at least he'd have his arguments all lined up about how whatever he was doing was technically legal."

"Did he ever deal with criminals, to your knowledge?"

"Well, he started in defense work. I mean, you deal with criminals every day, right?"

"Sure," I say agreeably. "But I meant more like doing legal work for mobsters."

I'd half-expected the idea to give her pause—brash guy who thinks he can handle himself does a deal for some hoods, deal goes south, hoods react the way hoods know how—but she brushes it off without question. "Elliot wouldn't have had any mob dealings, even legal ones. It's just not like him. Elliot was more of a one-man show. He wouldn't want to be beholden to any kind of boss. I mean, that was his whole problem at Richardson."

"He had problems at the law firm?"

She glances up at me like she knows that I already know this. "He never should have joined that partnership. Elliot was meant to be solo. He said so a million times. He just couldn't resist the prestige of an old waspy label, so he tried to play it both ways."

"You think he could have gotten himself in trouble with his partners?"

She answers simply. "Absolutely. I don't doubt that there was plenty of friction. Would they kill him? A bunch of lawyers?" She gives me a roll of her eyes. "Elliot may have pretended he was living a real-life Grisham novel, but I don't think so."

"They might give him the boot, though."

"Fat chance." She sits back from her work to give me all her attention. "Look, you have to remember something. Elliot was silly when it came to women and, yes, he cared too much about what strangers thought of him so he could look plenty silly there, too. It's called narcissism. But all that didn't mean he was stupid, by any means. Elliot could pull something off that other lawyers wouldn't have been able to maneuver. He anticipated better than those around him. That's why they disliked him at the firm. They could complain all they wanted about his tactics, but you can mark my word that there wouldn't have been anything illegal or, you know, in breach of the partnership. Elliot was that cocky SOB you so wished would cross the line enough to get himself burnt, but it never quite happened."

I dip my head. "Sounds like he could make people pretty mad."

She laughs. "You don't say?"

"So let me ask you this. How did Elliot afford his lifestyle?"

"Well, I'm sure he did pretty well at his practice," she muses. Then she cocks her head. "Like, what do you mean by lifestyle?"

"Maybe you haven't seen his condo. He only got into it last year. Beacon Street."

"Nice?" She seems a tiny bit curious in spite of herself.

"About nine million nice. Bit showy for my taste, all that glossy mosaic tile spreading out before you, the leather ceilings, and all that glass to soak in the unobstructed view of the Charles. Still, the elevator entrance thing is cool—straight shoot up, car to bar. And car means one of those mini Ferarris everyone's salivating over. Bar's rocking some limited edition vodkas. All this is news to you, I'm gathering?"

She looks baffled for a moment, then affects a shrug. "We didn't have any kind of arrangement, so it was pretty much none of my business how Elliot was doing after we split." After a long pause, she adds, "I'm glad he was doing well financially. That would mean a lot to him. And it certainly supports my gut sense that Elliot wasn't in a frame of mind to take his own life, right?" She's doing a good job trying to deflect, but she can't quite hide her shock and suspicion at how Elliot's nest egg had exploded so much since their split.

"Look, Bonnie, my partner and I, we keep dancing around this wheeler-dealer idea because the woman angle is so bloody easy, and we hate when life's easy. So let me ask you one more time, just for kicks, and I want you to answer without thinking. First words that come to your mind. You think it's conceivable that Elliot could have maneuvered some backroom deal that someone just couldn't tolerate? I mean, we all agree that Elliot had a big ego, but so do a lot of other guys who fashion themselves to be big fish. Some of those guys can't take being beat."

"So they'd kill the lawyer who outmaneuvered them? I mean, please." She does answer immediately, just like I asked her to, but it's clear she wants to quash the whole idea, and why not? One way, he's just her lovelorn idiot ex. The other way, he's a crook who lost his way after she abandoned him. She doesn't like the first option, but she likes the second option less.

"Yeah, sounds stupid," I agree. "Still, there's lots at stake, sometimes. There's liberty, in a plea bargain situation. Political capital, when you're doing business with the state. And money can be more than just money if it's old family money. Hell of a lot of toes out there waiting to be squashed by some guy who doesn't have quite the finesse to match his chutzpah."

The sun's gone down, so I hear more than see her gathering up her bag and trowel. "I've actually got a bunch of editing to get through tonight," she says. She sounds queasy.

I stand up. "Understood." I put out my hand. "And let me reiterate that I do get the difference between fact and speculation."

"Yes, well," she says, offering a weak, chilly hand. She nods, trying to convince herself that she hasn't helped me to suspect her ex of something that could blacken his name a lot more than infidelity. "Be sure you remember that, okay?" she says.

Glancing back when I hit the sidewalk, I see her in silhouette, the cheery house behind her. Best I can make out, she's staring after me, gripping the bag of bulbs.

I'm beginning to sense there's more than meets the eye going on with Elliot Becker's death, Zoey. I'm thinking that Elliot's ex kind of senses that, too.

SIX

I am Nightingale—

You know, my friends, when first I began circling in on Elliot Becker—following the girls from his office so as to catch tidbits about him, watching his Back Bay high rise to steal a glimpse of him sliding out of the underground garage in his silver coupe, trailing him to the gourmet market, the riverside jogging paths, his private Pilates class—my intent was to be unerringly methodical about this kill, and all my kills. I would observe all simultaneously, then enter the life of each man, seriatim and without pause between, position myself for the dispatch, and execute without passion. My touchstone would be my detachment. I would play the quintessential Moreau.

This did not prove to be the case. My encounter with Elliot was eye-opening, in spite of my painstaking efforts. Certainly the man was, to all appearances, a parasite, marinated in ego, incapable of conscience or remorse, his mentality differentiable from a child's innocent greed due only to his smug sexuality. It was on this that I focused, the last evening of his life. Still, you know, in killing Elliot Becker, I killed a child, as this was what he was in his innermost mind. There was something disquieting about it; it haunts me to this day as I observe my son, sucking esuriently at my nipple, his tiny fingers kneading the air, his infant eyes translucent with satisfaction. And back then, it made me realize that this adventure in serial killing would not be the tidy linear project

I had envisioned, five chores executed domino style, five dead guys in my wake. Murder, it turns out, is emotionally complex. Who could have guessed?

And thus I approach the killing of Rocco Petrianni, owner of Rocco's – A Gentlemen's Club, with some trepidation. It is not that Elliot Becker had caused me to question my resolve. But I come to my second kill looking for some confirming gesture. As you will see, I was in luck to have selected Rocco for this moment of affirmation.

For two weeks, even as I set my plans in place for Elliot and my other targets, I spend some of these choice evenings observing Rocco from the shadows of his bar, my wig askew, fingers palsying against my cigarette as I affect the persona of the self-loathing female lush. During this time I *fourrage* into his mind multiple times, but there is only one message Rocco emits—he is an unequivocal man, all told. A misogynist, certainly, and akin to Elliot in that way, but in this instance it is not borne of insecurity and yearning; Rocco is *au fond* distinct from his predecessor in that he yearns for nothing. He is exactly what he wants to be, and, more amazingly, he is aware of this. He thrives on cruelty, which he recognizes as the essence of masculinity and thus his birthright. His life, as such, is at once content and restless, his psyche at peace yet violent. But he is not devoid of wile, and in his aversion to those different from he, he is naturally both predatory and wary at all times. I wonder, slipping into his club through the employee entrance on the after-noon following Elliot's final flirtation, exactly how the dispatch of Rocco will proceed. A killer must stay loose, you see—the need to improvise will arise without question. I harbor no doubt, however, that I will accomplish my goal within the hour.

Emerging silently into the near-deserted bar, I find myself standing only yards behind Rocco himself. He sits sipping a blanc cassis. I settle an elbow against the bar and slip into Rocco's mind as he takes in the room. He has recently redone the place, I learn. Purple lighting. Sculptured carpet. Bucket-style chairs with an ox-blood leather finish. There are six glittering poles on the stage, which itself has been widened and can easily accommodate eight girls. Strings of minuscule lights rim the dance area, which is backed by a coruscating curtain of ruby and silver. And everything—stage, bar, all the furnishings—is trimmed in glossy mahogany. "A spectacle of excess." That was the phrase Rocco had kept in mind for the redesign, and he has achieved it. Last night some of the Cs had been in from Boston; one of them began tossing dollars at the stage and then others joined, their massive brown hands throwing bills until money was churning in the air like confetti. Rocco had six of his best girls out there, slipping on the bills, cramming them into their G-strings and bras. No fights, no injuries. Just a damned good time. Making a regional name for Rocco's.

He observes a group of young men just entering across the expanse. College softies, Rocco thinks, their jeans drooping, visors crested just so. Douchebags groping for some manhood. Rocco feels his spirits lift. Been a grind of a week for everyone. He taps a couple of fingers on the bar to get Pauly's attention.

Late afternoon, he has just the new girl on. He suspects she might be underage, although the broads are putting braces on their teeth at all ages these days. She amuses herself and the couple of barflies watching her by languidly swinging her dimpled legs around one of the poles, rolling her head so that her yellow corkscrew locks cover her face, and throwing in the occasional squat to show how far her thong cuts into her cheeks. She is part of the decor. The frat boys are settled along one of the banquettes now, if puds like them can "settle" anywhere. They call out for a "rub and tug" and "some tail." Rocco throws a glance over at Lenny, who flashes a quick grin. Lenny is a mixed martial artist with professional fighting experience. He enjoys the opportunity to flex.

One of the waitresses, a henna-haired tramp well past her lap dance years, heads over to take an order and maybe hint that it might be a good idea to tone it the hell down. Whatever she says, it does not do the trick. One of them starts yelling: "*Tell me that I'm pretty, honey! Tell me I'm pretty!*" Much cackling from the others. The boys order, then a couple approach the stage, pulling out their wallets. Rocco hears one of them giggle something about "all that slutty goodness up there." Encouraged, Goldilocks puts a little hip into her gyrations. Some of the regulars smirk in anticipation as Lenny saunters closer.

Party begins when one pretty boy goes to stick a twenty in Goldilocks's thong. Although this is commonly done, and without fail by newcomers to strip joints, the house rule is that patrons do not touch the girls. Sure enough, Pretty Boy flicks the twenty and Goldilocks swivels her way over, then squats so that he can shove the thing under her elastic. Pretty Boy does not quite make contact when Len gets his attention, moving behind him with his arms crossed. A conversation follows which ends with Pretty Boy tossing the bill onto the stage, where Goldilocks snatches it like a dog at a cookie. Pretty Boy heads back to his table, shouldering past Lenny with just enough contact to bump the other man sideways. Or so Lenny makes it appear.

As Rocco watches, he feels my presence behind him. He glances around and is surprised to see that I am a woman. Rocco usually notices when a woman enters the place. He nudges forward, assuming that I am seeking to pass by him.

Lenny has sauntered over to the rowdies. Rocco watches as Pretty Boy gestures with his beer glass. What's coming is predictable.

"Mr. Petrianni?" I say from behind him. I lay some Eastern Europe into my accent.

He tilts his head my way, then turns when I speak no further. I wait, my eyes without expression. Rocco is not fond of women with attitude. He hitches himself up a notch on his stool, letting me know that I have as much of his attention as I am going to get.

"I am from Tuscany Champagnes," I say. "You were expecting me, I trust?"

Rocco hears rattling glass and turns his head. Lenny's got one of the dope's heads pressed against a table. A bottle has toppled, and beer pools against the kid's face. Rocco snaps his fingers and Pauly throws a bar towel over.

Rocco swings round on his barstool. He absorbs what there

is to see: my turtleneck sweater tucked into tight pants, cinched at the waist by a thick suede belt. Tits rather inauspicious, hips round, but long legs that make up for whatever my flaws may be. The pants disappear into a pair of boots. When he raises his eyes to my face, he reads something other than what he expects. I look, for lack of a better word, patient. Eyeballing women is what men do, my expression says, and so we will begin conversing when the inventory has been concluded. My lips are painted a deep brown. My hair is auburn, pulled back smoothly and rolled into a French twist. Quite the fucking get-up, Rocco thinks.

"Excuse me," he says. He walks across the carpet. "Look, son," he says, gripping the kid's shoulder. "You want to stay, have a few drinks, watch the girls, sit your ass down and enjoy. If that doesn't suit you, you'll need to leave."

"What are you, funny?" Pretty Boy stands, and Rocco's hand on his shoulder is now reaching upward. The kid's got arms, too, which apparently has bred him some confidence.

"I'm a regular riot, most days," Rocco says tersely in answer. "But right now I advise you to take me very seriously."

Pretty Boy does not look scared, Rocco gives him that, as he casts about for how to salvage some of his self-esteem. Rocco does not wait for it. He drag-flips the clown over the table to land flat on his back on the carpet. It's loud and messy and takes about five seconds. Rocco straddles him, his feet spaced wide across the other man's chest. Action's over—Rocco actually heard his shoulder dislocate—but Rocco leans forward and looks him in the eye.

"Know your place," he says in a tight, quiet voice.

The guy's cap has fallen off, and Rocco is slightly surprised to see floppy curls where he would have expected a buzz. Rocco stands up and steps off him in one tight motion. All this happens so quickly that the guy's friends are only starting in with predictable shrills of "What the *fuck*?" Pauly and Lenny take over as Rocco heads to the exit, then holds it open as the twits get tumbled into the evening. Just before reentering, Rocco scans the parking lot. His eye grazes a car where a man with a goatee sits smoking behind the wheel, watching the scene with an affect of detachment as he taps cigarette ash across the rim of his open window. The car is an old model Mercedes, maroon in color. Rocco goes eye-to-eye with the man and gets an unpleasant vibe. He does not dwell on that fact. Lots of types visit strip clubs.

He reenters the club and walks toward the stairs to his office. He is not a man to gloat. Problem solved, he moves on. Someone, however, is standing in his path as he makes his way toward the dark end of the bar—oh, yeah, it's the chick in the Zsa Zsa Gabor getup who says she's selling champagne.

"Excuse the wait," he says.

"No matter. I am a representative of Tuscany Champagnes, as I stated earlier. We would like to add our newest malt beverages to your inventory, along with our signature champagnes. These fine new products are all offered at introductory prices." I extend my hand, a business card between my index and third fingers. My nails are thickly lacquered in a rich brown polish, whimsically dubbed Deathwish.

Rocco eyes me, ignoring the card. He thinks he knows what this is about and that I am no saleswoman, but he decides to string me along. "You got promos with you, I suppose?"

I smile briefly and lift my bulky sky-blue case, but I do not rest it on the bar. "Perhaps you will allow me to describe as you sample? Somewhere quiet? I would very much appreciate an opportunity to get to know your particular tastes, Mr. Petrianni," I say. "I am most certain that I can deliver whatsoever it shall take to satisfy you."

Rocco almost smiles. Why do women with shit English always talk like they are in a porno, he wonders? Do they not get what they are saying, or do they get it exactly, and is this simply the way they've learned to deal with men where they come from? He suspects it's the latter.

He leads me behind the bar and along the backstage corridor. Goldilocks is sitting on a folding chair, peering listlessly into the smudged reflection she casts in a little music player she has got balanced on her thighs while she uses two fingernails to pry at a pimple on her forehead. We can hear the whispery beat of a pop tune. When she sees Rocco she stands up quick, then throws back her hair so as to smile down her cheeks at him. Her face is brushed heavily with makeup, which contrasts oddly with the soft plump of untouched flesh under her chin. Her lips are thick with cherry gloss, a bit of which has smeared. That and the braces make her look about sixteen. Sweat trickles from her pits, staining her spangly bra.

"Afternoon, Mr. Petrianni," she slurs.

He tilts an eye at her. "What's your name again?"

She flushes. "Donnalinda. Donnalinda Tonite. But I can change it if—"

He reaches out and cups her face with his hand, pressing a thumb into one soft cheek and his fingers into the other. "How old are you, Donnalinda?"

She pauses, blinking. It occurs to Rocco that there is a possibility that she honestly does not know the answer to his question.

"I want you to leave, Donnalinda," he says. "I don't want to see you again until you can show Mr. Lenny some proof you're twenty-one." He squeezes her face. "Understand?"

He does not glance at me as we climb a narrow pack of stairs to his office. Rocco walks round behind his desk. Fishing out his cigarettes, he watches as I carefully close the door behind me. It is a large room, its walls covered in flimsy paneling, the floor laid with carpet that looks a decade past expiration. The single sash window overlooks a stretch of flat roof. My eyes rest momentarily on the doors to the closet, sliders that reveal some cases of liquor piled atop a safe. My eye does not pause again, as he watches me, until my gaze reaches the bathroom door. It is partially open, making it clear from where I stand that there is nothing in there but toilet and sink. We are alone. He sees that this satisfies me, but does not guess why.

"One of these?" he says, offering a pack of Chesterfields when my eyes return to him.

"Not for me, but I hope you will indulge," I say in my accent.

He laughs. "Thanks for the permission. So what you got for me, Miss, uh…" Here he makes a show of examining my card, "Nightingale. What's the F for?" He winks across at me, making it clear that he is onto me.

"The F is for Flora," I tell him, then smile. "A pretty name, yes?"

"Why don't we get started, Flora?" he interrupts. "I'm running a business."

My smile tightens. I heft my case onto his desk, then pop the latches. "I thought we would try a champagne. You seem like a champagne man."

"So where you from?" he says. "Russia or something?"

I polish a glass with a handkerchief. "Not Russia, no. My people were originally from Turkmenistan, but I have been in the States for quite some years. I speak well?"

"Sure, sure. Figured you for a local," he taunts me.

I place the two glasses on his desk and begin twisting the wire off a small bottle of champagne. I pop the cork and cast a critical eye at the waft of gas that drifts from the bottle's lip. "This one is my favorite of the three. Sells briskly everywhere it is carried."

He sips the champagne, his eyes on me.

"You see?" I encourage him. "Attractive undertones."

"Beautiful," he says. "So how's the poppy trade back home?"

I stop momentarily, then move my hand over to a thin liquor bottle made of frosted white glass, busying myself with its stopper. "There is much opium coming out of Afghanistan. I know a girl who carried product into the States for a certain Boston businessman. Very risky, but she received good money." I present the uncorked bottle. "Speaking of smuggled pleasures, this is Arak. In my country we call it 'milk of lions.' Mostly it is drunk by men, but here your women do as they like." I nod encouragingly. "Can I pour…?"

He sniffs and touches at his moustache. "Let's get to the point. You peddling dope?"

I stop, my hand holding a couple of chunky snifters. The Arak sways and shimmers in its bottle. "You flatter me, Mr. Petrianni."

"How so?"

"The girls who do this, they are quite young—eighteen, twenty, no more."

He continues to stare me down. "Are you offering trade or not?"

I hesitate, then tilt the Arak bottle over one of the glasses. "Let us enjoy what I have brought and speak of it only, shall we?"

Rocco stands up, reaches across the desk, and grabs me by the wrist, hard. "Damned straight you're not offering trade," he says in a calm, dead voice. "Because if an undercover cop offers drug trade, that's enticement, and you can't make the charge stick."

I look down at his hand gripping my wrist for a drawn-out moment. I do not try to free myself. I think about his interesting misinterpretation of my drop-dead perfect Jeanne Moreau—so I am a cop, now? Well, as I always say, you never can tell what you will stir up when you *fourrage* in a man's head. I raise my eyes to his. "In truth, Mr. Petrianni, I was a courier for two years, while in my twenties. I did not like it then. I would not go back to that life now."

He studies me for a moment, then, quite suddenly, yanks me closer, half across the desk, in fact. I cry out softly even as my free hand shoots out to prevent the Arak bottle from toppling.

"Your accent's slipping," he says. "Time to come clean."

I think about it, my breathing audible, then swallow hard and nod. Without bringing attention to it, I cork the Arak bottle. "Whatevah," I say in my best Southie accent. "But let go the arm, huh? I'm not a cop, but if you fuck with me I know a few ain't gonna like it much."

He shakes his head and pulls my arm even closer, so that I am dragged fully onto his desk, my feet off the floor, my shoulders awkwardly twisted. I cry out involuntarily from the pain. It is all I can do to keep from knocking the precious bottle of Arak to the floor. "Look, shithead, what is this getting you?" I manage to gasp out. "You made me, I admitted it. Game over. Now get your fucking mitts off of me."

"What's the scam?" He spits the word directly into my face,

then shows me a raised finger of warning. "If you say you sell fancy booze for a living I'll break your wrist, then ask again." He pauses to let me get used to the idea that I am about to tell the truth. Then he proceeds in a calm, friendly tone. "Now, who are you and why are you here?"

I nod at him, eye to eye as if I am truly frightened. "Name's Nightingale, like I said. Flo Nightingale. I'm a private detective, right? Not a cop. Not working with no cops. I don't know about no drug trade or why you think the cops are into you. I swear t'Gad, right? Swear t'Gad."

Rocco narrows his eyes. He believes me. Still, he enjoys holding me there, against my will, off balance and under his control. "You wearing a wire, Flo Nightingale?"

I shake my head. "It's just you and me, lover."

Again, he believes me, but he decides to check for himself. Adjusting his grip on my arm, he leans across the desk and feels around at my sweater, gripping each of my breasts, poking his fingers into my armpits, then running his palm down my side and directly to my crotch, which he grips harder than necessary. I utter a muffled cry and twist my face away, as if humiliated. Satisfied, he reaches up and feels around my ears, then notices that my hair, still in its elegant bun, is askew. He yanks off the wig and I grimace as the pins pull at my actual hair. He laughs at the idea of a PI wearing a wig, then leans back to assess the real me. He likes my hair, which is parted on the side in a classic boy cut, dyed in streaks. He softens his grip, just a touch, without realizing it. I am not some snotty European after all. I'm a scrappy local tomboy. He almost likes me. Still, that will not stop him from kicking my teeth in if the conversation goes sour.

"I seen you here before, now I think about it, with a different wig on. You been around now and again past couple of weeks. I seen you talking to Pauly down the bar, just the other night. Don't tell me it wasn't you, neither."

"It was me, yeah. I'm supposed to be checking you out. Today was gonna to be the end of it. Last day I'm paid up to, anyways."

Now that he knows he is not about to be busted, Rocco is enjoying the bit of drama we are playing out. He grabs the forelock of my hair and pulls my head back hard so my neck is stretched taut. "I said I want to know what's going on," he says into my face.

"And I just told you!" I spit back. "What are you, deaf or just plain dumb?"

It's the kind of answer he was hoping for. Letting go of my hair, he slaps me, a real stinger, then reasserts his grip in my hair.

"Easy, boyfriend," I pitch him. "Just trying to make a living here."

He slaps me again, hard enough that the side of my face goes numb and my ear rings for a long moment. "Ready to talk, Flo?" Rocco says in his even voice.

"Yeah, here's some talking: go fuck yourself," I say. I see a tiny spray of saliva from my mouth land on his collar. A few of the bubbles are pink with blood.

With a nasty smile, Rocco releases my hair, stands up straight, and punches me. It is an open-handed punch, admittedly, but still not much of a contest. I am propelled backwards and fall rather clumsily from desk to floor. With that, dear friends, I have reaffirmed everything I'd hoped for with the able assistance of Rocco Petrianni. It would not have saved his life if he had turned out differently, but it is far less troubling as it is. As if in response to my thought, I see my little pet, the Arak bottle, rolling around next to me on the carpet, toppled but intact. I tuck it behind me to protect it as Rocco walks around the desk. I put up an arm as if to ward him off.

"You made your point," I say. "You can hit a woman. Wow, ain't you the one."

"I'm waiting, Flo," he says from above me.

I shake my head around a little, testing for damage, then roll my jaw, glance up at him. "I'm looking into the Dorchester Five, okay? All five, not just you. I'm just supposed to see what all of yous is up to. And that's everything I know, so if you could keep your hands to yourself from this point forward, I'd greatly appreciate it."

"The Dorchester Five?" he interrupts. "What the hell are you talking about?"

I run a finger under my nose and check it for blood. Just snot. "What, you trying to tell me you don't remember being one of the Dorchester Five?" I say, pushing myself back against the desk as if worried that he might aim one of his pointy black shoes at my gut. "Like eight years ago up in Boston, you bunch of winners tipped a car with a guy inside. Went on trial and walked. Any of this ring a bell, or has life been just so goddamn sweet since?"

Rocco makes a cutting gesture to shut me off, then steps back and adjusts his shirt. I sit up and touch at my face with the back of my wrist. He offers a hand but I ignore it and get up on my own. I bring the Arak bottle back, setting it on the desk.

Rocco rights a chair, and I sit in it while he hitches a thigh onto the desk. "Who the hell would be interested in the Dorchester Five? That shit's ancient history."

I glance up at him like I am nervous that he is going to start using me as a punching bag again. "Guy whose car you rolled died. That bring it any closer for you?"

He sneers. "Prick had it coming," he says. "Some dick from the suburbs, thinks he can mosey on into the city to pick up his coke fix and then coast on out back to the mansion."

My turn to scoff. "They got a lot of mansions over in Southie? Myself, I never noticed. Anyway, it's been a slice, Romeo, but I got a report to write. And it ain't my finest piece of work, so…" I go to rise, but Rocco stills me with a raised finger.

"You know better than that."

I shrug like I agree and slump back in the chair.

"Who you working for, Flo?"

I sigh. "So Terence D'Amante got released from Walpole late August, right? Very same night, he's shot to death on his girl-friend's front stoop. Close range—execution style. It's got some attention, and that's all I know because the guy who hired me ain't my actual client."

Rocco ignores my false bravado. "So let me get this," he muses.

"Someone thinks that one of the other Dorchester Five was out to get D'Amante?"

"Might be," I say gruffly. "Like I said, I do not know because—"

"Don't add up," he interrupts. "If the guy's capable of pulling off an execution kill on a public street, why wouldn't he just have had the asshole killed inside? A guy in the pen's a sitting duck. Anyone like me wanted him dead over these years, he'd have been dead."

"Well, maybe the killer didn't know how to make that happen," I say as if uninterested. "It's not like all the others are connected with the gang thing, like you obviously are."

He shrugs. "Proves I'm innocent, at any rate."

"Ironic little world, ain't it, though?" I agree. "Got some ice, angel?"

Rocco is puzzled momentarily, then sees the way I am handling my jaw. He tips his forehead at the little fridge against the wall. "Help yourself."

I rummage, then turn to him with a few cubes in my hand. "Look, I think I could use that drink we was talking about before you, uh, broke my cover," I say. "You in?"

Rocco looks at me, slightly surprised, then cracks a smile to indicate his answer.

I fake smile back. "You break my snifters, tough stuff?"

He fishes them out of my case, where they managed to survive our scuffle. I walk over, drop a cube into each, and pour. "So, long as I did my homework, let me show off a little. See how this stuff goes white? Called louching. It's the ice. Purists drink it straight, but Americans like it foggy." Taking my glass, I raise it and sniff. "Whoa! *Ça déchire la tête*, eh?"

He cocks an eye at my French.

"Stuff'll rip you a new one," I translate. "I better take a little water. I'm driving." I head to the little bathroom. "Now, don't drink without me," I call out. "It's bad luck."

"I don't believe in luck," he says in a terse, automatic way, as if he is thinking about something else. Ah, but he does not know how correct he is. He is, at this point, just about fuck out of luck.

"No?" I empty my drink into the sink, retaining the ice cube, and add water from the tap. "Big fan of luck, myself," I say around the door. "My line of work, I rely on it."

"Yeah, well, it didn't come through for you today too good, did it?" he says.

I emerge from the bathroom, swirling my glass. "Day ain't over, handsome."

"Cigarette?" he says.

I nod. "Yeah, actually."

He shakes one partway out and offers it. "Look, Flo, I don't believe for a minute that you don't know who your client is. PI's don't operate like that."

"They do when some guy drops a fat money order on their desk and they got bills to pay," I offer. "What, you think we're like those human hairdos on TV, tooling around in two-seat convertibles, hopping in and out without using the door?"

I let him light me up. "I don't buy it, and you're not getting out of here without telling me," he says pleasantly enough. "I mean you get that, right, Flo?"

"I do," I say flatly. I draw on the cigarette. "Fact is, I got my ideas."

"So I figured," he says, lighting his own cigarette.

"Maybe I'll tell you, being as we're getting along so nice now," I say. "But only after you answer me something." I smoke and lift my snifter.

"Like what?" Rocco sips the liquor and bares his teeth to draw some air.

"Little while ago, you acted like you having been one of the Dorchester Five wasn't no big deal. But that was just bull, right? I mean, just between us A-rabs?"

He shrugs, uninterested. In spite of himself, however, he thinks it over. The fact is, he still remembers going after that douchebag in the VW, the rush of being part of a serious, spontaneous ass-kicking. And, for a moment, a full-sense memory floods his conscious mind.

Rocco throws the gym door out of his way, noting how a couple of gays flinch as they skitter by. Behind him, Ella booms, "Watch me winder, white boy." The heat hangs heavy, making folks woozy. His muscles thrum from his workout. He's restless.

He spots the car, then, bobbing round the slower cars, coming from a ways off, jagging in and out—some impatient prick. Somehow, Rocco knows. His eyes stick with the dull blue balloon of a car, and then an old lady darts out from the sidewalk. She's tiny and comes out from between two parked cars—she's going to get hit and it's her own damn fault. Rocco watches the old bag pinwheel over the hood to land on her neck, orthopedic shoes still trying to walk upside down, slip billowing in the heat. In the moment it happens, it's barely noticed. The dipshit behind the wheel never saw it coming—he doesn't even brake enough to slide. For long seconds, no one even turns. Guy on the sidewalk right by where it happened is eyeing a chick's ass and uttering a long, drawn-out statement of appreciation. A knot of church ladies, thinking the dead biddy's still among them, continue to fan themselves as they gab. A dog takes a languid piss against a hydrant.

The little bug rolls forward, shuddering as its engine stalls, then jerks backwards as it shifts into reverse—Rocco can see the sunlight reflecting off the windshield, but nothing of the driver. Doesn't matter. He knows, now, where the afternoon is heading. The twit, dazed and frightened, intent on nothing but getting himself out of the trouble he's suddenly found himself in, is going to bolt. The onlookers, waking up to the tragedy in their midst, will seize the opportunity to make the stranger a scapegoat. And, if someone takes charge, administers a little painful justice, the mob will respect that guy. Even as he's arrested, convicted, does time, they will revere him.

Rocco sees all this, but not as a spectator. He recognizes the moment on a personal level—it is his. This is how he makes his mark. He moves fast, pushing through the passersby, even as the little bit of the world surrounding that car begins to recognize the reality under their noses. Rocco hears a hoarse yelp as one of the old lady's cronies figures out what she's just seen. Rocco flexes, feels the blood in his shoulders and arms. The bug's engine revs, and the car jerks clumsily to the right, then left, as if the driver is attempting to turn the thing. Rocco jumps into the street, spreads his arms and slams two fists down against the flimsy hood of the car, then points through the windshield. "Get the FUCK out of that vehicle, cocksucker!" he roars. And that's when the guy really tries to rev and run. Rocco's one step ahead. He's so pumped full of adrenaline, he might actually stop the moving auto singlehandedly. But he doesn't have to. There's a rush into the street to join him—Rocco will never forget the thunder of that stampede. A man focuses when his defining gesture is upon him.

"It was no big deal," Rocco answers my question. "It happened. I moved on."

But I have skated along with him through this flash of memory, you see, and so I realize quite thoroughly that in spite of his affect, the Dorchester Five had been the profound moment in his life. All these years later, that memory and more—the arrest, the trial, even the sight of Jakey with his face and brains damaged beyond repair—all of this still gives him the huge rush. He is a man quite worthy of his life. And of his fate. Of this I am now certain.

"You're a cold man," I comment. "No insult intended, but…"

Rocco feels a pain in his stomach, a kick followed by a hot glow. Indigestion? He sips his drink to chase it away. "I am who I am. I don't pretend otherwise," he manages to respond.

"Well, then." I raise my glass. "Here's to you being you."

Rocco raises his own glass, when the intercom buzzes. He leans back across the desk and punches a button. We can both hear the tinny return from downstairs.

"Evening shift's on, boss. You wantin' anything?"

Rocco depresses the talk switch. "I'll be a minute."

He sits up. I am standing, my glass empty, looking for a place to staunch my cigarette.

"Time's up, huh?" I say. I go to where he tossed my stuff during our tussle and start puttering with it. "You gotta run, I can pull this crap back together and let myself out."

"Yeah, whatever," Rocco says. His gut is tied up in a knot made of white-hot wire. He feels beads of sweat break out on his upper lip. "Tell you something, lady. That fuck in the car had it coming. If it hadn't been that day, that incident, it would have been something else. No luck. No fate. No such thing."

I stand up with my case. It could very well be that Rocco is quite right about Jakey, his destiny. Wise, even. But I do not care. "No regrets, then," I say more than ask.

"I have never regretted a minute of my life," he growls, gripping his stomach.

I pick up the bottle of Arak, the last thing I need to collect. At his words, I uncork it and pour myself another hit. "I'll drink to that," I say, raising it. "No regrets."

"Damn straight," Rocco answers. He downs the rest of his, which tastes of aniseed but with a woody undertone. He has always prided himself on his palate. Makes him a cut above.

I drop the Boston accent. "You like the Arak?"

Rocco shakes his head. "Too much aftertaste. Too sweet. I wouldn't have ordered it, if you'd really been selling."

I empty my glass onto the carpet. "The aftertaste is not its fault. It's the cyanide that provided the syrupy tone. But do not worry. It will be quick."

Rocco shrugs, then immediately grimaces in pain. "That supposed to be funny?"

"*Pas de tout*," I say plainly, dropping my Boston accent. "Most of the time, I am a regular riot. But right now I would advise you to take me very seriously."

Rocco looks up at me sharply. Before he can think about it, he feels another explosion in his gut. This one erupts from his stomach into his chest, then courses like fire up into his throat.

It is enough for him to decide that I have, in fact, poisoned him. Always the man of action, he lunges even as a surge of lava rises in his mouth. "You fucking..." he manages.

His legs fail him. His pitches forward to land with his forehead almost touching the toe of my boot. Then comes the vomit. He cannot roll himself or even raise his head an inch, and so the mass of molten acid foams up against his face. He vomits again, drags air painfully into his lungs, and shrieks, very feebly, in pain. Or perhaps rage. I cannot say.

Rocco loses his bowels. The stench is feral, as if he has expelled half his ravaged guts. And perhaps he has—I do not know, as my study of cyanide ceased when I decided it would do the job. He raises his eyes and sees me, swimming, losing color fast. I am adjusting the auburn wig, a pin in my mouth as I secure the French twist into place. He cannot think, but if he could, he would nevertheless not have recognized me. It occurs to him that I may be a stripper he canned, back for revenge.

I crouch down near his ear. "You wanted to know the identity of my client?" I say. "Well I will tell you. I work for myself. I am *Nightingale*."

"You...fucking...cunt," he manages to croak.

And with that appeal to my feminine instinct to aid a dying man, he loses consciousness.

Two dead, three to go. The slices of cake, my friends, yes?

Très sincèrement,
Nightingale

SEVEN

Marina Papanikitas's Personal Journal

Well, Zoey, it may be me who has some sort of spastic psychic ability, but it's H.P. who made a major connection today. Gang-rushes me to his car on my arrival at the precinct, and then we're on our way to Rhode Island, my latte moustache still bubbling on my lip. Interspersed with the regular patter of mutterings about other drivers—hey, I finally figured out that "it's the long, skinny one on the right, lady," is a reference to the accelerator and not, as I'd imagined, some sort of phallic thing—he lets me in on our plan. Last night, he's doing his usual "three-way" over dinner, he tells me. This, turns out, is also non-sexual—just means he's conversing with the wife and also watching TV, all with his laptop open on the table so he can "hit up" stuff that piques his interest from anywhere. So in the midst of this homey mosh pit of info-overload, on the TV appears this face. It's one of those over-the-anchor's-shoulder flashes, on screen for maybe five seconds, and Harry entirely misses the accompanying headline, but it tugs on his nose—his expression, not mine—like he ought to know more about what's going on with that face. So he beads in on the crawl, and when he sees something about a Rhode Island strip club owner, there's that tug on his nose again. Hits up his favorite search engine and pretty quickly gets the story of Rocco Petrianni's murder. Couple more clicks and he's got the answer to his twitchy proboscis: Rocco's the second of the Dorchester Five to get whacked within a month. First Terence D'Amante and now Rocco. And so Harry and Pop go road tripping southward.

Now, strictly speaking, neither D'Amante nor Petrianni are any of our business, so, strictly speaking, we should have just thrown a heads up at the cops working on both cases. But it's no good going through channels when something curls its tentacles round your curiosity, and by the time H.P. finishes his tale, I'm in. As we do the freeway crawl out of Boston, I go to dial up Rhode Island's finest, but Harry shuts me down—makes his own call to a buddy in Providence and, with no detail and no trouble, gets us a promise of a guided tour of the death scene. Methinks I need me a buddy network. After that, we don't talk much in the car, as we have this more or less unspoken pact never to theorize about a crime until we walk the scene. Actually, this is Harry's pact with himself. I just get to live with it, a proposition that's not all that natural for me. I'm big into letting my imagination lead me to the truth, and I happen to imagine best with my mouth running. Bottom line, though, is that H.P. indulges my rather prodigious quirks, so I'm bound to indulge his. So silent we are, aside from the occasional grouse from Harry about the driving antics on display.

Rocco's – A Gentlemen's Club sits on a spread of blacktop between a sixteen-pump truck stop and some sort of gravel op along a light-industrial strip not far from the interstate. Not a terrible location for a naked lady lounge, all things considered. Essentially, the place is a warehouse—wood plank sides, corrugated roof, and nothing resembling a bush, tree, or weed anywhere near the place. Only clue it's a destination for fun and frolic is the signage that looks as if it would light up like a bunch of separate bulbs at night, reminiscent of an old burley house. Sheet glass doors down one end are the grand entrance, currently roped off with tattered yellow police tape and an official "Keep Out Crime Scene Violators Will Be Prosecuted" notice taped to each window where the "Live! Nude! Girls!" signs would normally dangle. There's one car in the lot—an unmarked Dodge complete with fancy grillwork and double side-views—affirming that H.P. has scored us backstage passes to the murder room. I should point out that while I'm pretty sure I would not have been totally straight-armed by the local fuzz, we've all met cops who get super turfy about their assignments, especially sizzly cases like a strip club murder. Nobody wants his shot at the we-interrupt-this-program press conference yanked out from under him.

The locals are waiting in the vestibule. Guy in charge is middle-aged and wire thin, with carefully razored white-blond hair, matching white eyebrows and lashes, and a hatchet-sized Adam's apple. Name's Jeff Shanko. Naturally, when I hear this, I barely refrain from a friendly crack about him playing "bad cop" during interrogations. Luckily I hold back, because it doesn't take all that long for me to suss out that I'm the only card-carrying Batman fan club nerd present. Shanko has a mild voice and an ice-cold handshake, and comes off as almost preternaturally humorless. The uniform he's brought along, Alec something-or-other, apparently takes his behavioral cues from his mentor. On the bright side, neither seems the least bit ruffled to be giving a couple of nosy parkers from Boston the crime scene tour.

Club seems like a typical strip joint—bar, stage, seats for ogling the deluded chicks who think their very own J. Howard Marshall's about to drop in. On our way up to the dead man's office, Shanko recites the story in a toneless way, just this side of sadistic. A couple nights back, Rocco was found dead by a bartender who went looking when he didn't come down for the dinner shift. I interrupt to remark on the fact that strip joints have dinner shifts, a fact that would not have occurred to me. All three men nod in a noncommittal way—either they share my surprise, or they're assuring me that all strip clubs serve steak tips and onion rings.

Rocco's office is a classic firetrap—clumsy egress, tinderbox paneling, one itty-bitty sprinkler poking through the asbestos ceiling tiles. Fire marshal's lucky day was when Rocco died some way other than a total conflagration. Body tape is curling back from the shag. We bend over to get a look at the stain remnants of whatever he'd been vomiting when he died.

"What am I smelling, garlic?" Harry makes a face.

"Picking up a licorice scent, too," I comment. "Like ouzo, but not. What was in his gut?"

"Might have been ouzo," Shanko hedges. "The other odor, possibly zinc phosphine."

"Providence lab a bit timid about commitment?" I ask, standing up.

Shanko drops one about life not being a *CSI* show. So he knows about TV, at least. I'm already hunting around for just the word to describe his particular brand of patronization.

"This zinc phosphine something a bar man like Rocco would usually use to chase his ouzo?" Harry asks lightly. Unlike me, H.P. always sticks to topic.

"It's a common rat poison, used less often than it was some years back," Alec offers. "But whatever he was drinking isn't what killed him."

Harry's incredulous. "Man dies in a pool of his own vomit and it turns out the rat poison in his system wasn't the cause?"

"No sir," Alec says, because every remark is meant to be taken at face value. "The vomiting expelled enough to make it nearly impossible for it to have been lethal. In addition, even a lethal dose of zinc phosphine wouldn't have killed him as fast as he died. Bartender spoke with him fifteen minutes before he was found dead and says he sounded fine."

"So?" I say, glancing at Harry, then back at our android counterparts. "This idea that Rocco was murdered at all comes from where?"

"Oh, he was murdered," Shanko says. "Someone strangled him. Used some sort of wire or plastic cord. The killer didn't leave it behind."

Alec lays photos on the desk. Rocco was early forties, if you can read a swollen face in profile and slimed in vomit. But I'm a woman in her thirties—I read crow's-feet and forehead creases like a forester reads tree rings. Speaking of creases, Rocco's got one round his neck that might have severed an artery with only a touch more effort. The fat ball of tongue, dead black, protrudes from between his teeth like a massy growth of fungus, making it hard to believe the rat poison didn't at least assist in the guy's demise. I note the gold potency necklace lacing his chest, the moustache carefully elongated into his cheek fur, the modified duck's ass up top. Everything says woman-hater so loud I can barely repress stating the obvious.

"So how do we know it was wire?"

"No fibers."

"Poisoned, then strangled? How's that make sense?" muses Harry. He's talking to me.

"Might have been electric cord," I say, thinking aloud. "An extension cord?"

They look at me.

"Something he found around the room," I say.

"Sure, okay?" says Harry, wanting more.

I explain myself better. "If someone slipped our friend a mickey, then found he wasn't dying fast enough, he might grab at something else to finish the job impromptu. Guy vomiting his guts out might be easy to strangle from behind, even by a person who'd thought they only stood a chance with poison."

"Like a woman," Harry observes.

"I could imagine Rocco being on a couple of girl-approved hate lists," I agree.

"Interesting," says Shanko woodenly. *Phlegmatic*! That's the word I've been trying for.

"Certainly plausible," Harry sides with me opaquely.

"The strangler had substantial muscular strength," counters loyal-to-the-bone Alec.

Meantime, I'm busy ignoring them. I take a go at the window. It's one of those cheap metal-framed sash jobs. Not a ton of room for anyone to hop through. Still, it would do in a pinch. Outside is rubber roofing. Judging from the number of exhausts piercing the expanse, the back wing's the kitchen. I get one of my tickly premmie feelings around the eyes and turn away quick before I find myself watching a ghost hurrying along the edge of the roof in a crouch. I cannot afford to go all vishie in front of the Rhode Island Robocops.

"Exit route?" I offer. "Anyone talk to the—whatever we call the guy dunking the fries at a strip club, and do not tell me it's 'chef'—about whether he heard the pit-a-pat of soft criminal feet overhead at any point?" That bit of snark was for you, Zoey—appreciate it.

"No prints on either the glass or the rubber," Alec points out. "Neither hand nor shoe."

I turn round from the window, shrugging stagily, palms up. "Guess our strangler whistled his way back down the stairs and slipped past an entire crew of professional men as they tarted up for a lively shift at Rhode Island's number one slut shop."

Shanko and Sidekick respond—or don't, you might say—with absolutely blank facial expressions. Harry, behind them, gives me his "what are you trying to do to me?" look.

We kick around the kitchen a little, thinking about routes in and out that someone could take unnoticed. I'm harboring this distinct premmie that I'm looking for something, and I find it out back. There's this ten-gallon canister, sitting amid the garbage spills around the base of the dumpster. White plastic, totally nondescript. Got a metal ladle handle sticking out. I remember the feeling that a near-identical visual gave me that night in the Hampstead. I peek—it's filled with some sort of greyish liquid, probably rainwater mixed with lard or whatever gunk had been in the bottom of the thing when set out. I prod around with the ladle and come out with a roll of thin cable wire. The Beantown Babe scores—oh, yeah.

"Have we found ourselves a murder weapon?" Harry gloats ever so slightly. I notice he does not sound surprised. More like he's been waiting.

I watch the water drip off the thing. Sometimes I think Harry's picked up on my so-called gift, but this is not something I'm ready to discuss. "Maybe someone did use the roof. Could have hopped down to the dumpster right over there," I indicate.

"Also hints that the strangulation was improvised," Harry adds. He turns to Shanko. "Might want to check if the cable connection's been ripped out in the vic's office."

Shanko seems indifferent to the idea. Nevertheless, he carefully bags the cable as Alec runs up to check out Rocco's office for where one such item might be missing. Sure enough, Rocco's TV is plugged in, but can't function without its absent cable.

Out in the lot, we let the local boys motor off first. Not that I was expecting effusive praise for my brilliant detective work, but the lack thereof gets me daydreaming about how fun it's going to be to have our Superintendent of Police call their Superintendent of Police to josh about how groovy it is when homicide teams cooperate—you know, just in case our new BFFs forget to mention who got their get for them today.

And that, Zoey, is when we get the real break we've been waiting for without knowing it. Harry's around the side taking a leak for the road when I spot this girl, trundling along from way, way across the median, heels scraping the roadway as she fools with her hair. She's got some hair, at that—so blonde let's call it yellow, and cast in fat ringlets that tangle amongst themselves to about halfway down her jacket, which looks to be constructed of a faux rabbit fur in brown, black, and white splotches. Her ample thighs stretch her fishnets to the breaking point. Weirdly, the overall effect is less of a car wreck than it ought to be, maybe because her face is young and essentially pretty, in that unobstructed-by-thought kind of way. In her hand she holds a little music player. Earphone cord disappears into her locks.

"Someone's missed the news," I think aloud.

Harry concurs. "Early for work, too."

The girl approaches, smiling at Harry, then noticing me better and catching on that I'm not a dude. I smile real nice, and she comes along, encouraged. It seems to dawn on her around then that there are no cars in the lot other than ours, and she stretches a piece of gum from her mouth thoughtfully as she makes to circle on past us toward the back, where she's probably been taught to enter. The gum's neon green.

"Excuse me, Miss?" Harry tries. She ignores him until he jogs around in front of her and waves, at which point she pops her pods with a gentle tug.

"Sorry, I'm not allowed," she says. Her pronunciation is slurry. I wonder if she's intellectually impaired. "Not on the premises, anyways."

Harry flips his badge. "Boston police. Not allowed?" he asks.

She stares at the badge but doesn't otherwise react. "To talk to the clients. Len says only when they're buying me a round." She looks from the badge to Harry's face. He smiles, so she does, too. "I'm of age," she says helpfully.

I come around to join them. "Back from a couple days off?"

"Yeah," she says. She pats a couple of red nails against a big plastic-coated purse, also red, that she's got over her shoulder. "Mr. Petrianni said to not come back till I could show Len proof of age. So I got it."

"From where?"

"Binghamton."

"Ouch. Long bus ride."

She shrugs. "They got TV."

I introduce us. "Mind telling us your name and answering a question or two?"

The girl glances up at the club. "I don't want to get in trouble," she says, taking a tentative step to one side. "I'm kinda in the weeds with Mr. Petrianni already."

"Club's closed for now, Miss," Harry says. "What can we call you?"

She looks past Harry again, staring at the club, her mouth open, the gum lodged patiently against her molars. "Donnalinda," she says, eyes now wandering to the police tape.

"Got a last name, Donnalinda?" Harry says, not unpleasantly.

"Tonite," she says, then turns more of her attention to Harry. "I mean Witzkowitz. Donna Witzkowitz. I go by Donnalinda Tonite, like, professionally."

"Nice," Harry says. "You come up with that yourself?"

She smiles at him and pulls absently at one of her curls as she shakes her head no.

Much as I have a feeling that this girl has something for us that's worth coaxing out, I figure we ought to drop the bomb. "Donna, we got some bad news. Mr. Petrianni is dead. Happened two nights ago. Were you here at the club that night?"

My turn for the vacant stare. Then she puts it together. "So I'm out a job?"

I admit it. "Temporarily, anyway. But the sooner we can get to the bottom of this, the sooner someone might be able to reopen the place."

She blinks at the dark front doors hopefully. "Len around? Maybe he's thinking of opening back up or something?"

"He's not around, and we don't know his plans. We're just investigating the death."

"Oh," she says. Once again, she catches up after a couple of seconds. "So Mr. Petrianni was, like, murdered? Is that what you're saying?"

"Could be," says Harry.

"Huh," she says. Then she refocuses. "So how come you're down from Boston? I mean, wouldn't the cops from around here be the ones doing this?"

I'm actually impressed that she put that together. "Mr. Petrianni had connections with Boston," I say. "We're looking into those. So, Donna, can you remember last Saturday?"

"Yeah, of course I can remember it," she says, adjusting her shoulder strap. I've offended her, but it's okay because now she's out to prove her memory. "I had the early, and after was when Mr. Petrianni told me about me needing to get proof of my age. I got my braces off, too." She displays her teeth at me in a fake smile, then closes her lips spitefully.

"Nice," I say. "You bleach?"

"Yeah, of course," she says. "Yours look good too." We're friends again.

"Donna, did you notice anyone besides the regulars at the club last Saturday?"

She nods, chewing her gum and looking down to concentrate. "There was some cute guys. Mr. Petrianni kicked them out after one of them gave me a twenty. I don't know what was so wrong about it. I mean, we're here for the tips, right?"

Harry jumps in. "Agreed. Those guys seem pissed about being given the boot?"

She shakes her head vaguely, shrugging at the same time. "I left the stage when it started happening, so I didn't see too much. Sorry."

"That's okay," I assure her. "So was that it? The last time you saw Mr. Petrianni he was escorting those guys out?"

"I guess," she says glumly.

"Except he managed to send you to Binghamton to get a copy of your birth certificate," Harry points out.

She looks up at him. "Oh, yeah. So that was the last last time, come to think of it."

"He did that right after he kicked out those kids?"

"I guess so. I don't know how long that took him."

"Anything you notice about Mr. Petrianni? He seem his normal self?"

She nods vaguely. "Actually, he did something kind of mean. He squeezed my face, like this." She demonstrates on her own face. "It's like a thing someone might do to be nice, like if they're saying you're cute, right? But he didn't mean it like that."

"Why'd he do it? Just because he was pissed about those guys, or about your age?"

"I guess. " She does her shrug-nod again and stares off across the parking lot. Harry's about to say something when she adds, "Plus he was showing off."

My ears prick up. "Showing off, Donna?"

"You know, like guys do. They have to show off they're in charge."

"Showing off in front of...?"

She feels at her face where she'd squeezed it. "The lady."

Bingo, huh, Zoey? Not that we got much of a description out of Donna—"the lady" was tall, old (my age, that turned out to mean), and in need of implants. Hair dark in a fancy up-do—Donna shows with her hands and a lot of rattling jewelry how she would fashion her own hair in the style, which made me think of a chignon. Cashmere turtleneck, top-of-the-line manicure, pricey kidskin boots. Other than that, "just some lady."

I give Donna my card and ask her to call me if anything new occurs to her. She looks at it, front and back, before tucking it away in the pocket of her faux rabbit jacket.

Good deed for the day completed, Harry and I head north.

EIGHT

Marina Papanikitas's Personal Journal

Yo, Zoey,

Back at the keyboard, m'sweet. As you don't seem to be showing up to throw dinner on the slab for your home-girl, I took a
break to slip a frozen pizza in the oven. Life in homicide—remind
me, next time you see me, of why I was so hell-bent on scoring this
gig. Better yet, Zoey, whisper it in my ear tonight. Just don't wake
me, babe. Beat detective needs sleep.

Driving up to Boston, Harry and I opt for quiet, both of
us kind of buzzing about what we have and haven't found out.
Donna's description of the woman she'd seen with Rocco had been
sketchy. Even with pressure all we got was that she'd had heavy
eyelids, sad lips, and ski pants tucked into the tall boots—I play
out how receptive Shanko would be if I were to tip him that he
should be on the lookout for Natasha from *Rocky and Bullwinkle*.

Harry waits until we're almost back up to town before breaking the silence. "Look, uh, you still in the mood to be nosy?"

I consider. "You know something? I am pretty reliably in a
nosy mood."

"Because I'm thinking that if we take the Mass Ave exit, we
can slide right over to where Terence D'Amante got shot."

"Well, we chewed up half the day dabbling in other people's

cases across the state line. Might as well polish off the afternoon catching some friction here at home."

I do a little GPS-ing while H.P. maneuvers us from highway to city streets. It's almost growing dusky when we find ourselves on the front stoop of one Neva Deunoro, the newly minted single lady, once girlfriend of the recently murdered Terry D'Amante. Girl lives pretty deep in the urban hood, by which I do mean to imply that the cement park across the street from her window doesn't strike me as a real estate plus. Quiet, though—I find myself wondering how startling the noise of a single gunshot would be to the folks lurking behind all the drawn shades. We're just about to give up on Neva's buzzer in the vestibule when the outside door opens behind us and a young woman starts in. Her hair's skinned back and she's pulling a laundry cart. Clothes trim and tidy. All that makes an impression, but the thing you really notice—what everyone cannot help but notice when Neva Deunoro comes into sight—is that the girl is drop-dead gorgeous. Tawny eyes, dark brown skin, full untouched lips, high forehead without a flaw—who knows what makes her features come together the way they do, but she is a nymph among mortals. Moves well, too. After barely a glance at me and Harry, she lifts her hand and flicks a finger gracefully back and forth at our faces, then over her shoulder.

"Get your goddamn cop asses the fuck out my building," she says.

"You Neva Deunoro?" We display our creds.

"No, I ain't. Now get."

"Just want a word with you, Ms. Deunoro. Won't take much of your time."

"Yeah, you got that shit accurate because we already finished. Now get the fuck out the way. I got shit to do, and it don't include talking to no fuckin' cops."

She squares off as if ready to pull her cart through us.

"Look, you want to make this fast or play it your way?" Harry says. "If you're worried about the message we're sending with our car idling at the hydrant, fast seems smarter."

She jams a hand in a pocket and whips out some keys, then steps forward and thrusts them. I swear I almost react defensively, but she's going for the inner door. "Fast ain't fast enough," she says through her teeth, slamming over the threshold with her cart. Her place is the one by the front door. Otherwise we'd have had the fun of being cussed all the way up the stairs.

We enter, and Harry shuts the door behind us. The apartment isn't bad—decent rug, couch, TV, couple of framed prints. Girl likes pastels. There's a blanket on the couch and a kid's book on the floor, looking recently abandoned. *Everyday Math for 1st Grade*, I read upside down. Neva shoves the cart out of her way, leans over by a table where she seems to smack something down, then turns around, arms folded over her still fastened jacket.

"Well?" Before we can talk, she seems to hear a noise, and looks off to the side, where a pair of heavy sliders block our view of the next room. A kid's curious eye and a bit of skinny torso barely appear between the doors. "No," Neva says. The child disappears.

"Look, we're sorry to intrude like this. We'll keep it brief," I try.

She walks across to the sliders and bangs them closed, then stands with her hands behind her on the door handles. "What do you want?" she says.

"Terence D'Amante was shot to death on your front steps a couple of months ago."

She freezes—just for a beat—then goes natural again. "That supposed to be news?"

"You want to tell us what you know about it?"

"Already talked to them other cops. You get it from them. That it?"

"We're here to get it from you," I say. "You home at the time?"

"Yeah. I didn't see nothing." Her eyes narrow. "What's different?"

I'm willing to give in order to get. "There's been another death. Someone associated with Terence."

She considers this a moment—I sense a breath of relief. Why? She maintains the 'tude, but now it's more of a front than genuine hostility. "So? That supposed to make me remember something I didn't know in the first place? 'Cause it don't."

Her eye seems to catch sight of something, and she walks across the room to lower the shade so that it covers a small amount of windowpane that may have been showing. She stands up again. "I don't know nothing about what he was up to. He was in prison. I wasn't."

"Didn't you visit?"

She looks at me like I'm crazy. "I don't visit prisons."

"Wasn't he the father of your child?"

"What's that to you?"

"Answer the questions, you want us out of here," Harry sticks in.

She's cowed, at least for the moment. She lowers her eyes, then nods.

"I mean, that's what he was coming here to see, right? His kid? Maybe you, too?"

She shrugs. "We wasn't in contact," she says vaguely.

Something occurs to me. "You mean he'd never seen the child in eight years? He was coming to see his child for the first time?"

She gives me a defiant eye. "Man want to see my child, man keep his ass out of prison. Simple, right?"

"Ever meet Rocco Petrianni?" Harry throws at her.

"No." Not curious, either.

"I ask because he used to live around here."

She stares. "So?"

"You remember the Dorchester Five?" I offer.

"What about it?"

"Rocco Petrianni was one of the Five, like Terence D'Amante was. Petrianni was murdered a couple of nights ago."

She wants to say something dismissive, but she holds it back and just stares us down.

"You there, that day when they turned over that car?"

"No," she says.

"You must have been a kid. What are you now, twenty-two, three?"

"I was eighteen at the time," she says defiantly.

"Yeah, don't worry about it," Harry says.

"I was eighteen years old, mister. I was working at the youth center over there, wasn't I? You think them sisters is gonna hire underage?"

"Oh, so you were working over at St. Brigid's, where it happened?"

"I just said so, didn't I? That don't mean I was in the street that day."

"Just trying to get the lay of the land," says Harry. "So, look, you say you weren't in touch with Terence, but did you know he was getting out?"

She nods reluctantly.

"And you knew he was coming over as soon as he got out," I prod her.

"Yeah. I knew."

"How'd you know?"

She sighs impatiently. "He told me."

"Thought you weren't in contact."

She fixes me with a look. "He phoned me up and he said he's getting out and he's coming over to see his kid. You want to call that being in contact, go ahead."

"He offer support?"

"I didn't want nothing from him, that's for sure."

"Why not? Could he be violent?"

She scoffs. "What he go away for, all the peace and love he spread round the world? We done here? I told you before, I got shit to do."

Harry takes out a card. She doesn't move so he sticks it between the doorjamb and the wall. "You think of something that might help us locate whoever killed the father of your child, you call." He pauses and she doesn't respond. "Thank you for your time."

"One more thing," I say, turning back. "You think there's any way it could have been a woman who killed Terence?"

She just stares at me for a beat, unblinking, just like earlier. For a second, it's like she's frozen. Then she walks forward, as if the silent moment hadn't happened, to shut the door. "Talking about a .38, one bullet behind the ear, through the brain," she says. "Yeah, that's good. It's likely a woman who did that to him."

Harry and I share a chuckle as he wheels us back toward town. "Fricking goose chase all around," I sum up the day.

"Fricking goose chase we're not assigned to, might add," Harry points out. "Wonder what she was lying about, though. Think she knows who killed him?"

I shrug. "Absolutely. Just not sure that anyone on this side of the law's any closer to prying it out of her by virtue of the fact that you and me spotted the fact that she knows."

"True enough." He nods in agreement. "Interesting fact, though?"

"Throw me anything, partner. I'm a drowning detective."

"Terence D'Amante was a dark-skinned guy. And Neva Deunoro I would call a woman of rich color."

"Agreed," I say.

"So how come the little boy who peeked in at us was white?"

"You saw the kid?"

"Just a glimpse. Blonde. Skinny. Bright blue eyes."

I think. "Maybe she babysits."

Harry does his sideways smirk. "That picture she turned flat soon as we went in?"

"Didn't see. Her body was in the way."

"Guess I had all the good angles. Same kid," Harry says. "Little younger, little blonder."

"Huh," I say. "No wonder they weren't at the window waiting for daddy that night."

"Maybe daddy was already home."

"Woah. So the kid's father whacks the old boyfriend just before he can see for himself that Neva hasn't been true all these years?"

Harry shrugs. "More to the point is whether she was true before he went in, back when she was his girlfriend. It's not her he was coming to see. It's his son he's been counting on for eight years." He turns the car into the lot at the precinct and kills the engine. "At any rate, time to make sure Jack's clued in on the fact of two Dorchester defendants biting it within months."

"Not that either of them was on a life path that promised a ripe old age."

"That's a point. And with D'Amante's death starting to smell domestic, there's even less of a pattern. But I got a feeling Jack may want to check on the others, particularly the city guy. At the very least, give him a heads up that the media's about to pick this up and run with it."

I think awhile. "You know, what's got my panties in a twist is that we abandon our case and go hunting in Rhodie for the day because we sense a connection with the D'Amante killing. But what we come back with is nothing much in common between the deaths of D'Amante and Petrianni, and instead, a couple of glaring similarities between those of Petrianni and Becker."

"Such as?"

"Well, they're both kind of splashy, as far as murders go—cinematic, you might say."

Harry shrugs. "If Becker wasn't a suicide, I'll grant that."

I look at him. "Becker wasn't a suicide."

He considers. "Maybe I'll grant that, too."

"And then there's this woman who cuts through both stories, the apathetic broad with a pout and a thing for yester-Euro fashions."

"There was a woman with Becker. Left prints and DNA on that coffee glass like she's out to make sure we know she's got no priors. Down in Rhodie, we don't even know if the lady with Rocco ever made it to his office."

"Yeah," I muse. "What really strikes me is that in both cases, the descriptions of the lady herself make it sound like she could go pretty incognito if she chose to. McD, Donnalinda, and Penny all seemed to be saying that this was a woman you might not notice if she hadn't affected a certain look."

"True enough," Harry concedes. "Doesn't really add up to much."

I sigh. "I totally agree. Just can't shake it out of my gourd that it will.

NINE

I am Nightingale—

I decide to take on an accomplice.

I spend the evening in the room I have rented in a house in Dorchester. My landlady is black and widowed, like Oleander, but the similarities end there. Tati seems to spend a lot of time screaming and laughing into the phone and thudding on her stairs with a dry mop, although the stairs do not seem particularly clean as a result of this attention. She often sings while she works, gospel, out of tune. The house is Victorian. My room is directly off the front entry, at the base of a long, straight stairway with an ornate banister. My room may have been meant originally to serve as a parlor. A short hallway that once connected this room to some rear area of the house has been walled off, and the resulting alcove serves as the closet. In my room is a bed, a rather fanciful velvet armchair, several additional pieces of furniture, and a fireplace in which sits a gas heater that may or may not work—I have not attempted to use it. I leave the doilies where they are so that Tati will not feel justified to go hunting for them when she peeks in my room, which I am certain that she does from time to time when I am out; I am quiet, which piques her curiosity. But she learns nothing from my room. Indeed, aside from my clothes in the closet and my wigs in their boxes under the bed, I have made no impression on this little overcrowded space. I keep my money locked inside a travel case atop the closet, in which I have also stowed my cyanide-laced lozenges. I keep the key to my case on my person at all times. All my private information—this diary I write and the music I listen to through ear pods—I store in the little portable device that I purchased for myself the day I left Southie for the last time.

Before tonight, I have never been upstairs, as I use a bathroom just off the kitchen, so small that the rust-trimmed shower stall fills half of it. I always wash late at night after Tati has retired to her own room. She must hear the pipes sing, but she never comes down, realizing that I value my solitude. I leave my rent money sealed in a cheap envelope on the front foyer table, in cash, once a week on rent day. To Tati, I am an actress who has run away from someone and is not looking to recover just yet from whatever pain this someone inflicted on me. I heard her once, talking on the phone, saying the words "actress with some love problems, looks to me. That kind of hurt take its own sweet time mendin,' in truth it does." So she is not unworldly, and not altogether wrong about me. I gave her the name Julie Truffaut.

In spite of my inattention to the household, I have noticed that Tati seems to enjoy gabbing with her other lodger. You would not think that this other lodger would be talkative, but apparently he listens. He is a skinny hipster with skin so white that his lips appear to be suffused with blood and his eyelids, both top and bottom, caked with soot. He smokes tiny brown cigarettes and often heads in the direction of the T, walking very straight with his collar up and his arms pressed against his sides, his eyes cast down like a teenage girl. When Tati converses with him, here or there in the house, I can hear pauses in her chatter, but until this evening I have never heard his voice. Tati refers to him, when she gossips with other ladies on her stoop, as "the young man with the ferret whut smokes the weed." He carries the ferret on his shoulder, nestled under his matted hair, and appears to take it to work with him, if indeed he works.

Until today I have had few thoughts about this lodger and certainly no curiosity about where he happens to be quartered in the house. But now it has occurred to me that he can help me, so I sit at the window, smoking—Tati is wise to recognize that in order to rent in this neighborhood one has to accept the pedestrian sins of the transient loner. For something to do, I watch the side gate of St. Brigid's, across the intersection from my window, as it fades into the dusk. The rhododendrons are clustered thick around the path up to the mangy rectory, so first it is the entrance to the youth center that is blotted out by the falling night. Next, the cement path recedes into the blackness, merging with the weedy undergrowth that lines the gate. Soon even the gate itself is barely discernable against the leaves that crowd through its bars.

It is a messy intersection in which accidents occur with regularity. Cars roar by, some blaring the music, more than a few skidding through the red light with an irreverent squeal of the tires. Drivers curse and occasionally expectorate loudly into the street. At one point, gunshots or noises very like them echo through the air and are ignored by all. Eventually the lodger appears from the direction of the train, walking his narrow walk, arms tight to his side, knees brushing one another. Strapped over his torso in the diagonal style of the day is a sort of rucksack in which I suspect roosts a portable computer. His face is a colorless dagger. He glances at neither male nor female that passes him as he makes his way. I drop my curtain and move to the bed. When he enters, I listen to the noise of his steps pacing up the long bare stairway. I picture his boots, black leather with large rubber heels and side buckles, and attempt to discern the direction that he takes when he reaches the top.

After giving him a bit of time, I pull on a pair of leggings and a fleece sweatshirt and slip my bare feet into a pair of padded flip-flops. I put on my glasses. I do not need these glasses, but I do not want to frighten my accomplice in any way. I walk quietly up the stairs. All is dark; the hallway is quite long with stairs leading up into the gloom at the far end. Muted television noises—shrieks of fright and jarring music—come from one room. The sound should make me feel nostalgic, but I feel nothing. I spot a door with a half-light striping the floor at its base. I knock quietly with my knuckles. There is a murmur from within, and I twist the knob.

His room is oblong, with windows all along one wall and shingling opposite, as if it were an upstairs porch that has been at some point insulated against the cold. He is sitting at a desk of sorts—a smooth board resting on some sort of supports—with the light from his computer screen full on his face and no other lighting in the room except for the glow of his cigarette. Directly across from the door is the single bed, unmade. He has shed the coat, but nothing else, including his scarf and boots. His eyes are set narrowly and he does not display surprise or interest at the fact that I have appeared in his room; in fact he barely glances over before returning his eyes to his screen.

"I think, perhaps, that you can help me."

He waits for a moment and then shrugs. "So?"

"I need a website. Quickly."

"Design takes time." His voice is thin without force, as if he puts no effort into how he might present himself.

"Maybe not." I move forward. The ferret watches. "I have identified one or two sites you may emulate. The man I will show this to does not care about my creativity."

He stops and turns to me. His eyes are limp.

"I need a site for a local order of nuns. They perform charitable functions, put young folk to work, collect old clothing, maybe a food drive is coming up. They are called the Religious Sisters of St. Cecelia. They are at an address in Roxbury of your choosing, as long as it does not exist. The charitable donations efforts are handled by a Sister Julia."

He thinks about it, then rotates back to his screen, where he raps a few keys. "Happy poor kids," he says in his monotone. "Street murals. Urban gardens. Announcements about pregnancy counseling and drop-off hours for the food bank."

"That is it exactly," I say. "Can you set up a voice mail with an electronic recording? Perhaps a fax number that malfunctions, as well as a broken link to the location finder?"

He shrugs. His fingernails are painted a glossy black, quite chipped.

"Five hundred, then?" I say. "Seven if you can have it done by morning?"

He turns away, taps a few things, checks what he's brought to the screen. I wait until it occurs to me that we have reached an agreement.

Down in my own room, I change to the clothes I have just acquired at a thrift shop located a safe distance from Tati's house: pale cotton underwear, a felt skirt with pleats, a blouse with short collar, knee-high stockings, worn shoes with tassels. I don my jeweled cross and stow my new wig in my macrame satchel, along with a well-fingered pocket Bible, some tampons, a large ring of keys, eighteen dollars folded into a silver plate money clip fashioned to look like a pair of praying hands, a dog-earred bodice-ripper published a decade earlier, a scratched-up cell phone, and a large box of jelly candies in assorted flavors. My little electronic device I slip into my skirt pocket. I wear my sweater-coat of brownish wool, wrapping it close. I do not apply makeup.

When I reach my destination, I don the wig. Its hair is chestnut, shortish, but with some thin locks that curl inward around my face, the longest of these tickling against the underside of my jaw. She is not devoid of vanity, our Sister Julia.

The streets are narrow in this area of Cambridge, although cars glide along rapidly, rattling the manhole covers and swiping by the parked vehicles that crowd along the uneven curbs. Only the upscale coffee and dress shops hint that the real estate here is pricey—there is no hiding that at one point it was all very "down in its heels," as we say, but perhaps for most this fact adds character. Van Ness Collectibles announces itself with an old-style swinging sign—the once-gold lettering is carved into the wood. The store's front windows are shielded by tortured ironwork bolted to the bricks. It remains open into the evening once weekly, according to its website. Inside, bleary porcelain plates and serving bowls decorate a massive rustic breakfront of scrolled wood that has been arranged to face the street at a diagonal. Beyond this, chests and tables and chairs, some polished and others lacquered in an oriental style, are set about in small groupings. The walls are a deep orange.

Although the shop is lit only by the antique chandeliers that dangle from its ceiling here and there, through the window I can nevertheless see well the man who lolls behind an antique desk with pen and account book on the blotter before him. He is much changed, Bruno Myeroff, now called Brewster Van Ness. He is perhaps a touch under thirty, but exudes a more seasoned man's cockiness, with dark hair rather daringly sleeked back from a widow's peak. He has grown a ring of curling facial hair to encircle his mouth, but it does not mask the slight pudginess of his cheeks and chin—he is teetering in his prime, once a stocky teen and, in all likelihood, heading toward a stodgy middle-age, but for now, temporarily shed of fat and probably quite muscular under his clothes. About his neck he wears a daring scarf in autumnal shades. His sweater-vest is knit of a hand-dyed braided wool, undoubtedly imported. His shirtsleeves are pink pinstripes.

He talks into an old-style desk phone, pausing to drag on a cigarette from which he flicks ash in the manner of the old film stars—palm upward, with a thumb tap to the filter and a careless feint at the tarnished ashtray. Perhaps he is talking to an older woman, I think, and so puts on these airs. Then I see him form the words "go ream herself" and hear the coarse blast of *bon vivant* laughter, and so realize that his tone of insouciance is not a put-on he adapts for playful moments, but is genuinely a part of him now, the way the studied youthful disaffection he exhibited through the trial those years back was a true part of him then. I watch, unseen, as he leans back and lifts his feet to cross his ankles on the desk, and then fusses a bit with the pleat of his trousers, still talking a blue streak to whichever of his gym pals—rich and cocky as he, no doubt—may be on the line. There is a glint off the heels of his boots, a curved bit of metal nailed into the edge of each that must make a little click as he walks. He is a natural actor, this one, a player on the world stage, but of course there is a core to him as there is to every person. He knows his core, whether or not he can present anything but his latest facade to the world. I know him at his core as well, I think.

I reach out, there from the dusky sidewalk, ever so gingerly, to *fourrage* about in whatever may be sampled in his mind. At the very moment I perceive myself to penetrate, he snaps his head around and aims his gaze directly at me through the glass. I see his eyes—vivid, pernicious black pinholes—the same eyes as eight years prior. Something in my head explodes.

I pivot away, my hand to my face as if in reflex to a blow. I try to run but for a few moments I can only stumble against the wall of his building in a drunken, off-kilter manner, as if suffering from some wild invisible assault. I will myself to move, clawing at the bricks ahead, motivated by the simple truth that if he emerges to investigate I will surely never complete my *hommage*. My brain is searing and I drag the wig down past my face and jam it into my satchel. I splay sloppily to my knees, then attempt to rise again, knowing only that I need to round the corner ahead before this— this Apollyon—has a chance to observe me.

There is a bakery at the street's end, a quaint un-American place with tiled floors and flaking plaster above, and the smell of toasting sugar emerging through its dust-clogged vents. I burst inside and rush straight through, stifling a sob, only to cower in a back hall against a thin wooden door marked W.C. A young dark man in baker's apron emerges—eyes wide, he jumps out of my way. I ram the door and flip the flimsy hook into place. My skull still burns but the pain is utterly internal—water will not help. Still, I turn the tap hard and in a moment have filled my hands and doused my head, once, then again, and then yet again, until I feel the water running down my arms, inside my blouse. I rake my nails up and back from the nape of my neck to my forehead until the pain subsides. Then I stand with my spine pressed to the door, my mouth open, my breathing raw and raspy like that of an animal. I can feel my shoulder blades, rattling against the wood behind me. It is good to tremble. Hell is out of my head.

In the mirror, my hair stands out like the wet dog, but I do nothing about it. I unhook the lock and wander weakly from the W.C. An elderly man in white apron stands waiting. They are mopping, preparing to close for the evening. The man takes my elbow and, although I protest and pull back, he is firm and seats me at a small table by the back wall. From the wide-eyed lad, also in apron, whose hands shake like my own, the old man takes a cardboard cup of tea, and also a square of wax paper that holds a slice of cake. It smells of clove. I nod my thanks without meeting his eye and reach into my satchel, but he shakes his head and lays a hand on one of mine. Turning from me, he crosses himself before returning to his work. It is a bit comforting, I must admit, to discern that for once some sweet soul has interpreted one of my disguises as I intended. As Sister Julia of the Order of St. Cecelia, I sip my tea and watch the water droplet fall from my hair to bleed into my seed cake.

When I reach Tati's, I change my clothes, rolling my Sister Julia outfit into my satchel, and then lie smoking in the dark, thinking. Eventually I take money from my case and am just exiting the room when I hear a crinkle and realize that I have stepped on an envelope that the upstairs lodger must have pushed under the door. Inside I find that he has printed a page of the Religious Sisters of St. Cecelia website. At the bottom is its web address. I use my little device to check the job online. I place seven hundred-dollar bills into the envelope and whisper up the stairs and past Tati's room. I push the envelope under the lodger's door. I can hear him in there, but he does not cease typing, even if he notices the envelope.

Downstairs in my room, I compose a letter on my little device in which Sister Julia asks those who have been charitable in the past toward organizations supporting the well-being of women and children in the greater Boston vicinity to consider offering their aid to the Religious Sisters of St. Cecelia, a Roman Catholic community of nuns operating out of Roxbury but servicing the entire Boston metro region, dedicated to aiding domestic and immigrant families in need. Near the end, I apologize solemnly

1

for perhaps having contacted some who are not in a position to offer aid and others who would prefer not to be contacted at all, promising to abide by their wishes in the future if they will inform me of such preferences in any way they choose. I sketch out several worthy projects in need of support—an infant nutrition drive, translation assistance, confidential rape counseling for both adult women and minors. I send the email to Van Ness Collectibles, finding the contact information on the store's website.

Although I am mortally afraid to do so, from my great distance I attempt to *suggére* in Brewster Van Ness a desire to respond. Or perhaps I do not quite do this. I have never claimed to truly understand how it works, and it may be that my fear causes me to flinch before I even try. I sit at my window smoking, deep into the night. Eventually I sleep, but not restfully.

The next day, while on the train, I receive his message.

> *Dear Sister Julia,*
>
> *In regard to your letter inviting Van Ness Collectibles to involve itself in your charitable mission, I delight to inform you that your timing was "immaculate," as we are positioned to offer you a sizable lot of valuable items. As always when lending ourselves to benevolent operations, we at Van Ness prefer to put earmarked items to auction and thereafter to forward proceeds to the institution. This approach may be appreciated for its practicality; however, it requires immediate action, as the goods under discussion will be auctioned in six days time to clear space for expected shipments. May you or a representative meet with me at our warehouse this Saturday evening at 10:00 pm? At that point, I will have the items grouped and we may review them in anticipation of transporting them for auction the following morning. I apologize for the shortness of notice and also the late hour of my proposed meeting, but the items in mind must be brought together from several sites. You will be happy to learn that our warehouse is located at the*

rear of our shop in Cambridge, and so may be reached by
public transportation.

In hopes that you and I may come together in the very
near future,

Brewster Van Ness

I respond immediately:

Dear Mr. Van Ness,
I will be at your warehouse at 10:00 Sat. next. God
Bless You.

Sister Julia Kohler

Within minutes, he replies:

Wonderful. You will bring the requisite tax forms, I trust.
—BVN

I stare ahead, out the train window at the city yards with their moldy trash and crumbling walls and back lots choked with weeds. The train clops quickly along as if stretching now that we have escaped the winding underground tunnels and can see all around us the gusty expanses of urban desolation. Litter dances playfully in the air, catching on the bare fingers of trees and the rusted spikes of fences. Somewhere—in a drab storefront office or perhaps a church basement along these streets—sits a grey-haired creature of God, perhaps even called Sister Julia, with opaque glasses, orthopedic shoes, a faint white moustache, sagging jowls. She is busy sending out emails in hopes of netting some funds for the poor. She knows nothing, of course, about the fact that her persona has been borrowed by a woman on a train that passes now, to set the scene for a murder that this woman who poses as a nun will commit. And will she not be implicated, this elderly person of infinite and exquisite grace, when my kill is successful? Will she not be a party to my crime? I do not see why she should not. We humans do carry our sins collectively, according to the teachings of Christ.

I think: *Who committed no sin, Nor was deceit found in*
His mouth; who, when He was reviled, did not revile in return...

who Himself bore our sins in His own body...by whose stripes you were healed.

I feel a shiver in my heart and a subtle nausea in my gut. I know not what it signifies.

Très sincèrement,
Nightingale

TEN

I am Nightingale—

La danse macabre begins afresh, and this episode of my crusade will not be anything akin to the "pigs to slaughter" murders I have enjoyed to date. The warm-up kills are over. From now forward, I must labor for my corpses.

I am seated amid the citizens of Roxbury in an urban middle school where Charles Wilkins Morley delivers prosaic phrases with gruff elegance from the auditorium stage. "This is a great city, a city on the move. Boston's *people* are on the move. Its technologies are greener. Its economy, during a time of severe economic trouble…" There are regular spatters of applause and the occasional whoop of support from here and there. "…must remember, however, how important it is that *all* of Boston's communities flourish, that *all* neighborhoods benefit, that *all* of us be on the train when Boston moves…" His voice is basso and full of vibrato. Perhaps he needs new lines, but it matters little what he says at this time of the evening to this crowd. He is chanting an incantation they know well, coaxing an evening toward its melodic conclusion. There is some homey comfort in the predictability of it all. "Ours is a decade not of promise, but of realization. We are the lucky ones. We are the offspring of promise. People, our time—Our Time!—has at long last arrived."

Wilkie raises a hand at the auditorium, his face in its characteristic expression of earnest seriousness. Sweat glistens on his brow. He turns to his hostess, who approaches him across the stage, leans in with exquisite grace to catch his hands in a double-fisted clasp. I watch carefully. Wilkie does not smile back at her beaming face. He is too full of vision. Too driven. Too hopeful to pause for a pleasurable moment, even with his elegant hostess, although he is aware of all she has done, all the crap work that went into her setting up this forum for him, and so he grips her hands hard in both his hands, expressing mute appreciation. She is black like he is, but with much lighter skin and long shining hair because she is also Asian. She wears a steel blue silk dress that sways in watery caresses around her hips and thighs when she moves, as if she is a dancer. Indeed, it would not surprise Wilkie if she had been a trained ballerina. From my program I know that she has an appealing name: Veronica Dahl, and an appealing position: City of Boston Cultural Liaison. I watch her lips as she murmurs something across at him and know from his expression that her voice, like everything else about her, is musical and lovely. He nods his thanks, looks into her almond eyes, and wonders aloud, right there on the stage in front of four hundred fifty tired and hungry members of his flock, if they might get together later, in private, to discuss personally some of the issues that hamper her efforts to promote the arts in the metro region. I do not hear him from my seat in the crowd, of course, but I watch his lips with care, and I know what he says as clearly as Veronica Dahl herself. And I know equally that her hands go senseless momentarily. She nods ambiguously and backs off a step or two, flashing her teeth at the audience as if to signal how much she is looking forward to the Q and A that will conclude the evening. Audience members are already lining up at the microphones that stand in the aisles. I grip my purse and offer a tight smile to the woman who sits to my right.

Wilkie turns to face the crowd, mopping his brow. A middle-aged male stands ready at the mic. He's white with scant hair scrupulously dyed a tint like molten caramel. Belligerent. Dumb. A true believer in neighborhood politics. Deep inside coils an almost toxic core of untapped racism. Wilkie knows this as well as I. He nods respectfully.

Councilman Morley, it's all well and good to support of the arts, but…

Mr. Councilman, I have stats I can send you about the impacts of city-sponsored recycling in ten major urban locations…

Wilkie is a big man and always sweating. It is part of his image by now. The intense City Councilman, C. Wilkins Morley. The real guy. Good clothes, but that is due to his law firm partner wife, a proud—dare anyone use the word haughty?—woman with steel innards. They are a pair of success stories, although very different from one another. Two young daughters. Gracious home in Jamaica Plain. There are whispers that they are estranged, maybe informally separated. People suspect he may be a ladies' man. So many pols are.

Now a black man takes the mic. He is old, thin, bent but not feeble. He holds his cap carefully in his hands out of respect for the young councilman. Wilkie leans an arm on the podium and waits for him to raise his eyes, then nods solemnly for him to begin.

Good evenin,' Councilman. We all been hearing a lot of talk about the inadequate rail system going on some thirty years now. Any truth to the story that the next mayor of Boston going to make something happen?

The audience laughs appreciatively, eager to pounce upon the implication that Wilkie might be Boston's next mayor—the city's first black mayor, in fact. Wilkie studiously ignores the compliment and launches an earnest seven-minute discussion of light rail and the ignominy of past promises about public transportation. He uses words like "ignominy" frequently. He uses "solipsism" and "cogent" and "anodyne" and "longueurs." He likes words, likes building his vocabulary and using it. Yet people still think of him as a real guy—he just happens to be a smart one. Wilkie is from Dorchester, and his history is well known. That has been his motto and the key to his success: hide nothing, and people will accept you as you are. At thirty-nine, he is the next big thing in Boston's black community. He never acknowledges his political momentum, even in private with his advisors. But it is true. People talk about him as a viable candidate for the state senate, the federal congress, the governorship. It all seems attainable.

He uses up his time. People are starting to slip up the aisles and out side exits. He himself could use a drink, a shower, some grub. Naturally, all that changes if Veronica Dahl takes him up on his offer. An image flutters in the back of his mind—her ass in the electric blue silk dress when she bent over to fuss with the sound system. Who could resist such a woman?

I am the last to arrive at the microphone—the people behind me are politely but firmly informed that there is no more time and that they must return to their seats. Wilkie observes that I am white and wearing a blouse with some scalloped bibbing down its front. He sees how my plaid skirt ends a half-inch shy of knee-length. My hair is white-blonde and teased so as to form a smooth, rounded curve, and my lipstick is a pale baby-pink. I could be, it occurs to him, a career backup singer from Nashville. My question is jotted in a plastic-coated stationery shop organizer, and I pause to raise my glasses, which have a subtle cats-eye cast to them. Wilkie knows what is coming. It is because of my question, which he anticipated well before laying eyes on me, that he remains assiduously solemn in all his public appearances. Is it due to this impending question that he will never speculate openly about his future.

I speak. My voice is untrained but my tone assured. I keep my eyes on the pad in front of me. I say: "Mr. Councilman, eight years ago you were one of the Dorchester Five. I have heard you answer many questions…"

I hesitate as soft hisses emanate from around the auditorium. His devotees are mightily sick of this topic, and why the hell should they not be, as they have heard it addressed countless times by an endless march of sanctimonious right-wingers. I glance quickly over my shoulder, as if suddenly nervous to be standing there, in this crowd of mostly black people, who might at any time rise up and do the unspeakable.

Wilkie speaks. "Come, come," he says to the room, his words loud yet nevertheless delivered with an air of quietude. "Each of us has a right to voice his concerns, here as in any public forum. It's the very root of egality, isn't it? I would like to hear the lady out."

The hisses fade but the room remains charged. I dip my head and adjust my glasses.

"Thank you, Councilman. I...I have heard you answer many questions about the Dorchester Five incident, mostly about whether you can expect the public to trust you with that incident in your background." Awkward pause to clear throat. "But what I have never heard you discuss is how you have learned to trust the public after having been through the incident, and I...I think it is important that we know that those who represent us respect and trust us. And...and as a follow-up...if there is time, of course...do you think that you were singled out in the mob that day...the day of the incident...because you are a powerfully built black man?"

In the moments it takes them to digest my words, the crowd's perspective changes. Some of the women begin to fan themselves audibly with their programs. They consider me a snooty bitch. Most of the men move about a bit in an effort to get a glimpse of me. They consider my legs. I lower my glasses and stand, lips pursed, waiting.

The stage creaks as Wilkie moves forward so as to lend my question the personal touch it warrants. He answers at some length—his phrases only partially canned. Taking my follow-up question first, he points out that three of the five men who were arrested that day in Dorchester were white. One was a local fellow Wilkie had known personally, another a college student doing community service in the neighborhood that summer, and the third white man arrested was a seminarian training for the priesthood. For this reason alone, he states, it is difficult to conclude that his own arrest was racially motivated. All told, it was a disconsonant group of defendants, and a very thorny group, from a political perspective, making it tough for him to believe that either the police or prosecutor's office could have chosen them based on a desire for quick or easy convictions.

As for his ability to trust the public—here he pauses to study the air above the audience for a stretched-out moment while I watch the light shift and reflect off his eyes—he admits that he has never received this particular question before. Indeed, he admits he has never consciously considered whether he might trust—and had I also used the term "respect"?—the public less than he would otherwise, due to his experience in that mob and subsequent to it. He was and remains daunted by the power exhibited by the mob that day, awed in both positive and negative ways, but only in retrospect, as he himself had been virtually unaware of the mob when he was up against that car. He himself had not been influenced by the shouts and jeers, because he had heard *none* of it. Indeed, he had been *astounded* at the size of the mob and the power of its rage, when viewing the video of the event at a later date. He attacked that car, Wilkie states to the audience and not just to me, out of anger. Righteous fury. Yes, he lost control of his reason, and he found in himself the physical strength to turn an automobile on its side, and he did it.

He lets this sink in for some moments before continuing. Even those who have heard him talk about Dorchester before are mute and attentive. Their creaks and coughs hang in the air. When Wilkie begins again, his voice is quieter, but his tone remains bold and penitent. He says that he has often been asked whether the public can trust him to maintain his composure in crisis—quite fairly asked that question, he must make clear—and all he is able to advise people is that they look into their hearts and decide that for themselves as individuals whether a man who did as Wilkie did on that day in Dorchester is a man they can trust. As for the question of how he can trust the public after the incident—the arrests, the media coverage, the trial—he rejects any implication that the public or the media or even the legal system was somehow to blame for his actions or the trial that followed. A young man was seriously and permanently injured. Wilkie had played a role in causing those injuries. There is no rationalization that he will ever offer publically, tempting as my invitation to indulge in such casuistry may be.

He finishes, and the hall is silent. After a long moment, he hears tentative steps behind him as Veronica Dahl approaches, preparing to shut down the evening. I remain at the microphone, my eyes trained not on him, but vaguely ahead of me at around stage level. Tentatively, warily, I reach out to *fourrage* in his mind. There is something that holds me back, but when I risk it, I am fairly certain I infiltrate his thoughts. He worries, I think, that I feel I have been chastised.

Somewhere in the auditorium, a pair of hands begins to applaud, and then another, but he raises his arm for silence, then quietly thanks people for attending. Disregarding his signal, the room breaks into prolonged applause, drowning out Veronica Dahl's words of thanks and appreciation. Wilkie, feeling for his handkerchief, stands alone at the front of the stage. He watches as I turn and walk up the aisle and am swallowed by the crowd that converges from both sides. He wants me to look, to give him a backward glimpse. He wills me to turn, in fact, and as I approach the double doors he sends a deafening mental order for me to turn NOW. Although he is not sure why, he needs another look at my face.

I drain from the hall with the rest of the audience, not thinking about the man who just spoke to me with such raw, honest, politically inexpedient words. Or so he believes.

As I leave, Wilkie feels several fingers slide tentatively onto the material of his suit jacket sleeve, where they press gently. He smells freesia…maybe Turkish rose…he senses more than hears her warm congratulatory words. He turns to envelop her fine-boned hand in yet another heartfelt squeeze. Veronica Dahl would indeed like to discuss the future of the arts program. Somewhere quiet, though, and private—the past week has been so hectic.

The following day, Wilkie spots me in another crowd. This time, it is at a food festival on Boston's City Plaza, a daring venture for mid-October when the forecast can vary from hour to hour. The wind is lively, causing trouble and even some comic moments. Occasional rain splatters and blows about, so sudden and sparse that it drives away very few. Volunteers and staffers work good-naturedly to stow tablecloths and lash down signage with rope. Food trucks are driven right onto the plaza to serve as semi-protected staging areas for the various displays. Natives and tourists mingle, fingering the usual bric-a-brac—ceramic bean pots, stuffed lobsters, Fenway Park snow globes—and scarfing down regional hors d'oeuvres, all while not quite listening to the upbeat rattle of the sound system as it pumps out speeches delivered by officials hailing from state offices with superficial appeal—urban initiative, small business partnership, renewable energy incentivization. Wilkie is not working the crowd. In fact, he is taking a break from a day-long symposium on vermin control in public housing, a more politically fraught topic than one might imagine. He is feeling frayed, but in that pleasurable way a man feels after having slept with a particularly desirable woman.

He is thinking about this as he spots me. I am in a pepper-and-salt boiled wool suit and grey-tinted pantyhose, and he recognizes me easily in spite of the white-rimmed bug-eye sunglasses that cover much of my face. Indeed, he has been looking for me, although the idea makes no sense to him. I am throwing a gauzy white scarf over my head and wrapping the long tail round my neck as he trains an eye on me across the plaza. He feels energized, all of a sudden, and a little playful. It could be the batty breeze, the tinny music, the aromas plucking at him from here and there while his stomach groans. It could also be me. He cuts across the plaza.

"Enjoying the chowder?" he says. He has a distinctive voice—unaffected and gravelly.

I turn, unsmiling. In one hand I hold a large Styrofoam cup containing a viscous substance with small colorless cubes and less well-defined wet chunks suspended in it; in the other I hold a plastic spoon, unused. "I am not, actually," I say. "I have never understood its appeal." I prod the stuff in my cup with the spoon, as if searching for an answer.

"So tell me," Wilkie says. "If you know you dislike chowder, why take a cup?"

"I tease myself," I say. "It is a thing I do, to challenge my presumptions. I dislike some food, so I order it."

"You expect a canned answer, so you ask a question."

I look up at him through my sunglasses as if surprised. "Yes, like that."

I spot a trash receptacle and step in that direction, and for a moment he wonders if I will continue walking. But I turn back, and I pause to observe him. He is a bit taller than anyone around him, dressed a bit better. He is wearing a double-breasted jacket, as only a barrel-bodied man can do without looking pompous. His suit is a deep navy, his tie silver and blue stripes against a bold orange shirt, reminding me that there is a stylish wife in the picture. I have seen pictures of him sporting a plain, crushed fedora and a rumpled raincoat—they are part of his trademark—but he has come out today looking rather dapper. Yet still, somehow, he blends. Maybe he is, in fact, the people's pol. Or would have been, but for me.

"You chucked the chowder without tasting it," he chides me.

"I observed it. I smelled it."

"And knew for certain that it was foul."

"There was no doubt at all."

"It's hard to change your mind, isn't it? Even when you give yourself the opportunity."

"This is true, yes," I say.

"And what you learned last night is what you already knew too."

I eye him through the shields of my sunglasses. "What is it that I already knew?"

"That I'm just another bullshitting pol," he clarifies pleasantly. "That the stuff?"

He does not quite break a smile, although he means to be friendly.

I move as if to take off my sunglasses, but my hand hesitates.

"You did not waffle. The crowd was impressed. I freely hand you all of that."

"I needed to answer directly," he says. I continue to look up at him. "Your question portrayed me as a victim. I didn't want to leave that impression."

"Yes, I can see why. Bad for the image." I taunt him a bit.

"Not the reason. I didn't want to leave the impression that I was the victim because it is simply untrue," he says. "I wasn't the victim that day."

"And so this is why my casuistry did not tempt you," I taunt again.

He nods, then relents with a wink. "Ain't good for the image either."

I smile. He smiles, and it sinks a dimple in one of his cheeks. "It's tougher to answer questions in a public forum than it is to ask them," he says frankly. "I think that true journalists acknowledge that fact."

I remove my sunglasses, needing to see him better. I am having a peculiar experience with this man. I have been attempting to *fourrage* and *suggère*, as with my prior conquests, but without success. I feel I am shooting blanks. He is meant to see me as the conservative schoolmarm—prim, self-satisfied, undoubtedly racist—a woman who (if you will excuse my *crudité*) could benefit from a rough fuck. Instead, apparently, I am a journalist. "You presume I have disdain for you, Councilman," I manage. "This is, in actuality, not the truth."

"Oh, I got the truth. See, I made you last night."

He gives my eyes a good long look, and for a moment I misinterpret his words. So he recognizes me! I back off a step, my heels unsteady on the plaza bricks. He is indeed the type to remember faces. "What do you mean?" I sound frightened and force a laugh to mask it.

He doesn't laugh. His eyes remain on mine. "Your question was a little too nuanced last night," he says. "And your poise—the heartland threads didn't hide it."

I laugh nervously once again. "I'm flattered and insulted all at once."

"You're some sort of investigative reporter? Maybe with a web platform?"

Not quite following, I murmur something about freelancing.

He looks puzzled, then chuckles loudly, his teeth showing. His smile makes his face quite pleasant. "I think this is where you go for broke, my good woman," he says.

I hesitate, then look at him directly. "Would you allow me to write your story?"

"Not sure I want it written," he says easily. "Not at this point, anyway. I'm thirty-nine, and I don't think of myself as having a 'story,' such as it were, just yet."

"Ah, but it will be written, and soon, whether you like it or not," I point out. I am quite correct, of course, although to Wilkie it sounds like part of my pitch. "You are a man in the public eye. This will only increase in the very near future. I can promise that with certainty."

He holds back his kneejerk response. "Maybe so." He checks his watch. "Unfortunately, you just reminded me that I have a meeting that's about to resume."

I smile, unbothered. "Until we meet again, then?" I have confidence.

He is about to agree and leave, but stops. "Look it, I get a sense about you. Can't put my finger on what it is, but I got some idea barking in my head that I'm supposed to let you chase me down. How about we meet? After we talk, I'll consider letting you interview me."

I tilt my head to the side. "An audition to an interview?"

"Sure, if you like. We'll set some ground rules—and, yes, I do mean both of us—and decide whether we want to go ahead. But I'll tell you here and now that I'm after an objective story, not a puff piece or an ambush."

"I am after just the same. I would give you my card, but…" I open my hands.

"Write your number on the back of one of mine," he says, forking one over along with a small, gilded pen. I hesitate—do I dare identify myself? He is sharp, this one. If I utter the word "Nightingale," perhaps it all falls into place for him. I write and hand it across to him. He glances at it. "J. Moreau." He looks up at me. "J for Jeanne, like the actress?"

I have my sunglasses back in place, so he cannot perceive my surprise. He even uses the French pronunciation. Quickly I shake my head. "I am Julie," I say. I decide to *suggère* to him that he should not think about my name any further, but something scares me off from even that, so I refrain. "Julie Moreau," I say, extending my hand.

He takes my hand, but at the same time gives me a penetrating look. For the second moment this afternoon, I am certain that he knows everything. His eyes say he knows. "But you must be related to Jeanne Moreau," he says. "You're so like her it's uncanny."

My hand remains captive in his. "Thank you," I say, sounding slightly defensive.

He waits, expecting more, but does not push for it. "It's been a pleasure meeting you, Julie Moreau." He pronounces "Julie" in the French manner, just as he did "Jeanne."

"You will call me? I am terribly grateful."

"Count on it." Wilkie walks back towards City Hall.

Like a coward who lashes out from behind, I *suggère* at him quickly, telling him that he wants to turn and wave a final time. He does not do it. I *suggère* again, more insistently. *TURN AND WAVE OR SHE WILL NOT FUCK WITH YOU!* I scream in his head.

He meets some people, young black professionals in suits, who undoubtedly work for him. They disappear into City Hall. Wilkie never turns, never touches at the breast pocket where he tucked my number. He has other things on his mind. I stand watching the stream of people entering and leaving the building.

It will be a challenge, this kill.

Très sincèrement,
Nightingale

ELEVEN

I am Nightingale—

At Tati's, I enter by the front and listen. She is a woman who cannot live without ruckus, so the silence of the house is a certain signal of her absence. I ascend the stairs and hurry along to the lodger's door. I hear the whispery clatter of his trade, but he does not heed my knock, so finally I enter unbidden. It is midday, but his narrow room is dark, the blinds drawn behind his computer screen. He glances my way, unperturbed that I have invaded. The air is thick with the merged odors of human and rodent.

"Was the payment enough?" I say. "For the website. I do not know if you expected more for a job like that, a night job, and done at the last minute."

He types for a moment. On his computer screen a photo depicts a muscular, shirtless male using an electric prod on another one, who lies hogtied with a ball-gag lodged in his throat. *Straight Lads Tortured in Secret Glasgow Location! Register Now for Instant Access to Live-Action Streaming Videos!* the headline reads. Perhaps he imagines that I cannot see it from my distance. Perhaps he does not care. Perhaps this is how he earns his living.

Finally he looks at me. He shrugs. "Whuddup?"

"I would like the same again," I say. "This time simpler, though. A dummy of a real website that must match its particulars. I need to make it appear as if an article I wrote was published in an online magazine, somewhere artsy and political that has not too much of the visibility. I have the article and several choices for the online publication here in my little device. My hope is to supply someone with a web address that takes them to a dummy site that resembles the publication's site. If they try to move elsewhere on that site after following my path, the connection should simply fail."

He shakes his head without looking over, then goes back to whatever he was doing. "Whoever you're scamming will know."

"No. He will not double-check," I say, closing the door softly behind me. "He does not care much about where I have published in the past. He is looking for an excuse to see me, you get it?" I pause to see how I am doing. His fingers whisper over his keyboard, but I can see he listens to me. "Besides," I point out, "I do not care, ultimately, if he discovers me. It is okay for me to be the fraud. I am looking for nothing but an entry, an invitation. I want to see him, that is all, and he wants to see me equally. Is that so dumb now?"

The lodger does not look over, and his lank profile gives no message. I see a movement in the dark at his neck, and realize that what I took for a scarf is the rodent. Well, to each his own. I notice that his fingers have stopped moving on the keyboard.

"I will pay you. Cash, of course," I say. "You will name a fair price, I trust."

He looks over at me, just a glance, as if to scoff at the money, or maybe because it is obvious that he would expect cash for this type of transaction. He points at the gadget in my hand, beckons it with a finger.

"Lie on the bed," he says. "Don't talk. I'll tell you if I need you."

He shakes me by the arm at 5:30 a.m. I look up at his grease-lined face. He silently throws a glance at the wall. I nod and gather myself together, then huddle by the door, listening. I can hear Tati singing to herself, dashing water about in the bathroom. I hurry downstairs, flip-flops in my hand, and ease myself in my room. The singing and splashing continue at their prior level. There is little doubt that she knows where I have spent the night.

Wilkie calls me late in the afternoon. We arrange to meet the following evening, at his in-town condo near the wharf in the North End. He explains unnecessarily that he often conducts business there on weeknights. Of course, yes, I am sure I will find it quite easily, I tell him. He makes a joke, signing off, about how he hopes I leave the French quips out of his piece. Just letting me know, you see, that he has looked me up and the evening he plans is not all about my appealing qualities. He is right—the evening is not about the sex we will undoubtedly have. It is about his death.

Afterwards, I put six hundred dollars into an envelope and slip it under the door of the upstairs lodger. Later I hear him come home, but he does not stop by to thank me for either my generosity or the promptness of my payment. I would have been troubled if he had done so.

Très sincèrement,
Nightingale

TWELVE

I am Nightingale—

"So you want a piece of me?" Wilkie throws out in his deep, shaggy voice as he opens the door. "That it?"

"Only a piece?" I try to bandy back. "Councilman, I am here for every last bit of you." Holding my eyelids at half-mast so as not to see him well, I affect a wry expression as I probe past him with all my senses. I smell dead fish—we are near the harbor. I feel a draft waft past me and out into the airless public corridor. I encountered no one in the elevator, but now I hear the echo of a door opening down the hall. A man's step approaches—light on his feet, he will come along the corridor quickly. I do not panic; this man may glimpse me but it is of no consequence, as I will be inside before the stranger can get a look at my face. From beyond Wilkie I hear music—a fey warbler from many years back, tinkling through his high notes, making beautiful harmony with a piano. The stranger passes. I hear only the metallic click of his heels against the corridor tiles before the door thuds. Wilkie has his own incentive to keep me invisible, you see.

Moving on in, I note the lighting—more of it gleaming through the floor-length windows than coming from the dimmed ceiling cans. Wilkie is a decent man, but only to a point, yes?

He puts a hand out for my shawl. My dress is a red kimono, knee-length, sleeveless with a high collar, trimmed in black piping. Ignoring Wilkie's offer, I wrap my silky shawl tighter and walk away, its long fringe swaying against my arms and hips. He interprets this as a gesture—well, maybe he does. I tell myself that I *fourrage* in his head and am not just reacting to outward signs, like other women need to, but I am not certain. I am trying to use my special skills, but something is off. I know that he is assessing the chances that we will couple tonight, and his confidence is rising, but who in my position would not know this? In any event, he may be correct in his assessment, but it will only postpone the terminal event.

"So, you think you're getting all of me tonight?" he jokes. "Sister, politics don't allow 'all' of anyone to remain intact. At this moment, Charles Wilkins Morley is sliced and diced into very tiny pieces and sprinkled all around the city of Boston."

"Such an image," I offer over my shoulder. "You are like the crumbs for the birds."

His laugh is rich. "More like so much cremation ash," he jokes. *Inside, I go numb—could he be reading me?*

He goes on. "What you're looking at tonight is an empty vessel, a ghost. This talking you think you're hearing? It's an echo."

"It is indeed." I walk ahead of him, calming myself, my heels marking time gently against his wood floors. I tell myself that it is just a coincidence—he is simply flirting, following my own lead. "Did you know I collect ghosts?" I quip over my shoulder.

"Do you now?"

"I have a few floating about, back at my place. They await your company."

He laughs some more in his comfortable basso, pretending he finds me clever. He will appreciate my little joke later, though. When it is too late.

We banter on. Some men may have telepathic instincts of their own, of course. If so, it would not surprise me if Wilkie were one of them. Under other circumstances, I would not mind the idea of having him probing in my head. But honestly, I do not need some male version of my own gift getting in the way of my plans. I need this kill, after my strange fiasco with Brewster Van Ness. I need it tonight.

Shying away from him, I do a slow, full circle turn. It seems as if most of the condo—living, dining, kitchen and office areas—is open space, rolled out in a sweeping crescent rimmed by a lot of glass sliders. Some of these are open, and the bronze-tinted sheers twist gently, billowing then drooping like sighing shadows. The bedroom must be overhead, where there looks to be a loft area that cannot be seen from below. The open design maximizes the view of Boston Harbor, which sparkles dully in the hazy sunset across a busy street and, beyond that, a public park overlooking a dock. I breathe in, absorbing the slick stink of low tide. I find the odor of rot soothing. Inhaling, I catch a prickly aroma as well and slice him a look under my eyelids.

"You are expecting someone for dinner?" I ask. "Or do you simply wish to display for me that, in addition to everything else, you can cook?"

"I can cook, matter of fact," he agrees, gesturing for me to sit where I like. "Used to cook at a little Vietnamese joint in J.P. Dangerous place to eat for anyone but an FOB, and I couldn't understand a word anyone would say, but somehow I learned a couple of tricks you can get on with a mess of crayfish. Now I cook once, twice a month."

I ignore the invitation to pry into his family issues. "What do you have on now?"

"This one's a bouillabaisse," he says, then adds, "And, yes, I do make my own rouille, if that was the next question."

I smile as if he's read my mind.

"This batch I froze last week and am just thawing out, but that's only between you and me, y'hear? Believe me, I'd never serve a reheated bouillabaisse to a guest."

"*Ça arrache la gueule?*" I ask, just to check.

"Yes, indeed. Spice is my signature," he answers.

"*Vous êtes coulants dans le français?*"

"I'm not fluent by any means, but there's plenty of Creole in the hood where I grew up, so I can catch the gist of the simpler stuff," he says. "Wine?"

"Ah, you speak my language now," I say.

So he understands French—or does he simply read my mind? Either way, I am relieved to hear that he does not expect me to eat with him. Apparently he plans to dine after popping me in a cab, still dewy between the legs. It is a shame, this—he is a man who likes to eat, and I would not have begrudged him a final meal if I could have thought of a way to convince him to eat without me.

"Have a seat, please." He walks off to where he keeps the wine.

The decor is sleek—walls grey, canvases unframed, furniture low and set about in a geometric fashion. The kitchen area is designed to look sterile as a laboratory. I seat myself on one of the slabby sofas, wondering fleetingly if Wilkie seduced the decorator or vice versa.

Arriving at his wine cabinet, he flicks on the overheads, and the scene alters. His shirt is a mass of creases, dark stains spreading from the armpits. An unwashed plastic container sits next to the sink while a pot bubbles on a burner, gently splattering the tiles. The seating area is out of kilter, as if the maid bumps around with the vacuum and does not realign things. Off by the glass wall, the desk is massed in papers. It is a tired working pad, and Wilkie just a professional guy, stuck in town on a weeknight, hungry, happy to jawbone about himself with some fawning amateur because his wife and kids are out at the house, and he is not the type who dwells comfortably in silence. But now I hear the wine pouring just as the singer's voice swells from the hidden speakers, and so I must reconsider once again. He keeps me vacillating, this one. He is pure and good, hardworking and inspirational. He is predatory and lascivious. Ah, well.

Wilkie brings me my wine. He has got something red for himself, which he has poured into a different kind of glass.

"I looked you up. I like to know my interviewers." He seats himself.

"Of course," I shrug. "So you know I am divorced quite

recently and have only just returned to this area. Well, it is sad enough, but not a secret."

He laughs. "I did not know that, in fact. Found very little on you. Just a few articles. Apparently you came to writing fairly recently. Before that, seems to be a gap." As if he does not know my story from my supposed "slice of life" articles. As if.

I laugh. "A suitable way to describe my marriage—the gap in the résumé."

"I didn't mean to be flippant," he says immediately.

"It is quite okay," I assure him. "In truth, I like it. When we met you asked about a French background. It is true, yes, but an odd fact is that I met my ex-husband, who is French, here in the States. So back I went, and spoke little English for almost eight years. We lived in a rural town not so far from Fontainebleau. Each and every house walled in. Outside the walls, nothing but drunken rabbit hunters and old women hatching chickens in incubators. Endless mud and rain, my husband traveling far more than he was home, and of course, the three miscarriages. Ah, but the bread, eh?"

"Eight years. That's a serious stretch of time."

I shrug and swallow some wine. "You know, I did not mind so much the idea of a husband who sees other women from time to time—you cannot change the French—but I believe that he owes his wife the courtesy of being discreet. Do you not agree?"

"I do." Wilkie is comfortable. "You kept his name, though."

"I did, in fact," I say, meeting his eye. "I took it when I married him, and it is mine to keep or discard as I wish, not his to reclaim. I like this name. It is, as you pointed out, the name of a beautiful and daring actress. One of the finest in French cinema history."

"We agree on that," he assures me. "So what are your own people called?"

I hesitate. "Oh, I see. You need to continue your background check on me. No, no—there is no need to protest. It is fine, and I will in fact provide all the pertinent information for you quite soon. My original name was…"—my voice catches in my throat for just that moment, and I know he hears it, but I must risk it anyway—"…I was called Nightingale."

He looks across at me, eyes narrowing. Ah, yes, he has made me, finally! But of course he would have been alert during the trial. Unlike some of his fellow defendants—Terence D'Amante and Rocco Petrianni and Bruno Myeroff—Wilkie would have read the papers and would have known what people were saying, even about the peripheral characters, as his personal nightmare played out. I sit there on his flat, modern sofa, heart thudding. The wine in my glass trembles. I like him, you see, but I fear anything that may derail my plan.

"Julie Nightingale," he says. "Lovely name. Poetic. You should repossess that one. When you're ready, of course."

"I will do so," I say. "But only when I am ready, as you say."

He holds out his glass and we toast—to me, I suppose. And so he knows who I am, or so he thinks. He needs no further reassurance. I am bound for home.

He brings the conversation around to the piece I am supposedly hoping to write about him. I chatter defensively about how a sheltered white woman may write with conviction about a black man who hails from the streets. He pretends to buy my argument. All the while I am trying to sort out my confusion over how difficult he is for me to *fourrage*. He is not like these other men, who were so simple. Yes, he too has the male vanity—the relentless throb of the libido and the competitive ambition and the rather mono-dimensional perspective on his place in the world—all of this. But it is obscured by his heightened sense of others, his innate ability to probe the minds of those around him. He is a successful politician and thus of course a gifted manipulator. But also he has the emotion, the empathy. He loves. Not his wife—or not her in any complicating way, I sense—but perhaps he loves his little girls enough to awaken in him an intuition that clouds my *fourrage* and frightens me away from trying to *suggère* in his head. He has loved others as well. Relative strangers. Even an elderly neighbor who took an interest in him as a boy.

"I plan to start the piece with Oleander Tidwell," I say.

It is like water dashed in his face. So I am, in fact, able to *fourrage* him, if only in the vague fragments.

"I see," he says. "You've done a bit of homework." Then he seems to recover. "Or are you speaking about that day in Dorchester—Oleander as the hit-and-run victim?"

I sip the fancy wine, then slide a smile over the edge of my glass. "The article is to be about you, not about the Dorchester Five. We will not hide from it, but there will be little if any sensationalism in this piece. Is it not time for this?"

He agrees, but I've aroused his suspicions. "You know, my personal history was never discussed in open court," he says. "I saw to that. My attorney attempted to use my prior connection with Oleander during the trial, but I shut that shit down, and I know that there is no publically available transcript of the testimony that contains that stretch of questioning. I know it because I saw to it. This leaves me wondering how you would have learned of any dealings I might have had with Oleander Tidwell prior to her being killed on the street that day?"

He studies me. He is right that some cub reporter wistfully scratching around the cold news files would not have come up with a connection between him and Oleander. Only someone who had sat through the trial, listening every day, would know about it, unless she was very lucky, and I do not strike him as a true nose-for-news kind of gal. But after he did not make me upon hearing that I am Nightingale, I am confident that he does not and will not recognize me. The persona I have taken on for him, even more so than the last two, is simply too far removed from the silent, expressionless drone with the colorless shingle-cut hair, through the weeks of testimony, never wavering, never raising an eyebrow, seeming perhaps not quite present enough to follow the proceedings even if she had wanted to, and not curious enough to try. Slouching my way in every morning. Slouching out, for breaks and at the end of the day. Standing at the "all rise" with the rest of them, although perhaps I could have escaped complying with that imperious command due to my particular role in the trial. The occasional tissue to the nose or lips. A sip through a straw. Little else, really. Still, it will not do for me to remind him in any way of that brooding, persistent presence.

"Perhaps I am more intuitive that I seem," I stall.

He waits for more. "Come off it." There is firmness in his tone. He will not budge—he will not even bed me if I do not come clean on how I know about Oleander and his past.

I sigh. "I sat through the trial. Some of it, anyway."

"You were there?"

I dare to send him a quick signal—I *suggère* that he should believe me—after all, it is the truth I have just spoken. Following this, of course, I lie. "I was in the States for a visit with my parents, already having trouble with Michel, you see, although certainly not ready to admit to it. This was after my first miscarriage. My parents had moved to South Boston, so I was not even visiting a familiar neighborhood. The case was gritty, steeped in tragedy from all angles, and I got it in mind that I would write about it. Not a news piece, and not junk, but a dispassionate study, you see? So I arrived early enough each morning to line up in front of the rabble. Each day I sat in the courtroom, and I took the notes. No one forbade it, but I worried that they might, so I wore the gloves and I held a little pad in the palm of one hand and a tiny white pencil in the other. I filled twenty-seven pads. I took stabs at beginning the piece over the years. Michel was dead against it."

He nods to himself. "And now you're trying to revive that ambition to write."

I shrug. "I never acknowledged that I had given up. Women do not, when they sacrifice a personal goal for a man. We call it postponement. We are good at self-deceit, you see? That is why divorce can be so nasty."

"She sees a sacrifice where he sees a free ride, that sort of thing?"

"That is it."

I look off, out the windows, as if through being frank about my life. For a moment, I dare to *fourrage* in his brain. He is a naturally suspicious man.

"Shall we talk?" I prod him.

"Oleander was the woman who made me try in life," he says. "She wasn't a relative. Not even a friend of the family, really. Just a neighbor while I was growing up, and then, when I became a man, a fellow neighborhood activist. Not an ally, mind you. Too strict by about half, and the old girl knew nothing of the art of compromise. But somehow, from all the way back when I was a kid, she was the one I was proving myself to in life."

"A grandmother figure?"

"I wouldn't say that." Wilkie smiles bemusedly. "I had a grandmother—well, into my tenth year, anyway—so I didn't need a surrogate there. It was kind of mysterious, that I would feel any kind of connection to this other lady. And for all her Bible preaching, Oleander was less benign than the typical granny. So it wasn't a gap, and it wasn't that she was so good. It was more that she took a serious interest in me—Lord knew why, because to my recollection I was just another neighborhood squirt, but she must have spotted something—and from then onward she was like, I don't know, a force of judgment. A voice, tsking away in the back of my head, proclaiming an ideal that I knew I'd never fulfill—that I was pretty damned comfortable not fulfilling, in fact—but which I liked having out ahead of me. A royal pain in the ass, she was, and I know for a fact that there were whispers, after she was gone, that the community meetings she used to attend made a lot more progress than they used to."

He pauses. "Here, let me try to put it how she might have— Oleander Tidwell was a tough old bird who insisted that life could be for us black folk what life was for the white folk. She scorned the reality that things will never be equal. And the mean old thing latched onto me, for some reason, as the black man worth pushing, and pushing constantly, on this point."

He runs dry, shaking his head. "Haven't thought about Oleander for a stretch of time. I probably should, more often."

"So," I say. "Turning over that car was personal for you."

He glances at me sharply. His eyes, dark brown, have a bluish ring around the irises that seems to glow when he is intense. "Seeing her die in the street was quite a shock. Damn near made me see fireworks when that little shit tried to motor off like he'd hit a dog."

"So you were punishing that boy behind the wheel. Street justice."

He studies me and I wonder if he is floating thoughts into my head. "I acted out of anger. But my intent—my sole intent—was to make sure that the driver didn't leave the area."

"For his own good," I say dryly.

"It damn well was for his own good. You kill someone with your car, accident or not, and you take off from the scene? Honey, you talking about some serious time. You hit someone, stay with the victim, see it through." He paused to wipe his mouth. "Well, a nice clean white boy with no record gets to go on with his life."

"Was the guy who hit Oleander Tidwell a nice clean white boy?"

"That I couldn't have told you at the time," Wilkie admits. "But I sure as hell knew that he weren't doing himself any sort of favor trying to hightail it out of there. Everyone saw what had happened plain as day."

I speak slowly, as if picking my words carefully. "I think that what you are saying, Wilkie, is that you were trying to do the right thing. Is that a fair translation?"

"Christ, no," he says. "Nothing that happened that day was right. Nothing." He picks up his wine glass, just for something to grip, and has himself a swallow.

"I went about this clumsily."

He shakes his head. "Oleander is an indelible part of my past. You were right to pick up on that. Her memory is an element of my decision-making on many an issue. Perhaps more importantly, she—what happened to her—was just about all that got me through the trial, back then. I did an unforgivable thing. You saw that kid! But I knew why."

"You are quite brave, I think, to explain this to me." When he doesn't respond, I hurry ahead. "What were you doing on the street that day? Wrong place, wrong time, was it?"

He seems about to nod at my cliché, then stops himself. "I was heading to a meeting, actually," he says. "The same meeting Oleander was heading to, at the church. About the drug problem. Sales on the streets, local gangs preying on their own, a rumor that drug deals were going down in the church itself. That sort of thing. The usual hand-wringing, the usual neighborhood watches and kids' clubs—weak as water, always seems, but somehow it must counterbalance the problem because if it doesn't happen the neighborhood goes straight to hell. So, no, actually, I wasn't in the wrong place at the wrong time. I was in the right place, and something wrong just happened to me on my way."

"Happened to you?" I say, jumping on his words before I think.

"Very true, very true," he agrees, unfazed. "That boy in the car suffered far more for his sin than the rest of us did for ours." He cocks an eye at me. "Is he—Jake Culligan, that is—someone you know? Maybe your parents got to know his family when they moved to Southie?"

I pause before murmuring that it is just as he says, but I am sure that my fear shows.

Wilkie shifts his gaze from my face to my wine glass, as if the shimmer there has him mildly distracted. "I hear that he is doing well, relatively speaking," he says.

"You hear this?" I am sure he detects the tremor in my voice.

He looks me in the eye. "Jake Culligan is twenty-eight years old. He's brain damaged for life. His condition has not changed much from what it was at the time of the trial."

"He is dead," I say, unable to help myself.

He shakes his head. "He isn't, unless it happened fairly recently. I've kept track. He lives in South Boston with his mother Prudence. Economically, they're taken care of completely. The older brother is trouble. Other than that, not much."

"Why have you kept track?"

"Don't want to forget."

I clear my throat and he chuckles sympathetically at my discomfort, then graciously changes the subject. "You know I was related to Terry D'Amante?"

"No," I say gratefully. "I never learned that."

"Well, not by blood. Terence was a distant cousin, second or even third. Barely had heard that his girl at the time was expecting, time of the arrest, but apparently it had happened a month or so prior. They never let Terence out. No bail, like the rest of us got—he'd already jumped bail on another charge and was about to be rounded up. Must have been finishing up some business before seeking to get his ass out of town when the incident occurred."

"What business was this, do you think?"

Wilkie spreads his hands. "Nothing he was prepared to talk about, since no one was offering him a deal. My guess is that he thought he could collect some cash from someone to make running viable. Or maybe he had a score to settle. He was like that. When the case against us reached settlement, they just took him straight out to Walpole for his other stuff. I tried to see Neva, offer what assistance I could, but she wouldn't have a thing to do with me. Possibly she resented me for walking away while Terence did time. I've never even seen the child. Went in to see Terence a few times, tried to talk with him about his paternal obligations. He said the right things, but…" Wilkie spreads his hands again. "Guess we'll never know. All we can say is that he tried to see his son soon as he got released."

"It is," I say, "quite chilling, this part of the story."

He nods. "Unfortunately, it isn't going into a piece about me. Neva isn't to be mentioned, nor my efforts with Terence."

I concede with a dip of my head. "Of course."

We listen to the sound of a jet taking off across the bay. It seems to remind Wilkie of the time. He crosses to the sliders and closes them with a soft thump, then skirts the seating area and pokes at his bouillabaisse. When he returns, he has brought the wine bottles. He tips, and I nod him on. I take a cigarette out of the pack in my purse and gesture with it.

He shakes his head. "Maybe later. But you go ahead."

I light one and drop the match on his stone table. "Perhaps I may take a look upstairs?"

Wilkie nods. "You surely may," he says solemnly.

The stairway is unassuming, around a corner by the front door. I had not noticed it earlier. Upstairs, the bedroom is more expansive that I imagined it from below. The carpet is blue-grey, matching a velvety coverlet that half-drapes the bed. At the foot of the bed sits a massive old carved chest, the only item in the room that isn't sleek and smooth-sided. A glass sculpture seems to be an image of African femininity. The music floats up. It is semi-dark, but I can see that the room is untidy, with the bed made carelessly, the closet doors hanging open with clothes dangling from hooks and knobs and laundry spilling in a loose tangle from a basket on the floor. I make out a plate next to the bed, a crumpled napkin, a beer bottle.

"You are separated," I say without thinking. I turn from the middle of the room, where I have just stepped out of my shoes. Wilkie is leaning against the rail, bulky—even fat, I see now that I'm viewing him in silhouette and he is not sheathed in a suit. His arms are massive, his shoulders slope smoothly, his gut makes a proud round bulge—he is the male counterpart to the cool, blue statuette that sits adjacent to where he rests, both of them watching me.

"I should not have said that," I apologize.

I see his teeth flash in the dim light, and he laughs, sounding almost shy. "That's okay. And, no, my wife and I are not separated. Not exactly."

"Ah, I see," I say across the space. "You are two mature, mutually supportive adults with an understanding. You comprehend the French, then, after all."

"We care about each other, Claire and I, but we try not to stand in one another's way."

"Ah," I say. "I think that maybe she started it. My apologies for presuming it was the other way."

"You miss very little," he observes quietly. "Not at all how you put yourself across at first, are you, though?"

It should frighten me, this remark, but somehow it does not. It does not matter what he knows, at this point. He wants sex, you see, and, like so the males of all species, he will copulate even with the certainty that the female will cut him down him shortly after. I raise my wine glass and sip. "Such flattery," I say. "Now where will that get us?" I sit down on the shiny bed-stuff with a soft plop, then cross my legs and gaze over at his silhouette. "Anything else I should know that might make me live to regret this?"

Wilkie walks forward, swirling his wine. "Haven't washed the sheets in a month."

I scoff and blow smoke off to one side. "I do not mind the human odors."

"I'm a damn good lay."

I laugh aloud. "I did not need to be told this. I am the one who first flirted across that auditorium, remember?"

He nods, studying me thoughtfully. "Look, bedding down visitors isn't particularly a habit of mine, if that's what you're asking."

"I think perhaps it is," I say, looking about for a place to park my wine glass and stub my cigarette. "But I do not really care."

"So you don't mind being just one in a line of conquests?"

"Not if you do not mind being the same," I say.

He barks a laugh. "I don't mind, naturally."

"That is what you say now," I coo.

Again, Wilkie laughs. "I won't say differently later," he says. "That I can assure you."

"I believe you," I say. Of course I believe him. But, truthfully, I would have believed him even if I had been planning to let him live out the night.

Wilkie stands close now, his leg practically touching mine. I turn from where I have stretched up so as to nuzzle my empty glass into the clutter on his bedside table and gaze up at him, leaning back on my elbows. I slide my legs up slowly so that they present themselves for him to do with as he will. He reaches forward, cups each of my knees in one of his large hands, and gently separates them. I relax, then, and lie back against the pillows.

I give him the best I am capable of giving. It is not that I am sorry that he will die tonight, which I am. I give him my best because I see the scars. The entire left side of his chest, along with a swatch of his belly and the inside of his arm on that side, form a twisted mass of white-pink flesh, more like exposed intestines than skin, each patch shiny in the middle and black around the edges. I do not flinch from the sight—I am accustomed to it. But the stories that the lawyers told in court about how he broke the VW's side window and tried with all his might to pull Jakey from the burning vehicle—now at last I know that these tales were quite true. So I give him my best as a thank you for this effort on his part to make up for what he did, and for his integrity in not displaying himself during the trial in some self-serving attempt at sympathy. Just as he finishes, when a man's mind is in its most unguarded state, I *fourrage* deep into his brain. I find the moment immediately, as if by instinct:

Wilkie stops, one foot on the curb and the other in the gutter, so as to make room for a woman to pick her way around a pile of dog crap. She darts him a smile, not quite sure of him, or maybe she wonders why he gives her such wide berth. It's a vestige of his youth, the myth that white women are afraid of black men. He's recently come to realize that at least some of them are not nearly as intimidated as all that. In fact, seems there's a tone of abandonment inherent in interracial sex that he has not tasted with women of his own race. All this has been an exciting revelation to Wilkie, not solely because his prurient tastes run to white women, but also because the eager reciprocation he's experienced of late offers him an entirely new take on his world. Suddenly he is part of the new century's political culture. He shares in it. He is not simply the underclass, the guilt trip, the weight. He is the

Mighty Negro—fertile, exotic, irresistible. Over time he can change that caricature, perhaps in part through the curiosity that stirs the sexes and, apparently, transcends race tribalism.

All that bodes well, sure, but today is sweltering—sweat weighs down his shirt, and no female of any race needs to smell the stink coming off Wilkie like heat off tar. So he gives the white lady her space, then watches her walk off down the busy sidewalk, the hem of her polka-dotted sundress fluttering in time to the bounce of her rump. Beyond that twitching derrière he spots Oleander, decked out in full church lady regalia—hat, gloves, Bible—marching off the curb on her side of the street, bright-eyed with righteous fervor. The old bird's out for blood, namely that of the diffident priest-in-training who runs the youth group. Claims he's a bad influence—won't explain further, although Wilkie himself is aware that the fellow's had issues. Serious issues, whispered around the parish. Wilkie's on his way to pow-wow, maybe avoid the lasting injuries that will come from a public scandal. Oleander is the enemy, this round. She is a crusader for mercy, but only for her own people.

With a sigh, Wilkie raises a hand in response to Oleander's raised finger. In spite of his efforts to work quietly, it surely looks like he is about to hear her out there on the street. But she's not focused on Wilkie, he realizes even as he thinks this. She's flagging down a VW, ordering the driver to halt. Wilkie recognizes the car, somewhat sketchily, as that of a lowlife from South Boston, the type who prides himself on plying his drug trade in neighborhoods other than his own. The type with no consciousness that all neighborhoods house someone's kids, someone's hopes. Someone's God. Wilkie frowns, pivoting so that he, too, is now in the street, heading toward the moving vehicles. He's seen the shark who drives that incongruous powder blue bug—guy's got eerie eyes, furry jowls, and a smirk like the devil's. If Oleander thinks that trade like him is likely to be intimidated by a scrawny lady with iron grey hair, she's mistaken.

She is fatally mistaken, turns out. Wilkie watches in dumb awe as the guy behind the wheel catches sight of the old girl. The Beetle swerves, but only to a point. Hits her—drives through her, actually—

she twists over the hood and through the air like so much litter caught in an updraft. When Oleander hits the ground, she seems to collapse into herself with no skeletal resistance, folding down in a seamless instant as if every brittle bone had just snapped upon impact. She's dead, Wilkie realizes—there will be no moment of clutched hands, no fruitless straining to hear the ambulance, no lingering breaths. She's off reaching for heaven, right before his eyes. In an instant, Wilkie's mind's eye jumps to the litany of ceremony that confront his community—the solemn public remembrances, the keening before the news cameras, the memorial fundraising.

Oddly—or perhaps not, in light of the suddenness of the event—Wilkie feels no emotional response during that long moment of standing there, staring across the lanes of traffic at the tatty yellow suit, at the Bible's pages riffling in an air current. He sees the car's driver blinking back at him, equally surprised, equally unemotional. It is not the dealer Wilkie had envisioned after all—it's a kid, beardless and shirtless in the heat, some foolish piece of macho bling round his neck, some ineptly executed tattoo scoring his shoulder. Wilkie feels nothing, looking across at that kid, until he hears the car start up, sees him throw it into gear, watches the front tires twist as the car backs away from the scene.

Wilkie moves forward just as the guy starts swinging into his U-turn. Having realized what was coming, Wilkie stands squarely in the bug's path. The kid looks him in the eye as he powers up the windows, locks the doors. Wilkie sees him scrambling for something—a gun? A phone? Whatever it is, it is far too late. Rocco Petrianni, a neighborhood hothead, rams his way in front of Wilkie and slams his fists down against the car's hood, bellowing, and it shudders to a halt.

There is no doubt about it. The kid hesitated—he paused and stalled—because Rocco is white. He would have taken his chances with Wilkie, maybe let himself think that Wilkie would surely step aside. But Wilkie, like Oleander, is expendable. Like a dog, in this kid's eyes. Wilkie will recover his senses, his equilibrium, quickly. But for a moment, he sees blood. For a moment, that kid's life is as meaningless to him as his life was to the kid.

We lie side by side, etherized by memory. Finally I speak. "Are you ever glad it happened?" I ask.

Wilkie lies there for a long while, then turns his head to stare at the side of my face, his gaze searching, intelligent. "What?" he says incredulously.

"Are you ever glad," I repeat at the ceiling. "About Dorchester."

He looks at me more closely. "I think I just fucked away whatever common sense you possessed when you came up here tonight," he says.

I laugh and feel for my little beaded bag, which happens to lie on the carpet next to the bed, within reaching distance. Extracting a cigarette, I glance at him. "Not glad about Oleander's death or the injuries to Jake Culligan. But for the ordeal that followed, what you went through. I am talking about being linked with those other men—in the press and in the court case as well—being associated in the public's eye with four truly bad men, when you are not and never were one of them. Do you recognize it, on any level, as a life lesson that has stood you well, now that you dwell in the public eye more permanently?"

I watch the suspicion recede in his eyes. "You're an interesting woman," he says.

"If you find my question offensive, do not answer." I flick my lighter.

"Not offensive," he says, raising a large palm. "That's not the word." He waits, then says, "Look, I feel like we can be open with one another, that you'll understand."

I glance at him as I reach for a second cigarette. "We have just had a damn good fuck. It is worth a try." I light the second cigarette against the first and offer it over to him.

"Truth be told," he says, taking a drag, "while it was happening that day, I felt proud to be part of the mob, to be right up against the car," he says. "As someone close to Oleander, this was where I belonged. And I felt no pity for the boy inside."

"Did you see Jakey's face, in there?"

"I did."

I close my eyes. "What was it like?"

He thinks about it. "He looked more excited than frightened. I don't think a kid like that can envision injuries like he sustained. I think he imagined he was going to walk away."

"I wonder," I whisper.

Wilkie smokes some more, then gestures in the air above the bed, as if dispelling an image he's seen there many times.

I sit up partway and pull the sheets up over my breasts. "You tried to pull him out."

"I attempted to correct what I'd done," he says in a simple tone. "Sometimes you do something terrible, you get a second chance. Not that day, though."

"No. There were no angels looking down on Dorchester that day," I murmur.

"Mmm," he agrees, "although there was one among us." Then he interrupts himself. "Holy mother, baby, you mind telling me what we are smoking here?"

"They are the Gitanes," I say. "Too much for you, I think?"

"Way too much." He draws again. "These soldiers kill without pretense."

I nod. "This is true. What did you mean, there was an angel among you that day?"

He goes to rise, seems to want to roll to his side and prop himself on his elbow, but after a small effort he sinks back and rests on his back. He lies silent for a long moment, the cigarette held between a thumb and finger.

I sit up a little straighter. "Wilkie?"

"Love," he says groggily.

"Love?" I almost smile. "The angel of love?"

"Not…" he says, shaking his head, "not being abstract here. Guy named Love."

"Ah, Simon Love," I clarify. "But he was one of the Five. He helped turn the car."

Wilkie smiles in the dark. The forgotten cigarette glows

between his fingers. "Love was a flawed man. But he didn't turn over no car."

"He did not?"

"Did not." Wilkie floats now. I reach over and take the glowing butt from his fingers.

"What did Simon Love want, then?"

Another long pause. "Wanted peace."

"So Simon Love did not deserve to be in the Dorchester Five? Is this what you tell me?"

Wilkie chuckles in a dreamy way. "Darling," he slurs softly, "the Dorchester Five is a media myth. There weren't no five. There was, like, fifteen. Thirty. Fifty. You think the cops nabbed the five guilty guys?"

"Why did not this Simon Love fight it, if he was just trying to save Jakey's life?" I argue. "Why did Simon Love's lawyer not defend him when the time was right?"

"Way I recall it...lawyer opted...for the out."

"And he allowed that? An innocent man who could prove his innocence would allow such a thing?"

Wilkie shrugs and works his thick tongue before answering. "Never talked about it...weren't allowed...separate defendants, different defenses." He pauses and then, after a long moment, breathes deeply, once. "The deal meant it ended."

I continue to argue. "How are you so sure about what was motivating this Simon Love on the street on that day? How do you know he was not just like you, angered about the elderly woman cut down by a hit-and-run driver?"

Again Wilkie takes a long time before answering. I can hear from his breathing that it is close, now. But eventually he speaks. "I know...because he got through to me. I tried to reverse what I done...because of Love."

I lay there awhile, thinking, then stand up, leaving Wilkie the sheet. "May I shower?"

He tries to nod through his stupor, then, to be polite, adds, "May I join you...?"

"Yes of course. But please give me ten minutes to myself."

It is while I am showering that he comes to realize that it must be the cigarette that has done this to him. He is more than high. He is paralyzed. He imagines me in the shower, crying, my face under the stream of water so that I may hide the fact of my tears even from myself.

When I come out, he remains lying on his back. I can see him in silhouette as the night sky penetrates the dark some small amount. I dress silently and only then approach him. It is safe, now, to be detected, and so I reach over quite openly to *fourrage* in his mind.

He watches me as I stand there. I am dressed once again, but I look different. My hair is short, my face younger without makeup. I stand brushing at the teased wig, preparing to put it back on. He is not afraid, although he knows that I have inflicted this paralysis upon him. He wants to meet me eye to eye, but I will not look him full in the face. He feels no pain, and in fact experiences very little in the way of panic as I fit a large clear plastic bag over his head and seal it around his neck with duct tape. He watches, and notes through the haze that I seem to be standing there to watch him die. He thanks me for that.

"*Think nothing of it,*" I shoot him telepathically. "*It is the least I can do.*" This is not a way I would choose to kill this one, but of course he must suffocate. It is Moreau's pattern.

I disappear for a while. I have gone to find the card on which I wrote my phone number for him. When I come back, he cannot see anything but a ghosted outline of me. It may be that I misperceive him as already dead, he thinks, for I come forward and remove the tape, then pull the bag off his head. I check his eyes and hold a makeup mirror to his mouth and appear to perceive no sign of life. He can feel nothing when I touch him. He has no fear anymore.

"*You knew him,*" he tries to say. His lips do not move. He speaks to me telepathically, his brain to mine. A man has never done this with me before. "*You were...?*"

"Yes, I was," I say aloud, not unkindly. "How did you know?"

"*Jakey,*" he says. "*You called him Jakey.*"

I eye him with curiosity. "*Yes. I am Nightingale.*" I light the lighter and stand with the fire flickering next to me. He watches it reflecting off my eyes.

"*They're onto you. I got a call.*"

"*It is of no matter,*" I cut him off. "*They will catch up with me in time.*"

"*You call yourself Nightingale. I understand why—it's after the Stravinsky opera. You are the near-invisible bird who waits nearby and whose song, sung in the night, forces tears from all who hear it. Am I right, Julie Nightingale?*"

"*No. It is not Stravinsky who inspires me. Now I must go.*"

I use the lighter to light one of the French cigarettes. Then I step back, take a drag, and toss the lit cigarette onto the bed. It sputters for a moment, then begins to smolder. The smoke, even in the first moments, is thick and moves heavily, as if clinging to the bed. Wilkie sees only the vaguest flicker, somewhere on the edge of his vision. He does not smell the smoke that will asphyxiate him. It seems more dignified, to me, than the plastic bag.

I quote scripture: *Let burning coals fall upon them; Let them be cast into the fire…Let evil hunt the man to overthrow him.*

Downstairs, I turn off the flame under his bouillabaisse, then find my wrap. I leave quickly, running across no other people in his building. It would matter little if I had.

Très sincèrement,
Nightingale

THIRTEEN

Marina Papanikitas's Personal Journal

Closing in on a week since Becker took his dive—pressure kind of building. That in mind, I start the day kind of random. Got this massive urge to take in the Dorchester Five vid, so I head to Harrison Ave first thing. Phone rings just as I'm arriving, and for close on a minute I do a shoulder-chin hold while wrestling the steering wheel through a tricky parallel park. From what I can hear, which involves a girl's wavering voice stumbling through some nonsense-talk, I'm on the receiving end of a junior high drunk dial. Fortunately I catch on just before hanging up. It's Donna Witzkowitz, aka Donnalinda Tonite, and she's trying to pronounce my last name. I stop trying to park and give her my attention.

"Hey, Donna, how's it going, girl?" I throw her, just in case her life experience has made her skittish about chatting up cops.

"I'm good," she says. "Is this a okay time to talk?"

"Absolutely. So what's up?"

"You said to call if I had any thoughts about Mr. Petrianni."

"I did say that," I assure her. Someone taps his horn, trying to clue me in that my front end is sticking out into the traffic. I resume trying to wriggle the car into its spot. "You had a thought?" I prompt her.

"Yeah, I did," Donna tells me proudly.

"Excellent," I say patiently, inching the car backwards. "So what is it, Donna?"

"Okay. So you know how you guys were all over that lady in the club, like she was the one who killed Mr. Petrianni?"

I stop working on parking. This seems like the time to remove the phone from between my chin and shoulder. "Yes, we were fixating on her, weren't we," I agree. "What about it?"

"So this thing was bugging me about that, but I couldn't figure out what. Then, last night, I got what was bugging me. Oh, I'm working again."

"Congrats!" I say. Another driver is trying to squeeze by and gives me a pissy horn toot. I wave him on. "You, uh, remembered this thing about Mr. Petrianni's death while at work?"

"Yeah. See, now I'm an escort. You know what that is, right?"

I feel a pang, knowing I'm about to blow by the opportunity to help her consider her life choices in the interest of getting what I can on Rocco's death. "I do know about escorts," I say.

"It's legal in Rhode Island," she says.

"Still, not the safest line of work."

"I know," she says, contrite. "Oh, but that reminds me of what I want to tell you. So I'm meeting this client last night, and I'm walking to his car where he's waiting, and I'm thinking maybe I don't want to meet him. And I happen to notice that the way he's smoking is just like the guy in the parking lot that night. You know, when I was leaving after Mr. Petrianni tells me to go get proof of my age. He flicked his thumb a lot, like to drop ash, the way they used to in the movies. I mean, that's not why I didn't want to meet him. It was just a thing he did."

"Okay," I say, "So give me a little more about the parking lot guy."

"Well, there isn't anything more."

"Just that there was a man in a car, handling his cigarette in a dated way?"

"Yeah."

I try my coaxing skills. "I would think that every night there'd be some guy finishing a cigarette in his car in that lot. This one must have made an impression on you, Donna, more than just the way he flicked his ash."

She thinks it over. "Not really."

I try to coax better. "But you thought it was worth calling me about, right?"

She thinks some more. "Alls I'm saying is that I saw this guy in the parking lot, and I remember thinking, 'that fuck's gonna kill someone.' Like a hit man, you know?"

I frown at my reflection in the rearview, ignoring the dope who's decided to really lean on his horn at me. I talk slowly, not wanting to discourage her, but needing to squeeze out of her whatever she's got to offer. "So you're saying that when you were leaving the club, you noticed a guy in the parking lot and somehow got the feeling that he made a living killing people."

"Yeah. Well, no." She ponders. I hold my breath. "It's more like this," she finally says. "I'm leaving, and I notice this man in a car, staring at me, and I don't think nothing much. Then, when I meet you, and you tell me Mr. Petrianni got murdered, first thing I think is, 'so that guy was a hit man, like I thought.' Then when you and your partner start talking like it was a woman, I think, 'Oh, I was wrong about that guy.' But last night I'm heading to meet this client in a car, and I decide I'm blowing him off. We're allowed to stand up a guy if we get a funny vibe off him. And so that reminded me of the vibe from the other guy, and that's when I thought maybe I should tell you."

"Got it," I say. "Hold on a sec, would you?"

I turn my head and yell, "You mind? I'm on an important call, here!" and give a twist to the steering wheel, finally rocking my car into the spot. I go to display my badge, just for kicks, but the guy's already flipping me off as he roars on by. I catch a glimpse of him—older exec type, silver hair, clean car. Probably en route to his job running a multi-million dollar charitable foundation, and he gives the finger to a girl just the age to be his daughter—nice.

I apologize to Donna, but she seems psyched that I referred to her call as important.

"So I got the lay of the land, Donna, and it makes sense," I say. "You must have had a powerful reaction to this parking lot guy to have held onto the memory in spite of all the distractions between then and now."

"Yeah, like, that's exactly it."

"So give me whatever you can. Description, clothes, car make and model?"

"Car was the kind with the peace sign. Old. Dark color. Like maybe brown."

Mercedes. I smile a little. "Okay, let's go for the guy."

Here Donna fails me. "Looked like a real dick," she offers.

"Don't most guys, to someone, Donna?" I point out. "What about race, age, features?"

"White," she says. "Dark hair, or maybe just wet. And one of those chin beards. For age, oldish. For weight, don't know. For height, he was sitting, so…"

"Oldish like me and Harry, Donna, or oldish like your dad?"

She seems to realize her blunder and tries to think her way out of it before admitting, "Maybe not all that old. More like your age. But mostly he seemed…"

I wait for it.

"He seemed, like, a guy chicks need to watch out for. You know what I mean?"

"I do, actually," I say. I tell her I'm going to call Shanko and Alec and that they'll arrange to have her sit down with a sketch artist, just to go over some brows, chins, and noses. Then I ring off before she can back down. The call to Shanko is as warmly received as I would have expected. He certainly gets that a skittish witness warrants fast action, so maybe that's why he foregoes any feint at thanking me for the tip. I'm not delighted about siccing him on Donna, but I tell myself that she's a girl who needs some unadorned contact with the law while she's still teetering on the correct side of it.

I'm still pondering this new development as I sit down in Archives in front of the Dorchester Five vid. I watch Petrianni and D'Amante earn their five minutes. The speed at which that crowd materialized around that bug was probably the most startling part about it. You don't see the old lady at all, as the vid starts with the bug in mid U-turn and a much younger C. Wilkins Morley stepping out in the street with his hands spread. Rocco thrusts himself in, playing rough, and within the minute you got Terence D'Amante jumping up on the hood, screaming at the kid through the windshield, and a bunch of guys shoulder-ramming the side doors with a crowd of screaming lunatics wedged around them foaming for blood and guts.

Bruno Myeroff, also one of the Five, distinguishes himself by stepping up with a brick to smash a window, then reaching inside to try to get the door open. Guess his angle was that it might be fun for the crowd to take apart the driver and not just the car. Bruno's the one the press dubbed "the college student," but that label's deceiving. He's a beefy guy with a dyed blond skullcap of hair and a studded dog collar around his neck, a sleeveless jean jacket and chains everywhere. Apparently he was from money, going through an acting-out stage. Simon Love, the final defendant, is barely noticeable, but if you do focus he comes off like a strung out longhair. Maybe he got arrested because he was there to clean up when the squad cars swarmed in.

The bug flips more easily than I'd have thought. Crowd goes bananas—chills me to the core, watching them cheer as yellow smoke boils from the interior. There could be no doubt in any person's mind that the driver is going to die or suffer serious injuries. Morley seems to be trying to climb up onto the vehicle, ignoring the flames. It's impossible to guess what's going on in his head, but I want to think he woke up and got what was going down. All of this I'm describing to you, Zoey—we're talking one minute and forty-two seconds. That's the amount of time it takes for a crowd of human strangers to join together for an impromptu slaughter.

At around this point the cameraman turns round to film the

circle round the old lady. More screaming here, with a keening tone to it. Shrill, though, and a lot of fists shaking in the air. If I were a cynic—and I am—I'd say these creatures were doing their part to add fuel to the fires. You don't see the old lady, the dead one, for a moment. Whole thing ends abruptly, as it seems like the guy doing the filming starts getting hassled himself.

I watch it three times. Not sure why—something fascinating about the horror of it all. Just to pretend I need to sit there, I try to make out what D'Amante is screaming through the windshield before he spots Myeroff and scrabbles over the roof of the bug at him, probably after his brick. Whatever he says ends pretty clearly with "ass man." That part he managed to enunciate. It's what comes before that's a garble. I get "hollered you, hollered you, no Chopin disco, ass man," with varied repeats. I dutifully write it down, agreeing pretty readily that classical études should never be laid over a four on the floor beat, but does that seem even a little helpful? I'm thinking not.

Returning the vid, I lay my jotting on the counter. Janai glances at it.

"This is what one of the guys is saying. I can't make it out except like this. Care to play?"

She's skeptical, but her day job's a bore, so she gives it a minute. "Well, 'hollered you' is like 'I told you this in no uncertain terms earlier.'" Then she looks up. "Lemme get this. This is like ghetto talk, so you figure the black girl in the evidence cage going to be all over it?"

She has a point. I blink a couple of times, then say, "Actually, my idea was to stick it in front of every BPD employee I come across. I...didn't think."

She kind of smirks, and something tells me my blush is the most effective part of the apology. "Yeah, well, lucky thing you got to me first. I don't what this stuff about Chopin and disco is, but sometimes these gangs got their own code going on, right? Then he calls him an ass man, probably just to insult him and not really as part of what he's saying."

"As in 'not a tit man?'" I say. "Seems a little off topic, doesn't it?"

She stares at me, then says, "I'm going to retract that 'black girl' thing I laid on you a little earlier. You come to me directly when you need to translate some street talk, and we'll keep you from embarrassing yourself unduly, hmm? So, like you say, an ass man might be a guy who prefers what's in the trunk to what's up the rack." She points to each of the areas on herself—and she has quite the example of each. "But in a situation you might call unfriendly, it would probably be more a comment that the guy wants to get with other guys, like that he prefers a guy's back door over lady parts?"

Again, I feel the blush. "I'm grateful for the explanation. Thanks, truly, Janai."

She looks satisfied. At the very least, she's got a story to tell all day. While I'm signing out she says, "Weird, isn't it though? Two of those guys dead, space of two months."

I agree, finish signing out, and am actually leaving the cage when the dime drops. I catch the door just before it clicks. "Uh, Janai?"

She's walking away. Turns halfway back with a major hip shift. "Honey?"

"How do you know about the second one?"

"Oh, I was upstairs when they were getting the call, so I just overheard. But I know it's all supposed to be quiet, so I won't be telling a soul."

I shake my head. "Tell about who? What's supposed to be kept quiet?"

Her turn to look quizzical, then she realizes I don't know. Fortunately her recent vow of secrecy doesn't include me. "City Councilman C.W. Morley got himself murdered. I mean, that's why you're looking at this here, right?" She gestures with the video.

I stare. Then I nod a couple of times, nothing much else coming to me. When I go, I move fast. No idea what I left Janai thinking, but if she's confused, she's not alone.

FOURTEEN

Marina Papanikitas's Personal Journal

Major breakthrough time, Zoey. Does not feel triumphant, though. Feels like I was blind to the obvious for one major beat too long. Ready for some psychic-babble? Sometimes I think the bloody premmies and the bloody vishies actually inhibit my perceptiveness. I'm so busy trying to normal up and be less in tune with my baggage that I get in my own way. Harry's feeling some pain himself. Gets all businesslike and surly—that's his tell.

So after I leave Harrison Ave with the news on Wilkie Morley, Harry and I get over to the guy's North End address. Naturally, Harry had reported our Dorchester Five coincidence—the D'Amante and Petrianni murders—to the Super last night, but we should have done so before our road trip south. Fact is, we didn't want to be told not to head to Rhode Island. Now with Morley murdered, someone's going to have to take some heat, and it doesn't take a premmie for me to predict who.

Morley's final home is just another residential building living its normal weekday life—quiet but for some distant vacuuming and the occasional dog walker jangling through the lobby. We hit the intercom and—oh what fun—it's Dick Farnham. Asks Harry what we're doing there, like he's weighing whether to buzz us in.

"Covering your ass," I say. It's my tone that makes him hit the buzzer.

Upstairs I brush past Farnham and also sidestep Landis Pomerance, his partner and overall a decent cop. The crime scene is up some slatty stairs and I sense a need to see it—my premmie thing's bouncing off the walls of my skull, and this time I'm not resisting. The place is very much a pad, with a platform bed and halogens dangling from wires. Someone's burnt an ugly hole in the velour coverlet and the sheet below—still smells like melted plastic fibers. There's another odor, kind of chalky, that's about to become lost evidence. I pull it into my lungs as if to save it. Sitting open at the foot of the bed is a carved chest covered in Far East designs—elephants, owls, snakes, maybe dragons, all chipped into the wood. Pile of once-folded linens sags next to the thing, looking freshly dumped. Someone has half-pulled some duct tape from where it must have been used to seal the chest's rim, all the way round. Now it dangles from the gaping mouth of the thing. Body's gone, of course. One of the lab guys, a lanky Hispanic kid with his hair shaved in a pattern, I half-recognize. He's working with powder and a brush over by one of the built-in nightstands. Got his headgear on, including monocle. He blinks at me like a curious cyclops, then gets back to work.

"Who found it?" I ask, glancing into the chest. Cedar inside, very solid. Looks like some fluid's pooled at the bottom.

"Wife came over this morning when some staffer called to say he hadn't shown for work. Didn't notice the tape at first. She actually sat there, wondering about the bedding. Took the Super some time to convince her that Morley'd already been dead some hours and that he hadn't suffocated while she sat on top of him."

I glance down into the living area. Harry's talking with Landis, behind the hand like a couple of sideline coaches. Techies are brush-working the sliders and some surfaces in the living area. Jack Finlayson, Boston's Police Superintendent for about a year now—Super Jack, just between you and me and H.P.—is looking solicitous, even from above, as he hovers down a ways behind a big-shouldered woman. She's dressed in a grey sheath with a stylish sheen to it and a matching short-sleeved jacket. Hair brown-red and semi-relaxed, coifed just the right amount. Expensive all around. "That is what I said, Jack," she's saying, "and therefore it is what I meant." Expensive and coiled, ready to lash out.

"Any idea when he was killed?" Lab kid's name comes to me a beat late. "Sterns?"

He takes a second to catch on that I'm talking to him, then shoots me a glance and snorts as he goes back to his task. "Foster," he says. "Wasn't in full rigor when they lifted him out but he was heading that way. They had a hard time."

"Big guy," I muse. "Must have taken a lot of doing to fold him into that thing."

Foster pauses, looking at his work. He sighs. "Wife touched a lot of stuff."

"So, Pop. Anything we can help you with?" Dick Farnham has trailed me up there. Guy grates on me. It's a competitive profession, sure, but so's car sales, and it always strikes me that Dickie should have set his star on that one. Right now he's jumpy that we're homing in on his action—wants to be the one standing behind Finlayson at the press conf. Used to make dyke jokes all the time, trying to persuade me he was cool. If any one of them had been funny, honest to God I'd have laughed.

I walk down the stairs with him, trying to sound like I can stand him. "Someone suffocates a man in his hope chest? I mean, what?"

"Crazy," Farnham answers, pretending to think we're just shooting the bull.

"Let me guess—he was naked?"

"Not quite," Farnham confides.

I get his hint just before we emerge into the condo's entryway. "Condom?"

He hesitates, then nods. "Should yield a sample."

"Yeah, except the lady doesn't care about our having her DNA or she wouldn't have left it on him. The fact that she used sex to get at him doesn't mean she's dumb."

We emerge from the stairwell. I'm unhappy to see that

Finlayson and Morley's wife have made their way toward the door. And, apparently, overheard my last remark.

"And just where does that get us?" Morley's wife challenges me. "Do tell."

Super Jack tries to throw an introduction between us, but she's not having it. She's also not repeating herself. She stares me down, her lower lip trembling in anger.

I keep it simple. "Appears there was a woman involved," I say. "I'm sorry."

"Excuse me, are you saying you're sorry for me?" She steps across the space between us and slaps me one across the face. Woman's got a healthy wallop, too. Lets it go like a nun from the old days. "You think you going to hide the nasty facts from me, like wifey doesn't know what her husband got himself up to? I can spot someone trying to hide something across a busy courthouse, lady. Don't you ever soft pedal anything to me. You got it?"

Jack goes to intervene but I shake my head once, sharp. Let her get it out of her system.

"I got two girls to tell that their daddy got murdered last night. What do you think of that, detective, huh? I got a public out there that loved this man and counted on him to make a future for them—it's me who has to face their disappointment now. You think I need handling? That what you think?" She includes the room with a glance. Well, she certainly has everyone's attention.

I clear my throat, give her what she wants. "Evidence indicates he'd been copulating shortly before it happened."

"You damned right it indicates that," she says. "So what do you think, detective? From the gut. Was the lady just some diversion, or did she do the deed?"

Jack's signaling from behind her, but I keep my eyes on her eyes. I swallow. "From the gut? She did it."

She nods firmly. "You betcha," she says. Then she steps back, still full of energy, her hands on her hips. She sways back and forth, kind of jauntily, as she assesses me. "So let me catch you up. Lady calls herself Julie Moreau, puts herself across as a freelancer.

Jack's got her so-called résumé, but it's bogus. So you want to know what's puzzling me next?"

I keep it simple. "Yes, I do," I say.

"How is some woman going to shove a man like my husband down into that chest, huh? Man weighed two-sixty. And don't tell me something stupid like she could have rolled him off the bed, because that chest lid would be in the way and there weren't any signs of that thing being moved. That's carpet up there, right? So what do you think now, lady cop, huh?" She breathes down a bit, at least it seems so from how her nostrils go from flaming to hot air.

I look across at her, thinking about Donna's mystery hit man. Is there muscle behind some black widow's Dorchester Five spree? Time to keep it simple, though. "I could have got him in that chest if I'd decided to."

She nods angrily, glancing around at the men as she shifts to her other hip. "I could have, too, my friends. If I had a mind to, I could have lifted some damned fool, too."

She moves in a circle, pointing the spiked fingernail at each one of us. "So now that we're all finally talking, let's talk about something else. Terence D'Amante got murdered two months ago. Man's a convicted felon and a known gang member with countless personal enemies, but the media is all over dredging up the Dorchester Five, trying to flog that old nag one more time. And does it occur to any of you fine protectors of the peace that maybe some hater out there might try getting at the other African-American defendant from back then?"

She's aiming it at me, but Jack answers from behind her. "I spoke to the councilman's people just last night about that. They assured me they'd spoken with Wilkie. He promised to talk soon, but his message was that he saw no indication, Claire, that the D'Amante killing had any connection with the old incident. You just said it yourself—D'Amante was a man with a lot of violence in his past."

I notice that Jack says nothing about Rocco, although he must have in his call to Morley. Nor did he make clear that last night's call was the first conversation about a potential threat to Morley. Claire Morley is definitely in a "shoot the messenger" mood.

"Well, now you got your indication," she says, not bothering to turn to Jack. "The two black men involved in the Dorchester Five incident are dead. A woman's involved. Calls herself Julie Moreau and poses as a freelancer who writes fluff about living in France—sounds mighty white to me, but what do I know?" She pauses to nod firmly as she wipes a fleck of spittle from her lip, then aims her closer around the room. "So now that we've settled all that, let's find the bitch. And Jack?" She points at me. "That one. She's the detective on my husband's case. Got it?"

In the elevator, Harry goes to talk and I raise a palm before he can say it. "She was right," I say. "But we're even slower than she thinks. Why the hell didn't we tip Jack about Petrianni first thing yesterday, Harry? Morley wouldn't have been tough for Jack to get to."

Harry shrugs. "What was there to tell?"

"Could have saved his life," I say stubbornly.

Harry's equally stubborn, and also has logic going for him. "It's only Morley's death that gives us a pattern. Until this morning, two wildly differing killings in two states meant nothing but two more guys who moved in dangerous circles—very separate dangerous circles—got themselves murdered. Claire Morley's dealing with her own shock in the way she knows how. Give us a break."

"Look, Harry, we are not your 'just the facts' kind of detectives," I argue.

"Occasionally, however, they get in the way." I go to respond, but Harry plows ahead. "Especially when they're missing."

I don't like the idea of letting us off the hook, but then neither does Harry. He's just doing it because I took the brunt of it upstairs. "So what do we do?"

"I laid the pattern on Pomerance, complete with the lady angle."

"Reminds me. We got a guy angle now, too. Creepy vibe. Drives an older Mercedes."

"Umm?"

"Donnalinda gave me a jingle. Funny thing is, I think we better heed."

"Duly heeding. We will update Pomerance. He'll consult with Big Jack and my guess is someone will be making some phone calls very soon to Dorchester defendants number four and five. Incidentally, as thanks for all our work, Landis made it crystal clear that Morley's death makes the whole serial threat part of his case, and not our thing. Took pains to point out that Claire Morley, strong-willed as she may be, isn't running the BPD."

I pause before ducking into Harry's car. "Meaning?"

He slaps his door closed and hits the ignition. "Meaning that we are to share what we know in detail as soon as we can all get together, and we're not take it upon ourselves to go calling on the two remaining defendants. Makes sense, of course."

"Making sense sucks," I say childishly.

Harry shrugs as he eases the car round the garage ramps. "Hey, it's the system. Got something else to do right now, anyway."

"That so?"

He nods and gives me his sideways smirk. "We're dropping in on Jake Culligan." He rounds the wheel, one-handed, pulling us smoothly into the flow on Atlantic Ave.

"We are, are we?"

"Sure," Harry says. "Officially, he ain't part of anyone's turf. But who better to have a grudge against the gang of five?"

And here, Zoey, you see the difference between me and Harry. I'm the cop who blunders in, all psychic nerve endings and far-flung connections, and winds up on the collecting end of an angry citizen's fist. Harry's the classic image of the muscle-head flatfoot, but, end of the day, the man's got finesse.

FIFTEEN

The Culligan house is clad in faded green siding with white metal shutters and a matching storm door, all streaked with soot. Wheelchair ramp runs round the side and into the driveway, where there's a white Crown Vic nosed up against its base. Fender dents make it clear that it took the driver some getting used to the fact that the car and the ramp need to share the parking space. Harry noses his own car half onto the sidewalk, following the example of others up and down the street. A container truck roars by, explaining the custom.

I hit the buzzer. After a while, a lady with what looks like a permanent sneer opens up. Later forties, arms crossed, jaw set—probably used to be a looker, but life's left her decidedly unimpressed, and it shows. Blonde frosted hair with a synthetic sheen to it, coifed in a kind of tiered mound, velour top with a plunging neckline, pink stretch pants, fuzzy mules—the kind with clear plastic heels. No cigarette to talk around but my guess is we caught her between.

"Sorry, sweets," she says to me, "I'm on a call." Both Harry and I flash our badges before she can swing the door shut in our faces.

I identify us as her mouth sinks into the surrounding flesh and her eyes go kind of hooded. "So now I gotta talk to detectives too?" she says. She walks away, leaving the door open, presumably an invitation for us to follow. We watch as she shoves her way through a swinging door muttering a couple of choice words that she's happy for us to overhear. I glance at Harry as we follow her through to her kitchen.

"I'm assuming you're Mrs. Culligan?" I say. "Jake's mother?"

"Wow-wee, got it in one. How do you people do that?" She settles at the table, her phone call ruse forgotten. We can hear some tense dialogue from the next room.

"They got soaps on before noon now?" I ask, casting about for how to break the ice.

"It's SoapNet," she says, like everyone knows. She holds a mug between her hands, not offering us a seat. Looks like a World's Best Mom mug. It's the little ironies, huh, Zoey? She lifts the mug and has herself a sip. I don't smell coffee, but the rich, fizzy scent of rum hits me as she lights herself a Parliament. Must hit Harry too.

"Little early for the sauce, huh?" he says. H.P. knows who not to make nice with.

She lets her lighter clatter to the table. "Got my reasons."

"Maybe," I concede. "How's it been for you?"

"Not easy," she says, picking a piece of tobacco off her tongue with a fingernail. She likes me a little better for asking. "But it wasn't ever gonna be easy, was it? Not with those two. Not after Wayne left us. One day here, next day gone, like that." She makes a motion vaguely reminiscent of a leaf in the wind.

"Husband been gone how long now?" I ask.

She squints, thinking, then half shrugs. "Jakey was just a little brat at the time. God, he made it hard on me. Not Jakey—I'm talking about Wayne. Jakey wasn't ever trouble till he started getting ideas from his brother."

"Where's Jakey's brother now, Mrs. Culligan?" I ask, encouraged.

"Pruddie," she says to me. She shoots Harry a look to signal that he shouldn't presume that he's in on the first name invitation. "Dylan's out in Concord again. Breaking and entering, intent to burgle. Facing a max of five. You want to know what? I don't care if they toss the key. Kid's in for one mistake, I'm all full of a mother's rage." She taps her chest to signify where these emotions lodge, then takes a moment to adjust her breasts in her bra. "Kid goes in a second term, I'm finished wringing my hands and talking about lessons learned and that nonsense. Guy's determined to be a felon, so be it."

"Hard for you, though," I say.

She shakes her head stubbornly. "Not anymore it isn't. I'm through with that one."

Harry decides to get to the point. "Anything going on with Jake, Mrs. Culligan?"

She sighs angrily. "Look, what's it to you? Like that snot they sent over from the law firm said, that stuff's between me and them, and there's not one reason for you or anyone else to be involved. They want to contact me, they can go ahead. I got a phone, don't I?"

"Sure, we hear you," I say, no idea what she's talking about. "Where is Jake, anyway?"

She breathes down. "I put him next to his father, down in Calvary. That's done and, frankly, it's all I got the energy for right now. The hell with the rest of it, got me?"

Harry and I exchange a glance. "Look, whatever it takes to cope," I say.

"Exactly how long's Jake been gone, now, Mrs. C?" Harry asks.

She looks down into her mug. When she raises her eyes I see the same hooded expression she'd used on me at her front door. "Month or so. I don't know—it's all a blur."

"But you must know," I say without thinking. "I thought Jake lived here."

She moves in her seat. Out in the living room, a shrill argument gives way to an ad—some loudmouth trying to fast-talk viewers into phone-ordering the latest piece of junk—and guess what, you get "much, much more" if you dial up in the next five minutes. "Jakey lived here, sure," she says. "But that don't mean I go running upstairs all of the time. I got a back thing, a disc. So when the man comes by from the lawyers, I'm as surprised as anyone the kid turns up dead. Guy said it looked like he'd been dead a couple of days. I'd been coping with the arraignment and all the crap Dylan got himself in, and Jakey was always okay. He—" She pauses for a breath. "He was always okay up there."

I go to say something sympathetic, but she cuts me off. "You know they took Dylan straight into custody? No trial, nothing." She eyes us resentfully. "Thought this was supposed to be a democracy or something." She lets it die out, heaves a sigh, shrugs. I see her slide a glance toward the sound of the TV, but I have a feeling it's something else out there she's after.

Harry sees, too. "Mind if we go upstairs to Jakey's room? Need to take a look around. Death scene—you know how it is."

She makes a feint at rising, but sinks back to her seat readily when Harry tells her we'll find our way. "Suit yourselves," she says, cupping her hands round her mug.

Upstairs the place is far less of a mess than downstairs, probably attributable to Pruddie's bad back preventing her from getting up there much. They'd had a stair rider installed, but the piles of junk that block its track make clear that Jakey hadn't been going downstairs much near the end, either. As another part of the conversion, they'd opened up doorways between the various rooms, removed all doorsills, and covered the floors in a smooth grey linoleum, so that the bathroom connects to a jacuzzi room—clearly a former bedroom—and from there you can cut through to what must have been Jakey's bedroom, all without a bump or a hitch. Handy for a wheelchair, a couple of which are lined up, folded, in the hallway. I peek through a door to the outside world, where a switchback ramp ends at the chain link gate to the sidewalk. Nice to know the guy had some access to sunshine. Bedroom's got a hospital bed, built-ins for various monitoring devises, and a largish flat screen angled from the ceiling. Another former bedroom is set up with a shiny silver weight machine that would allow a guy in a chair to do various upper body exercises. There's also what looks like a massage machine in here. The last room's a mini-kitchen with printed medication schedule taped to the refrigerator door.

Got red checkmarks penciled down the days. The checkmarks end about three months ago.

I open one of the few hallway doors that remain and find the bare stairs to the attic. I'm drawn to see where they circle round to, and start getting my premmie tingle as I hit the landing. Not happy about this, but I follow my instincts. It's hot up here, and the ceiling's at a slant, but, in the way of old row houses, it's useable space. Ancient bathroom's got a rust-streaked tub tucked under an eave. The largest amount of space, behind a door, is attic storage. That leaves room for one smallish bedroom with a single bed, rumpled like someone expected to return. There's a bureau, empty except for the contact paper, and a through-the-wall air conditioner above it. I open the closet and pull the swinging cord to get the bulb, and suddenly I'm confronted by an insanely vivid vishie—I see this wriggling creature all tied up with duct tape. At first I think it's an animal being tortured, but then I realize it's a naked man. He struggles to look over his shoulder at me—not really, of course, because I'm not wherever he is—and seems to be keeping his knees folded up in an effort to shield his genitals, but from what I have no idea. There's blood on his face—it's not pretty to see his bulging eyes rolling around, surrounded by all that wet, red stuff. He bellows something incoherent through the tape that's stuffed in his mouth, his cheeks puffing from the effort. He screams again as I shut the door. It fades slowly.

I stand for a long moment, hand on the crystal knob, waiting for my senses to return. When I can hear Harry's tread on the stairs, I reach in with one arm and pull the light cord without looking again, although I know that the man won't be there anymore.

Harry finds me. "Seen the family ghost?"

I force a laugh. "If it was Jake Culligan, I'd have asked him his date of death."

"So you're thinking what I'm thinking." Harry keeps his voice low. Not that we're worried that Pruddie Culligan's going to light-foot it up there to eavesdrop.

"Loving mother is hoping there's a way to slip a death through the cracks and keep the care deposits coming?"

"One too many social security scam stories gave her some big ideas," Harry agrees. "Although you'd think she'd catch the fact that they all end badly. Her luck, actually, someone coming over to check on the situation when the body's still relatively fresh. Hopefully that will keep her from being exposed in a couple of years as the mother from hell. Question one is why this guy from the law firm—which I assume handles the care arrangement—hasn't stopped the money tap. Question two: you'd think there'd have been a nurse who'd tie off the benefits once he's deceased."

"Maybe there's a bunch of paperwork that has to happen before the gravy train stops. Might even need a magistrate to sign off on it." I gesture around. "We'd have to know what type of arrangement it was. The set-up downstairs looks like someone put some real thought and funding into Jakey's care—that suite was not what I'd call government-funded. And as for nurse, could be they were between. I hear it's hard to keep them."

We tramp down, and Harry gestures me back into the room with the hospital bed. "Thought you'd want to see these. I know you're into—what do we call it?—genre films?"

There's an old video cover on the meal tray. On the front, a monster about to lock lips with a babe. "Man alive, this is literally one of my fave flicks of all time. No disc, though. I bet it's in." I pick up a grimy remote and power up the entertainment unit. Sure enough, the movie starts to play from where it was abandoned. I see a sleek, dark-haired woman dressed in an otherworldly get-up, including a cap with antennae, dancing in a cavernous hall. The orchestra is made up of mechanical men. An old guy in gloves and a mask sweeps in to join the girl for a waltz. His mincing, eerie voice begins to narrate.

Harry snorts. "Vincent Price did some real schlock."

"Don't I know it," I say. "This, however, is what we call a schlock classic. That's the abominable Dr. Phibes you're watching, dancing with his lovely accomplice Vulnavia."

"No message in that name," Harry remarks.

"You'd like her. All guys do. She's hot and mute." I find myself drawn to the wall of videos. "Nine have killed and nine must die," I murmur, more to myself than to Harry.

"Pop?"

I crouch in front of the shelves, looking at titles. "Dr. Phibes's pledge to his dead wife. Always loved a countdown slasher. Mostly because my mother thought it inappropriate for a girl. Jesus, this is like my brother Nikos's entire collection. *The Screaming Skull, Peeping Tom, Dead and Buried*—that's with a pre-Freddy Robert Englund—*Dark City, Bay of Blood, Dawn of the Dead*—can you believe I know every frame of these sick pieces of misogynist propaganda?"

"All because Mom said 'no?'"

"You'd have thought she would have learned to play me. Down here are the oldies. *I Walked With A Zombie*—I love a good nurse-versus-jungle-voodoo tale, don't you?"

"I mean, doesn't everyone?" Harry says.

"And here we have *Carnival of Souls, Vampyre*—oh, wow, remastered! *Fury, M*—early Peter Lorre, can you beat that? These down here are original European horrors from the '30s. Couple of additional French entries: *Un Chien Andalou*—God, the eyeball scene alone—and, hey, look, an old favorite, *The Bride Wore Black*. That's early Truffaut and a serial kill flick but in my view not a horror—ah, but I see *Leave Her to Heaven* and *Laura*, so evidently we're shading into a classic noir shelf here. I love it. Oh, and lookie here—*Rashomon*—that Kurosawa with four radically differing viewpoints on a horrific rape-murder. Definitely not schlock. You must know it—no? And, yep, here's the Vincent Price collection—*The Fly, Theatre of Blood*—you know that Diana Rigg was in that one? Phew! Kid had some upscale taste in his slasher entertainment, anyway."

"Pop?" I look over and Harry is watching me funny. "Kid was brain-damaged."

I stand up, feeling myself color. "Well, he'd have to be to watch some of this crap."

Harry laughs. "I swear I've never seen you quite so—I don't know—animated."

"Blast from the past, is all." I try not to sound defensive. "Look, my mother wanted a girlie-girl. Actually used to urge me to tattle. You believe it?"

"Well, you got her back."

"Damned straight. Watched every sick blood-fest I could lay my hands on."

"Oh, you got her back better than that, Pop."

I give him my dry look. H.P. can be a hole like the best of them.

Mostly to change the subject, I give the remote a random thumb squeeze. A home video flickers into view in place of Vincent Price. We watch a dark-haired kid, young, skinny, shirtless. Doing his silly best lip-synch dance to an oldie.

"Ah, Numa, Numa," Harry remarks. "The original YouTube anthem."

"Kid was truly cute," I remark. "Dimples for days."

"Looks like a wise guy in the making to me," Harry says. He reaches over and pops the pause. "Guess Dimples forgot to check what was in the background. That or he's advertising." Harry points. If the plastic bag of yellow-brown moss sitting on a desk behind the frozen boy isn't clear enough, the one-hit bong propping it up is. "How much he got there, you think? That a pound?"

"Half-gallon bag," I concede. "Think he's doing his Numa number here in the house?"

"Could be, if it's pre-rehab. Now they got the double-glazed storms."

I hunt about further, find a couple of additional lip-synch vids the kid made of himself. Either no one bothered to load up a lot of personal pictures or someone scoured them. Can't figure why—it's the type of stuff you suddenly cherish when your kid dies.

Pruddie Culligan's parked at the kitchen table, biting off smoke rings, reading what looks like an old library book through drug store half-specs. She marks her place with her finger and tips the specs off her nose so they fall against her chest as she slides an eye over at Harry.

"You know, you look just like that cop on TV. Anyone ever tell you? No? The good looking fellah they're always putting in the shower. The hell's his name again?" She taps a fingernail. "It'll come to me."

"Mrs. Culligan, just curious, were there any women in Jake's life?" I ask.

She looks at Harry like I'm crazy. "You're not quite getting it, hon. Jakey was burned—half his face was, like, a mess. And he didn't have hardly any brain function. He'd bang a cup and yell to get attention, you know, like a baby. Sure, before it happened all the neighborhood girls were stickin' their hands down his pants, but not after."

"What about a nurse? He must have had one of those?"

She shrugs. "So?"

"What happened to her?"

"You notice anyone in need of nursing while you were up there just now?"

"What home health aide service did you use? We might need to talk to them."

She pauses. "There wasn't, like, a service company, per se."

I'm surprised, mostly at the sudden display of Latin. Somehow I've gotten her back up. "You're kidding."

"I did a lot of the caregiving myself. What, you think it was such a hard gig?"

"No, except for the fact that your charge was a grown man with severe brain injury and burns over half his body, right?"

"And you with your back problem," Harry throws in.

She brushes it off. "Have it your way. I'm a saint and a nun, rolled into one."

Harry lets it go. "Hey, you know how you mentioned someone coming over from some law firm and giving you the bad news about Jakey? Some snot, I think you said?" He's doing his head-scratching thing, like he's puzzled and needs help.

She frowns, smoking, looking from one to the other of us. Harry's hard to resist when he plays dumb. "Sure," she finally admits. "What about it?"

"You get the guy's name?"

"Didn't catch it. Frankly, I didn't like his attitude. Actually put on a pair of plastic gloves when he went to climb the stairs. Imagine. Like, excuse me, buddy, but we all wipe with the same motion."

"And he's the one who informed you that Jake was dead?"

"I said that, didn't I? Could be I don't need to go over it a thousand times."

"Okay, I hear you," Harry soothes her. "So, if you didn't catch his name, how about the law firm he's at? I mean, we can find out by talking to the coroner, of course, but it would save us some steps if you knew. Get us off of this and onto something we should be doing, right?"

She nods to herself, smoking, apparently trying to think something through. Finally she expels smoke. "Not sure I got the name of the firm either," she admits. "See, my lawyer was on his own, back during the trial, and only joined up with this firm after. I never had dealings with anyone but him directly. I mean, until this other guy showed up."

I've about had it with the cat and mouse. "Okay, then, the coroner it is. Thanks for your time," I say, making to head out. Harry starts making noises about how to contact us if anything comes back to her.

"My lawyer's name I know, of course," she says. We stop.

"That would help," Harry says.

"Becker. Elliot Becker." She picks up her cigarette and taps it, then nods thoughtfully. "Or the late Elliot Becker, I suppose I ought to say, as of last week."

Harry and I sit in his car for a minute, just running all of it around in our minds. Finally he starts the car. "So I guess it's pretty much like Claire Morley said," he mutters.

"Oh, yeah," I finish for him. "We're the original Keystone Cops. Although at least you sensed a connection between Becker and the Five, which is what dragged us down to take a whiff of Rocco's final hurl and then over to get chewed out by Neva of the miraculously blond son. I, on the other hand, am just a bunch of sparked out synapses. I need a serious course in dot connecting."

"Other hand, you're the one who went over to Harrison Ave to view the tape. We've been dancing around the obvious all week without quite clenching it."

I snort a laugh. "And then to get clued in by Mother of the Year in there."

"Time for another talk with Big Jack."

"Yeah," I say, the tiniest bit trepidatious. "It's Super Jack, by the way."

He starts the car. "Around my house it's Big Jack. Around yours it's Super Jack."

"But he's not all that big, and he's the Super."

"True enough. But when he finishes chewing us out and hands this case to us, I'm seeing him as both big and super. So let's think next steps. I mean, after we pay visits to Dorchester defendants four and five."

"Law firm. We need to know the deal Becker cut for the Culligans."

"Plus we want anything that was fit to print on the Dorchester Five, from then until now. I'm thinking Malloy in front of a microfiche."

"I can picture that surprisingly well."

"Yeah, but the best part's yours, Pop."

"What?" He's doing the smirk. I actually laugh. "Holy shit—you mean I get to tell Dickie Farnham?"

He pulls out between container trucks. "Wow-wee, got it in one," he shouts above the roar.

SIXTEEN

I am Nightingale—

He becomes conscious of me first in the church nave. It is a late weekday Mass, and so I am among mostly single parishioners, who pace their way through the Mass with their evening plans in the forefront of their minds. He sits just off the altar, his violin resting across his raily thigh, facing us, making it easy for him to observe me. It does not surprise him that I have captured his attention, as he has discovered that it is not uncommon for him to focus on a particular parishioner during any given Mass. He does not think about why he picks his targets—random faces and postures draw his eye irresistibly. It is not an air of religiousness or desperation that brings his attention to these people. And it is not lust.

He sees that I am a tallish woman of indefinite age. Today I wear the long wool sweater-coat over a cream-toned shift, rather unclean. He notices my hair, black, chopped in a coarse horizontal just below my ears. He knows that I am wearing a wig today because he has noticed me during prior Masses, and sometimes I have had auburn, kinky hair that brushes my shoulders, and other times I have had thick brown hair that I wear in a braid pinned into a bun. He does not wonder why I choose to wear these various wigs. He does not wonder what my real hair may look like. He is familiar with the fact that I do not receive Communion, but he notices that I murmur the responses and participate in the rite of peace as if on autopilot. So I am, in fact, a Catholic, he conjectures. Or I was, at some point.

I observe him as well, although not with his own brand of placidity. Tonight, as always, he wears a thin suit of a washed-out blue color and no tie, although his poorly ironed shirt is buttoned to the collar. His black-framed glasses do not hide the aqua-toned brightness of his eyes. His lips are thin and colorless, but at the same time somehow feminine. He has allowed a bit of blond scruff to grow round his chin and also has allowed his sideburns to reach his jaw line, although it appears that he shaves the rest of his facial hair—or it may be that he shaves only weekly, and in between his beard just happens to grow in this spotty manner. His shoes are black and look to have been picked up at a thrift shop. When it is the time, he rises and plays the chorale *Dostojno Jest' No. 3*. His playing is competent and gentle, the effect unassuming. The deacon nods in thanks afterwards, but he does not notice. When he turns his back for a moment while reseating himself, the light reflects off the bald crown of his skull—otherwise he might be quite young, perhaps even in his twenties. Later he will play again while a small choir sings *Preterp'ivyj*. It is Slavonic and means "having suffered."

After the service, he stays in the church to collect his payment and discuss the next week's musical offerings with a motherly contralto who often attempts to draw him out. She makes her usual reference to some unmarried friend, much younger of course than she—naturally there would be no expectation that he follow up—women understand how men rely on visceral responses when making connections of this nature. He remains noncommittal as always, which prolongs the conversation more than if he had been more definite in declining her efforts. Still, he is not particularly surprised when, forty minutes later, he notices me in the subway station. I have stuffed the wig into my satchel and so he sees my hair for the first time, baby short and freshly dyed a platinum blonde with streaks of black here and there around my ears and the nape of my neck, but it does not throw him even for a moment, because it is my posture he recognizes, a curious manner I have of wavering ever so slightly from the heels to the balls of my feet when otherwise standing still, almost as if preparing myself for a leap off the edge of some imaginary precipice. He has seen me stand this way during service, and he notices it now as I stand near the edge of the platform, waiting for the same train as he. Because he is behind me, he allows himself to observe me quite minutely, the long sweater hanging with its wool belt undone, one end of it drooping nearly to the station floor. My hands, he notices, are rather long, the fingernails untouched. I clench and unclench the hand gripping the shoulder strap of my satchel. I appear to be listening to the still-vague thunder of the approaching train, although I do not turn my head to gauge its distance. It is chilly out. Night is falling fast. Some young people are insulting one another and giggling, well down the platform. "Cheer up, sad drunk guy!" a girl sings out gaily. "It'll all be over quick!"

He watches as I step forward, anticipating the train. I stand with my toes at the very edge, my feet pressed together. He moves in, not so near to me that I will feel crowded by him, but close enough for him to see my face. He leans out a little, sees the train approaching from some ways down the track, past my profile. My eyes are closed. He sees the sallowness of my cheeks, the greyish hollows around my eyes, the melancholy droop of my lips. My shoulders have ceased wavering, he notices. Without thinking, he walks over and takes me by the arm, his hand closing around my sweater sleeve, gently but firmly, just above my elbow. I open my eyes, but do not otherwise react to his touch. He tugs at me with-out speaking, moving me backwards and away from the edge, one step, then several more. I do not resist, although I could have easily broken free. The train rushes into the station and settles. A door opens, directly in front of us. I turn my head and blink at him, my face expressionless.

We go to a bar, a depraved old cesspool. Men are clustered around a pool table in the dark, smoking. The low ceiling is painted blood red. I am the only woman aside from an ancient drunk sitting by herself at the end of the bar, who is quite fat, with feet that waver in the air—she may in fact be a midget. He goes to the bar, where he orders a whiskey and asks if the man will make some hot tea. The bartender eyes me as I unwrap a pack of cigarettes at the table, my eyelashes against my cheeks, the violin case in the chair across from me. He says he will bring it over to us when the water boils.

"Simon Love," he says, seating himself. I nod but do not otherwise reply. When his teeth show I notice that they are almost translucent, like his eyes, in his otherwise jaundiced face.

I smoke. The tea arrives in a dented pot with a slice of desiccated lemon balanced on the rim. I drop the tea bag in. Simon nudges his whiskey in my direction. I sip, raising my eyes to meet his as I swallow. I nod and have another swallow before passing the glass over to him.

He nods at me encouragingly. "I remember you," he says, "from the trial."

I play with my cigarette, rolling the tip on the rim of the ashtray, watching the embers drop. "They said you became a priest," I say.

"People seem to like the idea," he apologizes.

"You went into seminary."

"I was a seminary student at the time, out on pastoral work. I left, though."

"When?"

He thinks, then shakes his head. "Didn't happen all at once. Pastoral work is part of the obligation, but I haven't been back for religious education since. The rector prefers to leave it open, in case I decide to return."

"But you will not return?"

"No."

"Lost your calling?"

"You need to be compelled," he says simply.

"I see." I watch my cigarette for a while. "So now what for you?"

176

He ignores the question, instead half-turning with his glass upraised. When he turns back, he says, "How is he? Do you know?"

I look up at him. "Yes I know."

He is not surprised. I blow across my tea while the bartender brings a second whiskey, and Simon digs in his pants for a couple of bills.

"He is dead," I tell him when we are alone again.

He pauses, studying the table. I *fourrage*. In his head he is saying: *We are dust. Our days are like those of grass…. The wind sweeps over him and he is gone, and his place knows him no more.* Aloud, he says, "When?"

"Three months."

"That is why we are together?"

"Yes."

He thinks about it. "Some of this?" he says, tilting his glass. I decline.

We sit in silence. I sip at the tea. In time, he finishes his whiskey. He wipes his mouth with the back of his hand.

"May I take you home?"

I gather my sweater around me as he retrieves his instrument.

He lives in a brick row tenement where the tenants do not complain about vermin and broken lights. The street is wide and would be busy, but is empty now, when the nearby transfer station is not receiving trucks. The grind of machinery from that direction must continue through the night. When we enter his building, the door to the apartment on the first floor cracks, and someone watches us go up. Simon lives on the third floor in one room overlooking the street, large enough for both the double bed and a table with some mismatched chairs, plus there is a kitchen in the back, where he has rigged up a hose and a curtain ring round the tub, for showering. The toilet is enclosed in a closet beyond this. The bed has an iron headboard and footboard, but no sheets on the mattress.

"I sleep between the blankets," he apologizes, noticing me looking at this.

"It is not of concern," I say.

He stows his violin in a small wooden armoire that is built into the corner—the room has no closets—and then he begins to undress, carefully hanging his suit and shirt on hangers that he takes from the back of the armoire door. In his underwear he looks healthier than when dressed. He is thin but not without some girth across the shoulders and some muscles running up and down his upper arms and thighs. He lifts out some old corduroy pants and pulls them on over his boxers, then strips off his t-shirt and shoulders his way into a denim shirt, which he does not button. I see the gold cross lying in his sparse blond chest hair, and glimpse a tattoo of Jesus on the inside of his arm.

"Do you want to shower?" he says. "Or to eat something? I have a robe you can wear." He takes it out and holds it to his nose, then drapes it across the footboard for me. It is a plaid flannel. "I have to practice. I'm sorry," he says.

Slowly, I rise from the bed. I take up the robe. "A shower, then," I say. I go through to the kitchen and shut the door, although it slowly swings open on its own behind me.

I shower for a long time. The water spurts from the hose end in a tired tread, first hot, then icy, then practically not at all. Afterwards I stand in the tub surrounded by the water-stained plastic curtain for a long while, listening to him playing. It is Vivaldi, he tells me later, a concerto that some consider a difficult work, meant for two strings with accompaniment and, according to Simon, beyond his capability. He has been commissioned to play it in a concert in Cambridge that is scheduled to occur in some days. To my ear it sounds like a piece of painful beauty, still playing in my mind as I lie back on the bed, so I nod mutely at his explanation.

When he finishes practicing, he stows his violin. He strips once again to his underwear, folding the pants into the bottom of the armoire and hanging the shirt. Then he turns to me where I lay against his pillows.

"One of those and the top blanket, I think," he says.

I do not follow him. I am reluctant to enter his head after

hearing him play. His despondency, I believe, saps me. He comes over and gently eases the pillow from behind my shoulders. Then he grips the blanket and smiles at me, raising his eyebrows. I lift my hips so he may pull it from beneath me.

He turns out the light. It is one a.m. Later I wake to hear him struggling in his sleep. I leave the bed and make my way across the floorboards on my knees to where he sleeps and lean over him to see his face. He looks agitated, troubled; he moves his lips as if preparing for a kiss. Perhaps he dreams that he is in church, now. I reach over and grip gently at the blanket where I know I will find his erection. I hold it firmly, stroking it very little. He finds peace, as I knew he would. Eventually his erection subsides and he sleeps on in silence.

The next day I retrieve some money and also some of my clothing from Tati's house. The rest of the money and my canister of laced ibuprofen I leave locked in my travel case. I leave some rent money on Tati's mail table.

Simon is out while I stow my few things in his room. I take his suit and shirt and walk along the industrial boulevard until I find a dry cleaner. Then I buy a fifth of whiskey, a thin steak, a carton of salt, and some colorless Brussels sprouts. When he comes in, I sear the steak in salt and allow the Brussels sprouts to roll in the same pan. He eats it. He plays the Vivaldi and another piece, this one a Bach chorale. I lie smoking on his bed, listening. When he reaches for the pillow I grip it. He looks into my eyes with his strange glittering irises, and I tell him that he sleeps on the bed. He looks away, then nods.

I wake. He is next to me, facing away, twitching and grunting like a dog. I *fourrage* and find him dreaming about being beaten. He cowers as men kick him brutally. It appears we are in a dungeon—some sort of dark subsurface, but there are stars, far above us, or candles. It may be a cathedral, where Simon is beaten. Some of the men appear to push to get to the front; the number is growing until they come in waves. The men are wearing robes, I notice, thick and hooded. Occasionally Simon shrieks like an animal that has not been taught pride and therefore knows no shame in fear. There is no other noise. Next the floor below him begins to burn—it is metal, he discovers, and now his face is seared against it. He must rip his face free, losing half the skin from it. He forces his hand from the floor, stripping the skin from his palm, then his arm—he is being flayed alive. The pain is beyond screaming over—he weeps feebly, almost mutely. The men in the forefront grip him now. The robes are gone and his attackers are recognizable. I see Wilkie, sweat coating his face. I see a young man with empty eyes, a blond skullcap of hair, and a tattooed neck peering menacingly into Simon's face. I see Terence D'Amante, screaming, his mouth distorted so that he almost appears to be laughing in a frenetic hysteria. Simon is deaf and baffled—he is like a woman accepting her fate, asserting a sort of negative power in willful acceptance. There is a girl, somewhere in the layered dream—black, pretty, naked with her legs spread wide. Somewhere also the difficult passage from the Vivaldi concerto repeats itself.

I have seen enough. I roll the sleeping Simon so that he faces me. Stealthily, I untangle the blanket from his two-fisted clutch. His face is smeared with warm saliva, like that of a child. I grip his sweating skull, clutch it, press his mouth and nose against my breasts until his breathing calms. Later, I lower his undershorts and open my robe, then ease myself against him. Gently, I reach around and push at his buttocks with my hands so as to get him inside me. I move against him, cradling his head against my neck. Soon, without warning, he finishes.

I slip into his head and *fourrage*. Like every man after sex, his mind is blissfully blank.

Très sincèrement,
Nightingale

SEVENTEEN

I am Nightingale—

He lies on his back, his eyes tracing the bloom of a ceiling leak over in the corner by where he has tacked up a picture of Leopold Auer. The mattress smells musty, or perhaps it is me, lying next to him. We are naked. A vague current of chilly air seeps through the room from the window next to him. He can feel it touching at the sweat that has pooled in the hollow of his chest. He hears the strike of a match, then smells the cigarette.

"Should we not try again?"

He feels the mattress depress as I roll to one side to tap ash onto the floor.

He considers, then shakes his head in the negative.

"It will make you play better," I say. "You owe it to the music. When is this concert?"

After awhile he swallows audibly. "Sunday."

"And it is important?"

He shakes his head at the ceiling. "No."

"Ah, you lie." I smoke and pass it to him. "It is your life. The acoustics alone! If you do not do your best, I will blame myself. Would you like that?"

"If I play poorly, the failure will be mine."

I gesture and let my fingers come to rest gently on the downy surface of his damp, chilly stomach, which spasms at my touch. "But I come here. I distract you. I remind you of some terrible moments from the past. You dream horrible stuff. Always *le péni-tence*, the torturing, of yourself. You are so miserable you have forgotten to be afraid of death, I think."

"I've never thought about suicide."

I tap a rib sharply to get his attention. "Do not bother lying to me. I *fourrage* in your mind, remember? I told you about this talent I have."

He considers this. "When do you read my mind? Now?"

"Anytime, whenever I want. But not now, no. You are screwed up in a big way, and I am afraid to go in there so much."

He sits up and throws his legs off the bed. "I need to play."

"It is all because of the kid in the VW, yes?" I say to his rounded back.

"He wasn't a kid. He was a young life. I destroyed that life."

"But you were not to blame."

"I was guilty. You didn't bring the guilt with you when you came here. So your presence has nothing to do with my problems playing, or…with any other problems."

"Wilkie said different."

"What?" He half turns his head. His profile is gaunt, his beard spikes out, dirty blond, from his jaw. I have been sculpting his stubble, and I make him look better.

"Wilkie said you were innocent. He said that. Only you, he said."

"You spoke to him?"

"I did."

"Wilkie Morley's dead. It was in the papers."

"Yes, well," I chuckle without humor. "I do not pretend to speak with the dead. It is only the minds of living men I *fourrage*, and only that from time to time. I spoke with Wilkie before his death. He told me you did not help to tip that car."

Simon considers this, then stands up and walks toward the kitchen. His rump is quite thin. It is yellow and pocked, with deep hollows on each side.

"An angel, he called you," I call after him. "That was the

word he used. You think about it, and maybe later we will try again, huh?"

He shuts the door. I hear the shower and watch him step over the rim of the tub as the door slowly swings open.

Later he is playing the Vivaldi while I prepare to go out. I am wearing my Jeanne Moreau wig, adjusting the heavy bangs so that they frame my eyes closely. I apply a mauve lipstick and adjust my pale shift on my shoulders. He plays like a master, fast and faster; it is sharp and insistent but he is right that there is no life—the instrument does not sigh and weep when he slows. It is because he is thinking all the time, a state that is not healthy for a man.

There is a knock on the door. A male voice, polite but insistent. The police would like to speak with him.

He looks at me, seeking instruction, his instrument under his jaw, his bow across the strings. His eyes are pale green-blue, almost transparent. I nod to him, then lower myself to the floor and slide under his bed. It is a clumsy spot to hide but there is no other. He walks to the door, flicking the blanket so that it hangs down further on that side as he goes by.

"Nice music. Sorry to interrupt," the cop says. When he speaks, his sentences begin from deep within his chest. I picture a mountain, so imposing that he can afford to be pleasant wherever he goes. "Hope we didn't startle you. Buzzer's broken and so's the latch. Might want to get on your landlord about it. Seems like this could be an unpleasant neighborhood at night."

The male cop has a woman cop with him, introduces her as his partner. She wears short lace-up boots with low heels and a pair of wool pants, cuffed, dusty green with a herringbone stripe. Walks springy on her heel like an athlete. Her voice is fluid and she accommodates the male cop, but she is not aware of this. Likes to see herself as hard and in charge. A man of the clay and a woman of the water. This is what their voices say to me.

"Leopold Auer," the female cop says, noticing the poster. "You know he was related to Mischa Auer, the character actor? Played the first victim in René Clair's *And Then There Were None*. Rolled out the movie's theme on the piano just before throwing back a glass of cyanide. Had these long musician fingers, like yours." They continue to toss topics round to warm Simon up. They get to the point when they ask whether he has picked up on the recent deaths: Terence D'Amante, Jake Culligan, Elliot Becker, Rocco Petrianni, Wilkie Morley.

I hear him laying his violin in its case. "Rocco Petrianni?" he says. "I didn't know."

"He'd relocated. Wasn't local news."

There is a short silence while Simon prays in his head for Rocco's soul.

"You heard about the others, though," says the male cop, not disrespectfully.

Simon mumbles about wishing Jake Culligan's death was a peaceful one. I come to realize, lying there within inches of these cops who would do anything to stop me, that the guy trying to protect me cannot lie. Apparently he also knows this about himself, and so he tries instead to prevaricate. Unfortunately, at this he sucks massively as well.

"We don't want to make anyone paranoid, Mr. Love," says the female, "but as you know from the papers, at least a couple of these deaths were not peaceful at all. We thought it was fair to check in with the remaining people associated with the case."

Simon says that he is grateful.

"Look, we'll be frank," the male cop throws in. "The police don't have the capacity to provide round-the-clock protection. Any way you might be able to get yourself out of town for the next little while? Maybe your church could help you arrange to play out for a change?"

He says he has obligations. They seem disappointed that they did not scare him well enough. Maybe his surroundings gave them hope that he was a drifter at heart. Maybe he struck them as cowardly. Reluctantly, they go somewhere new with the conversation.

"Mr. Love, there's some indication that a woman's been involved in at least a couple of these deaths," the female says.

"Descriptions have been vague, so the best we got is that she's white and in her mid-thirties, maybe with an accent. She might wear a wig, but her real hair is short and at one point it was dyed blonde. Might call herself Julie Moreau."

"You seem to be nodding to yourself, Mr. Love," the male cop cuts in. "I don't suppose you've seen a woman that meets this description lately? Maybe in a church where you play or here in your neighborhood?"

"I was just thinking." Simon sounds nervous. "About whether I've seen her."

"And?" Male cop's shoes rock like he's shifting up onto the balls of his feet.

"Yes," Simon says in a tight voice. "I remember her from the trial. Short blonde hair, and she…she'd be in her mid-thirties now. I didn't know she was French back then."

"How do you suppose you remember her?" the woman cop throws in. "I mean, it must have been a hectic time for you, crowded courtrooms, all that public attention. How does one woman stand out?"

He pauses. "She was someone to look at. She seemed not to judge."

"And you haven't seen her lately. You're sure of that?"

Simon gives them some mute indication.

"I ask because you said that you didn't know she was French back then. Almost as if you'd learned that fact about her since the trial."

There's a pause. "You didn't say she was French?" he tries.

"No. We said that a woman who may have been associated with some of the recent murders may speak with an accent."

"Oh. Her name, though."

"Moreau? Sound French to you?" Male cop is playing it dumb.

"Yeah," Simon says. He sounds testy that they toy with him. But this is what they want, of course, the cops with their psychology.

"Point is you haven't seen her," says the female cop. "Right?"

Simon mutters something.

We wait, none of us moving, to see what will come next. The two cops must know that a person who cannot lie often cannot tolerate a long silence while his lie hangs in the air. I take a risk and *suggère* a strand of thought at Simon. Just a gossamer prod to stay quiet, not get duped by the double-edged psychology. I do not know if I am able to *suggère* him, as I have been out of his head for days now. This was not the time to test.

The female cop, who is standing by the window, suddenly turns. "What did you say?" she asks Simon. Her tone is not hostile—more startled.

"I said I don't know," Simon tries.

"Not that," she interrupts. "Someone said…it was something like, *taise-toi*…" She pronounces it roundly, as if she has not spoken much French.

"Pop?" says the male cop. "You okay? Could have come from outside."

She walks directly at me, over to the bed, but she does not make it, quite. She misses her step, in spite of her sturdy shoes, and rolls onto the outside of her foot. She murmurs, "Holy shit, Harry," sounding very gruff and needy, and then she collapses to the floor. You ever watch someone faint, my friend? It is not at all like they do it in the horror classics, gracefully into the hunchback's arms so he can carry her off, drooling, to his master's lair. In reality, every part of the person falls at once, straight down—it is quite a fright, how the gravity hurtles us earthward when we do not resist. The skull is heavy and starts highest up, so it lands with the violence. This female cop is lucky. She sits straight down on her bottom, taking the bulk of the fall in the spine, then from there she continues onto her back, her arms in their stylish jacket cascading about her, her bare head set to smack the boards quite hard.

Simon is closer than the male cop. He sprawls forward and somehow slices his hand between the female cop's skull and the naked floor. He is the Good Samaritan, Simon, but perhaps he moves so quick also out of the fear that this cop will see me, as indeed she lands beside the bed, side by side with me, with perhaps four feet between us. Simon tries to thrust himself so as to block her view of me. He does not succeed, however, and as his shoulder rams the shuddering bed frame and the male cop's feet pound from across the room, the female cop's head lolls about, quite loosely, and for one long and drawn-out moment she and I look directly at each other.

I see much in that sliver of time—she has a strong face, her skin porous, her nose somewhat broad, her lips elegantly shaped, nude of lipstick. She is delicate but decidedly masculine—hair cropped, chin cleft, brow furrowed. There is a humor, however, perhaps even a child's mischief in the lines around the lips. I notice this even as her mouth sags and falls open to allow a heavy foam to pool against Simon's callused hand. Mostly, however, I look across the floorboards and into the eyes, in that split second of time that we lie close to one another with no obstruction between. They are large eyes, colored the darkest brown, liquid and clear, and bright even in sightlessness. These are eyes that yearn, and stubbornly deny whatever pain she has suffered. She wants something, this cop, or maybe there is no particular thing but it is just that she will live out her life grasping, always, for whatever is beyond. I think it is normalcy that she is after. Stability. Why, when she has so much more?

She cannot see me, of course, as we stare at one another, but on some level she discerns my presence; and indeed she snaps out of her faint only moments into it. She blinks and her tongue protrudes in a spasm just as Simon insinuates his narrow torso between us and as the male cop asserts his ownership of her, lifting her bodily from beyond, his powerful legs spread wide, and lying her on the unmade bed directly above me. The springs depress toward my face, and as I hear her cough and struggle to sit up I close my eyes and will my mind to go blank.

As if from some distance I hear them arguing, him for her to stay put, her for her right to rise, and in the mist of my willed semi-consciousness I realize through their blurred words to one another that they are in love, these cops. They laugh uncomfortably, she as if scoffing at what has occurred, he as if to help her rise above it. Both of them are frightened, for their own reasons. Both are the whistlers in the dark.

"Someone step on your grave, Pop?" he quips.

"More like stuck a finger in my brain socket," she says back, not quite lightly.

"Head hurt?"

"Wasn't like that. I swear I heard something for a second."

Male cop tries to solve it with common sense. "You got a radio playing in there, buddy?"

"I don't own one," Simon offers. I can tell from his voice that he is more scared, even, then the two of them. He has me to protect, you see.

Male cop says, "Maybe someone in another apartment turned on their TV, then cut the volume. You never know."

"Spanish station," says Simon. "I remember now." Fortunately they ignore him.

Female cop gets her way. She rises, plants her feet on the floor, her heels inches from my nose. She stands there, right up against the bed, leaning with her thighs against the mattress, for a moment. Finally she murmurs, "Get off, would you? Honest, I'm fine."

Male cop steps back and they stay put, all three of them, as she tests her legs. I think she is also trying to figure out what she heard, and perhaps also what she saw. The silence stretches, and then finally the female cop breaks it. I can tell from her voice that she is dissatisfied. She knows she was close, but she does not want to admit how she knows this, maybe even to herself. We are kindred—a cruel irony, as neither of us hunts for the soul mate. But there is the hand of fate for you. I do not know, yet, whether it bodes in my favor or against, but I cannot believe that it is random, the fact that this cop with psychic ability has crossed my path.

They give Simon their contact information and finally leave. Simon closes the door, then crosses the room to his violin. He strikes several harsh introductory chords, pauses to tune, and then resumes playing, picking up with a wild and furious passage.

Lying under the bed, I rest my cheek against the floor. He has done better than I would have expected. It is the guilt that has broken him down, diminished him. As I listen to the music, I see a shadow underneath the crack of the hallway door. Then another shadow. Two feet on the landing. Simon stops playing, kneels by the bed. I reach for his lips but am too late.

"Don't worry," he says. "They drove off."

I shake my head and shoot a look at the door. Simon rises, crosses, and yanks it.

"What the hell do you want?" he says.

"Chill, bro. I heard the classy tune and stopped to listen. No big deal."

The steps clatter down the stairs, but not before I catch the faint metallic clang from the heels of his boots. The voice was masculine and quite sure of itself—someone who sees himself as in command, although perhaps the world does not agree. Not a personality I would expect in this building, although life may play the dirty tricks on any of us. Where have I heard a footfall that makes that noise? There is an answer, but it eludes me. So yet another twist arises—one that I do not fully recognize at the time.

Ah, but now my bus arrives through the fog, late, the water spinning from its tires as it wheezes to a halt, half on the highway macadam and half on the rocky soil that erodes toward the gully beyond the guardrail. I make the dash. The men, they must be fed in all weather. It is a need we create, we who compel them to rely so absolutely on our care.

Très sincèrement,
Nightingale

EIGHTEEN

I am Nightingale—

I go today to Wilkie's memorial service. Not to the church or the cemetery—those events are being planned for God and the select—but to the public event on Boston Common. It does not seem a risk for me to be there; it seems indeed as if the city had ripped open its gut and poured its writhing bowels into the park this Saturday to mourn en masse. Chants of "black lives matter" rise and fall, sometimes nearby and insistent, sometimes like a far-off cheer. The crowd is so dense that there are many long moments when movement is not possible and one simply closes one's eyes and curls inside oneself to endure the crush. Others interpret this as prayer, and reach out to squeeze a stranger's arm or pat a shoulder. They pat my shoulder—yes, this killer's shoulder—quite gently. And indeed, I too am saddened and moved by what I have done.

At a distance from where I stand, on the steps of the State House beneath the massive gold-leaf rotunda, speeches are delivered—the governor, a senator, the local cardinal. We who stand deep within the crowd watch these speeches on screens that have been propped up amid the trees. Wilkie's widow is reflected on the screens now and again, and appears each time like an Amazon, fifteen feet tall, her skin jet black in the crude outdoor lighting, with the tattered autumn boughs swaying to her left and right. I recite Scripture to her, just in my head: *Your men whom I cut down shall consume your eyes and grieve your heart.* At one moment I find that

I am whispering aloud the word "*salope*," repeatedly. Most people near me cannot understand, but one young Haitian woman turns to stare in frank disgust. Perhaps it is something about my tone. I move along, putting on my sunglasses.

I spot a cop, at one point, and it is my cue to leave. He is in the typical patrolman's uniform, his weapon secure at his hip, and he appears to be checking something that he carries in his hand and then glancing about, his eyes penetrating the crowd. I wonder if it is me he seeks in that audience. It is not inconceivable that they are onto me. The detectives who visited Simon are not stupid, and of course she possesses the extra sense. Has this female cop seen me in her mind's eye? Has she done up a composite sketch, mystified as to its origin, and spread it about amongst the street officers? Such a day will come, sure. Perhaps not yet, though.

At Tati's, I gather my remaining belongings, which fit snugly in my case. Tati chats at me in the front hallway. "I hope we are taking care," she says, reaching out to pat my stomach meaningfully. "I know how these 'second chance' things can go, honey, so if it don't work out—and I pray to the good Lord that it do but if it don't—you just remember Tati's address, and if it ain't this room I got available, well, there's plenty more upstairs, you hear?"

On the train, staring through my reflection into the blackness beyond, my thoughts wander to memories I have not visited in years.

I am behind a bar where I work, pressing trash into a can, pushing down on a greasy bag with the cover. I turn and a couple is approaching, back-lit, the man with his hand on the girl's shoulder. I think nothing, but when I go to reenter the kitchen he grips my arm. I see now that the girl is a younger man, slight, practically a boy. The older brother grips my neck and thrusts me to my knees on the cobbles as the younger one undoes his pants. Afterwards, the man shoves me over with his boot and then throws some rolled up money in my face. $600.

Perhaps he feels guilt. Perhaps he thinks my keeping this money makes me complicit.

Some weeks later I see the younger brother by chance, on the street. I follow him onto a crowded T and stand so near him I can hear the music through his ear pods. He listens to "Dragostea Din Tei" and reads a Watchmen *comic book. When the train jostles us, I rub the front of his jeans with my thigh. I do it again when the train does not jostle. Suddenly aware, he looks at me, startled. His face is inches from mine, and I see that he barely shaves. I look into his eyes and touch his chin with my nose. He smiles.*

One day much later I read to the dying ladies about Jakey in the paper. The Dorchester Five is big news and I am stirred. That night I lay out some clothes: a loose blouse covered in flowers, white pants, clogs, cardigan, and a quilted satchel. Around my neck I string my cross. Next day, I find his lawyer's office and sit in the tiny reception area as the girl chats into the phone while darting me the sour glances. Late in the afternoon, Elliot bangs the door out of his way, ignoring the girl as he laughs into his phone about "not budging on escrow until the wire goes through, my friend." He is about to elbow his office door closed when he happens to glance over, still sparring. I rise, presenting my parts for his examination. Perhaps I suggère—*who knows?—but after some moments, he waves me in. I wait while he finishes his phone deal. Afterwards, we reach an agreement quite easily, as we are of a mind and he has, so he says, been looking for a woman such as I. "A presence," he calls me repeatedly. He wonders aloud about my hair, whether I might cut it short, and when he touches it, I do not flinch. He touches my face, gently, rubs a thumb across my lips. We meet eyes. The girl has left for the day, but he locks his office door out of propriety. Fifteen minutes later, I leave with a sum he calls my retainer. I understand my life.*

I find Simon sleeping, partially covered by the thin blanket. Working quietly, I stow my case under the bed. His violin sits on the table, the bow across it. I study it—it is old, and the stain has worn away in places. I move my head minutely to read the yellowed label affixed to its inside. *Moinel Cherpitel*, it reads.

I am wearing a dress, black, very simple. I slip it down over my hips. I flick the blanket from Simon and climb on him and lie upon him, undulating slowly until he is quite erect. Then I slide down his body until I am folded, on my knees, between his legs. I have become quite a master over the years, and when his body begins to twitch, I roll off the bed and step into my dress. He begins to wake. I leave before he sees me.

Outside, I lean my elbows on the hallway banister rail, looking down into the stairwell, smoking. The ground floor is tiled in little octagonal white tiles, trimmed with a rim of blood red tiles, many of them chipped. I tap my ash and watch it float in the still air. I listen to the violin, warming up with a series of rapid, vital arpeggios. I listen for an hour, maybe more, then enter quietly. Simon is standing with his eyes closed, playing. He is naked except for his black-framed glasses and the small cloth he drapes on his shoulder under his instrument. I lean against the door, listening. He begins to walk up and down, repeating a passage, then playing a variation of it, frowning. When he opens his eyes, he is surprised, not having heard me enter.

"What you did before," he says. It seems to be a question.

"I want you to play well," I say.

He puts down the instrument in its case and walks over to me. He cups my face and studies it. He undresses me himself, this time. The room is quite dim.

Afterwards I smoke, using the damp hollow of Simon's chest as an ashtray.

"You don't owe me any of this," he says.

I nod, idly singeing one of his chest hairs, then another.

"We do it while I'm sleeping," he says. "I thought I'd dreamt it."

"It is something that I used to do," I explain. "Cures the nightmares."

He nods. "And I have nightmares?"

"I see them in your head," I say simply. "I am sorry, but you are a mess in there."

He studies me, then gropes for his glasses and puts them on to study me some more. "Are you seeing what's in my mind now?" he says.

"It is not like that. I do not guess the playing card that you are looking at. And with you I only looked inside to see if I can stop the nightmares."

"Do you only see images or do you hear thoughts, too?"

"With most, words. With you, the pictures. And music. Sometimes the screams." I turn on my side, putting my face against his. "Maybe you want to punish yourself, for one reason or another. Maybe this is why you do not defend yourself when you are arrested and even the other defendants know that all you did was to try to stop that riot."

"I was guilty," he says.

I sit up. "You are a liar."

He puts an arm around my shoulders. "I'm happy now," he points out.

Later I walk over to the church through the lifeless afternoon. I sit in a pew near the back and watch them. The other player is very different from Simon—he is beefy with hairy cheeks, and so effusive when he plays that his black ringlets shake and the stool squeaks. Simon, in contrast, is uncommonly still. Only his eyes move constantly as he picks up signals from the other man's minutest flourish. He is a dog reading the body language. They speak little, instead conversing with nods and head nudges and the occasional scribble of a pencil against the score.

Afterwards I stand in the aisle while they pack. The big man blows his nose and slaps his case closed with a loud report, while Simon studies his instrument closely. His attention is caught by my swaying sweater-coat and he does the double-take. For that moment, I see fright in his eyes. Then he smiles.

I take his arm as we walk and can see this pleases him. We pass a diner, and I stop and we retrace our steps. We sit in a booth by the cash register, and I order tapioca pudding with my coffee but find that I am not hungry. He shakes his head when I offer the spoon, but I insist and he lets me feed him a mouthful. Finally, I take his hand and pull it across. I examine the fingertips, which are calloused and stained with the rosin.

"You play well now," I say gloatingly.

He scoffs, pleased. "The other part is being played well. Werner is a master."

"That is shit. You know you are playing well because if you did not you would be dissatisfied," I say. "But you are content."

"I'm content," he admits.

"So you are ready, I think, for the performance?"

He leaves his hand captive in mine, but it goes cold to my touch. I look up into his eyes that look naked without his glasses.

"You'll let me do it," he says. "Before…?"

I turn my head away sharply. For a moment I almost rise, but he does not release my hand, and I lose the urge to flee as quickly as it comes upon me. Finally, I nod at the table. "I love you."

"I love you, too," he says, then adds, "you're my Nightingale, just like you were his."

I look up and see the world grow starry as the tears block my view of him. I am still clutching his hand. "My name is Agnès," I say.

"Well, I love you, Agnès," he says. He pronounces my name correctly.

Très sincèrement,
Nightingale

NINETEEN

I am Nightingale—

On the night of his final rehearsal, he tells me. I have just twisted the shower handles and am standing in the tub with the curtain all around me. He passes a towel through, and I begin to dry off. He has made coffee, and I can smell it as it begins to perk. He says, "Do you know why I'm guilty of Jakey's injuries? Have you seen it in my mind?"

"I have told you that I do not read your mind," I say.

"I need to tell you, then."

"You are guilty because it is what you want," I say.

"And you want to abandon your plan because you don't know the truth."

I feel a chill when he talks of my *hommage* this openly. "So we are not objective, either one of us. But Wilkie told me you are innocent. A third party."

"Was that on the night of his death?"

"Yes. He would not lie in his last moments. He would be honest, just then."

"He was wrong."

"He said that you were responsible for his own attempt to save Jakey's life. He was mistaken about that?"

"He was correct about that," Simon admits. "But not about my guilt."

"How do you know all about guilt and sin?" I say, a shrill

196

undertone entering my voice. "You think that because you wallow about in guilt you understand it?"

"Wilkie was grateful for some work I'd been doing, but he was wrong in what he thought, even about that. His view was as subjective as any of ours."

I fist my hands in the towel. When he goes to speak I stamp a bare heel against the wet porcelain. "Enough!" I say from inside the shower curtain. He waits.

"Some day you'll want to know," he says.

"I don't!" But, for a moment, I realize he is right. I want to know, and in that moment his memory explodes in my head.

He waits on the steps of the church, in the darkness cast by the shadows of the overgrown yews. He has failed at his vocation; he is foul, and they come to cast him out.

He wants for nothing, standing there in his filthy linen shirt, his jeans worn to thread at the knees and hem, his sandals, ponytail, beard. He rejects mercy and pity, empathy and compassion. God's love, he's come to suspect, is a hallucination. If he has a yearning, it is for anything that will make him imagine he can feel God again. He does not fear remonstration or humiliation or condemnation. As a vessel of the Lord, he's deformed and unworthy. He personifies the perversity of God's flock, the extent to which Man may stray, yet dwell among the pious. He is floating, there on that hot summer day, amid the fray. He floats because he is closer to death.

He sees the woman, down the cement path, beyond the gate, across the sidewalk and the street. The traffic slices between them. The old lady, out in the glare of the day with her brigade rolling behind her, all of their dresses splashes of pink and yellow and rioting flowers, all of their faces etched with righteous fury. She has come to claim her church. Her sanctity. Her God's purity. He doesn't blame her for her efforts to protect her domain. He is not one to condemn anyone's crusade. His fate is to bend to the will of others, to be trampled by the hoard of the righteous. This is his calling.

"Simon, dammit!" He hears the sharp whisper from the youth center entrance behind him. No—it comes from below, from the metal hatchway under the stairs. "Come on, pussy! I got the key to the gate out back the nave, and I got to get it back before one of them bitch sisters find it missing. What are you, stoned? Look, do this for me now, I fuck you good later. You like? Yeah, I think so..." He steps away from the girl's urgent voice. He is finished with temptation. It is time for retribution.

He sees the car, then, up the street, swerving to pass a bus that pulls out from the curb. It is the pale blue bug from Southie. There will be no salvation today. He steps forward, grips the rail, watches.

"Simon, you fuck! Get back here, goddamn you!"

He throws his satchel off, over his head. He begins to run down the path, his sandals slapping the pavement. He knows he must try to stop the inevitable. He knows, with absolute certainty, that he will fail. His is an ironic God...

I begin to cry against the towel. When he is sure I will listen, he speaks.

"I was taking crack. We had a policy at the youth center that if they turned over their drugs, we wouldn't ask questions. This girl said she could have flushed it herself, but she was trying to prove she was going straight. I congratulated her. That night I smoked it. I don't know why; maybe I wanted to humble myself, to prove that I, too, could sin. The next day she asked me if I wanted more. I pretended to think she meant she wanted to turn over more of her own stash. But it was a tactic. She was getting me hooked."

"Why?"

"Her boyfriend was a dealer."

"Her boyfriend was Terence D'Amante."

"Yes."

"So you became his customer."

"No. Bruno caught on. Must be easy, if you know what to look for. Pulled me aside, offered to set me up, said he knew someone safer than D'Amante. I told him I was getting clean. But later he came back, and I said yes."

"What was in it for Bruno?"

"At first he seemed like a punk, or maybe a petty blackmailer, just wanting to score some piece of whatever action he set up. But it was more than that. By the end, he started talking about my testifying at his probation hearing."

"Lying under oath. But that was the point, eh?"

"He liked testing people."

I digest all this. Finally I speak up, my voice laced with phlegm. "How long?"

"Months. Maybe four, five."

"Others knew?"

"Oleander Tidwell. I heard she wanted to publicly shame me—the seminary student running a youth center, hooked on crack, buying it on church property. She was right to feel that way, but Wilkie Morley was trying to talk her into letting him work it out privately with me."

"How do you know all this?"

"The girl told me. Neva."

"Why did this girl do that?"

"I think she realized that things would go violent when D'Amante discovered that another dealer was on his turf. She went to Bruno, tried to warn him off."

"A girl hooks a guy on crack, then suddenly develops the conscience."

He glances at me. "I think she figured out her boyfriend."

"He was perhaps uncontrollable, that one."

He sighs. "I am worse. I raped her."

I open the curtain. He stands in profile, staring through the trail of steam that rises from the coffee pot to fade into the foggy window. The water in my lashes makes him little more than a silhouette. I see the gleam off the crown of his head as he lowers his gaze to his clasped hands.

"She made the move when you were high?"

He nods.

"She wanted a child. Your child. She got you stoned. You call this rape?"

"She was sixteen. Unable to consent."

I think about all this, my face buried in the towel. "You may condemn yourself for that if it suits you, but none of that makes you guilty of what happened to Jakey," I say.

He turns and meets my eye. "The dealer Bruno set me up with was Dylan Culligan."

The air between us seems to yellow. I shut the curtain abruptly and finish drying myself. I hear the door close, and when I come out, Simon has left the apartment.

Très sincèrement,
Nightingale

TWENTY

Marina Papanikitas's Personal Journal

Yolanda Myeroff is…let's go with idiosyncratic. Gorgeous kitchen—black and white tiles, take your pick of ranges, pantry with a rolling brass ladder so the scullery maid can scamper up to the high shelves—you'd have forgiven her all foibles, Zoey, just to get your foodie mitts on that cook's playground for an evening. For us flatfoot types, however, all the lady had to offer is a lot of the ritzy-ditzy.

Had our little sit-down with her a couple of hours ago. Incidentally (if I can be off-hand enough about my iconic mental condition to relegate it to the "incidentals" category), the partner and I have entered a kind of neutral zone about my "fainting spell," as Harry has dubbed it. I insist that it's a nutrition thing and that I'm scheduling a check-up, soon as I get around to it. Just to let me know that he's pretending to buy that story, Harry detours through the Tex-Mex drive-through and tosses me a scrambled egg burrito. Extra hot sauce. I eat it, and it actually helps. On some level, of course, he gets that I am a spastic psychic with no control over when and how I pick shit up, and on some level I get that I need to come clean about it. Sigh. Just couldn't settle for an average gal, could you, Zoey?

So, anyway, we leave Mr. Love's place, I pull it together, and, you know, we work. Let's take it from sunset, with Harry and me

201

down the South Shore checking in with Dorchester Five defendant
number five. Or trying to. All at Super Jack's urging that we move
quickity-quick on this one—Jack himself had phoned the lady and
ascertained that young Bruno was living with mother, à la Norman
Bates. We figured we'd do the rest face-to-face.

As you know, Zoey, the bulk of the South Shore is pretty
nondescript—lot of raised ranches, hamburger stands, billboards
advertising deep sea fishing tours. Nevertheless, anywhere there's
a shoreline in New England, you're going to have your Newport-
style mansions, and the Myeroff place, called Briars according to
the tarnished brass plaque, is one of these. Picture a mass of worn
red stone shaped vaguely like a medieval castle, streaked with the
soot of the ages where it isn't strangled in ivy, and stamped here
and there with lead-framed windows that seem to emit a kind of
algae glow as night enfolds the grounds. The gravel drive goes right
up to the door, in the style of the great manors. I half expect a
couple of loping hounds to burst from the swaying scrub pines
that crouch on either side of the spreading wings, so I'm relieved
when we get away with just a wild gust of sea spray and a couple
of angry gulls.

Ancient fellow who hauls the nail-studded door inward never
explains himself, but, Zoey, this was a butler—talking the kind
who graduated butling school. Interior's a lot of oiled paneling
and ten-foot walls, solid with unreadable-looking books. The old
gent has us park in the drawing room with an invitation to "please
be seated." Neither of us is tempted by the horsehair-stuffed relics
she's got poised about as furniture, so we stand, making eyebrows
about the stuffed grouses.

We hear the lady of the house before we see her. She's tottering
along on heels somewhere, warbling into her cell. "Mercy, dearest?
Yolie," she says. "I can't do the twelfth, don't you know…But the
poor dears knew about the Oppenheimers and that's been for ages.
Love to Bats, won't you?" She's got one of those old-style Long
Island accents, like the rich folk who hire Philip Marlowe. She
stops, then, and seems to listen to the butler's murmur, then sighs

and says, "Well, let's have at it, then," and appears through a cur-
tain-trimmed entrance at the far end of the room. She's short, just
shy of tubby, and clad in a dressy suit that seems like it was made
at the same factory as her upholstered stuff. Everything about her
from hair to makeup to the tint of her stockings is kind of pressed
and primped but just a bit unraveled, except maybe the sleek little
phone that waves back and forth with her upraised hands—this is
a lady who walks with both hands raised, palms facing you, almost
like a poodle on its back legs. Not stupid, though—no, this type's
more resolutely obtuse.

"Detectives," she says, trying to be fearless. She paces her way
forward across the rug. "Tell me nothing terrible has happened?"
She seems to discern from our wooden smiles that the news isn't
the worst she's gotten over the years from cops at the door, and
makes a quick assessment that ends with our shoes. "Is it wet out?"
She doesn't seem to need a reply, and then finally she allows a bit
of fear to flash in her eyes. "Is it Brewster again?"

I imagine she means the dog, but apparently she's less scattered than she comes off. "It's about your son Bruno," Harry says.

"That's what I was afraid of," she says, pursing her very painted
lips. "Well, you'd better tell me. Don't hide anything please. Mother
must know."

"It's not that he's done anything, Mrs. Myeroff, but we need to
locate Bruno. We understand he's been living here at home."

"Brewster," she says patiently.

"Excuse me, ma'am?" H.P.'s always super polite with your
older women.

"Bruno. He's gone over to Brewster now."

Scatty ladies always throw me. "Would that be Brewster, New
York, Mrs. Myeroff?"

"Not at all," she explains pleasantly, evidently pegging me as
the limited one. "It's Bruno's name. He's going by Brewster now.
Brewster Van Ness, in fact. And I go by Mrs. Van Ness, these days,
at Brewster's insistence. It's terribly flattering to have him embrace

my family name, now that his father's gone." She doesn't look as sure as all that.

"So it's Brewster we need to talk to," Harry says.

"Indeed." She seems genuinely pleased that we've reached this point of understanding. "But you can't, of course."

"Ma'am? Is there some problem?"

"Well, no, not exactly a problem. It's just that he isn't here at the moment." She looks at us and we wait. Then she seems to remember our wet shoes on her rug, and cocks her head. "You know, perhaps we'd be more comfortable talking in the kitchen? It's warmer there, and Gunther can dry your outer things. Gunther?"

We concur on going to the kitchen, but reject Gunther's offer to take our coats and do whatever he does to magically dry off people's outerwear. Soon we're settled with Yolie at her kitchen table, an antique English slab that could seat fifteen. Yolie cuddles a cup of something hot between her fingertips—I'm guessing from the scent that it's some sort of custom tisane. Definitely not ginger echinacea. We've assured her that we're not interested in a cup.

"There, that's better," she says as the sea wind beats furiously against the bay behind her.

"So about contacting Bruno—uh, Brewster," I prompt her.

"Oh, yes." Her face falls a little. "I'm happy to give you his number, but it won't do to call him. I tried a bit earlier, and he's got the cell off. Must be at auction. That's usually it when I can't reach him, or so he tells me. You know how strict they are about phones at auction."

"Where is the auction house?"

"I'm afraid I don't know which one Brewster might have been planning on attending tonight. I try and let him run the business in his own way."

"The business?"

"The antique business." She forages with one finger in a few of her little decorative pockets and comes out with a card, which she lays flat on the table for us to admire, kind of the way people show off their kid's artwork. "Van Ness Collectibles. Brewster operates it quite on his own, these days."

"Does he, now?" Harry picks up the card with interest.

"It's so good to see him keeping busy. I do think that it's running a business that so often keeps a youngster out of trouble."

"Actually, we'd like to sit down with him, if possible," Harry says. "Will he be at the shop in the morning?"

She hesitates. "I couldn't say, really. I don't often know his schedule. But certainly Armand will be there, and you can get in touch with Brewster through him. Will that do?"

I think I see the issue. "Like we said earlier, Mrs. Myeroff—Mrs. Van Ness—he's in no trouble as far as we know, but it's important we see him." On our way over, we'd worked up an explanation designed to keep her from worrying unduly about the potential threat to her son's life, but by now I realize that she is the type who would never ask about someone else's private business, so no explanation is going to be necessary. Unfortunately, this code of conduct is also keeping her suspicious that Brewster's gotten his spoiled ass in trouble again. I can't blame the lady for not liking the idea of being the one to divulge where he might be.

She looks a little hopeless. "I will deliver the message next I hear from Brewster," she says. "But I can't say that he always listens to Mother. Not anymore. It's all been so hard on him, and I do believe that he can sometimes behave perversely, as an assertion of independence." She looks across at us sympathetically. "His father's death, you know."

"I'm so sorry. When did your husband die, Mrs. Van Ness?"

"Seven months ago, now." She nods back and forth, her little button eyes going from one to the other of us. "Stomach cancer. It happened rather quickly, all told."

"Must be hard on both of you."

"Oh, I'm over and done with mourning." She bops a fragile fist against the air. "Can't hang onto your grief. Not healthy. But Brewster, you know he and Hiram never reconciled, so of course it's harder for him. He's always been the sensitive one in the family."

"When you say they never reconciled, do you mean after the Dorchester Five incident? I only ask because it's pertinent to our reason for needing to reach Brewster," Harry says.

She nods at us. "Such a difficult period. Our friends were quite supportive, but I worried so that the Van Ness name would be pulled into it. How Father would have hated that."

"Your father is alive?" I ask stupidly.

"No, dear, he's quite dead, but that's not exactly the point, now is it?" she says politely.

"I know it's tough," Harry says, "but would you mind telling us what Brewster was doing in Dorchester that day, if you know, Mrs. Van Ness?"

"Why, yes, of course I don't mind telling you in the least. He'd gotten into shenanigans at college, and so was taking a bit of time to, well, to give back to the community. I believe he was working at a youth center for some period of months. It was quite a wonderful charity. We gave it a little gift of our own afterwards."

"That was very generous of you," Harry says solemnly.

I have a mini-revelation. "You were very generous toward the Culligans, too," I blurt. Luckily it comes out as if I already know and not as the guesswork it is.

"Indeed, we were," she says a tad pompously. "Hiram insisted on providing for that unfortunate young man in the car, and it was we who set up the trust so that he could enjoy home care for his lifetime. Hiram's only stipulation was that the source of the funds would not be made public or known to the Culligans, as it has not over these years."

"It was the right thing to do," Harry says. "Shame that it caused bad blood between Mr. Myeroff and Brewster."

"You know it wasn't that part of it, really," she says. "The money was—well, you know how it is—that was just money."

"So what caused the friction between father and son?" Harry prods her.

She pauses, then looks up as if with an admission. "It was

that lawyer, actually, although I hate to say so. The one who died recently in that rather terrible way."

"Elliot Becker?"

"Yes. Mr. Becker."

"The Culligans' lawyer."

"Well, you see, that's just the point. Mr. Becker had been our lawyer, or I should say Brewster's lawyer, before the incident in Dorchester. One would assume that he would have offered to represent Brewster again. But right away we learned that he was representing the injured man. It felt like a betrayal."

"I can see how that would be. Now when you say that Becker was Brewster's lawyer, in what capacity are we talking about? Did he manage Brewster's trust fund?"

"Oh, no, no. If he'd worked for the family on that sort of ongoing matter, there would have been a conflict that would have prevented him from representing the Culligans. But he'd helped us out on a number of discrete matters. On a case-by-case basis, but regularly. So it wasn't as if he were not a part of the Myeroff team, as it were."

Harry says, "So what types of cases had Becker handled, you don't mind my asking?"

"Oh, you know." She waves her fingers evasively. "Brewster had his little peccadillos. Young men will."

"Little criminal peccadillos, I'm gathering?"

"I suppose some of them must have been." She nods sadly. "Seemed quite fond of pharmaceuticals, that sort of thing. He had an experimental streak, I always said."

"Did he straighten out after the Dorchester trial closed down?" Harry asks.

"He did," she says, brightening. "Became quite grown-up and responsible."

"Although he still lives here," I can't help noting.

"Yes, indeed," she says, smiling, apparently not seeing any contradiction.

"So I'm a little confused," I say, seeking to nudge us back to topic. "If Elliot Becker was your regular lawyer for criminal matters involving Brewster, why wouldn't he have wanted to represent Brewster in the Dorchester Five case?"

"There, you see? You've hit right on it!" She reaches over and pats my hand like she's proud of me. "It seemed wrong to Hiram as well. And then when Mr. Becker also got to manage the trust that Hiram and I so generously created, I think Hiram rather resented that."

"And so he resented Brewster, too, for putting him in that position with Becker."

She nods sadly. "I must admit, Hiram and I never spoke a word about it, not between ourselves."

"No?" Harry clucks in concern.

"Oh, no. One didn't."

"Not even when Mr. Myeroff knew he was terminal?"

She shakes her head sadly. "He was very ill, but it didn't make him any less angry. I begged him to at least allow me to put some money into The Old Lady, but he wouldn't. He knew that Brewster always loved The Old Lady so much, and that he might have read it as Hiram's giving in to him if Hiram had allowed me to fix her up." She pulls a handkerchief from her sleeve and goes at her eyes a little.

"The Old Lady?" I ask, almost afraid that it's yet another gaff.

"The Nantucket house," she says tearfully.

"It's name is The Old Lady?"

She nods, still fighting the tears. "She's on the cliff, and there's an erosion problem, quite a famous one. Of course she needs to be moved. Well, it's a hardship, getting something like that done, but I always say "just have at it and get it right!" And she really is mine, from my side, so it didn't seem quite fair for Hiram to deny me the privilege of giving her the help she needed. I think Hiram wanted to see The Old Lady crash into the sea. Well, he didn't manage that, and now I've started the work so that the old dear will be saved. Brewster is very pleased, but it doesn't change the fact that father and son never reconciled. Nothing will change that."

"No, nothing will," Harry says sympathetically. "You know, I don't suppose that Brewster could have been thinking about heading out to Nantucket, staying in The Old Lady, just lately? Maybe checking out some antiques on the island? Must be some sweet deals during the off season."

"Oh, no, that wouldn't be possible. The Old Lady isn't habitable. Holes in the roof, some windows missing, rot everywhere—she's a beautiful old place, but she's become quite battered over these past few years without her regular maintenance—and I believe they've even begun digging round the foundation in preparation for the move. So no, he couldn't be heading there. Besides, the weather would have prevented it tonight, regardless of The Old Lady's condition. He'd never be able to maneuver the sloop through this."

"The sloop?"

She nods proudly. "Brewster's forty-footer. Handles her like the grande dame she is. You know he was planning a solo circumnavigation for a while? Wanted to be the youngest sailor to take a boat round the world nonstop."

"Wow," I say. "What got in the way?"

She looks at me, and her eyes go from proud to puzzled. "Life, don't you know? Life always does get in the way."

I'm getting the premmies like there's bugs under my skin. It's all I can do to stay seated, much less to sound offhand when I say, "So, uh, where does Brewster keep the sloop, anyway?"

"She's moored down in Falmouth," Yolie assures us. "It's really quite handy. Brewster can drive to her from here in less than an hour, and then it's an easy day's sail. I've never done it myself. Don't have the sea legs."

"That makes two of us," I say, straining for casual. "Say, um, what's her name?"

She shakes her head, smiling politely. Old thing has picked up that I'm too curious.

"It's just a thing with me," I say, putting my pad away and trying to sound sheepish. "My brother has this little fifteen-footer—nothing you'd even try to call a sloop. Named her the *Lizzie Dane*—that's after the ship in the flick *The Fog*. I always think you can tell a lot about a guy by what he names his vessel."

"Ah, I see," she says, brightening. "I suppose that's true. Brewster's boat is called the *Jane Guy*. Do you know where that name hails from?" She likes this topic.

"Old girlfriend?" Harry guesses, playing along.

"Not at all," she says. "It's the name of the boat in *The Narrative of Arthur Gordon Pym of Nantucket*, which was written by none other than Edgar Allen Poe. Imagine that!"

I laugh. "Well, I guess it displays a fundamental difference between the artistic tastes of my brother and your son, Mrs. Van Ness."

We stand and make our exit, which happens not so quickly as you might hope, once you've flattered Yolie Van Ness about the one part of her life that makes her want to preen. We walk by Brewster's sailing trophies on the way out. Gunther keeps them shiny.

Heading back to Boston, Harry's curious. "Nikos has a boat?"

"No," I assure him. "He did for a little while, couple years back. Turns out they don't attract the babes like a puppy, and they're a lot more work, so now he just has Romeo."

"Retriever?"

"Bulldog."

"I think chicks are supposed to like goldens."

"Nick wanted to be better looking than his animal."

Harry absorbs this. "So what was up with the boat talk back there?"

"Oh, a few things," I say, poking about in one of my phone apps. "First, I wanted to leave it kind of chummy with the lady. Maybe she'll actually get Brewster to contact us."

"Agreed," Harry concedes. "Plus, I do get that you're about to call around to every Falmouth boatyard until we're satisfied that the *Jane Guy* is chewing its cud at its mooring."

"If we're supposed to keep a protective eye on Van Ness, we do want to know where he is," I say practically.

"Uh-huh," Harry says. He's not buying that I'm giving him everything.

"Before I start that, take a listen." I peruse the online encyclopedia app that's replaced my long-term memory. "It's exactly like I remember it from *SparkNotes*. This *Arthur Gordon Pym* is the most surreal, hallucinatory downer of a sea voyage book ever written. Every ship in the thing, including the *Jane Guy*, meets with disaster. The narrator, turns out, might already be dead while he's telling the story, so, like, yikes to that. But here's what I was looking for: at one point a captain abandons his son onboard a ship during a mutiny—there's some suggestion the old man thought the son was in on it, though the kid was not—and the son ends up starving at sea. Oh, yeah, that's the key to Brewster's naming his boat. Very telling."

Harry shrugs. "I bet there's some messy family junk in *The Fog* that we could claim was behind your brother's choice to name his boat *Lizzie Dane*."

"No, that was about Adrienne Barbeau's ass," I say. "Nikos doesn't do family junk. When I came out, my parents were all freaked about whose 'fault' it was and offering to pay for therapy, in case I needed to figure out whether I was really gay. Nicky gave me a list of women from high school he thought I should try to bed."

Harry chuckles. "His hottie list?"

"No, that's just it. These really were the chicks he figured were gay."

"Was he right?"

"Not the point." I start looking up numbers for boatyards in Falmouth, then relent a little. "He was right. In one case, anyway."

"A man with girl-on-girl gaydar. Very handy," Harry says idly. Then he meanders back to subject. "So, uh, you didn't have some other reason to jump all over the boat issue?"

I glance at him. "Like I said, I just thought it might prove useful," I say opaquely.

He looks at me for a long beat while the highway lights paint his face yellow. I'm busy listening to my phone when I hear him say, half to himself, "It will."

TWENTY-ONE

Marina Papanikitas's Personal Journal

About last night—nothing like a midnight beach walk to clear the head. I know you were exhausted and the last thing you were up for was a windy stomp over frozen mountains of pebbly sand, listening to me grumble at the stars. So, Zoey, you think it's just me, or are all female cops closet wusses who spend their lives failing to prove the opposite? And why try? The world is kind to wussy women. I myself am extremely considerate toward the gentler members of our sex—and toward the wimps from that other sex, too, for that matter. I *like* gentle! Sure beats the alternative. So why can't I tolerate it in myself?

Case in point: Bruno Myeroff—'scuse me, that's "Brewster Van Ness" now that the old man's dead and can't disown him. Not that I got anything against a man bucking patriarchy by owning his mother's name, but something tells me that Brewster made the swap because he prefers the timbre of his maternal great-granddaddy's label to the mercantile clank of his birth name. First clue? Man wears an ascot, and it's Hermes. His only excuse—I am giving the dude every benefit here—is that having the neck tattoo removed, the one I recall seeing in the video of his rock and roll days, probably left a scar that the ascot covers. I'd have opted for the scar, but that's me.

H.P. and I arrive at the Van Ness antique shop well before

opening time—silly us, thinking a Cambridge shop might pop the lock at ten, but apparently it's shades up at half past for the Brattle Street crowd. Being the way we are, we rap and rattle on the pretty iron bars until we get a special entry from some little monkey with fancy moustaches and a comb-over who apparently thinks you get to respond to a couple of badges through the window by mincing up your face and pointing at the little dangling clock that says "Open at 10:30." Harry's natural way with words clears up that little misapprehension, and soon we're standing in the dark while our host flips light switches and rattles off his coffee order to the monkey, who scurries out the back way. So at last we meet the fifth of the Five.

The Van Ness place is a typical high-end antique shop, maybe a little less cluttered than some, so I'm not coping with that break-it-and-buy-it paranoia you sometimes get. Brewster's clearly put two and two together after having heard from Yolie, so our news isn't surprising. He's wise enough to act like he's taking us seriously, although he's got this sort of "we're all men of the world" bluster that I can tell H.P.'s not enjoying. Me neither.

"Eight years ago you were pretty young, Mr. Van Ness," Harry explains. "Going through your twenties brings a lot of change, it's true. I can also see why you'd want to get as far as possible from your Dorchester days." Here, Harry indicates the guy's fairly convincing metamorphosis from shit rebel punk to pukka sahib. "But let's not overestimate the amount of water that's gone under the bridge. From Jake Culligan's perspective, life hasn't moved along too swiftly since he got tipped in that car. For Terence D'Amante, it's been on hold while he's served out a term in Walpole. Something that happened eight years ago can be a pretty fresh memory when the good times haven't rolled."

"Agreed," Brewster says airily, taking a cigarette from an inner jacket pocket and tapping it hard a few times against his case. "And I suppose the list of possibilities for who could have killed three out of five of us is fairly endless."

"How do you figure?" I cut in. My turn to be dumb cop—again.

He lights up, then trains an eye my way for the first time, through the smoke. Dislikes me. I can't really gripe, though—I started it. "I would think it's obvious," he says. "It could be someone as close to the case as Culligan's brother. Other hand, it could be some psycho who saw C. W. Morley at a podium somewhere and came up with an elaborate ruse to obscure his simple motive for killing a black politician on the rise."

"Huh," I say. "Sounds like what Morley's wife was talking about, don't it, Harry?"

"Well, there you have it, then," says Brewster. "Every political spouse's fear."

Harry shoots me a look to not play it as dumb as all that, but I'm on a roll. "So, Mr. Van Ness," I say, "you mentioned Culligan's brother. Dylan, I believe is the guy's name. Why would someone like that wait until now to start taking on his brother's revenge? Any ideas?"

Brewster sits himself on the edge of his desk and neglects to bother meeting my eye. I'm playing it too dumb, and he's onto me. "Endless number of reasons, all of which you've undoubtedly identified," he says patiently.

"Humor me," I drop the naive intonation.

He smokes, apparently considering whether it's worth blowing me off, and then decides it isn't—shrill dyke who imagines she rates your respect, no telling how she might lash out if you put her in her place too, too openly. He sighs. "Maybe he was waiting for D'Amante to get out. Maybe he had a hard time locating Petrianni or the priest. Maybe he's a slow boil, or a slow planner, or has been in prison himself. Maybe it just took him this long to get bored with the other sordid pastimes that occupy his time."

"Like what?"

"Excuse me?"

"Like what sordid pastimes?" I push.

He levels me a look. "I could not know less about the activities of Jake Culligan's lowlife brother. I'm actually somewhat surprised to discover that I'm aware he exists."

"But you are aware," I say. "And you're aware he's a lowlife."

"Meaning?" he says.

"Just seems like you've been keeping tabs on the Culligans. Have you, Mr. Van Ness?"

"I have a lawyer for that. The one who doles out the support my family provided."

"Elliot Becker. Ouch—another unlucky fellow. Who takes over managing the Culligan family trust now, by the way?"

He flutters an eye in my direction. "I'm afraid I do not know, detective. Forgot to even consider it."

"It's a lot of money, even for a Van Ness," I say skeptically.

He laughs silently, then speaks as if to himself. "I'm being interrogated."

"No, but that's an idea that's crossed our minds," Harry cuts in. "I mean, there's just you and the one other guy left."

He frowns and shakes his head. "Why on earth would one of us want to murder our fellow defendants? We were 'in it together' and all that, weren't we?"

"Maybe one of you felt you didn't belong."

He blows smoke abruptly. "Oh, well then it's definitely the priest. Sanctimonious little deviant." He glances at me. "Sorry."

I shrug, not getting why I rate an apology—later I realize it's the gay thing. "Wasn't he the one you worked with? I mean, at St. Brigid's youth center."

"Yes, but he was there voluntarily," he explains, "while I'd been naughty at school."

"So when you call him 'the priest,' you actually know his name," Harry clarifies.

Brewster waves the air. "Simon something-or-other. Anyway, we all called him 'the priest' because he was holier than the rest of us."

"Well, he was also in seminary school at the time," Harry points out.

"That bastion of moral behavior," Brewster says, snorting a laugh. "All I remember about Simon was that he always seemed to be behind closed doors with one young weepy thing or another. Boy or girl—didn't seem to discriminate."

"Thanks for grossing me out," I throw him.

"You asked," he says. We hear a rap out back—the monkey must be back with his coffees, and it's his turn to be locked out. "Be a mo. Hope you don't mind?" Brewster says, stepping through the curtain.

"Not at all," Harry says. He motions at me with his forehead and we follow Brewster, just to bug him. To my mild surprise, it turns out the back is actually this mini warehouse space with a corrugated ceiling about three stories above this complex of exposed metal scaffolding, most of it occupied by cardboard boxes, crates, and some larger items of furniture wrapped in huge swatches of plastic. Couple of boxes that sit between us and the back door Brewster is just pushing through are open, their mouths foaming with bubble wrap. Brewster pauses to give some instructions to his little minion, Armand. You think there's ever been a "Bob" or a "Bill" in the antiques trade? I'm guessing not.

"Would you look at this beauty?" Harry whistles. Sitting in one of the open boxes is a glossy wood crossbow. "Mother of pearl, this thing must be valuable."

"Please be careful with that," Brewster calls out.

"Calm yourself," says Harry. "Won't say I'm an antiques hound, but I think I'm up on weaponry etiquette enough to keep my hands off other people's crossbows."

"Other people's is right," Brewster says, rejoining us. "There's been some sort of mix-up. I never ordered the thing. And it's not valuable, incidentally. It's a reproduction, probably made in the sixties. You can see that the handgrip in the stock isn't chiseled. The string is twisted; an authentic string for one of these would be braided."

"Authentic one of what?" I ask. "I'm vaguely familiar with a crossbow, but this is odd."

"Ah, well that's of some historical interest," Brewster admits.

"This is a copy of a Chinese repeating crossbow, circa 1894. Would have held ten to twelve smallish arrows."

"The Uzi of its day," Harry comments. "But with all due respect to Chinese ingenuity, it don't look all that deadly."

"Poison-tipped arrows," Brewster says over his shoulder. "Anyway, it makes no sense that it showed up here. Addressed to a Ms. F. Nightingale, and we don't have anyone with a name even vaguely resembling that. Damned delivery people just don't think."

We follow him out front.

"So, look, Mr. Van Ness, we won't take up too much more of your time, but can I ask if you've noticed anything suspicious lately—someone watching the shop or following you, maybe a car parked out back or near your home?"

He shakes his head, frowns, then shakes his head again.

"You want to go with either one of those?" I prod him.

"It's nothing. There was just this woman…" he says.

I exchange a glance with Harry. "What about her?"

"This would be days, maybe even a week ago. I was sitting here, I looked up at the window, I saw a woman, and she ducked out of the way. End of tale."

"Want to describe her?" Harry says, sounding casual, like we're just being routine.

"We're not worried about a woman," he says dismissively.

Harry starts to throw him a line about how women are often used to case a place by men planning crimes. I cut him off. "Why not? Why aren't we worried about a woman?"

Brewster looks at me patiently. "I thought it was common knowledge that there are male crimes and female crimes. Don't mean to be expose my gender bias, but your sex does comes out on top in this area. Now, a female maneuvering a cretin like Elliot Becker off the edge of building I could buy. He was a fool for women, like…" he snaps his finger, searching.

"Miles Archer," I give him. "*Maltese Falcon*. Spade points out that only a woman could have gotten close enough to shoot a lech like Archer at point blank range."

Brewster chuckles. "Exactly," he agrees. "But shooting that felon D'Amante, execution style, right out on the street? And Petrianni was also just a tic up the food chain from a gangster, as I recall. How was he killed? Don't bother telling me—whatever it was, these are not the murders of a woman. When someone spikes the priest's tea, I'll start worrying about some dowdy female I spied peeking in my shop window."

"You know, it's pretty clear there's no love lost between you and the rest of the Five," Harry observes. "Occurs to me that when someone remarked before that one of the Five didn't feel like he belonged with the set, maybe you'd have been a better choice than the priest."

"Oh, I belonged with the set," he says, "but not in the way you mean."

"Care to explain?"

Brewster lays a fist on his desk and leans on it, observing us eye to eye, the supercilious drawl forgotten for the moment. "Look, the police—your colleagues—arrested maybe twenty-five men that day. They made a judgment about whom to charge based on their usual assessment criteria. Fortunately, because my family has resources, a jury of so-called peers was never allowed to ply its collective stupidity in order to carry out further injustice. Now protect me from this vigilante freak if you will, whoever he or she may be, or occupy your waking hours in some other way if you prefer. But don't condescend to me, threaten me, or preach to me about anything to do with Dorchester. I owed society and the Culligan trash nothing more than any of the other hundred losers on the street that day. And because of what happened to me and did not happen to most of them, today I actually owe far less."

I can't stop myself. "Why you, then? Why were you charged? I mean, look, we're not here to challenge whatever rationale you've constructed for yourself on why you five were singled out back then, but since you bring it up yourself, I'm truly curious as to your reasoning. Because I want to tell you, Mr. Van Ness, I've watched the video. The five of you were up against that car, and if there were any mistakes about who was attacking and who was defending, you weren't one of those mistakes. You went at the window with a brick."

"Maybe I was trying to help the kid get out. That's what the suddenly sainted C. W. Morley kept claiming."

"He had the body burns to back him up."

"I'd wager the underside of a running car is hot if you press against it while turning it."

"Okay, so let's hear it, then. How'd the five of you get picked for charges?"

"Let's see," he muses stagily. "Two niggers, a second gen wop, a drugged-out fag, and a rich punk. I think the crowd that day was a little more average than that, don't you?"

"So it was all based in police prejudice? But there are plenty of African-Americans on the force," Harry points out. "Italians, too."

"And gays as well, oh, sure," he agrees readily, slicing me a look. "But not among those who were positioned to decide who got charged in such a politically dicey case at that particular time." He pauses. "I've checked. It was white Irish, all the way up. And we know how clannish that sort can be."

"Eight years ago don't seem that far back all of a sudden, even for a chap like you who's moved along so nicely, huh?" Wasn't Harry's words—it was more his tone that shut the dialog down right there. Must say, I never saw H.P. display his hostility toward a law-abiding citizen quite as openly as he did toward Brewster Van Ness at that moment. That's usually my area.

Getting in the car, I hear him mutter a couple of choice words about the ascot.

"Aw, give him a break, partner," I say, just to rag on him. "It's a fashion statement. Goes with the antiques turf. Or, hell, maybe the guy's gay and wants to dress the part. Gonna hold that against him now?"

"That guy ain't gay."

"Think not? All that over-the-top hostility toward 'the priest' hints otherwise."

Harry gives me a knowing look. "Brewster Van Ness hates women too much to simply coexist with them. He needs to fuck them to feel fulfilled."

"Huh," I say.

Every once in a while, Zoey, I come in contact with the fact that H.P. thinks more about these social psychology issues than he gives off.

TWENTY-TWO

Marina Papanikitas's Personal Journal

Seems like old times, standing around amid all that burled cherry. Can't say I was surprised to find that Roger Coburn would be in the office with a full schedule on a Saturday afternoon. Surprises me a little more that the whole place seems to kind of buzz quietly. So, like cops, lawyers work weekends, just without as much chatter. I catch glimpses of a couple in designer ripped jeans and ponytails. Something tells me that ol' Roger doesn't dress down for those weekend hours, and I turn out right. First I think that maybe he's left his top button undone behind his tie knot, just to be daring, but it turns out he wears his shirts one neck size too large. Harry and I are dying to make it a quickie, as we've got a ton going on and no time on our hands. Ol' Roger is apparently of the same mind. Starts our interview while we're still treading the corridor carpet.

"Busy as all get-out—well, but you must know how it is when tax season approaches," he says. I'm picking up fast that Roger Coburn's the type who only works—even his small talk's about work. Golf's a waste of his time, and he even resents doing lunch as a means of wooing clients. Except that at least over lunch you can talk shop. No way this man is married.

"Isn't tax season early spring?" H.P. humors him.

"Not for the trust clients," he assures us, shaking a finger in the air. "Got to get the charitable donations out before the close of the calendar year." He stops by an office door and ushers me ahead with a flourish. "Shall we be quick? I have a three o'clock."

"Depends on how direct we are in our answers," Harry says.

I smirk to myself at Harry's royal "we."

For the head honcho at a reasonably high-profile firm in a reasonably high-profile city, Coburn's private domain is on the tight side. Not too surprising, as he strikes me as the minimal overhead kind of manager. Walls are painted a non-distracting green-grey, two computers with oversized screens, skinny blinds covering the view, and very little in the way of desk clutter. This is a man who likes his distractions minimal. Cops, of course, thrive on distraction—observing the trivial in its natural habitat is the name of our game. I kind of have a hankering to vomit my overstuffed pockets across his desk, just for balance, but I keep it together.

"Naturally, I'll do whatever I can to help you out," Roger is saying, "but the clients do have this little bug in their ear about their privacy. How close are we to putting the Elliot Becker matter to rest?" In my head, this translates to his wanting to know how long it's going to be until he gets to unfreeze Becker's client matters and start making money on them. Not that I blame him for needing to know that, but I always get a headache when people make you figure out their motives because it would be indiscreet to state them aloud, while they have no compunctions about pursuing those motives single-mindedly.

We sit and Harry takes the lead. "Three of the five Dorchester Five defendants have been murdered recently. Becker's death falls between the first two killings. We know he was the Culligans' lawyer."

"The killings are all connected, in your estimation?" Coburn says. Like a good lawyer, the man presumes nothing.

"You don't usually have a string of slayings carried out by multiple killers," Harry says.

"But the *modus operandi* vary, am I to gather?"

"True enough," Harry admits. "In fact, they vary remarkably."

I add, rather honestly, I think, "To the point where it took us until pretty recently to even connect Becker with the others."

He looks surprised. "Why, it occurred to me the moment I read about that other fellow's death in the paper. The one who ran the Rhode Island establishment."

"Guess you could have put two and two together for me last time we spoke," Harry says dryly. "Shucks, if only I'd asked."

Coburn eyes him, tapping a finger against his nose. "I, too, wish I had thought to state what I'd presumed was glaringly obvious," he say dryly.

"Maybe it's obvious if your focus is the law," I say, trying to push ahead. "You probably identify a case by the lawyers who handled it more than by any other factor. The rest of us focus more on the salacious elements. For example, seen anything in the papers indicating that the media has picked up on the Becker connection, even after Wilkie Morley's death?"

He looks astonished. "Why, I'd presumed that the serial killer angle was being kept quiet by your department," he says.

"Nope, not us," says Harry. "You're just way, way out ahead of the pack. It's why we're here, sir. Looking to catch up, any way we can." I have to say, this is one of the rare times that I can't tell if Harry's using a tactic or someone's actually rankled him.

"So now that we finally know what we're supposed to be asking you," I say, "care to tell us about the trust Becker set up for the Culligans?"

Apparently comfortable at having been acknowledged as our superior at our own job, Coburn turns to one of his computers and taps the screen to life. "I pulled it up, in anticipation," he says. "It's essentially a care and provision arrangement. Allowed Becker to make decisions about the needs of the patient, upgrades to medical equipment and services, etcetera. Needed to consult with the creator, but I don't see anything here that gives that party veto power over an expenditure that falls within the terms. That's standard."

"Sounds remarkably simple for a long-term arrangement," I comment.

"If all parties are in agreement, straightforward is best," he says. "Complexities can allow all manner of hobgoblins into an arrangement."

"What I'm hearing is that Becker exercised a remarkable amount of discretion over the money," Harry says.

"Naturally, all spending would be on the beneficiary's behalf," Coburn says comfortably.

"Justified when, though?" Harry throws at him. "To who?"

"To any interested party who sought an accounting, in a timely manner."

"So I can think of the Culligans as interested parties, but they weren't likely to question Becker's actions as long as they got the meds, the meals, and the full cable package. How about the creator—might as well call him Myeroff, since we know. Could he demand an accounting?"

"Conceivably," Coburn says. "Although, as Jake Culligan is still a young man, it's unlikely that there will be much principal left when the terms expire."

It strikes me that Coburn is still unaware that Jake Culligan is dead. I decide to save that juicy tidbit for later, and jump into the conversation before Harry has a chance to spill it.

"Can you give us the dollar amount for the principal, Mr. Coburn?"

"That I cannot," he says readily. "Confidentiality, you know. But I'm sure that if you put your mind to it, you can ballpark it."

"Okay, I'll play," I say. "So if I were to ballpark it at, say, eighteen, twenty million, would I need to put my mind to it much more?"

He wags the finger at me cheerily. "I'd say you'd be safe to start putting your mind to other matters." So what do you know? Apparently I get to play smart cop, this round.

"Mr. Coburn, if Becker was supposed to be keeping Jake comfortable, would he need to be in relatively steady contact in the Culligans?"

"That's the way it generally works," Coburn says opaquely.

"So was he, to your knowledge?"

"There is evidence to that effect. There have certainly been no complaints from the Culligans."

"Well, we've already talked about how the Culligans wouldn't be likely to demand much once they were settled into a care routine," I say. "So was there some other form of evidence that Becker was tending to them regularly?" See, that, Zoey—told you I should have gone to law school. Witness evades, Pop pursues, barracuda style.

"Yes, there'd be Becker's own record of the time he put into managing the trust."

"Like billable hours?"

"Not unlike those," he concedes.

"So what might Becker have been doing to keep tabs on Jake? Maybe send a junior lawyer or a paralegal out to the Culligan place once a quarter to make sure their needs are met?"

"It might be handled that way. Many lawyers, including myself, prefer to keep in touch personally with the beneficiaries of the trusts we manage."

"So you make the rounds yourself? How often, once a month? Sounds like a gravy train, if you don't mind my saying so."

He colors visibly, if only for a moment. My gut impression, however, is that this is because he is essentially ethical and doesn't like being accused otherwise, rather than because I caught him pulling the old "billing for breathing" caper. "Clients under a care arrangement can be greatly aided by a vigilant attorney. In most cases, however, regular site visits aren't necessary unless an alteration to the arrangement is under contemplation."

"Okay, my bad, and cancel one gravy train," I say agreeably. "Maybe in this case there'd be a need to make sure the trust money is being put to the right use? What if Momma Culligan sells her kid's massage table to fund a trip to Vegas, or the nurse is putting Jakey's meds into her own arm? Guys like Jakey can't complain."

Coburn nods like a pleased schoolmarm. "Well, I think you've just explained why Becker would need to keep regular tabs on the beneficiary in this case. And of course he'd pay himself out of the trust; hence the record of hours."

"Sure, but the point here is that it sounds to me like you're saying that most lawyers don't keep such close tabs on what's going on with their trust beneficiaries unless someone starts complaining, and we don't actually know if Becker was making an exception in this case and keeping close tabs on the Culligans, except for the fact that he paid himself as if he were doing just that. I mean, not to put too fine a point on it, but if Becker was feeding himself from the trust—not so greedily as to risk depleting it, but enough to keep himself in oysters and champagne—there's just him to say that he's earning that bread through his dedicated service to young Jake, am I right?"

"I think we have a cynic in the room," Coburn says coolly, "but I follow your logic, yes." I get the feeling that the indignation is, at least in part, an act. Fact is, I think that on one level ol' Roger's relieved to discover that at least someone else has cottoned to his own theory that Becker was an immoral SOB who could have caused the firm some serious embarrassment if anyone had been—or started—keeping tabs on him.

I nod, satisfied. "So now that Becker's dead, what happens?"

He recites. "We at the firm meet with both the trust creators and its beneficiaries to identify a suitable replacement to manage the assets."

"Creator's dead too though, right?"

"Hiram had a co-creator."

"Yolie carries on?"

"You'll have to ask her."

"Okay. Have you met with her on it yet, if you can answer?"

"Put it this way," he says. "Step one is to pull together the figures so as to inform all parties of how the firm has performed insofar as investing the principal and whatnot."

Harry gets back into it. "Meaning you're still dressing up the dog-and-pony show to convince the clients to allow the trust money to continue to sit with you."

"We have an excellent return on our managed investments and several partners with significant experience in overseeing medical care situations, myself included," he says. "I see no reason why anyone sensible would contemplate moving this trust to another fiduciary."

"You've sold me already," I say. "And in the meantime, I guess the payments keep coming out of the trust department as they did when Becker was alive?"

"I've seen to that personally," he agrees.

"Handy. That makes you the guy I need to ask about the nurse."

He steals a glance at the corner of his computer screen—today's way of checking the time. "Jake Culligan's home health aide, do you mean?" he says.

"That's the one. I don't suppose she's named in the file?"

"Not in the creating document," he says, but he's game to bang up the expense account. I like a guy in a hurry—tends to get me the info I need with a little less of the lunge and parry crap. "Monthly care payments are wired directly to Prudence Culligan."

"The mother? I'm confused. We met Pruddie Culligan, and she may have a lot of talents, but nursing does not appear to be one of them."

He shakes his head while scanning the document some more. "The home health aide payments can go through the client. Happens from time to time."

"Why, if you don't mind giving us a lesson?" Harry asks. "Seems like that would be almost tempting fate as far as a potential misuse of funds."

Roger nods mildly while continuing his perusal. I watch the pages scroll by, reflected in his glasses. "There are various reasons we might set it up that way, the most common being that the patient insisted on a particular nurse, and the lawyer does not want to be on record as having been a party to the arrangement. Someone uncertified or an illegal—that sort of thing."

"All about covering your ass, huh?" I muse, totally dissatisfied.

"Much of life is," Roger agrees comfortably. I can tell by the assertiveness of his keyboarding that he's shutting both the trust doc and the interview down.

"Could it be that the person who actually tends the books might know something?"

"Be happy to check for you, but right now, unfortunately…" he says, clicking away.

On cue, Coburn's phone buzzes. I rise, and both men follow suit. Harry gives me the wink, and I have to agree that I've earned the right to drop our little closing bomb.

"Hey, since you've been so helpful to us, Mr. Coburn, I thought it would be fair to give you a little intel in return."

"Just trying to help clear the air in connection with Becker's death so we can all move along," he says, coming round the desk to herd us the few feet toward the door. "I've got another opportunity to be helpful, right on your heels, so what you could really give me in return for my assistance is that you allow me to stay somewhat close to schedule."

"Ah, but this you're going to want to hear," I say. "We went over to see Jake, just to satisfy ourselves that he hadn't miraculously recovered and jumped into the revenge racket."

"And of course he hadn't," Coburn says to press me along. "Brain damage like his doesn't mend itself. Wish we'd spoken earlier on that, too. Could have saved you the trip."

"You're right again. Jake Culligan hasn't recovered," I say.

"Indeedy," Coburn says perfunctorily.

Harry decides I'm stringing it out too long. "He's dead," he says flatly.

Coburn stops short, then looks from one of us to the other, waiting for the punch line.

I give it to him. "Leaves me wondering who is chowing down the meals-on-wheels you've authorized to continue going out this month. But—not my hunt, eh Rog?"

He looks across at me and for the second time reddens very briefly. "You simply must try the crow," he says. "It's absolutely marvelous."

Gotta say, I like a man who takes it like he dishes it.

Downstairs, I shoo Harry. "Go cool your jets—bug Malloy or something," I say, punching my cell. "Got some girl stuff."

I call the law firm—good reception, too, being as I'm standing right outside. They bounce me around, and then Penny Dupris picks up. Looks like Roger's got the whole team trained to hop in for Saturday duty.

"Marina Papanikitas. Remember me?" She does, but then I've got a good name for that. "Mind joining me for a butt?"

She shows up squinting into the wind just like last time. I get a flash memory of our prior conversation, and how I'd gotten the sense that she'd known there was something off about Elliot Becker's draw from the Culligan trust. Plays it close to the chest, our Penny. She's a tiny bit full in the face, I can't help noticing, and since this is not a girl who is going to let the pounds creep in on her, I figure congratulations are due. She catches me snatching a glance at her left hand. Looks kind of bare where there used to be the dime-store engagement ring.

"Boy, you don't miss a thing, do you?" she says. "I'm having it resized."

I smile in apology. "How far along are you?"

"Like fourteen weeks."

I can't help my maternal side from coming out. "Todd still into it?" Or maybe that's my vigilante side, come to think of it—the side that wants to break bones when a guy leaves a girl high and dry after she turns up pregnant.

She makes a face like I'd better believe it. "He's walking on air. Anyway, even if he weren't still into it, the wedding would be very much on. It'd be me in my big white dress, walking Todd down the aisle with my father's shotgun. We're moving up the date, just so I don't show. Personally I think it's crazy in this day and age but his mother's old school."

"Sounds good all around. Hope you're real happy."

Her hair's loose today, and she holds it at her neck with both hands to keep it from whipping her face. "So what's on your mind?"

"Was just upstairs talking to Roger Coburn about the Culligan situation. He had to run, and I have a couple of questions that I think you'd answer better than he would anyway."

She shrugs. "I can't say anything that wouldn't be okay with the firm."

"Fair enough," I say. "You be the judge. First, I was talking to Pruddie Culligan and she mentioned that a man came by to check on Jakey. Described him as a lawyer type, whatever that means. Said she didn't know him and that it was the first time anyone had dropped by to check on things. Do you know if Mr. Becker sent someone out there shortly before his death?"

She frowns. "That's totally weird," she says. "Maybe they called, and Mr. Becker went himself. There wouldn't have been any reason for him to bother telling any of us that."

"Mrs. Culligan seemed to think it was at the firm's initiative. It couldn't have been Becker himself, either, because she knew him and she said it was some man she'd never met. Said he was young and snooty. Ring any bells?"

She shakes her head. "I can tell you that no one asked me to make a payment, so it wasn't like we hired anyone to go over there, like from an insurance company or home health service or something. And we don't have any male paralegals in the trust department. Look, I'm totally comfortable checking to see if any lawyer or para billed time to the matter. I can do it when I get upstairs. It'll take, like, a minute. If you don't hear from me, there's nothing."

"That'd be great," I say. I pass her my card with my cell number, subtly hinting that I'd just as soon not have her emailing me in a way that gives away to anyone checking firm emails that I'd met with her right after seeing Coburn. Something tells me that Roger wouldn't like the smell of that. "So, I also wanted to know a little something about Jakey's nurse."

She nods. "Really amazing for them to have had the same live-in for all those years."

"Yeah," I play along. "Seemed like a rare piece of luck to me, too."

"That's, like, the understatement of the decade. It's one of the biggest problems you deal with when someone needs hospice. You get a decent nurse, she finds something better. You get one who can't find something better, you end up having to fire her."

"Any idea why this one was different?"

"I never had any contact with her. Payments didn't go direct. Guess she was just content there. Jake Culligan would have needed a lot of care, so probably she felt needed."

"Mrs. Culligan seemed like she could have been a handful herself," I point out.

"Yeah, but that could make a nurse want to stay even more. I got a sister-in-law who does it. She says that some of them develop this need to take on the toughest, saddest cases they can find. Calls it the Nightingale syndrome." There must be something frozen, all of a sudden, about my facial expression, because she says, "You know, after that famous nurse who started the Red Cross." She frowns. "Or, wait, that was the other one, I think."

I try to pull it together. "Hey, you've been great," I say, "but I don't want to keep you. If I, uh, need to get in touch…" I start stumbling off aimlessly, groping for my phone.

She watches me for a moment, then points. "Partner's over there in the Mustang."

Sure enough, she's made Harry. I glance back at her, in spite of my desire to rush off. "If you ever get tired of bookkeeping, give me a call," I say.

She laughs and shakes her head. "Got enough cops in my family."

Even before I hit the car, I'm dialing Brewster's cell. He's not picking up. I call Van Ness Collectibles and get the piss-and-vinegar Armand on the line, who disclaims knowledge of Brewster's whereabouts. Not sure I believe him. I tell him that it's important for me and Harry to take another look at the crossbow they received, including the box, and that in the meantime no one should touch it. He makes a supposedly jocular comment about "Nancy Drew and the clue of the crossbow" and then goes off looking for it, just to let me know it's safe. Comes back and claims he has no idea what Brewster did with the thing.

"It wasn't valuable, you know," he tells me perfunctorily.

"Depends on what you value," I note sagaciously, breaking the connection.

TWENTY-THREE

Marina Papanikitas's Personal Journal

"Aw, Christ on a cracker," Pruddie greets us. Hair's kind of mashed on one side, making me suspect we'd caught her napping. "So when do I get to call it police harassment?"

"Couple questions, Mrs. C," Harry says, a warning note in his voice. "Let's go with the truth this time, and maybe we can scratch the trip to the station for a recorded interview."

She crosses her arms and leans a shoulder against the doorframe, aiming her best jaded look at us through the screen. "You got questions, ask," she says. Guess not allowing us in seems like a victory to her. Well, whatever lubes her up.

"Last time we spoke, you indicated that you served as Jakey's nurse all these years."

"I got eight years of dishes, diapers, and sheets behind me. You don't want to call that nursing, be my guest."

Harry's ready. He opens the screen door with a jerk. "Okay, I can see we have to do this downtown."

"What are you talking about? You asked, I answered. I thought that was how this worked," she tries. I can see, through the bluster, that she's scared.

"You must have had help, at least with the meds," I say reasonably. Harry stops, his hand still holding the door open.

She settles against the doorjamb again, but she's learned her lesson. "I mean, you couldn't exactly take Jakey to the store, or say I want to go for a drink with a girlfriend, right? So of course I had someone to watch him when I needed to get out of here."

"A nurse?"

She shrugs dismissively. "More or less. Most of these home health aides aren't exactly trained up. Seemed to me they did a lot of sitting around watching the box up there. She was into creepy movies."

"Did she live in?"

"She had a room up top for when she wanted it, yeah."

"And did she use it?"

She sighs. "After a little while she was here permanent. If she had another place I guess she gave it up. Look, what do you want to know for? How was I supposed to know the nurse was important? It's not like she would be killing anyone."

I'm curious about why she thinks this, but Harry jumps in. "What's this nurse's name?"

"Anyer," she says.

It occurs to me that the 'r' at the end is optional. "Anya?"

"Like Tanya without the 'T.'"

"You have a last name for us?"

"Something foreign, started with 'R.' I never got the knack of it."

"Woman lives in your house for eight years, and you don't catch her last name?"

"Well, we wouldn't have been using last names a lot, now would we?" she snaps. "It's not like I hired her. A home health aide was part of the package, and the lawyer sent her."

"Okay, okay, no need to get all hot about it," Harry says.

She nudges at her breasts, signaling that she's over her ruffle. "She was always a weird one," she says as some sort of reconciliation. "Frankly, I would have replaced her, but Jakey was attached and would go bonkers if she was gone too long."

"So she was local? You knew her?"

"She was around Southie a while, I guess." She pauses, then adds, "And I don't know about her people, so no need to start asking."

"Okay, I get it," I say agreeably. "But how'd you know of her at all? Was she in Dylan's crowd? Maybe in school with him?"

She thinks. "She's his age," she muses, "but he was in and out of juvie. I wasn't exactly President of the PTA, if you get my drift." She examines the paint job on her nails contemplatively, then glances at me in a confidential way. "Someone killed himself, janitor at the school, and people whispered that she'd been involved with the guy."

"Around when was this?" Harry asks.

She shrugs. "Had to be fifteen years back. Maybe more."

"Which high school?"

"St. Francis. The one with the vigil to keep it open." She squints at the sky. "They're demolishing it anyway. What are you going to do?"

"So where is this 'Anya R' now? You know?"

She considers. "I don't have the foggiest."

"How did it end with her?"

"What do you mean, end?"

"I mean when Jakey died. Didn't she talk to you about her plans?"

"Oh, you wouldn't get something like that from that one. One day she's here, caring for Jakey, and then next day she disappears. She was out when that snot from the law firm came by and tells me Jakey's upstairs dead. Then later I hear her sneaking in by the ramp, so I yell for her to get in here. I tell her Jakey's dead for days and where the hell has she been—she's supposed to be keeping him alive instead of taking these long walks she's suddenly so into. I mean, you call that nursing, I say, walking around for hours, going on close to a month, talking to herself like she's doing drugs or something?"

"Eight years his nurse and that's how you broke the news to her?" I can't help saying.

Harry interjects. "Think she was doing drugs, Mrs. C?"

She chooses to go with me, and points a finger. "I'm the mother. I'm the one been suffering." She's pretty ravaged looking—I believe her. Then she turns to Harry. "I don't know about drugs, but I was starting to think she was cracking up. Hadn't figured what to do, but I was thinking about calling Becker to get her checked out."

Harry and I glance at one another. "So what happened?"

She blinks past her memory. "What do you mean?"

I try to sound patient. "After you told Anya that Jakey was dead, what did she do?"

"I don't know. I mean, she turns around and leaves with not one word. Goes upstairs, probably because she thinks no one but a nurse can tell if a guy is dead or not." Pruddie starts to cry, I'll give her that—just tears, no sobbing or sniffing, so it's not a put-on.

"After that?" Harry pushes.

She's full-on crying now, but tries to ignore it. "She just leaves. Then she comes back and she's got this case on wheels, the hard shell kind, and she rolls it up the outside way. She doesn't answer when I call up the stairs—it's like she's here but she's not, you know? So I leave her to herself and just wait for her to take care of it, get the coroner over and take the body, but she never does. Like a day later I realize she's gone for good. I got my son dead and rotting right over my head and my other kid in the can. I never even saw her leave. Half expected you to be telling me she'd cut her wrists and was up in the attic with the flies circling." She pushes aside her tears and pretends to laugh to signify that this was a joke, but her heart isn't in it.

"So you never went up to check on Jakey yourself? I'm just wondering about where he was, exactly, when he died."

"I told you, I can't really do stairs with my hip."

"Thought it was your back," I say without thinking.

"It's both," she says, giving me a dark look. "They're connected, you might have noticed."

Harry's probably ready to smack my head. "So let me ask you one more thing. Then we'll get out of your hair."

"That a promise you're prepared to honor?" she tries to joke again, but she's pretty dreary.

"When did Jakey die?"

She rubs her cheeks, erasing the tear tracks, then covers her mouth with her hand, thinking. "I don't know, exactly."

"Well, when did you discover he was dead?" I try, then I have a flash memory—the pill chart on the fridge upstairs. "Three months ago?" I throw out. "Something like that?"

"No, no," she says. "It was more recent." Her heart's not in the lie, though.

I let it go. "And you haven't seen or heard from Anya after?"

"Exactly," she says. "And never is soon enough for me."

In the car, I play around on my phone. Turns out there are a number of ladies going by "Anya R" on the internet. One has a pop tune she's peddling. One's a model. One rates books on Goodreads—seems hard to please. All of them look guilty as hell to me. Harry hangs up after leaving a message for Bernie, his pathologist pal, about needing a death date on Jake Culligan.

"He's going to tell you three months," I remark, scrolling. I explain about the meds calendar on Jakey's fridge. If I'm right, Jakey died around the same time as Terence D'Amante. I try to picture an avenging nurse, finding her patient-cum-lover dead and loading up her .38 to head to Dorchester. Can't quite get there. Hey, turns out there's an Anya R advertising herself as a domina-trix. Never realized they used LinkedIn.

I look up. "Where are we going?"

"Concord. Want to phone ahead and clear it?"

"What's in Concord?"

Harry swerves into the left lane. Every inept driver's a new surprise. I think he keeps presuming that this time he must have maneuvered his way past the very last klutz on the road. "Dylan Culligan," he says.

I like it. "Best bet for someone who knew our nurse."

I put my phone to my ear, waiting for the connection to Concord MCI. "Dylan's going to ask for a deal, you know."

Harry laughs. "So what?" H.P. likes getting tough with cons.

I hear the connection go through. "At least we know this guy's at home," I throw out.

TWENTY-FOUR

Marina Papanikitas's Personal Journal

Driving out to Concord Correctional, I don't look over at Harry, but I have good peripheral vision. He's doing his silent talking thing where you can see the eyebrow tics and dimple flexes and other nuances of a person conversing, except his lips don't move.

"You mind if I get in on that?" I say. Normally I wouldn't bug him, but I've got this giant itch in my brain about us being a step behind, from Elliot Becker on forward. Plus, to be frank, we're heading to a mid-security prison, and prisons make me a little freaky, even when they're tucked in among the trees next to a sweet New England town center.

"In on what?" Harry says innocently.

"I'm just wondering if we can break the silence rule and talk it through now."

He gives me a glance. "I have a silence rule?"

"You do, Harry."

"No I don't."

"Yeah, you do."

"Don't even know what a silence rule is."

"Then how do you know you don't have one?"

He bops the horn and gestures like the guy in front of us is simply beyond all reason. "Okay, tell me: what's the silence rule?"

"You don't us like to think together. You want us to come at everything separately, then compare. Were you, like, ultra-competitive with your brother?"

"Don't have a brother."

"See, that explains it. So, okay, if there's no silence rule, what are we thinking about?"

"Becker. Got to admit, Pop, the guy had game. I mean, he sees the Dorchester Five story in the paper, maybe even on TV before they can get it through the presses, and he's already down with how to maneuver it."

"His ex said he was smart in just that way," I agree. "A player's player."

"She knew the man. I mean, it's not a stretch for him to predict that Hiram Myeroff will pay big money to make the whole nightmare go away. After all, Elliot Becker was familiar enough with young Bruno to be confident that the little hell-raiser was going to turn out to have been right in the vortex when Dorchester went mean. But where any lawyer might be pumped to represent a rich defendant in a media circus, Becker's thinking years ahead to who's going to be in the driver's seat when it comes to administering the trust Myeroff will undoubtedly ante up. Becker doesn't want to be facing off with some slip-and-fall shyster the Culligans stumble across from an ad on the tube. No, it's better to *be* that shyster. All he's got to do is woo Pruddie Culligan and he'll have carte blanche to deal with the mess as he will, including creating an endless gravy train from the grateful city officials who hate his guts *and* creating a generous golden goose for himself as the Culligan trust manager. Guy had a lot of balls."

"I recall that very fact, actually," I agree. "And, on the bright side, this is why no one's called us in to eat carpet for failing to solve the man's murder within a week."

"True, but all patience with us ends about a week from Morley's death date."

"So that brings us to the bird."

"This ubiquitous Ms. Nightingale."

"Want to start with the myth?"

He looks wary. "Am I about to regret asking the obvious?"

"'What myth?' you ask? Well, after striking out on the Anya angle, I have been refreshing my sketchy memory of the ancient tale of Philomela."

"One of my favorites," Harry mutters.

"Not even close," I push ahead. "So there's a bunch of versions, but essentially she's a princess who gets raped and then the guy cuts out her tongue so she can't tell."

"Couldn't she point him out in a line-up?"

"Sometimes he cuts off her hands too."

"She couldn't figure out another way to let the authorities know?"

"Harry? It's a myth."

"They must have had a justice system or the perp wouldn't have needed to disfigure her. Besides, if she's a princess she'd have connections."

I decide to keep it simple. "It's a myth."

"I see. No wonder I hate myths. So how do they catch him?"

"In some versions he kills himself in remorse. In others, her sister or father gets revenge by grinding up the perp, cooking him, and serving him up to his own father or mother."

Harry thinks. "Where's the nightingale?"

"Vic turns into one."

"What? Why?"

"It's a myth."

"Guess it beats having no hands or tongue."

"It might," I say patiently. "The female nightingale is mute, by the way. But I think the point is we've got a woman here who may be looking to get revenge on some guys she sees as having done violence to her in the past. Could be why she's calling herself Nightingale."

"From everything we've heard, this woman was in no way mutilated."

"Jake Culligan was mutilated."

"True enough, but Jake Culligan was no princess."

I look at him. "You're kind of literal."

He laughs. "My English teachers used to write exactly that in my grade reports, all the way up. I always took it as a huge compliment. Are you saying maybe it wasn't?"

"Course not," I say, clicking around on my online encyclopedia. "Which Nightingale should we tackle next? Syndrome? Historical figure?"

"The one in the wig."

I nod agreeably. "Multiple wigs, I'd be willing to wager, and I have a theory about that. She assumes a persona that she knows will give her the siren touch for each victim."

"Siren touch?"

"Elliot's striking out with one-night stands, so he gets a strangers-in-the-night pick-up. Rocco wallows in lady flesh all day, so he gets the class act. Wilkie's a middle-aged divorcée, for all intents and purposes, so he gets a lady casting about for a new beginning."

"Cool. So what do we warn Simon Love about? Lady cellist?"

"It's what he would fall for, not his female other. Homeless waif? Lost soul?"

"Got it. For Brewster she invents a Mayflower descendant name of Lacy Tewksbury."

"Exactly." Something niggles at my brain. "Why'd she send Brewster a crossbow?"

"Maybe it's supposed to mean something, symbolically, like your myth. Scare him."

"Didn't seem to."

"Maybe he's too thick to get the message."

"Didn't seem thick."

"Maybe she's better at reeling guys in than at sending messages. Maybe the message is like, 'Remember my beau? I'm still very cross.'"

I eyeball Harry while he holds back his smirk. Same doofy sense of humor as my father—oh snap, have I just figured out why Harry and I click? This is something I do not need to explore right now. "So you want to give the silence rule another try?" I offer.

He nods. "For now."

We dig out our badges as we hit the turnoff for MCI Concord.

One problem with talking to someone in prison is that it takes a lot of time to get at them, even for cops. Cops have gone haywire before, just like lawyers and social workers, and prisons have all these procedures when you enter to ensure that they'll discourage you from trying to engineer a breakout. You go through quite a few layers of security. You shed a lot of your stuff—wallets, ties, belts, which, for the novice, can strip you of some dignity as well. They don't mind that, though, the prison people. They want you to feel small when you're in there.

Once you're in one of the little interview rooms, you get to wait some more while the inmate goes through the several phases of similar routine that they have set up between him and you. For understandable reasons, they don't like the prisoners to be cooling their heels in an interview room while their lawyer or some cop is running late. None of this is news to me, although I can't say I've been in the house as many times as Harry. Truth is I don't think I'll get comfortable with it no matter how many times I go through it.

Guard brings Dylan in and Harry sits across from him at the little table. I prefer pacing around near the tiled walls, zoo animal style. Guard leaves, shutting the heavy door. My once-over on Dylan pegs him as your typical Irish playboy—got the green eyes decorated all around with deep dark lashes, the lips that make it look like he's always just about to crack a grin, hair that brings the word "tousled" to mind. Even the tips of his ears suggest a bit of pointiness—could such a chimerical lad as he possibly do any harm? Nice pecs and biceps, too, even in the baggy jumpsuit. Runs his bright-eyed gaze down my body and gives me a little wink—probably an involuntary reflex, as his life isn't filled with babes just lately—then turns his attention to Harry.

"What am I gettin'?" he says. Voice deeper than I would have thought. Accent more Irish than his Ma's, meaning he must like the affect. Presents as if he's got a real sense of dominion over himself. Something tells me this boy is going to handle his term just fine, and when he hits the streets, the time inside's going to be nothing more than a step up.

"You know how it is," says Harry. "You talk to us, we write it up. When it comes time to make room for more baddies, you get sprung for behavior."

"You calling that an offer?" he says in his polite quasi-brogue.

"We're not making an offer."

He snorts, amused. "There's always an offer, scratch round a bit."

"Maybe we want to talk about something you happen to want to talk about too," Harry says logically.

This time he shows his teeth and chuckles silently for a while. Guy's hoisting one huge Adam's apple, particularly when he leans back. "Now that's rich."

I decide to step on his patter. "Anyone tell you Jakey died?"

That stops him. He considers it, then flips me a look. "All respect, ma'am, Jakey died eight years ago," he says. "Just forgot to stop breathing."

"Well, he finally got there," Harry says.

"Sorry to break it to you this way," I give him. "Figured your mother would have told you the news. Maybe she thinks you have enough on your mind."

He just levels a look at me for that one. Sainted mother off-limits, or is Pruddie a sore topic for another reason? Having met her, I'm going with door number two.

"Along with Jakey's death, a string of murders have taken place. Terry D'Amante. Elliot Becker, your brother's lawyer. Then Rocco Petrianni. Then Wilkie Morley. All men your brother might have had a reason to resent."

"Yeah, some people started wondering about you as a suspect," Harry throws in, "before we figured out you've been hanging out here at the country club."

He lets his eyes slide back to Harry. "Lucky break for me, that," he says.

"We're interested in the nurse," I say.

He lets his eyes wander the ceiling for a moment, like he's considering. But I see that Adam's apple of his do a little jerk. His nostrils go tight, too, for a tick.

"The loyal Agnès," he says with sarcasm.

And so we learn that "Anya" was Pruddie's attempt at pronouncing "Agnès" the French way. Dylan says "Ohn-yay," like the French.

"Loyal is an understatement," I affirm. "Eight years is a long time to stick it out with a patient in your brother's condition."

"Half-brother," he says, kneejerk.

"How's that work?" Harry throws in. "You're both Culligans. Your Ma take in some other woman's kid after Pop strayed? Mighty big-hearted of the lady if she did."

Again the neck jerk. "No," he says. "It weren't that way."

"Not here to judge," I say, brushing past it. "Point is, Agnès must have cared for Jakey a great deal to stay as long as she did."

He chuckles noiselessly. "You got a sweet way of putting things."

"Okay, how would you put it?"

"Caught her rubbing his face in her cooch once. Barely flinches when she sees I'm watching, then gives me a look like I can go bugger myself."

"You report this to anyone?"

"What, and spoil the fun?"

"Did it seem like fun for Jakey? I'm not trying to be crude, here—I ask because I don't know what his capabilities were."

Dylan snorts. "Jakey shat in a bag. He couldn't talk so you could understand him. He weren't watching any French art films or Hitchcock nonsense no matter how often she played them up there. I gather you think she's the one been killing these fine gentlemen?"

"Would the idea surprise you?"

He almost smiles. "She's just fucked up enough, that one."

"Kind of harsh," Harry comments.

"Sure, sure," he agrees easily. "But reality's harsh, ain't it?"

"So give us a dose of harsh reality," I say. "You knew her just from her years with Jakey, or from way back?"

"Never really knew her at all, ma'am, but I knew of her in some way or another from way back, as you put it," he says politely. "And I'm beginning to see that you know even less of her, or perhaps nothing at all. So what's in it for me to aid you?"

"Got a lawyer friend I can get in to see you," Harry says.

He keeps his eyes on me, probably to display to Harry how uninteresting his offer sounds. "Mighty weak tea, that. Already got a lawyer," he says.

"Lawyer I got in mind comes to work sober," Harry points out. "Hear you waived trial. So how's the challenge to that brainy maneuver coming along?"

He scratches at his whiskers, unimpressed, and goes to say something.

"What if we're thinking she killed Jakey," I cut in. "Would that move you?"

"Lad's dead either way," he says mildly.

"Look," Harry piles on. "You give us a hand, lawyer who can pass a breathalyzer comes to see you. You get to boast to your block-mates about how you had a chokehold on us in here—scoring some quality counseling while only helping us chase down whoever did in your own flesh and blood. Trust me, you'll look good."

"Got a good rep as it stands," he says. "Not sure I want to jeopardize it."

I've had it. "You know, Harry, he's right, and we're wasting our time. We've got more than enough for a warrant to search Pruddie's house. Bound to be more fruitful than trying to do trade with this one." Fortunately, I mean it, so I say it with conviction. Harry half-stands.

"Hasty retreat, ma'am," Dylan says. "Place make you jumpy?"

I turn, genuinely surprised that he's acting like he's biting, and ready to cut him off if he tries any more of his smarmy brogue stuff on me. "Yeah, it does, quite honestly. So make it worth my hanging around or stow it."

He plays it calm, contrasting my overt frustration. It occurs to me that I'm actually playing the "on the rag" card and it's working. It also flits through my mind that the threat to invade Pruddie's place struck home, and not due to filial instinct. Guy's hidden something in Ma's house he doesn't want found. Classic Southie maneuver, sure, but not my hunt right now.

"The good nurse Agnès." He parks his feet, ankles crossed, on the chair across from him and clasps his hands behind his head. "What can I tell you?"

Harry settles back into his chair, glancing at me. This is mine, he's saying. I get that. I also get to not ask the obvious stuff I desperately want, like her last name. I need to come off like we know more than pure squat. "You knew her far back as high school?"

"Didn't attend high school all that religiously, myself. Nor did she, I'd wager. But I do recall her from then. Perhaps before, but that'd be stretching it."

"Any idea where her people were from originally?"

"Don't recall. Thinking Chicago, maybe Canada before that, but can't tell you why."

"Had something going on with the high school janitor, according to rumor?"

"That'd be me mam's ballsch," he kind of spits disgustedly before thinking. Then he shrugs. "Agnès was the poor fellow's daughter, I recollect."

"Why are we pitying the janitor?"

"Bit of a sad tale. Man killed himself on the high school premises. They covered it up but everyone knew. Pinning that one on her, too, are we?"

"No, but I'm noticing that your memories of this woman are better than you thought."

"I was a young fellah on the make. She seemed like the type might give it up. Sullen sort. Loner. Nice enough to look at, sure.

Had that accent, too. Worth a go, especially once the father was out of the picture."

"You ever get with her?"

He chuckles, but I'm not buying that there's nothing there. "Lot of last-call hookups o'er the years. Lot of moments a better man than myself might regret."

"You're telling me you wouldn't remember picking up some woman you half-knew growing up?"

"Shameful, ain't I?"

"What about Jakey?"

My second turn for the evil eyeball, leaving me wondering what he thinks I'm hinting at. "'Fraid I'm not following you, ma'am," he says blandly.

"Eight years indicates some sort of meaningful connection between her and Jakey. Did they go back?"

"Kid was quite some years younger than me. Barely entering school when she'd have been drifting out the other end. As for her devoted years as a nurse, what can I say. It was a gig, and, like I told you, she was an odd duck. No sayin' what she'd get for work if she walked."

"You don't seem to have much respect for her."

"Neither did your mother, from our conversation with her," Harry throws in. When there's a button to press, H.P. thumbs it hard.

Dylan throws his head back to study the ceiling, then lets out his breath. "Nursing Jakey was a step up from earning money on her knees behind the Claddagh. I'll give her that much."

"Memory's coming back stronger and stronger," I note. "Is that a personal recollection or did she make little brother Jake a man, back behind the Claddagh one night?"

"Big happy family, we Culligans, eh?" He shakes his head like he's mildly disgusted. "Fact is, father walked out a quarter-century back. Never heard from the man again. Since that moment the place my mother lives wasn't my home."

"Walked out?" I'm surprised. "I thought he died."

He lowers his gaze to meet my eye. "Mother likes to tell it her way," he comments dryly. "Never had much success keeping track of her little spoofs."

"You went round, though," I chide him. "You cared some for Jakey."

"Got my interests to protect, don't I? Keep me needy mam from giving it all away to the next Canuck comes calling."

"Jakey must have looked up to you. Impressionable kid and you such a legend."

"Oh, he did, he did," he says mildly. "Used to smoke like me, dress like me, hoist his plums just like me. Such a crush he had I started wondering if the kid was a bit of an ass man."

Harry's done. "I don't think you got a lot to give, Mr. Culligan. Then or now."

"Never claimed much to give," he answers lightly.

Harry stands to leave just as something clicks for me—Terence D'Amante screaming through the windshield at Jakey Culligan: *no Chopin disco, ass man,* and then Janai explaining to me that ass man was slang for guys who are into other guys. But I looked it up in my handy online dictionary of slang and it doesn't only mean that—ass man also means gopher, delivery boy, as in assistant. The rest of it tumbles into place: chop is dope and code is ZIP code. *No chop in this code, ass man!* Terence was yelling at the driver of the faded blue VW to get his dope out of Dorchester. And he claimed he'd told him as much before. *I hollered you!* But it was Dylan's car. Dylan's dope. Dylan's delivery. I swing round—this is not a time to think out my next move.

"How's the guilt, now he's dead? Better or worse?"

Harry stops as Dylan shifts his sleepy-eyed gaze to me.

"I mean the guilt over sending Jakey into that neighborhood where you knew you were infiltrating the turf of a guy like Terence D'Amante," I explain.

Dylan shakes his head like he's not going to honor me with an answer, but I've got more.

"Why'd you send him that day?" I say. "Getting a little hot for you over there? Might as well let little brother test the waters, see if anyone makes good on the threats you'd received?"

Dylan stands abruptly, his chair clattering over.

"Steady, friend," Harry says.

I got more, though. "I get it now. That's why Bruno was going at the back window with a brick. He realized there was dope to be scored from the blue bug. Bruno was your old customer, I'm guessing, but he'd be drug-tested while on probation, so my guess is he was getting off on helping you recruit some new users. Heck, maybe that's why the old lady herself ran into the street—she recognized your car. She was one of those clean-up-the-hood types. What a day to send your kid brother in your place. Excuse me—I mean the half-brother you resented for being born to your ma and driving off your dear da all those years earlier."

Dylan trains a fiery eye on me that I won't be forgetting for a long time. Then he strides across and raps on the door. Inches from Harry, who doesn't move a muscle.

I speak at Dylan's back. "You weren't all bad, though, were you, Dylan? You forced Pruddie to let Agnès stay on, even live in, after the court case. You didn't like her much, or Jakey for that matter, but you owed him, and Pruddie owed you both, your way of thinking."

Dylan gets cuffed and walks down the corridor. He doesn't look back.

TWENTY-FIVE

I am Nightingale—

I ride the subway to Cambridge. I have thrown over Sister Julia in favor of a raw Jeanne Moreau knockoff—brunette jaw-length wig, deep red lipstick, black leather jacket and matching hiked skirt, dark patterned stockings, and of course, the loaded gun in my purse. They check you, these days, getting on the subway, but these are random checks, usually performed by male officers, and so I *suggère* my way through quite handily. I stare through my reflection in the dark window across from me, watching the tunnel lights slash my face, again and again. I play my Vivaldi but when I draw near my stop, I turn it off. I need to be sharp with this one.

The Cambridge neighborhood is dead, the autos packed end to end against the narrow sidewalks. My heels click quietly with the occasional strum across an off-kilter brick. The Van Ness storefront is dark, although I can make out a vague red glow that seeps from behind a curtained doorway in the back of the shop. I am reluctant to *fourrage* carelessly after my prior experience here. Instead I push two fingers against the front door that sits slightly ajar and sniff the air from inside, deeply, like an animal. Like an animal, I smell blood.

All is silent, or so it seems for the first few moments I stand there, listening. Then I hear a thudding noise and perhaps a distant call. It repeats quite regularly, almost is if someone is singing while hammering and just happened to be taking a bit of a rest when I first began listening. There is another long pause, and then the noises resume. It is not hammering and singing, in fact. It is pounding and shouting. Someone is in the back, calling for assistance.

I am not here to help, and feel no compulsion to do so. But I am drawn forward, into the dark shop, to explore this muffled bedlam. Of course I realize—realized immediately upon receiving Brewster's invitation—that no one awaits Sister Julia here tonight. Nevertheless, mine is not a mission that covets safety and predictability, so I allow myself to be lured forward. Whatever is happening, there is plenty of space for retreat. And, also, the noises are those of a victim, and a victim who can make so much noise does not fear that his attacker lurks near. Mostly I am drawn forward because I must learn what has become of Brewster Van Ness. After all, this is my victim. I have a responsibility to him.

I move silently among the furnishings, stepping from one rich, old carpet to the next. I pass the desk where I had spied upon Brewster Van Ness a day earlier, and, sure enough, I see now that there is a doorway with something heavy splayed half across it, and what appears to be a vast space beyond. The light, such as it is, emanates from here.

I glide forward and observe the warehouse—the stacks of inventory, the mini-forklift, the distant exit sign glowing red. The thudding is louder in here and originates to my left where the place is its inky darkest. I hesitate, considering what I will do, and as I stand there a shadow before me on the cement floor begins to materialize into a more definite shape. I focus, and it is as if I have been playing a trick with myself, purposely avoiding looking at something that I have realized all along is the very thing I seek. It is a small mass, dense and uneven, perhaps some wrapping materials wound haphazardly around itself, or a rolled rug that has been dropped and partially unraveled. Near it, something catches the light of the distant exit sign. It is a puddle. It grows even as I stare across at it.

I step across the floor toward this mound, which compels me. When I get close I can discern much more—a hand, a pair of glasses. A shoe that has been dislodged from its foot but remains tied. I move further forward, hungry to see. The little man's throat is sliced, the blood still draining from him, but slowly, settling by his ear and in the hollow of his neck. In spite of the movement of blood, he is not dying—he is dead, and his eyes stare at a great nothingness. He is a middle-aged man with a cultivated moustache, elongated sideburns, one earring. I have never seen him before, although at times I have wondered if in death our faces take on a bland conformity, abandoning at the last moment the quirks of individuality that we value so much in life but need not at all when we enter the void. I scan his body quickly—for the last day of his life he has worn a cardigan sweater, frittered away to nothingness at a cuff and along the base, plus worn corduroy trousers and argyle socks, one with a run. Most importantly, for my purposes, he is not Brewster Van Ness. No one has cheated me of yet another of my deaths. I remain in business.

I hear, then, the vehicles. They move fast but silently. They are wise to forego their sirens, but I will escape. I turn and flee quietly as they close in.

It is from the relative safety of the bakery's entryway that I watch them arrive. The blue lights pulse silently against the windows across the street as uniformed cops confer in silhouette, the yellowy splashes of light from their torches spiking out to snatch at walls and trees and occasionally the sidewalk just off from where I crouch. The spears of light do not, however, penetrate the dark that clusters round as if to protect me. An ambulance arrives, then another, and soon the antique shop's interior glows, and for the cops it is the aftermath of murder.

When the first gurney rolls out, I watch with interest. There is a man strapped down—his face is not covered. He is not still; indeed he complains angrily. This is Brewster. Care for him well, men in blue! They will take the anonymous corpse later, after photos.

I slip from my spot and around the corner at a crouch. It is good to be back in the game.

Très sincèrement,
Nightingale

TWENTY-SIX

Marina Papanikitas's Personal Journal

Upstairs you sleep, Zoey, and down here I sprawl, laptop askew across my legs and the TV ablaze behind it, me with my eyes trained on my double layer of screens as simultaneously as I can manage. Taking in *The Abominable Doctor Phibes* at super low volume. Why I have a boner for Vincent Price right now, I cannot tell you, but it's a feeling akin to my premmies and it's driving me to suck down as much black comedy high-end slasher schlock from the sixties as I can handle. Right now psycho sidekick Vulnavia is doing her thing, decked out in ski resort get-up—all white, including the fur touches at wrists and boot rims. She's just faked her auto break-down and is luring dirty old gentleman number five to his icy demise. This junk is tripping synapses in my head, Zoey, but I'm not quite getting the connect I need.

On the bright side, we can check the box on another of my only-useful-in-retrospect vishies—based on an anonymous tip received earlier tonight, Cambridge's finest discovered Brewster Van Ness hog-tied inside the temperature-controlled stockroom he's got built in his warehouse for storing rare valuables of a humidity-sensitive nature. Being as he'd been stripped to the skin and wrapped with duct tape, I'd say it's pretty safe to cross off the visual from Pruddie Culligan's attic. Now why at that moment, and why in that spot, would I pick up a vibe about an event that

253

was to take place in another town and days later? If I understood that it could be a turning point in the case. Pondering all this, my love, is what's got me hot-wired.

Vulnavia is playing the white violin now—makes my stomach knot up. Goll-dang, I wish we'd done a better job at scaring professional fiddler Simon Love out of town.

But first, my evening. Harry and I get a call about the assault on Brewster Van Ness as we're leaving Concord and coast directly over to Boston Med, making good time only to flip our badges and get the usual Saturday night jaundiced response in the ER. Upstairs, we huddle with Brewster's doc outside his room and pick up the basics: flesh wound across the forehead measuring eighteen stitches, plus some superficial pokes, nicks and slashes to his arms, apparently collected while deflecting random lunges inflicted by a frenzied but inept attacker. No permanent damage except perhaps the grudges the nurses and orderlies are likely to harbor—apparently our Brewster makes an imperious patient. One lucky gal on the ward got the honor of stabbing his ass with methohexital, with the result that he's now a docile patient but not much of a witness. We peek in on him and find he's wrapped pretty good and more coherent than I'd have figured. The nurse feeding him lemon ice chips is black with a cute side flip hairdo, glasses on a beaded chain, and no smile for anyone. That's our Brewster.

Nurse taps her wrist, setting a two-minute deadline as she leaves—not sure what happens then, but it turns out we don't need to find out. Brewster tries gamely to be his supercilious self, but even he can hear himself slurring and so wisely keeps it brief. Essentially his claim is that he'd had some sort of meeting set up with a nun—not a joke, it turns out, but something about a charitable donation. Instead of a nun, a whore in grapeade-colored lip gloss came out of nowhere to attack him with a major blade, just as he was exiting the temperature-controlled storeroom. Sliced his face, then forced him to strip at knifepoint, trussed him with duct tape, and closed the door. Before leaving, she identified herself in dramatic fashion as *the Nightingale*.

His tale is altogether tough to buy, I'm finding, even for a major Selina Kyle fan like me.

Harry takes a more companionable tack. "Toughest part's going to be telling your mom," he says. "Lady Van Ness seemed very reliant on you when we spoke. She needs you, especially with your father gone only six, seven months."

He breathes for a while, mouth hanging slack and his one unbandaged eye closed, the lid trembling. I'm thinking we've lost him to the anesthesia when he opens his eye and gives me a look. Like what'd I do—I might have been thinking something vaguely uncharitable but it's not like the guy can read my mind. "Mother," he drawls, "is tougher than people think. Father…" Here he takes time to try to hitch himself up, without much success. "Father was more a burden than a support. House was hers. Money hers. Business…all hers."

Harry's interested. "That so? Always thought of Hiram Myeroff as a market wizard."

Brewster almost musters a sneer. "Made a pile," he admits. "Lucky to have died before the pyramid collapsed. Violent bully."

"It's a type that often does well in life," I say agreeably.

"Least he's dead," Brewster slurs. "One decent thing he did for us."

Harry nods like now he sees. "Say, what happened to that crossbow?"

"Ask," he stutters, then reaches up to wipe the spittle from his chin, "Armand."

"He doesn't know."

"Then she took it. Nightingale. Said: 'I am Nightingale.' Did I tell you that? Swear, this was the line she planned I would die hearing."

"So why didn't you?"

"Why didn't I?"

I gesture logically. "Die with the line 'I am Nightingale' in your ears."

He gives me a sidelong look, and I can tell he's trying to muster up his contempt mojo but the drugs won't let him. "After she said it, she looked…behind. Then left."

"Heard something, maybe," Harry says, giving me a glance.

I say, "You've been a big help, Brewster. Look, uh, there's something else you need to know, so I'll give it to you direct, the way you Van Nesses take your news."

He nods.

"I think that noise this woman heard was Armand arriving. Response team found him dead out in the warehouse, not all that far from where you were found yourself. Attack matches yours, except he wasn't so lucky."

He considers this for a long moment, then nods vaguely. We figure that for a signal that our time's up and start backing out of there. Harry's giving him a few words about healing and staying in touch, when he interrupts.

"Something else," he says. I look back and find it interesting that he's aiming his gaze past Harry and at me.

"What's that?" I say.

"Woman, when she heard the noise," he manages, "she… said '*merde*.'"

"What's that?" Harry asks. "Didn't catch you."

"That's French," I say, "for the world's favorite expletive."

So, Zoey, as you can see, we're on. Agnès, code name Nightingale, native tongue French, where are you? I'm going to junk *Phibes*— it's just not getting me there. Next up: *Theatre of Blood*. Diana Rigg aids and abets Vincent Price's frustrated nutcase. His murders mimic Shakespeare. Rigg wears a lot of wigs and changes persona a lot, so, you know—a couple of shades closer toward what we're learning about our vengeful bird.

P.S.—I keep thinking about Penny Dupris telling me that she'll put on her wedding dress and march her fiancé into the church with a shotgun if necessary. Why is that giving me a premmie flutter? Why, why, why, Zoey?

TWENTY-SEVEN

I am Nightingale—

He has attempted his life. A yearning for peace seduced him. Death, through which all pain dissolves—its soft call must thrill him. Or perhaps, instead, it is a yearning for justice that compelled him. Perhaps after his years of quiet misery he cannot tolerate the fleeting specter of joy with which he has been flirting—the moment when he and the instrument through which he speaks pour forth their joint soul, bringing those who listen to a collective ecstasy, if only for the moment before the chords fade. He does not deserve this, he thinks. It is simply too perverse, for him to bask even momentarily in the warmth of the public's heart, when he escaped its wrath on that earlier occasion. If he had been punished he might have moved along, humbled by his sins. But, like an unclean magic, the law arranged for him to slip free of his absolution. And so he must prevent fate from further diluting the condemnation he craves.

But neither of these explanations is the real reason he did it, you know. It is on my behalf that he attempted to take his life. He believes I am too weak to persevere. He dwells on the three lives cut down that will be rendered the random amusements of a psychotic, no more to be elements of a mission charioted on the one hand by terrible power of vengeance and on the other by the even more terrible power—love. He seeks to right the chariot, to

257

put in my hands again the reins to carry me through. He is *le naïf.* Does he not have faith I will kill him in time?

I never thought to lock my travel case once I was with him. Why would I? My money is his to take if he likes. But I did not see how close he was to the edge. And so he found my stash of poisoned pain relievers. When I come in from my fright at Brewster Van Ness's shop, exhausted yet strangely energized, I see my case has been dragged from under the bed, and it gives me pause. Between us, Simon is the tidy one. But I do not get it, not yet.

I drop my clothes and enter the steep-sided tub, then stand with my face under the erratic beat of the shower, thinking about that little man lying dead on the warehouse floor. There is no doubt that Brewster Van Ness killed this man, as I saw it myself just as I leaned over the corpse. Brewster stands with the box cutter unhidden—it must be that they use it often for opening packages. The man is complaining. He is saying, "When someone says fifteen minutes I don't expect to wait forty-five. So when she came back I told her exactly that—well, you know me, I don't mince words— and do you know what she had the nerve to say to my face? Oh, you're going to love this..." Brewster thrusts the blade into his neck and rips it across, then steps back. It is a precise pairing of motions, balanced well between his feet—perhaps he trained in fencing. The little man continues with his story for several seconds, even as blood begins to spurt from his wound, and then he blinks, quite amazed. He fades to invisibility, and so for the remainder of the vision I see only Brewster. He steps forward and grasps something with an open palm, his fingers somewhat curved as if this object would be spherical, then raises his hand hard, toward his chest. I imagine that the injured man has spun away as he sinks into himself and that Brewster has now lifted the man to a standing position, grasping him by his forehead or perhaps his face, so that the smaller man's spine is brought up against Brewster's abdomen, and the back of his skull nests against Brewster's chest. I watch Brewster cross over with the knife and slash it back with a great muscular rip. At this, his hands release. He has, perhaps, come close to decapitating the man before he allows him to fall to the floor.

He looks at what he has done with a tiny smile, like an artist who dares, in seclusion, to gaze with open affection upon his own creation. There is nothing but this inquisitive pleasure discernible in his facial expression. Then he strips. Once naked, he begins rending his clothing with the blade and stuffing the pieces down a large rectangular drain in the cement floor just by where the body rests. His torso is muscular. Standing, he begins cutting his own arms, moving them as he does so that the jabs are shallow and jagged. The entire vision fades as he begins whistling. He is whistling "Dragostea Din Tei." Is he aware, somehow, that I will have this fleeting vision? Is it he taunting me?

I pull the shower curtain and reach toward my towel, and this is when I see Simon. He is outside the small kitchen window, his head leaning against it, his back to me. I have never seen him out there, sitting on the fire escape. It gives me a momentary start. Then I walk over, quite naked, and open the window. I say, "I could use a fuck. What do you say?"

He slumps, then begins to fall backwards into the room. His violin is in his arms, and it slips free. I fumble to catch it. His body begins to slide and I grab at him so that for a moment his momentum stops and his head hangs, upside down, a foot above the floor. I heave at him, seeking to lift him back up, and as I do he vomits across his own face. It is a heavy vomit, thick as paint. It is black.

I reverse direction then, dragging him to the floor and then across the room to the sink. I turn on the water hard and attempt to lift him up so that I may shove his head under the water. I cannot do it, though. He is not just dead weight, but he is also slippery and slides between my arms, so I switch directions once again and drag him to the tub. Here I am successful at rolling him up over the edge. I turn the cold tap and the water smacks down hard upon his face. He vomits again, and I see his eyes blink in response to the water. I turn from him and scramble through his kitchen cabinets, spilling items about, searching for I know not what. I give up, and instead run to his armoire, where I bully myself into a pair of his pants and his sweatshirt with a hood. I jam my feet into his shoes. I run, slamming the door out of my way and leaving it open behind me. A woman, old, Hispanic, opens a door as I clatter by.

"Ambulance!" I say, pointing up the stairs as I continue down at a dangerous speed. She stares stupidly. I do not wait for her reply.

There is an all-night drugstore, I know, about ten blocks away. I run up the empty industrial boulevard, Simon's shoes smacking loudly against the cement. I encounter nobody. After several blocks, I take off the shoes and hold one in each hand. I run faster.

The drugstore is large and old. I have passed it many a time with its window filled with wheelchairs and walkers, the outdated mannequins wearing nurses' smocks. I have lost one of the shoes, but I would not be pausing at this point to clad my feet regardless, and I throw the other shoe aside as I push through the folding doors. I race past the register—I catch only the smeared image of a heavy woman in a pink vest staring at me—and straight to the back where I slam my hand against the little bell rapidly until it shoots out from under my grip and cascades off somewhere. A man comes out, annoyed, putting on his white jacket. He is older, with a hooked nose and glasses.

"What's the damned rush…" he seems to be saying.

"He has taken the poison! What do I give him?" My voice is hoarse, practically all rasp, from running.

The man's visage changes as he takes me in. "What form?" he says, but he is moving around the corner of the counter already.

I follow him. "It is solid. The rat poison, maybe."

"Your child?"

"A man. He has been vomiting."

He takes several things from his shelves and bundles them into my arms. I fumble for money but he pushes me toward the door.

"I'll come with you," he says, emerging into the street. "You shouldn't do this alone."

"No, no!" I say. "I must run!"

"I'll call the ambulance, then. The address!"

"They have called already," I cry out. I am running.

When I am still many blocks from the apartment, I come out on the boulevard, still running, and I can see the building, far ahead. There is indeed an ambulance at the curb, and lights in a number of windows, like I have never seen before. I slow in spite of myself, my breath ragged in my chest, and watch as a stretcher appears—all of this silent at my great distance—balanced by two anonymous males in uniform. One is a white man, the other black. They disappear behind the ambulance, and I hear the doors thud and then again, or maybe it is an echo I hear. The ambulance takes off, circling round to coast off in the other direction. I hear the siren wail as the lights disappear in the distance. It is like a song sung by an immortal. I hear it in my ears after it is gone; it seems too rich an anthem to die. It means he is alive.

I arrive at the clinic an hour later. I have stopped only to borrow a pair of sneakers from the boys in the first floor drug den. I have lost, somewhere along the way, the mix of plastic bottles the pharmacist had bundled into my arms. I have lost also the money I had grabbed on my way out. There would be a path of crumpled bills and bicarbonates behind me, I suppose, but all have undoubtedly been snatched up, so my trail has disappeared as if by magic.

The clinic is small, its walls white stucco, its only artistry the thin blue neon cross that pierces the dawn sky from its roof. I enter the place—this kiosk of tragedy, always agitated with traffic—mechanics of the soul toiling under the constant cross-tides of sufferers and their lovers, their mourners, and, of course, the flowing stream of freshly deceased, both coming and going. I pass through the automatic sliders, groping for the hood of Simon's sweatshirt against the sudden bright, pass through the waiting area where silent figures sit staring at nothing with leaden eyes. At the desk is a round Latina, her hair combed back smooth, pinned in place like a waitress.

"Simon Love," I say. I am hoarse, practically voiceless, from all my running, and perhaps from fear as well. My accent thickens in my throat. "He is alive?" I tell myself that I would know if he had died. He would have come into me at that moment. It calms me.

She checks and even from her face in profile I can see that he does live. "You kin?"

"Excuse?" I cannot comprehend her through the rush in my ears.

"You are his kin?"

"What is…?"

She refrains from meeting my eye. "You are his brother, yes?" she hints.

"Yes," I parrot. "He is my brother."

I follow the red line of tape down the linoleum hall to the men's ward. He is behind a curtain, amid the weary old palsied men who lie in rows, listening to one another groan. He is pale and thin. He has a tube in his arm and one in his nose. His eyes are sunken and the skin around them grey-black. He sees me.

"The violin?"

I stand against the bed. "It is well," I say although I do not know.

"They can suffer a hairline. Sometimes to a seam. It can be something you can't see with the naked eye. You didn't bring it?"

I lean over and look into his face, then ease myself up and lie upon him so that we are face to face, the hood practically covering us both. "You have survived, then."

"Your stuff was no good. You can't kill with that."

"When will they remove the tube?"

He shrugs.

"You will do the concert now? For me, at least?"

"I'll do it."

"You have a—how do we say—'comp' ticket for me? In the front row?"

"The sound is best further back, in the middle."

I shake my head. "I want to be at your feet. I want your sweat to spray me."

He doesn't answer. Eventually he says, "Bruno? Did you finish that tonight?"

I flick gently at his feed tube. "He himself has killed another. They will get him for that—there is no doubt. And you have killed yourself. So think of it as over. All of it."

"Until you're caught," he points out.

"Sure, sure—until I am caught," I agree readily.

Steps approach. A voice, firm but polite, addresses me as "sir." I peer into Simon's face.

"They think I am your gay lover." I kiss him. "*Adieu.*"

"Get my violin. I need to leave this place."

I nod and climb off him. The nurse checks Simon's tubes to make sure I have dislodged nothing. She does not scold me.

Très sincèrement,
Nightingale

TWENTY-EIGHT

Breakthrough today. Have I mentioned lately, Zoey, how glad I am to be a spastic psychic? Not even kidding, for once. Check this out.

So I'm up relatively late due to my all-night blood bucket marathon. I stumble through a shower while you throw down some sour cherry French toast for us. Absolutely love your French toast—never knew French toast till I met yours. I hit the road early afternoon with my phone under my chin and my latte warming my inner thighs.

Phone rings and it's Malloy. Starts getting into something, but I've got static and am not getting the gist. I try to clue him in but he barrels ahead, apparently not hearing me, and I have a flash memory of the night on the Hampstead Arms terrace, Harry sending him galloping after the lady's scarf that our Agnès had entangled in the roof's cornice. This, in turn, trips a memory of some facetious comment Harry had made a little earlier that night about Elliot taking his plunge to escape the upcoming wedding nuptials, and suddenly I start getting an acute premmie tingle. First time ever behind the wheel—occurs to me I should have started wondering long ago about how I was going to handle one of these bad boys in traffic, but I guess I didn't want to face the question. I drop the phone and steer for dear life. Fortunately, there's no visual to this particular premmie, but it's scary enough to start going brain-numb at sixty-five mph, so I'm grateful to shift over a couple of lanes and roll to a living standstill in the breakdown lane. I wait—turns out there's nothing more to it then the temporary numbing. After a minute or so it occurs to me that I can hear talking. I fish the phone from under my seat and tell Malloy to get over to Calvary Cemetery in Mattapan, find Jake Culligan's grave, and call me. Then I sit for a while, sipping coffee and pondering the many great unponderables of my first major homicide case. Don't know everything. Don't even know much. But essentially I just solved it. I know her MO. I'm in her head.

Phone rings and I decide to kick Malloy's ass round the block, just to celebrate. It's Harry. "Where are you?"

"Late."

I'm not ready to be plied, but, fortunately, he's got his own tale. "So listen to this. Tried to get in touch with Simon Love this morning, just to see if he's harboring your homeless waif. His phone's off so I drove to his place on my way in. Apartment ransacked. No blood, but someone puked his guts out in the tub. Kitchen window open, and I found a couple of old ibuprofen capsules scattered on the fire escape. Elderly woman who lives below told me Love got rushed to some clinic, middle of the night. I went there but he was gone. Didn't check out—removed his tubes himself and vanished. That includes a nose tube, meaning he was damned determined. Nurse at the clinic wouldn't quite say, but they think it was an aborted suicide. She did say there was a guy in to see him, claimed to be Love's brother. My sense, Pop, is that they use 'brother' as code for a same-sex partner who isn't a spouse. That sound about right to you?"

"Standard stuff," I assure him. Actually never heard of that, Zoey, but I feel pressured to come off as hip to the whole gay scene, male and female. "So Love is...?"

"Melted into thin air, Pop. I'm not happy. One additional fact the neighbor told me—she figured Love's place would be fleeced soon as the ambulance took off, and so she herself shuffled up there to nab Love's fiddle. She's heard him practice all hours and figured the instrument meant more to him than the rest of it combined. Said she's felt blessed to live below him and hear that music all times of day and night. Kept an ear out and opened up at dawn when she heard someone on the stairs. Turned over the fiddle to Love's girlfriend, who grabbed it and a suitcase and ran off to Love, wherever he may be. So this girlfriend either thinks Love's alive or is trying to make the rest of us think it."

I consider. "Maybe the old lady meant 'boyfriend' when she said 'girlfriend.' You know how people mess up their gender pronouns when they're talking in an unfamiliar language."

"Crossed my mind," Harry concurs. "But it didn't read that way. This lady seemed very 'old country,' like she might not even recognize a same-sex couple as what they were if they were necking in her doorway."

"Takes but one gay kid of your own to see the light."

"Maybe so, but I'm still confused about who's who in Love's life, all due respect," Harry says.

"Maybe the man's busier than anyone would figure."

Harry laughs. "It's always the quiet type. Anyway, the doc who'd treated him at the clinic told me he'd ingested some over-the-counter rat poison, enough to do damage to his stomach lining, but not enough to kill. My guess is that it's in the ibuprofen capsules I found on the fire escape—these are the type you can open and reseal."

"Thought they banned those years ago."

"That they did. Those Chicago deaths were in '82, which makes these doctored pills just that old. We'll let the lab tell the tale. Hey, speaking of labs, Pop, Bernie just got back to me on Jake Culligan's death. Apparently there were no obvious signs of violence, and the guy was in a condition where death is not a surprise, so they called it natural. Bernie says that from what he's read of the report, however, Culligan's condition was consistent with asphyxiation."

"So maybe he was smothered?"

"And maybe he wasn't. Interesting detail, though. Bernie says the doc who received the body said he was dead no more than a day. We know Pruddie let him lay there overnight, so that accounts for the lapse. In other words, whoever told Pruddie it looked like Jake had been dead for several days up there was not correct."

"That would be our mysterious snooty law firm guy," I say. "Well, well."

"Well, well, indeed," Harry agrees.

"So, what about the ten-million-dollar question?"

"Date of death? Three months back, as you predicted, but get this: Jakey died at least ten days after D'Amante. This blows our avenging angel theory."

"Not totally," I say slowly. "Not yet."

"If you say so. Hey, and speaking of our case unraveling, just now I called the uniform we got on watch outside Brewster's room over at Boston Mem."

"And how's our fifth would-be D-5 vic?"

"Checked himself out. Nothing mysterious this time. He was, in fact, good to go and Yolie picked him up to do his driving for him. But when I call his cell, it's not receiving, and when I dial the homestead, butler says they're not in."

"On the way, maybe? Can't see Yolanda Van Ness as a speed demon. Might even be the type to avoid highways altogether."

"Maybe," Harry agrees. "I'd just like to know. Speaking of which, where are you?"

"I'm heading in soon," I tell him with a twinge of guilt. "Got some stuff first."

"Stuff?"

"Just need to check on a couple of things on my own," I say reluctantly.

"What, the silence rule?"

"You started it," I joke weakly.

He chuckles just as the static takes over and our call breaks up. I consider redialing, but instead pull out. I hit up the GPS and feel my way toward Mattapan.

Cemeteries tend to give me a sense of peace. Maybe it's morbid, but I think of burials, headstones, the act of tending graves, as an orderly part of the life-death ritual that most of us get right. It's a chilly afternoon, cloudy enough that the frost's still clinging to the grass. People crunch along the cinder paths, immersed in memories. I get Malloy on the phone, and he guides me through the maze toward Jake Culligan's grave. When he spots me, he kind of swaggers down the path, then palms his ginger hair before taking off his shades and folding them in a single deft motion. I'm in a cop show—an overacted one.

"So what do you know, cowboy?" I ask, walking back the way Malloy had come and eyeing the headstones.

"The nurse," Malloy says, flicking on his tablet. "Name of Florence Nightingale, according to both court docs and news stories on the trial. Don't know where we got Agnès."

I look at him. "Malloy? Florence Nightingale's the symbol of modern nursing—you know, the Lady with the Lamp from the Crimean War. Agnès was tending Jake Culligan at the trial. Calling her Jakey's Florence Nightingale was Elliot Becker's courtroom flourish. I'm sure the papers loved it and couldn't have cared less about her real name."

"Ah," he says, scratching his neck, "ah." His ears go red as he thumbs through what looks like fifty pages of notes he's taken. Since those ears kind of stick out, the effect is truly heartbreaking. "So that's what that Grand Duchy stuff was about. And the pictures not matching up. Famous nurse from olden days. I get it now." He starts tapping notes.

"Yeah," I say. I spot Jake Culligan's gravestone ahead. Looks like someone's recently stuck some fresh flowers in a jar that leans up against the base. Same set-up at the neighboring stone. I read the stones, then look around and spot Pruddie Culligan, wrapped in a full-length quilted down coat, her eyes sheathed in oversized black sunglasses, sitting on a bench, smoking. I raise a hand and she half shrugs, which I take as an invitation. "So I need you to find everything you can for me on Agnès Rossignol," I say to Malloy, loud enough for Pruddie to overhear. "Pretty sure that's her name."

"Spell that?" Malloy studies his tablet, prepared to type. After I spell the name, he clears his throat. "This'll really speed up my research," he says opaquely. "Don't suppose you remember when you picked up on the last name?" I picture him slaving away in some archival basement, spinning through old newsreels.

"Learned her name just this second," I give him. "Look."

He looks at the gravestone next to Jake Culligan's. "Rudolph Rossignol—The Life Everlasting," he reads. "I get it now. Uh, no, maybe I don't."

"I'm only just starting to myself," I admit. "I need you to verify this, Malloy, but I'm guessing you're going to find that Agnès Rossignol dropped out of St. Francis high school around fifteen years ago. Another guess—she went through some program to be certified as a home health aide between then and now. Here's another wild guess—born in Chicago to Rudi Rossignol thirty-five years back, relocated to Boston just around the time of that string of ibuprofen murders."

"Whuh?" He blinks at me. "How's any of this connected?"

"Just do the research," I assure him. "So, a little while back you said something about the pictures not matching up. Does that mean you found some picture of this Florence Nightingale where she didn't look like a nineteenth-century lady in ribbony headgear?"

"Yeah," he says. "I got one of the Florence Nightingale from the Dorchester Five trial." He reddens again. "Agnès Rossignol, I mean."

"Excellent. Got it on your tablet? Okay, why don't you go to your car, and send it to me before you get going on this new research? I see someone I need to talk to. And Malloy?"

He glances up from where he's rapid-tapping instructions to himself with one finger.

"Good work."

I don't know why I encourage him. He swaggers away, flipping open his shades. I approach Pruddie.

"Good time of day to visit a loved one," I say. "Quiet." She sniffs in acquiescence. "So you heard me guessing away just now. How off was I?" I ask.

She nods, not quite looking my way. "He'll find what you said he'll find," she admits. "And the rest of it is pretty much the way you're figuring it, too."

I sit on the other end of her bench. "Rudi was Agnès' father and also Jakey's. Last time we talked, you said you put him in next to his father. Then I found out Dylan's father is alive."

She throws a butt aside. "One fling. One fucking mistake in all those years. You know how many broads he was doing? Couldn't count 'em. I let one lousy, sad drunk have his way, then decide to keep the kid, and he walks out. Never heard from him again, not once. I used to kind of fantasize that he got killed, early years. Not for revenge, either."

"Just to explain it," I say.

She lights a fresh cigarette, then glances my way and offers it. "I don't," I say.

"Smart." She smokes it herself.

I hear a ping and thumb my way to the photo Malloy's sent me. It's one of those courtroom artist sketches, depicting Elliot Becker in mid-oration. The five defendants are cartooned in, all in profile. Jakey is depicted from his good side, looking young, hooked up to a drip tube. Beyond him is the single female in the sketch, a young woman with a cap of short blonde hair and sad lips, checking Jakey's tube. It would be less than helpful, except for my purposes. She is, without a doubt, the falling woman in my vishie from the night at the Hampstead Arms. So now I know. This is Agnès Rossignol. This is Nightingale.

I pass my phone to Pruddie. She glances at it and nods, then passes it back.

"Got any actual photos?"

She shakes her head. "I looked after she left. Feel free to poke around yourself, though." She fakes a chuckle. "Or send the hottie." She gestures in the direction Malloy took.

"Appreciate it," I say.

"She the one killing everyone to do with the Dorchester thing?"

"I honestly don't know," I give her. "I'll only find out when I find her. Last time we talked, you said it couldn't be her."

She shrugs. "What do I know?"

"You want her to get them for what happened to Jakey, don't you," I say more than ask. "You figured out it was her from the start."

She looks away, not answering, and rewraps her coat. "So, look-it, about the elephant in the room. I knew they were half-siblings, of course, but I didn't pick up that they were—how do I put this—playing doctor up there till they'd been into it for awhile. Then I didn't know what to do. If she was away any amount of time, kid went ape. And you couldn't reason with her, so I didn't even try. She doesn't live by the rules any more than Dylan."

I glance at her, not tempted to mention that I suspected Dylan of instigating some sort of sexual contact between Agnès and Jakey at some point prior to her taking on her nursing role.

"Devil spawn, that one," she mutters, almost as if she's heard my thought.

"You going to be okay?" I say, getting to my feet.

"Why not?" she says, looking my way. "Fact is, I'm getting sick of hiding everything. What the hell is wrong with the truth, every once in a while?"

Fact is, I kind of agree. I walk off, homeward bound for one last slasher flick—the right one, at long last.

TWENTY-NINE

I am Nightingale—

He is brilliant. He plays, and it pains me. There is anger in him, and verve, and even moments of swagger, as he rips his way through those two allegros and the larghetto e spiritoso. Mostly there is precision, his hallmark. He is at the same time humble and proud.

He stands by himself on the stage, looking narrow and pale in comparison with the beefy virtuoso who plays opposite. I have clothed him in the lovely old tuxedo from a thrift shop. Its black is faded and textured, as is he, in contrast to his partner's raucous blast of shimmering black silk and ruddy emotion. Behind the two soloists, ranged about the stage, are the six or seven acolytes who echo their remonstrations. Two of these disciples sit at cellos, and the rest stand about like observers at a burial. Two with violins, a black man with snowy whiskers and a shorn-haired woman wearing sleeve-like black pants as if dressed as a pallbearer, stand to each side of Simon. One other, a blonde with a childlike face who sways sorrowfully in a rich mourning gown of red velvet, stands off beyond the cellos as if engaged in her own solo brand of lamentation, which she etches out in deep, sonorous tones on her larger, more doleful violin—a viola, Simon has told me this is called.

As I experience the music, I am drawn in and out of hallucinatory moments. The hotel where we encaved ourselves today, a joyless baroque structure of battered brick, slowly sinking amid the brusque high rises at the edge of the financial district. Rooms are let by the hour. Simon is in delicate shape—there is no doubt he will die soon, with or without my *adieu*. I feed him squares of unsweetened chocolate, playing it gently into his closed lips until they are coated in brown juice, and then rubbing this into his mouth with the bowl of a spoon dipped in tea so that it seeps down his throat unnoticed. He seems to ingest next to nothing but he swears it makes him quite strong.

The opening allegro ends, and Simon launches into the precise but solemn larghetto e spiritoso section. His violin creeps toward a vision that is very black indeed.

Later in the hotel room I ask him to fuck me—I want him calm and without memories while he is playing. We strip ritualistically and then separately explore the dark recesses of the room, circling slowly, watching one another blend into the mossy maze of the wallpaper and the dreary excesses of old furnishing. Simon without clothes is already more a memory than a man. The carpet and drapes are musky, the atmosphere drowsying as an opiate. At one point, I rip open those lugubrious drapes and splay myself silently on the dense embroidery of the bed, but the window gazes upon a brick wall and the shaft thrown is dull and shadowy. Simon snakes his body against mine, his pelvic bone ridges sharply into my hip. We kiss like lovers who barely wake in the dead of night, not noticing where our lips touch. I reach down and nestle his lazy slug in my sodden thicket. Later, he buries himself in my plot, and I reach round and with both hands help him push deeper until he has stuck me to the hilt. I hold us there like that, very still, until he shudders. I think he has pierced my soul at last.

He waits until I am dressing to divulge his plan. I brush my hair in the age-stained mirror. Behind me, he is dressed, his jacket square on his shoulders, his tie tied. He stands up from the bed and shoots his cuffs, and then, through the mirror's reflection, he displays for me the gun. I watch him in reflection as he approaches. Then I turn. He grabs both my hands in both of his and holds me there until I will agree to listen. He presses my fingers against the gun, forcing me to feel it, to hold it. He looks into my eyes as he explains what he wants.

In the final allegro, Simon and his partner lead a solemn dance—it is a ceremony, a requiem for a lover. I stand and walk up the aisle by myself. I can see the faces of others, rapt, joyous, frightened at this spectacle of raw refinement before them. What would they do, this crowd, if I circled around, raised the gun, and shot Simon through the heart?

I turn, there in the aisle, to watch. At first Simon carries the canticle, but then he draws back to touch me far more deeply as he ticks out time with an intense quietude while the flamboyant other takes the melody, relating a tale of humor and grace.

What if I were to aim the first bullet low, clipping him in the gut, so that he immediately curls in upon himself but stands, teetering, his silence the only sign of his pain? What if a second bullet enters his heart, shattering the precious instrument along its way so that the wood explodes before our eyes, revealing the surprise of its hollow innards, and the released strings spring askew, curling back in fright? What if a third bullet were to pierce his skull just as he begins to topple, so that a perfect black spot appears abruptly in the center of his forehead, bringing him instant peace, only just beginning to seep as he drops against the stage floor?

They end together, with their five devotees joining them in an emotive *fin du siecle*. If I shot him now, would the members of the audience instantly abandon their emotional connection with the moment and run, clawing and tumbling in their panic to escape this sudden scene of carnage, each worried only about the possibility that a stray shot might come his or her way, ricocheting off the stage, or perhaps aimed randomly about the auditorium? Or would they instead go to stone in their seats, minds gripped by the magic before them, and simply stare through their paralytic awe as this slight form from which they have been sucking a newfound vitality crumples into itself, folding as if to disappear before their eyes?

I turn again and walk slowly up the slope, one foot carefully before the other as if counting steps in a duel. My wrap dangles behind me, its silky fingers brushing against my ankles. I measure my steps, my gloved hand caressing the gun in my tiny jeweled purse. When I get to the very top, Simon has played the last note. I grip the gun and pivot slowly, taking in his applause. I have never been happier for another person than I am at that moment.

Perhaps, when I shoot, instead of shirking away the people in this crowd that now pulses with the very spirit of joy would find themselves blind-sided, their deeper artistic consciousness unchecked, and would in the moment turn their unleashed, inarticulable spirit upon she who has dashed the narcotic from their lips? Could they not rise up as a collective and leap upon me, there in the aisle, first tearing the gun from my hand, next the arm from my shoulder, and after that the eyes from my face and the tongue from my throat? Would it not be right of them? Would they be deemed heroic? Or would they be a mob? Would a handful be arrested, dubbed the Cambridge Five, put through a trial, tortured in their own hearts for years?

They bow simultaneously. Several audience members rise, and then a few more, and then with a boisterous ripple, most of the audience is on its feet.

I cannot see him now. I crane my neck and catch sight of his face for a moment. He stands with eyes downcast. For a split second, just the time it takes to blink the eye, he looks up and he smiles, unseeing, at the front row where he imagines I stand. Then he looks down, solemn again. He waits.

But I am weak, as we know. I back out of the auditorium, clasping my purse.

Très sincèrement,
Nightingale

THIRTY

Marina Papanikitas's Personal Journal

I am writing on the fly, Zoey, kind of literally, or maybe I should say it's about to be. H.P. and I are at Boston Med, on the roof, actually, waiting to hitch a helicopter ride. Pilot's about to whirlybird on over to the island of Nantucket for a patient transfer. Shouldn't be too long, now—I understand that when they decide it's time to load you on the airborne gurney from the island hospital to the big city, you're a patient who's in some serious trouble. So if I cut off mid-sentence, it means I'm boarding. Mostly I'm sending this so you won't worry about why the bed's empty and the TV downstairs is napping for once.

So earlier tonight I laid out my case to Harry, and he does get some credit for his lame one-liner about the groom dying at his wedding. It's all there: the scarf on the terrace, the bottle of Arak, the philandering pol asphyxiated. And now the artist. And a bow and arrow. Our killer is doing her own *The Bride Wore Black*. Or should I say *La mariee avant en noire*—that cult Truffaut in which Jeanne Moreau slaughters five guys, all seemingly unconnected, until it comes out that they accidentally cut down Moreau's husband on the church steps while she and he were pausing for a kiss, bride and groom, amid the rice. Agnès Rossignol thinks she proving her love for Jake Culligan by imitating Moreau's MO. Never had to prove anything like love, myself, but then this woman did hitch her wagon to her brain-damaged half-brother-cum-patient. Might give her something to prove. Might make her lose it. Might make her truly dangerous, in the end.

So when I leave Pruddie at the cemetery, I go home and watch the film. Moreau is just shy of middle-aged and smothered in retro fashions heavy in feathers and gauze, yet irrepressibly tantalizing. I know just about every frame of the silly thing, but it's been a while, and in spite of my motive for watching I'm drawn in. I find myself thinking a lot about Simon Love. In the film, Moreau poses for days while the artist paints her. They give his friends the slip at one point, hinting that they're in a bit of an artist-model affair. He finishes his portrait of her, professes his love, and she takes him out with the bow and arrow he's had her hold as a prop. Could Agnès be following the pattern that literally?

Now the true genius of H.P., Zoey, is that he gets what he gets and he gets what he doesn't get. Harry's a slab of granite—grounded, built to last, and destined to some day run the City of Boston Police Department. Solid is his forté, see, and no one's got anything on him there. He's too sane by half, though, to be able to think like a psychotic romantic gone off the edge. His genius is that he gets that my having a link with the lunatic element is what makes us work as a team. Maybe I'm just gushing, here, Zoey, but how many cops you know you think would take my *Bride Wore Black* theory in stride? After Moreau takes out her fifth victim with a bread knife while serving grub in prison—lady purposely got herself arrested so as to take him down—I hit the road and get Harry on the phone. I start jabbering about paintings and bows and arrows—this after Malloy's already entertained him with his tale of two Florence Nightingales. I explain that I spent some time online, even as the film circled in on its final twist, looking for upcoming concerts featuring the artistry of local violinist Simon Love. Lo and behold, he is playing tonight, perhaps even as I drive.

"And get this, Harry. Concert's at an art forum in Cambridge located just off the intersection of Bow and Arrow Streets."

"There's a Bow Street and an Arrow Street in Cambridge, and they intersect?" Harry says. "Now that's fricking unbelievable."

Out of everything I've just unloaded on him, that's what gives him pause. "Toward Central Square," I assure him. "I'm about to hit the tunnel, where I'll lose you."

"I'm closer," he says. "Should get there first."

"Harry," I throw out, "Agnès loves this guy. She wanted that to happen, but now that it has I'm sure she's confused by it. Could make her trigger happy. And remember, she's killed at least three times. She needs all that to have been for a reason."

"Pop?" he say. "I've been listening."

"I'm just saying that you may be forced to take this woman down."

"See you there."

I plunge into the yellowy netherworld of the Tip O'Neill. Tunnel's wide open but Storrow's a bloody mess. As a cop in a hurry, you just can't win in this town.

THIRTY-ONE

I am Nightingale—

His life seeps out through my arms. It is of no comfort, that fact. Not even now, a year and some months later. But I still believe that it may be of some solace in the future, and thus I put it down in this memoir so as to not forget. He dies in my arms, and as he fades he looks into my eyes and I push his glasses away, what is left of them, and I study his eyes, for I owe him much and will witness his transition from flesh to mud, from the nightingale's song to the silence in its wake. He is with me. I daydream, now and then, that this mattered to him.

That night, I stroll the chilly sidewalk outside the art center, my Spanish shawl wrapping my bare upper arms, my legs strangely warm in their patterned fishnets. The hip neon lettering splays the letters A-R-T into the night—pink and orange and blue, they paint the sidewalk and even tint the mist. I walk with energy, out of their range, then back a bit, then nowhere, just turning about, rubbing one velvet-gloved arm with the opposite hand. The gun in my dangling clutch knocks heavily against my hip, reminding me of what I had promised and failed to do—otherwise, I am lighter than the mist. As I wait, some other audience members—denim-clad couples clucking into their cells at their nannies—escape through the curved glass doors. We wink at one another conspiratorily, unable to refrain from sharing our delight. How could a person possibly top this high? Shall we drink until we topple from our stools? Shall we fuck so hard it hurts? Shall we drive with wild abandonment along a riverside road until we burst through a guardrail to sail in a slow spiral through the air, then pierce the black waters so that we may sink upside down to the bottom of the Charles? Who knows! Whatever we do, it stands to reason, we will never achieve the same high that we ride on this Cambridge sidewalk.

He emerges at last, but it is not through the public lobby. A door far down the sidewalk swings to, an unmarked, unobtrusive door of a backstage area. I watch it from some distance, expectant, eager, but for the longest while there is no movement, no figure emerges from behind that metal shield. He is talking to someone behind him, it must be, accepting some final word of congratulations, offering the same in return, promising to reconvene for an even more challenging concerto. He is once again a social creature, communicating with others in the language of their craft. I begin to walk, one heeled shoe carefully before the other, my steps measured, my stilettos hitting the sidewalk in steady tempo, punctuating the night. I reach into my tiny handbag—such a frivolous bit of velvet and sequin, bumping so insistently against my thigh. I hold the gun steady, keeping it from swaying so as I tread the bricks.

The door swings wider for one moment, then begins to recede. He appears in silhouette, illuminated only by the headlights of a car approaching from well behind him, but there is no question that this thin form with the small, high head and the black oblong case at his side is he.

I quicken my pace as he approaches, his step steady but slow. He is exhausted, powered only by the adrenaline that wafts in his nostrils and skitters electrically up and down his limbs. He drifts like a man who knows his own Lethe, who floats down his own current toward the close of his life.

I say his name, but he does not hear. Again I call, and he spots me. He walks forward with more vigor. He does not raise a hand,

and I do not see his face, as the auto that approaches from behind has drawn closer and its headlights throw Simon into an even blacker shade so that he is no longer even a silhouette, but rather an oblong dagger that only partially eclipses the insistent blaze from behind. I see his glasses glint as he turns his head slightly, distracted by the oncoming glare. I am afraid, then. I pull the gun from its satin holster.

He must see me quite clearly, I realize later. The overpowering dazzle in my eyes makes the opposite for him—a spotlight on me. He must see the gleam of my garnet choker and the rippling velvet of my dress, the spatter of my flowery shawl on my shoulders and the sway of its trailing fringe. He must see the glint of my sequined purse and the matching sparkle of light reflecting off the gun in my hand. He sees my smile and the tear that fogs one eye while the other eye's tear disappears off into the air, just a spark. He stops—perhaps he is struck by the perversity of fate, that it is his misery and my misery that should bring us to this moment.

"It's me!" I announce, squinting and stopping in the headlight glare, which is, at this moment, almost overpowering. We meet and he puts his hand out to take mine, to envelope my own hand as we come together. "I love you," I say.

"*I have been half in love with easeful Death,*" he whispers—it is a quote from a poem. He goes to kiss me as he slides the gun from my hand, but our lips never meet. Instead he jerks forward, almost throwing himself into me, quite suddenly and violently, and when he falls he takes me down with him. I do not understand, and think that he has shot himself, that he has, in fact, remained true to his morbid obsession and turned the gun I just handed him on himself. There was no noise, but perhaps I have somehow not allowed myself to hear it. I roll him, there in my lap, so I can see his face.

From the look in his eye, I do not think he is so convinced that he should die at this moment. I will never know whether it is the performance and his ability to accept that moment of pride that makes him realize that he wants to live, or whether it is, perhaps, the terrible pain of dying that he experiences as his heart is shredded in his chest and the blood floods his lungs and then pumps like madness itself from his mouth and nostrils and runs from his ears and his tear ducts. One way or another, he has changed his mind. I throw myself mentally into his brain in a wild *fourrage* as I crouch there on the street, gripping him by his shuddering arms, my skirt growing heavy with the weight of the blood he pumps into my lap. I invade his brain, greedy for just a moment with him—he who I have refused to *fourrage* for days, out of some asinine notion about respecting him, although numerous times he invites me to rummage about in his thoughts and memories—too late, I try to fill his head with the message that I love him. He goes alone, but maybe he imagines I can be with him. Maybe he likes that idea.

"*Je t'aime!*" I think at him. "*I am with you!*"

He thinks: "*You've killed me.*"

Brain communication, I have found, carries no inflection. It is not a conversation, not language, although my clumsiness with imagery has made me present it as such throughout this memoir. Telepathy, at least as it works for me, is closer to a communication between human and animal than human and human. So when Simon thinks up at me that I killed him, it is not fully clear to me what he means. Whether it is a statement of profound thanks and love for my pulling the trigger and doing the deed as I have solemnly promised him, or a simple accusation that I am his murderer, I will never know. Either way, his last thought is a lie. I did not kill Simon. I did not keep my promise.

The arrow that has pierced him through the heart is short, made of a thick, blunt metal, sticking out like an erect quill from his back. I try to pull it out, but I cannot at first, and it is only with a great second effort that I drag the thing out of its hole. Blood follows—thick and so fast that its beaded bubbles wink at the rim of the wound. I press at it with the heel of my glove and feel my hand grow wet and then fill like a cup, heavy with the tide of it. I cry out, but weakly, like a wordless child mewling at the world. He will not live out the minute.

His eyes, so strangely luminescent in life, remain bright even after he dies. I see those bright eyes often; to this day I conjure them up, while I am serving the men their mashed potatoes, while I am riding the bus through the wire festooned gate, while I am lifting the baby and feeling for wetness below, the baby with those same other-worldly eyes. Perhaps Simon's eyes are bright, still, in the box under the earth where they laid him. This idea makes me strangely uncomfortable. I let myself think about it often, though, and I believe I always will. It is my penance. A word from Scripture: *Man's fate is like that of the animals; the same fate awaits them both; as one dies so dies the other.*

A small group approaches, two laughing girls and their escorts, out for a night and feeling quite gay about it. I can hear the stuttering heels of the women as they punch the bricks. They come nearer. Simon and I remain in the spotlight of the auto, which has stopped and hovers just over from where I sit on the sidewalk. One of the men laughs in disbelief—can people be so drunk at this early hour as to have collapsed in the gutter? A woman catches on to what she is seeing—the blood, so much blood—and screams. I am grateful. She is screaming the scream I cannot dislodge from my chest.

Très sincèrement,
Nightingale

THIRTY-TWO

Marina Papanikitas's Personal Journal

False start, Zoey. Rugged guy heading for the copter turned out to be the mechanic who does the check. Pilot's on the way up, he assures us. Hey, I got time, but some poor Yank over on "fog island" who needs intensive care better get his second wind. It is breezy up here at rooftop, Zoey, but the mechanic assures us it's not gusting nearly enough to abort. I'm thinking we got rain in our future. I could get a little uneasy about that if I allow myself to think about it.

So, back to Cambridge. Harry gets to the crime scene first, as predicted, but some witness has dialed emergency so he only beats the ambulance by minutes. Me, I miss the show entirely, so essentially I get everything secondhand. Simon Love lays dead, having bled his heart out—that's literally, Zoey—on the Arrow Street sidewalk, just off Bow. By the time the Cambridge cops show, Harry's already got a bead on a couple of Lesley College undergrads and their MIT escorts, wandering around before the late show at Davis Square and apparently harboring some confusion—the split running along the gender line—on whether they're on a double date or just out as a platonic gaggle. The one girl who can actually articulate herself relates a story about a woman crouching on the sidewalk, more or less under the dead man, as if she'd shot him point blank, then took his weight when he toppled. Girl's claim is that some man came round the front of a car that was hovering in the street—a male accomplice—and he grabbed the woman under the arm to help hoist her up. The woman seemed to come to her senses around then, and went hurrying off with the man, hopped into the car next to him, and away they whisked.

One of the male witnesses—tall Indian kid, very certain of himself—claimed he saw a gun in the woman's hand. Small, black, snubbed—he claimed she dropped it into a little bag she had strapped over her shoulder. The Indian kid was the only one who gave Harry a detailed description of the female suspect—she's my vishie from Elliot Becker's death scene, down to the stockings and shawl.

Unfortunately, not a one of the college kids got a decent read on the guy from the car—too busy watching the geyser burbling its way from Simon Love's back. Still, the getaway vehicle was an old model Mercedes, black or brown. Never noted Brewster Van Ness's wheels, myself, but it sure sounds like a match. In any event, all of that was certainly enough to send me and Harry southward while the Cambridge cops took care of carting off the corpse and hosing his innards down the storm drain.

Heading down to the South Shore, I get Yolanda Van Ness on the line. Lady picks up all by herself rather than making me bully my way past the butler, which feels lucky, but only for a minute. Yolie assures me that Brewster is right there with her, safe as mice. I ask to speak with him and she demurs—the boy's been under a terrible amount of stress what with the threat to his life looming out there, and so is heavily sedated. Seeking to prepare her for our momentary invasion into her domain, I make sympathetic noises about Brewster's injuries and the death of his little friend Armand, and that's when Yolie gets kind of strung out on me. She accepts my condolences but there's a tone change.

"Poor Armand," she says. "Is he—will he pull through?"

I don't do a gentle build-up that well, particularly when I've already spilled the beans, and the person just isn't hearing it. Maybe Brewster's been soft-pedaling the ugly facts to her, but they're about to emerge, and I remember that the lady does pride herself on taking it straight.

"Look, I'm very sorry to have to tell you this over the phone, Mrs. Van Ness," I say, "but Armand is dead. He was killed at the shop. Throat cut. Died instantly."

She's silent for a long moment, during which it occurs to me that this is the first she's hearing about Armand having even been present when her son was attacked. What this signifies to her, she's keeping to herself. I ask whether she's still on the line, and she murmurs something about the man having been with them for years and years.

"Such a very long time, you see, I'd begun to think that he was like family to us...to all of us." She sounds vague because she's sad, but she doesn't sound spacey, if you get the difference—Yolie Van Ness sounds like she's suddenly very sad about something she's also quite lucid on. She sounds heartsick, actually.

"Mrs. Van Ness?" I say. "Would you like to tell me something?" It seems fruitless to try and insist that she wake her son. Besides, at this point I don't think there's a chance in a million that he's actually there, or that she'll admit it if she has any idea about where he may be. "Mrs. Van Ness?" I repeat. "There may be other lives at stake."

The line stays live for a long, drawn-out minute or so, but I don't think she's deciding whether to talk to me. I think that it's that she's moving in slow motion. When she hangs up, it's like she's finally lowered her arm enough to drop the receiver gently into its cradle. It's like she's finally accepted what she's always suspected. Must be a frightening jolt, that moment when you realize that your son is the raging psychotic everyone's always hinted he is.

We're ten minutes from the Van Ness place. "I think we better turn it around."

"Where we heading?"

"Nantucket. I think Brewster's taking Agnès Rossignol to the old summer place."

"What, on his boat?"

"It's a way to get there."

Harry nods. "Mother say something just now to make you think he's heading out there?"

I shake my head. "She's in shock. No one's pulling anything out of her."

"So we know it's Nantucket how, Pop?" I sit there as he takes the exit to reverse us. "You have one of your sighting things?" He says it more than asks it.

I must blanch in response, because my hands and forehead go to ice for an eerie couple of seconds. I have to clear my throat before I can talk. "What?"

He shrugs. "Don't know what you call them. One of your psychic events."

I go from cold to hot, clear my throat. "I call them premmies," I admit, then try to fake a chuckle. Comes out sounding like I'm choking on a cracker. "For premonitions. The more intense ones I call vishies, for visions. And, yeah, I had one."

"So what'd we see?" he wants to know, busy slicing across traffic to hit the on-ramp.

I breathe down. "Saw Rossignol. Outfit that witness gave you—the fishnets, the shawl, everything. She's falling through the rain, like she went off a cliff."

Harry nods. "The Van Ness Nantucket place is on a bluff. I'm with you." Back on the highway now, he picks up speed.

"If you're waiting for more, that's all I saw," I say, kind of miserable.

"Logan or Hyannis?"

I shrug, dissatisfied. "Logan. I'll call ahead. We're going to need a charter."

I'm doing the phone bullshit when Harry puts out a hand and touches mine. I almost start. Cripes, Zoey, it's like when I was in ninth grade and people would bring up the L-word. You kind of think you got your private stuff wrapped up tight, you know, and suddenly you realize you're out there naked. Takes some getting used to, apparently at any age.

"Got a better idea," Harry says. "Guy I know flies the emergency helicopter shuttle at BMC. Let me get him, see if he'll let us hitch a ride."

"There's a chance they'll carry us?"

"They carry Chinese takeout. I'd say it's worth a shot." He beckons without glancing over, and I hand him my phone. I wonder if he gets that I'm looking for a wing to hide my head under. If he does, he knows not to notice.

Ten minutes later, Harry's pilot buddy has come through and we're sweeping back into the city while I dial Super Jack and ask him to make the connect with the Nantucket cops. He's weirdly accommodating, considering I offer no explanation for how we know that our guy's heading out to sea. "No Coast Guard and no sirens, Jack, right? Stress the fact that this guy's got a hostage and he's planning on killing her one way or another. And we got time, Jack. He's heading over by boat. Going to take him all night."

Super Jack knows his job. He reminds me of that before he hangs up.

Good thing we got all night, as we just found out we've been postponed due to weather. Harry's pal sits it out with us. Kind of a little fella—I'd have pegged him for a horse jockey before I'd have guessed he's the helicopter kind—but maybe size is a disadvantage when you have to walk underneath those whapping blades all the time.

Talk later. Pray for me, Zoey. And not about the flight.

THIRTY-THREE

I am Nightingale—

I sit on the deck against the side of the boat, knees up, arms embracing my legs. The decking looks slippery, but Brewster has no trouble working the sail and the rudder and the ropes. The salt wind bats his hair about—occasionally one of the front locks sticks to the still-raw slash that dissects his forehead, left temple to right eye. I can discern the stitches from where I sit, even in the dark. Earlier on, while we were still chugging along on engine power, he had invited me to duck down below, clean up, try to rest. There is an old-fashioned bathing tub and quite a comfortable mattress in the stateroom, he assured me, and Simon's blood must be drying stiffly on my pretty dress. I suppose this superficial chatter was meant to taunt me. I do not know for certain, of course, as I dare not delve into this one's brain. Not after that first time.

As we get some distance from shore, the boat seems to fall into a rhythm against the waves, and Brewster switches off the engine and crouches by the rudder for a while. He seems invigorated by the sea air and obviously enjoys the spray in his face. I notice that he has changed to navy blue rubber-soled shoes and abandoned his socks—possibly back in the boat house. The ascot and cashmere jacket's tail flicker in the wind. Above us, the sky is deep and black—there are no stars, no clouds. The moon clings to the horizon, cowed by the expanse of night and sea.

I am strangely confident. I will not die before Brewster. I have met and accepted each of my victims as he was, each as he was shaped by what happened to Jakey—the opportunist, the misanthrope, the penitent, the martyr—and, as you see, I have done what needed to be done, one way or another, to achieve my end. But my fifth victim—the one who interpreted the event of his past only as a signal that he is untouchable, free to snatch life up and smash it without conscience or consequence—he imagines he has dashed my plans. On my side, I see nothing to prevent me from accomplishing my task—not my sorrow, not my inhibitions about using my mental abilities on him, and most definitely not the fact that this time I dance quite openly with another killer. I have got my Jeanne Moreau on, one might say.

Apparently Brewster misreads my silence, there in the boat. "Don't fret over Brother Simon, dearest," he calls to me over the wind. "He'd been playing the sin and regret game for a long, long time. It was bound to catch up with him, one way or another."

I ignore the invitation to exchange quips and instead stare past him at the stretch of foaming wake and the dark waves beyond. The last glimmers of coastal lights are just blinking into oblivion. It soothes me—I prefer the unbroken blackness of sea and sky.

He tries to goad me. "I do realize that you imagine yourself to have been in love with the creature," he calls to me. "I suppose all women like the idea of defrocking an instrument of God. Did you fantasize about being some biblical figure when you were fucking—the great whore of Babylon, Delilah castrating Samson? Maybe Eve with her wicked slice of fruit?"

I continue to stare past him. The crests breaking against the hull become choppy, and the gusts whimsical, so he has his hands full for a while. I can tell, from the way he twists the ropes and brings the sail round, that his arms are quite strong. Strong or weak, I will take him.

"Like that Neva creature," he throws over his shoulder. "D'Amante would have cut off her tits if he'd imagined she was straying, but still she couldn't resist seducing Simon. It's got to be something about corrupting the devoted—proving that your vagina has more authority than God. It's a battle easily won. I mean, who among us can stave off a horny teenage slut?"

I talk in spite of myself. "You know less than nothing."

He sneers happily, encouraged by my foolish words. "Not quite. Infiltrated the empty flat above Simon's, you see, and it was a simple matter of removing a bit of flooring to allow myself to watch you through those antiquated ceiling fixtures. You know, technically it was rape, the way you fucked him without his consent. Don't think I'm censuring you—he certainly turned out a willing subject when you decided to try him out awake."

I give him a glance of disgust. "You would lie there, face pressed to the mouse dung, watching others live their lives? You are one to cast the disparagements."

He smiles, but I can see I have cut him. "There's a device they call a spy cam, love. Quite reliable these days if you're willing to go top of the line. Little devils work in the dark and record only when there's action. Anyway, don't worry your pretty head about my life. I've been a busy boy between our little dates with death."

"Our dates?" I do not want to engage, but I cannot help myself. "You imagine you have a kinship with me because you watch me kill?"

He chuckles, focusing on sailing for a bit. "I'll give you D'Amante," he calls over to me. "Wasn't even there for that. The rest were mine, from Becker to Love."

I turn my head away. If he could read me, I would have welcomed him into my head to hear what I thought about him. But Brewster is only psychotic. He has no other talents.

"My dear, don't pout—it isn't becoming, as Mother always reminds me," he calls over the noise of the sail. "You simply hadn't the strength to tip Elliot, and that stuff you used on Rocco—well, you saw how it worked on Simon. And, sweetness, velour bedding is fire resistant these days. As for Simon himself, shall we be kind and say I beat you to it?" His tone takes on a mocking quality. "Or were you truly giving it all up?"

I plan my answer. "I knew what I was doing," I say.

"You're saying you were aware that I was closing in? I doubt that."

"He is dead, is he not?"

"Good girl," he says approvingly. "You're a credit to Moreau."

I glance sharply at him and he gestures grandly. "You must remember that I saw you tie off the scarf that night we were both stalking Becker." He kisses the air in my direction, then winks. "Of course it didn't hurt that I happened to notice the film in your little stack of unshelved videos when I called on Jakey. Don't worry—I tidied up. We needed to keep the cops guessing. The lady detective in particular seems like a lot of fun when it comes to mental chess."

I shrug. "I care nothing about the chess. And whether you follow me about adding your foolish touches to my crimes means nothing to me."

"Your botched crimes," he calls through a wind gust. "I complete you, darling."

"My ears are deaf to your claims."

He shakes his head as if marveling. "So inimitably cool, you are. And that deadpan sexuality, no matter where, no matter what. You know, if we spend much more time together, I really may start to believe that you are Jeanne Moreau."

We don't speak for a while. It starts to rain, softly, and then it abates. I watch the drops as they cease pattering upon the soft black swells. After that I go into a trance of sorts, not quite sleeping, but numb to the world. I cannot say how long this lasts.

"Look out there, my sweet," he says eventually. "The little dark mass off the bow is Muskeget. Off that way is Tuckernuck, and then we're home. Of course, we'll need to circle round, so sit tight—the cuts are tricky. Can't wait until you see The Old Lady, though. I can tell you're a woman who appreciates a place for its bones."

I sit watching as the dark island creeps along the horizon. The sails snap and rattle, and the hull groans gently as Brewster turns us into the current. I can hear, off somewhere, a steady thump, immersed within the wind, as if someone beats a tom-tom against the sky. A helicopter, I think. Surreptitiously, I finger the tiny purse in my lap, where it sits amid the frozen velvet of my dress.

Later, we walk along the beach in the driving rain from where he has anchored the sailboat. Behind us somewhere in the dark sits his little rubber dinghy with its hollow metal paddles. He enjoys the drenching surf. He enjoys the dead expanse of beach, the wind and the crackle of dismembered crabs beneath our feet. The sand is hard as stone, but I stop to remove my heels and allow the bits of crust and claw to pinch and pierce my soles.

"Nature is a cruel parent," he says. "She beats at us out of spite."

The cliff rises two hundred feet or more from beach to crest, where I can discern blowing reeds and the tops of wind-whipped trees and the occasional peak of a shingled roof against the night sky. Thunder rumbles and rain ripples in the gusts. This is a strange place.

"Come, my sweet," Brewster bellows, cupping his hand to his mouth. "These are the final remaining cliff steps, just beyond the sandbags."

The rough wooden stairs up are precarious at best. He recommends against relying on the handrail, and so we feel our way with feet only, eyes closed against the wind. The steps number in the hundreds. I am calm inside. I am as patient about nearing my goal as he is exhilarated to be nearing his. He reaches the top and turns to offer a hand and assist me up the final stairs. They say breeding is innate and I suppose they may be right. I feel safer, touching his bare hand with my glove, than I would if we had gone skin against skin. I do not want a vision of how he plans to kill me. I want my mind clear of him.

We rise above the cliff's edge behind a tidy cottage that's shuttered for the season. It sits far back from the cliff's edge, with plenty of foliage between it and us. We walk across the kempt grasses toward the snarl of scrub bushes that divide us from the next property, and proceed this way, lawn after lawn, for some little while. The expanse of grass diminishes from house to house, and likewise the foliage become increasingly spare and rough. Finally, we duck under the limbs of a heavily gnarled scrub pine, and Brewster catches my arm to make sure I do not step too far to the right. I look down and see the steep, naked cliff beside me.

He then leans into the wind, waving over his shoulder for me to follow. I clutch my shawl to my neck as we cross the unruly patch of land yet intact behind the Van Ness place. The house looms, only twenty yards from the cliff's edge. Just down from where we ducked through the bushes a wooden outbuilding, perhaps a shed or an old workshop, hangs partially off the edge of the cliff, its back end broken and jagged, its front intact but for a few sagging shingles. The shed door shudders and flaps and occasionally bangs closed, then shudders and flaps again.

"The Old Lady," Brewster bellows, gesturing a welcome as he backs across the whipping saw grass toward the porch. "Watch out for the trench."

The house is black from the rain, but I can see from the drier part under the porch roof that it is a battered grey cedar shingled structure, its fanciful trim once painted a yellowy shade of green. It appears to be Victorian in style, or Gothic—perhaps a daring entwining of the two—with tall narrow windows and numerous gables from which heavily decorated dormers steeple against the approaching dawn sky. Several pieces of heavy digging equipment sit on the landward side of the place, still as resting beasts, and from the mounds of soil and sand peppered with wind-flattened tufts of grass, it appears that workers have been excavating the earth from around the foundation.

Brewster leads me onto the porch, then uses a shoulder to wrench one of the French doors open. "*Après vous, Madamoiselle,*" he says to me.

I step past him and into the house.

THIRTY-FOUR

Marina Papanikitas's Personal Journal

Pretty drained all around, Zoey. Arrived on the island about an hour before dawn, just as the big drops start to splash down. This was my first helicopter ride, and although it was pretty smooth and quick, I was real content to be touching rock again. We're on the hospital grounds, like right out front on the lawn in a little square of amber footlights, and as I duck and run I can see the sedan with its blue lights pulsing, rolling toward the pad. Harry's pilot friend hustles off toward the hospital with a couple of orderlies, and we go for the squad car. Harry bundles me in the back, then slams the front passenger door behind himself just in time for the rain to start coming down heavy duty. I watch it hit the parking lot with a rush that sends out a shuddering hiss.

"Did we miss Nantucket and wake up in the tropics?" Harry says.

Guy behind the wheel twists round as best he can—he's a big fellow—and smiles as he offers a hand. "We can call it a nor'easter around these parts, but it's the same damned thing," he says. "I'm Granger Hill, Chief of Police." He's about fifty, African-American, soft-spoken.

"Look at that, Pop—picked up by the man himself."

"You think I'm not going to be in the middle of this shit?" he laughs. There's a tiny photo of a happy-looking white woman and

295

two tiny brown-skinned boys taped to the center of the steering wheel, and he notices me eyeing it. "That's my on-the-job cue card," he says. "Keeps me from doing things any more stupid than necessary."

I nod. "I'm sure it works."

"Like to think it does," he assures me.

He turns the car and starts wheeling down the hospital drive. "So am I heading to headquarters where we can talk about this with some of my guys, or are we in more of a hurry than that? Van Ness place is out on the east end of the island, and we're about in the middle now. Talking nine miles. No such thing as traffic here this time of year, so it'll take us ten minutes."

Harry looks at me. "Pop, got a sense of timing?"

I feel myself blush, reminded of what we're relying on as our basis for being here. "We want to be there while it's dark and the rain's still coming down," I say. "Better head straight out. If we're early, we'll sit tight. After we talk, you can call your guys and explain what kind of back-up we're looking for."

"Can do." Granger doesn't seem at all puzzled by my answer—kind of weird to be with two men who come off as utterly down to earth but apparently have no problem with the idea of operating off of someone's psychic vision. He turns out of the hospital lot into a rain-swept roadway lined with ragged masses of stunted, pale-leaved trees. The sandy soil merges with the blacktop, giving the whole place a soft, wild feel. "What are we looking to find?" he asks.

Harry gives me a glance over the back of the seat, deferring.

"Look, I don't know how tight you are with the Van Ness clan," I say, "but we may have a situation on our hands with Brewster—that's the former Bruno Myeroff."

He absorbs this. "Yolanda seemed like a nice enough lady, few times I met her," he says. "But from what I hear, I'm not sure she was up to dealing with that son of hers. Don't think there'd be many old timers around here who'd be surprised to learn that the boy grew up to have some mighty serious issues. Father was considered a feisty one. Couple of famous stories, not the least of which was his refusal to touch the Van Ness place after his son got himself in trouble one too many times. Understand that most of what I could tell you, I myself came by second-hand. Been Chief out here coming on five years."

"The permanent newcomer," Harry remarks.

"That's the stuff," the Chief agrees. "Island's always a unique kind of community."

I resume, encouraged. "Our suspicion is that Brewster may be heading for the 'Sconset house with a hostage. He may have murdered one or more people back in Boston. Most recent vic died last night on a sidewalk in Cambridge. Vic before him was Brewster's own assistant, and that one, we think, was just to throw us."

"Am I to understand that my old friend Wilkie Morley is among the victims?"

"There's a possibility that Morley's death is part of this, yes," I admit.

"Who's the hostage? Anyone we know?"

"The woman we suspect that Brewster has with him is Agnès Rossignol. She may also have been involved in one or more of the deaths, so it's probably safest for us to presume that they're both armed and dangerous, but not working in collaboration."

"Armed with what?"

I sigh. "We know very little. A witness said that the woman was armed with a pistol. And the last man that one or the other may have killed appears to have been shot with a crossbow."

He glances sideways to see if I'm kidding. Then he chuckles. "My, my, my," he says.

'Sconset, turns out, is a swank little colony set up in isolation out on the eastern tip of the island. Drive out there is about seven miles of straight, brush-lined macadam, and you barely see a light the whole way. Then suddenly you're slowing to twenty and watching the sweet fences and lawns go by as the pillared summer mansions peek at you from between the rows of fat maples. All of the houses are dark, as is the tiny post office. The shingled village-style grocery stop is boarded for the season, and no cars line the tiny roundabout marking the community's center. The rain has abated a bit, and dawn shows signs of drifting in, so we can see up a few lanes. A bunch of tiny, trellis-covered fishing shacks seem battened down. Remind me, Zoey, when I finally get around to writing that slasher screenplay we like to joke about—I need to set it in 'Sconset in the off-season. We're talking spooky oo-key.

"Let's take the ocean view," says Granger. He punches out his lights, and we coast down a long sandy road in the dark. Ahead is the beach—even on a night like this I can easily make out the breakers, throwing their weight against the grey sand. Granger turns the car, and we travel parallel to the beach for a while. There's a smattering of cottages down here below the main village. One and all are dark.

He stops the car and heaves himself out. Harry and I join him. Guy is about six foot four, turns out. Makes even Harry look kind of grounded. As if to emphasize it, Granger hoists himself up onto the cement seawall that sits between the dunes and the road. He stretches himself up tall and peers through some massive-looking binoculars. Harry and I stand below in the wind, watching him. Bunch of icy sand suddenly smacks me in the eye. "Son of a fucking bitch," I mutter.

"Night goggles?" Harry calls up to Granger, ignoring me.

"Oh yeah," he assures us. His quiet voice disappears practically as it comes out of his mouth. "We got us a sailboat," I think I hear him saying. "Take a look?"

Harry goes to climb up, then thinks better and laces his fingers together. "Use a boost?"

I go to stick my foot on his hands, and he takes a moment to wink in my face. "The old premmie comes through, eh, Pop?" he says, just for me to hear. "Not that I had doubts, but…" He blows his cheeks out in relief.

I lean on his shoulder, preparing to hoist myself up to the sea wall. "Plenty of space for doubting this shit," I assure him. "Trust me."

Up next to Granger, I teeter around, reluctant to grab onto him. Fortunately he's less reserved, and he grips the shoulder of my trench with his fist and yanks me over so I'm leaning against him. The dunes are just below us in front, although the drop back to where Harry stands is five feet. Somehow it lends me a sense of balance to have sand grasses blowing against my ankles, so soon I get my legs and can take the binoculars Granger offers. I train them down the beach and out over the water to where he's pointing.

Amazing what they've done with night goggles. I've sampled the green glow type that make everything look all sci fi. These deluxe babies Granger is sporting give you more of a real life day glow around your subject. Still got the tint, but just barely. I find myself gazing down a long, wildly desolate stretch of beach. Lots of grassy patches, and even some gnarly growths that might be tree-like when they're not underwater. The cliff starts gradually, with lots of tough looking viney vegetation holding together a gentle slope. Dark houses nestle at the top, chimneys poking skyward. Further away, the situation changes radically. The vegetation patches disappear and the cliff becomes a vertical wall of sand that dwarfs any bits of grass or tree that dare to crouch at base or zenith. Several houses, probably lofty structures from another angle, seem to cringe away from the edge, dark because they dare not peek at the fate that seems pretty damned inevitable—strangely, it's the fact that these cliffs are pure sand, and so must erode, that gives them their terrible aura of power.

Granger guides me a little by moving my shoulder, and I look out over the water more. The waves are small and choppy and seem to move with no flow or pattern. Out there looking very small is a boat—probably a forty-footer with a mast up around forty-five feet from the water. The hull is white, undoubtedly fiberglass, and the trim and interior seem to be covered in wood siding. Definitely a schooner. No sign of life aboard. No way of telling how long the thing had been there, although how long could a lone boat hang out off the coast of the island without someone taking note? Just before I move the glasses along, I catch a glimpse of the name painted on the hull: starts with a "J." As in *Jane Guy*. We're on.

I play the glasses back over the water, the beach, up the cliff. The rain begins coming down in earnest. Granger pokes me to signal that he's going, then jumps down behind me. I go to follow, but just before I lower the glasses, I hear this voice. Seems distant, exactly like it's someone yelling at me through a heavy wind, but I don't know, Zoey; I mean, it might have just been in my head.

She calls out *"Vous me donnez la force pour continuer."*

I jump down a lot more nimbly than I would have if I'd been thinking, and race for the car. Hop in and slam the door hard. The guys are just settling in the front. They turn at the amount of bang I make. Both of them give me a bit of a study, each in his own way. I busy myself hiding my face by running my hands through my hair, spraying water about.

"Eerie night, all around," says Granger kind of carefully.

"Damned straight," I reply. In spite of all efforts, my voice comes out about a half-octave above normal range.

"Ready to head up there?" he says.

"Ready, Chief," I say perkily. "Good to know they'll be there."

"That's affirmative," agrees Harry.

I just nod, finished trying to talk for the moment. Granger hesitates as if he wants to say something, then thinks better of it and starts the car.

THIRTY-FIVE

I am Nightingale—
    "Cigarette?"
    "I will."

I take the cigarette with my wet gloved hand and allow him to ignite it, then sit back. He has lit a few candles and placed them about the room strategically, so as to avoid the occasional gusts that sweep down the stairwell from a broken upstairs window. The house is only semi-furnished as workmen prepare for its relocation, but Brewster acts pleased to find that they have heeded his instructions to refrain from touching the living room and, he reports, a small first floor bedroom, so that he may spend the occasional night here as the time draws near. Thus, the scene is quite strange, with the lovely threadbare rug and worn silk-covered settee and matching armchairs, along with a delicate table or two and a rather massive glass-fronted sideboard, surrounded by dusty floors covered in brown paper, boarded windows and dangling wall fixtures. He taps his cigarette ash like a 1940s swell, explaining all this.

Brewster has offered me a towel to dry myself and has used another for himself. Both of us have limited our ministrations to our faces and hair, and neither seems bothered in the least to be sitting in the chilly room clad in our sopping clothes. Brewster comes through from the bedroom, which appears to be beyond a dark kitchen, carrying a dusty bottle of bourbon and two glasses. He seems quite cheery about this find, and pours liberal drinks for both of us. I touch mine to my lips as a gesture, familiar as I am with poison, then place it aside. We smoke in silence for a while, rather companionably, considering the circumstances. He drinks liberally, perhaps to prove that the stuff is not laced. But one cannot be overly cautious.

"Now, you do understand that I've brought you here to kill you?" he says in a civil tone.

"This is clear to me, of course," I reply.

"Yes, well, nothing personal, but it's quite a decent little set-up you've provided for me. Once the police finally figured out you were after me and you made your move to get me alone in the warehouse, I staged my phony attack in which you did this." He points to his facial wound. "Now you'll have followed me here to finish the job, determined little viper that you are. I'll overpower you. You'll die. Poof! All the murders solved."

"Yes, and in the interim you kill your partner to pretend I am surprised by him," I say. "But maybe you want him dead, too, huh?"

Brewster eyes me over his glass as he drinks, then sits up and wipes him mouth with his knuckles. "Partner," he says petulantly. "My father was in favor of turning the business over to the little mouse and letting him run it solo. A plan designed to torment me, of course, but Armand was all for it. So he got nothing he didn't earn." He gestures around us at the ruined house. "Mother talked Dad into making Armand and I partners, playing up the fact that a Van Ness should be at least partially at the helm of Van Ness Collectibles. Good of her. Still, I think once the old man died she should have forced the usurper out, don't you? A family business ought to be run by family."

Not waiting for an answer, he hops up, apparently having noticed a flicker of headlights through a slice of exposed window out by the front door. He creeps out there and peers round the edge of the plywood. "Oh, the Carlton lady," he says, half to himself. "The old buzzard must be about to move into town for winter. Bit late this year. Good for her for holding out."

He returns and eyeballs me as he heads for the bottle. "Shouldn't you be begging for you life?" He throws himself roguishly across the settee and waits, ankles crossed.

I shrug. "I have nothing to say. In the end you may be found out for your crimes and I may be found out for mine. It is a likely eventuality, I think, yes?"

He absorbs this, then throws his head back and belts out a loud laugh. "You are really so fucking deliciously cold-blooded. Even about yourself," he says. "You know, if I could trust you, I might actually be tempted to try and devise some way to let us both live on, trading murders like two old club cronies. We could—oh, I don't know—frame old Mrs. Carlton down the way? What do you say—beg me just a wee bit?"

I gaze across at him. "You owe me nothing. I am certain of that."

He sits up, snapping a finger. "But of course I do owe you, modest thing. Your killing D'Amante is what launched everything."

I scoff. "I have already told you that I did not kill him."

"Don't be tiresome." He smokes. "You know, that man represented a serious threat to me and mine. I mean, our settlement with the Culligans and the Commonwealth had absolutely no bearing on the fact that D'Amante was already bound to be handed over to serve time for the multiple sins of his past, but I'm sure he was far too intellectually crude to see it that way. No, he'd been stewing in his own diseased testosterone for eight years, blaming my family money and his skin color for the fact that he was the only one of the Five who saw time. One skillfully administered bullet to the skull, and the D'Amante problem was resolved. So kudos to you." He rises and crosses to where he's left the bottle and pours for himself, then turns. "And you know, far more importantly than removing D'Amante as a threat, what you did by killing him was to awaken in me my own resolve to tidy up my life's loose ends." He gestures. "What do you think my reaction was, when I first read about D'Amante's death? Do you think it was relief? Wonder? Simple joy? What do you think?"

I know his reaction, of course, because it was mine as well. What was awakened in me was awakened in him as well—for far different reason, however. I say, "I will not guess."

He doesn't care. His asking was but a flourish. "My first reaction was jealousy! Jealousy that I hadn't pulled that trigger. And that is when it occurred to me that deep down I so very, very, very much wanted to obliterate Elliot Becker. I began tailing him, a tad on edge at first about being spotted, but then he and I went face to face a few times, and I realized that I was too unimportant for a self-absorbed prick like him to recognize." He laughs and cocks his head at me. "You must have had the same thought when he didn't recognize you."

I shake my head. "I did not expect him to remember me."

"But he hired you in the first place, for the trial."

I shrug. "I was nothing. A courtroom prop. Why would he focus on me?"

He eyes me steadily for a while. "Well, I knew you. Never really paid attention to you during the trial—as you say, what were you to me? But I realized something was up when he trailed you out of The Underground that night, and I made you while you were with him on that roof deck. You have a way of staring at nothing when you're concentrating—your eyes go cloudy and your jaw goes a bit slack—and I got a flash memory of you checking Culligan's tubes during the trial. Interesting twist for me, by the way, watching from that ballroom while you angled in on my murder for me."

"So you admit I did my own killing?" I say, slicing him a look from under my eyelids.

"You failed," he assures me. "Don't worry, as the deed was yours, morally. But I stepped in and tipped him when you blacked out. Imagine his surprise, with you in a heap below—heaving himself back onto the safe side of the rail, already beginning to breathe down, when yet another righteous avenger attacks from out of nowhere! No, my dear, Becker was my murder. Petrianni and Morley—well, who knows what that gut-dissolving crap you fed them would have eventually done, but each was alive when I entered to tidy up after you."

"And why this level of hatred for your own lawyer?" I ask, knowing.

He sniffs. "His maneuverings came between me and my father. Do you know how much money he siphoned off my family alone?"

I wave it away. "You said yourself that you hated your father."

"Why should Becker benefit from that? Besides, the fact that I hated my father, and had for years, didn't mean that the old man hated me back, now, did it? Becker's deal made it mutual. And once he hated me, Pa became very cheap. You know he intended to write me out of my inheritance? I mean completely!"

"Ah, so why not kill him too?" I say offhandedly.

He studies me. "I would have if I'd had the time to work it out. Cancer got him first."

"So," I say. "What was this plan to bring down Elliot Becker, as you put it?"

He brightens up, back on track. "We knew he'd been abusing the trust for years and had arm-twisted his way into a lot of other goodies involving state or private funds. You know how they have all these charitable trusts for nonsense like charter schools and green energy. People owed him for defusing Dorchester, but they wouldn't remain grateful if they were publically embarrassed for putting so much dough under the care of this obvious shyster. You launch one ethics board complaint and with a few deft tips to a few sleazy pols about similar set-ups involving sizable pots of money, some of them fairly sacred, well, pretty soon it all comes out, one leak after another. All we had to do with file for an accounting of our own trust.

"Pa wouldn't hear of it. Thought he'd come off as the petty Jew he was. After Pa did the decent thing and died, however, the path forward was simple. I simply had to eliminate that bathetic commemoration Becker had set up to his betrayal of my family by terminating the support needs of the beneficiary." He eyes himself in the dusty mirror, then takes a small comb out of his breast pocket to smooth his hair back. He studies his stitches for a long moment, then turns to me, suddenly aware of what he's glimpsed in reflection. He smiles, seeing the gun I've taken from my purse, then gives me a look like I've been sneaky in an amusing way. "Yes, I thought you might have caught that little slip on my part while we were sailing," he says. "I did, in fact, make note of your film collection while in the process of smothering the heir apparent of the Culligan fortune. The Beast to your Beauty, the Caliban to your Ariel, your brain-damaged half-brother and lover."

I stand, the gun on him. "You have a plan. I have a plan. We each carry them to this point. The difference is you harbor a delusion that you will escape."

He backs up a step, raising his hands like in the old movies. "Doll-face, I just love you when you're cold as ice."

"Perhaps I like you that way as well." I lift the gun.

"Now look," he says, eyes on the gun. "Be logical. I needed Jakey dead to launch the trust accounting. And you have to admit, his life was rather repetitive. What's another half century of the same old routine when you can't remember a day as it passes?"

"He was aware," I say.

He makes a face like he doubts that. "Well, then I was mistaken, and for that I'm deeply regretful." He raises his eyebrows, as if this apology should satisfy me. "Look, if it's any consolation, let's remember that he really did have it coming." I say nothing. "Oh, come now, sweetness. I assume that at some point during the trial you caught onto the fact that he'd hit the old biddy on purpose?"

In spite of myself, I listen. The gun, still aimed at him, lowers to my waist. He laughs.

"New perspective? Yes, granny was out to drive the wicked drug-dealers from her neighborhood, but the Culligan boys were equally determined to resist. She knew the car, but she didn't know that it was Jakey behind the wheel—impetuous young cub, out to prove his manhood and thus even more dangerous than his animal of a brother. The old lady flags him down and he takes her out like he's bowling candlepins."

"You know this?" I scoff.

"Everyone knew it. You saw him jerk the car at her in the video, didn't you?"

"Then why did it not come out in the courtroom? Would it not have justified the crowd's reaction all the more?"

He chuckles. "But darling, we were all out to prove that the car got flipped by accident. The more justified the violence, the more retaliatory our actions. And Jakey could have flatlined at any time during that trial. For a while it seems quite likely, matter of fact. No one wanted to be in a position to have to rely on a justified homicide defense. No, no—much better to keep it simple—assault without reason, mob sympathy for granny, that sort of nonsense."

"So you all lie," I say.

He smiles at me sympathetically. "Gosh, does it bring you down to have done so very much for a soulless little monster who deserved everything he got and then some?"

"That makes no difference to me," I say, raising the gun.

He sips his drink. "Mmm, but it does," he says with assurance. "And do you know what? I'm beginning to believe you when you say you didn't kill D'Amante. I don't think you're really able to shoot that thing."

"Do not trouble your mind about that," I say, pulling back on the safety.

"No, it wasn't you," he muses aloud. "After all, it doesn't fit into your artistic theme. In fact, I think you were inspired to action by that killing, just as I was. I think we're a couple of vigilante birds of a feather, you and me." He snaps a finger. "The girlfriend did it. Neva herself. You know how resourceful those welfare mothers can be when protecting their whelps. Neva wouldn't have had to follow D'Amante around or known exactly when he was being released. Just have the gun ready, come out into the vestibule when he buzzes, get your hand up behind his head—a welcome home smooch, easy to pull off—and let him have it." He smiles across at me. "Maybe we could all learn a lesson from Neva. Simple is best."

It happens all at once, then. Brewster springs across at me, going for the gun in my hand. The kitchen door kicks in, and a male voice yells at us to freeze as another man kicks the front door out of his way. Behind me, I hear one of the porch doors crash to the wall, its glass shattering. The candles are snuffed by the cross breeze. One falls over, igniting a lace runner, which flares up the wall against the old peeling paper.

I shoot Brewster. I like to think that I shoot with conviction but I cannot say this in honesty. I do not know where I hit him, but he rams his body into mine, still aiming for the gun in my hand. He rips it away from me, and I am flung backwards quite hard. My skull smashes into a person's face, someone who seems to slip on broken glass and fall to the boards. The cops—more than two of them now—are yelling at all of us to get down, but they are focused on Brewster, who is on his knees, holding my gun and his own gut. I continue stumbling backwards over the legs of the female cop, and finally fall out onto the covered porch. I twist over and climb to my feet, then run into the rain. I see the sun beginning to emerge—white, eldritch, swollen, it raises itself slowly over the edge of the blackened sea, a great cold leviathan peering out of its lair.

I have no thoughts of escape. Freedom is not a priority. I am not afraid of death, either. I want to finish my task, and for that life is essential for the moment. What I seek is a mere shaving of time, a shiver of space, in which to regroup. That is my earnest need. That is my motive in merging into the rain and the grey of this dawn—I hide among the elements.

I hide still. But soon I will emerge again, never you worry. I have not yet had my fifth.

Très sincèrement,
Nightingale

THIRTY-SIX

Marina Papanikitas's Personal Journal

Excuse the abrupt hang-up, Zoey. Had to see a doctor about some glass in my hand and a broken nose. Not to worry unduly. Talking about a lot of "owwie" and not much damage. When my nose swells, I'll be plenty pissed—count on it. Right now I'm kind of marveling at how the whack I took actually seems to have straightened the thing.

But to reality. It is true that I am still groveling with thanks before whatever great god of fate there is who allowed my half-baked premmie and even more convoluted vishie to actually get me to the right place at the right time to prevent a capital crime and solve a handful of others. Too bad three experienced detectives and a swarm of back-ups utterly effed up one of the arrests. I'm almost ready to tell you that forces beyond common understanding came between us and our quarry. But that'll just be between you and me, Zoey. And H.P., in a backhanded way. To Super Jack, it comes off as botched. Still, he's satisfied. Claire Morley's off his sassy ass now that Brewster/Bruno is going to be formally charged with her husband's murder.

I think it's Granger who comes up with the plan that we coast by the Van Ness place and then pull into a neighbor's driveway.

This is an elderly year-rounder who stays out in 'Sconset every fall until her relatives fly over and force her to shift her bones over to an in-town residence for winter, where they claim she's safer, and she complains that there's nowhere for the puggies to romp. Granger's idea is that Brewster will see the light and assume the old lady's holding out. The effect will be to slacken his attention to every creak and crackle he may hear from outside. Life's just playing itself out when the Carltons are prying old Lillian from the face of the cliff in mid-October. Plus it gives us a chance to shine Granger's headlights on the Van Ness property and get the lay of the land. Apparently they're well into the process of digging up the foundation, so the land's literally got its own new lay every day.

Granger calls for backup, making himself nice and clear about how invisible every single one of us needs to be. Soon we three wet cops are wheeling on over to the semi-deserted cliff neighborhood—picture maybe a half-mile square of classic weathered summer mansions, showing themselves in brief pulses provided by the rotating gleam from the lighthouse that marks the tallest point on the bluff, some fifty feet beyond the last of the doomed residences constructed right up against the cliff. Tires crunching on the shelly streets, we get our oh-so-brief-and-hazy study of the Van Ness place. Talking about a haunted wreck of what was once a period summer estate, with stables out by the road, some funky connecting out-buildings and the ghost of a vast kitchen garden running behind, and then the multi-chimney four-story Victorian rising high against the windy sky. Can't help feeling a thrill of resentment against old man Myeroff myself for letting the place start to fall in on itself. Spite's a nasty motivator.

We mark where the excavation ditches are, as well as the scattered piles of earth and deserted equipment—not cool to trip over a backhoe—and then move along to park at the tidy antique saltbox down the street. Granger's got a plan of the layout that he picked up from the house moving crew's foreman. He passes it round, warning us that the place is in the kind of shape where every floorboard, door hinge, and windowpane could give way on very little provocation. We decide to let Granger take the front entry, as he's the biggest and thus less adept at sneaking about noiselessly while also pretty confident about getting results when he applies a shoulder to a slab of bolted oak. Harry opts for the servants' entrance, where we understand the door is broken—he's light on his feet and thus stands a decent chance of getting the gist of what's going on inside before anyone in there detects his presence. This leaves the French doors to the veranda around on the cliff side for me. Scratch the surface, Zoey, and you'll catch that all of this means I'm the weakest link. Well, the cliff side's bound to be wild and woolly, so good thing I'm not fussy about my hair. The backup cops know to hang behind and wait for Granger's signal. Our jump strategy is to let H.P. take the lead. He'll be in the best position to hear and see what's going on. When he blasts in on them, the idea is for Granger and me to make it a 3-D surprise party, just before the rest of the force swarms.

Works pretty darn well, as far as the set-up goes. I pick my way through the mud without losing a shoe. At one point, I crouch under a window and listen to some occasional loud banging until I'm quite sure that there's a random sort of repetitiveness to it, making it nothing more than a loose door or shutter out back. When I peer round the corner of the place, it's reassuring to see that we've guessed right. Someone's lit some candles in the main room that looks out over the cliff-top veranda. A couple of the windows are boarded over, but a vivid glow comes through the French doors. I study the expanse of planks that makes up what's left of the veranda—not much you can tell about the condition of the wood with the amount of dust and blown sand strewn across it, but then I see the wet path that must have been cut by the two inside. Naturally, the boards may creak if I follow the soggy prints, but at least I won't go through and find myself trying to flash my badge and command some respect with one of my legs three feet shorter than the other.

I creep up to porch level, pausing a lot but feeling pretty covered by the noise of the rain and the endlessly banging door somewhere behind me. From the wet trail, looks like Agnès walked in there in her stocking feet while Brewster's in canvas shoes with grooved soles. I work myself forward at a near crouch, my service revolver out and ready. When I get about five feet from the French doors, I can hear their voices. Brewster is saying, "the Beast to your Beauty, the Caliban to your Ariel…" Sheesh.

Then I see Agnès. She's been sitting in a chair with her back to me, but she suddenly stands. I see her hair, plastered against her skull, and a vivid flowered shawl that she holds tight round her shoulders. She says something like, "you harbor the delusion that you will escape." Her voice is low, her intonation even and unaffected, her accent faint, but definitely French. It occurs to me from the way she carries her back and arm that she may be holding a gun on Brewster. I also occurs to me that she must be facing Harry, and if I know H.P., he's figured out a way to get a gander at the scene in front of him. If it is a gun she's holding, Harry will have the best take on whether and when she might decide to use it.

They exchange barbs for a while. I can't catch a lot of it—too much wind. At one point, Brewster raises his voice, and I catch some stuff about Neva having killed Terence D'Amante. Can't say this hadn't occurred to me, but it's not why we're there, so I park it in the back of my mind. Finally, he says, "Simple is best." Harry must realize it's time to move. The swinging door some yards behind Brewster gets kicked hard. I'm ready to spring, and I do. And that's exactly when the French doors fly open and slam me in the face. Mother *effing* wind. Nature's just totally with Agnès and against me tonight.

I recover, more or less, and propel myself around the door and into the room, yelling for everyone to freeze. I hear Harry and Granger yelling as well, and someone's gun goes off once, which doesn't stop any of the yelling, so it comes off as more random than deadly. Can't see, of course, because the gust killed the candles, but one of those suckers must have fallen over because there's a sudden flare-up by the back wall. I'm down low, of course, and manage to look up in time to see Agnès backing into me, fast. If she had a gun a moment ago, she doesn't have one now. I go to stand, hoping to catch her as she falls, but it's all too slippery, and her skull cracks me in the face. We ricochet off one another, and I sprawl in a bunch of broken glass from when the French doors blew, while she kind of cascades out onto the porch. I scramble after her, leaving the men to handle Brewster and the fire. I'd have sworn that Agnès would be splayed on her back across the porch, feet on my side of the doorsill, but she's nowhere. I stare at the spot where she should, by all laws of physics, be lying. The dust isn't even unsettled, except where my own scrabbling footprints made a mess. I stumble outside and stand, baffled by the rain and wind. Then I see her. She's not running. She's out there, facing me, her arms wrapped around her, her back to the cliff. The shawl flaps and snaps in the wind. There's a grey-white glow, just beginning to tint the skyline behind her. Soon she'll be in silhouette; right now I can just make out her face.

"Agnès," I yell.

She seems to be waiting for me.

"Agnès, you'll want to come away from the edge," I yell. "Ground's not stable." I step forward, bending at the knees to slide my gun aside very visibly so she can see I'm unarmed. "We need to talk, you and me."

She reaches up and takes a swipe at her eyes, as if clearing her lashes of rain. "Some day," she says.

"Agnès, I get that you didn't kill them," I call out to her. "Brewster was trailing you all along. They've got him, inside."

She looks off into the sky, maybe distracted by the distant pulse of yellow from the lighthouse, maybe considering my words. "I killed them," she says.

"Trying isn't the same thing as doing it—not to us law and order folk."

She whips her head across and looks off in the other direction. I realize, somehow, that I'm actually insulting her, or agitating her, anyway. "They are dead," she insists.

"Yeah, they're dead," I yell across in agreement. "Like you needed."

She looks directly at me in an odd piercing way. "So you know. You read it in my head?"

Involuntarily, I duck and shield my forehead with a hand. "Hey, no, don't," I yell. She hasn't, or at least I can't feel anything like what I went through back at Simon's place. I look up at her, and she's staring across at me through the rain. Her mouth is open. She looks far more curious than hostile.

"Look, it hurt like hell when you did that. I would ask that you not," I say. Of course, I'm begging, here—not too cop-like, all told—but I try to sound authoritative.

"It does not hurt the men," she says simply. "They feel nothing."

"Yeah, well, stick to poking them in the brain, then," I say. "And to answer your question, no, I didn't read anything in your mind. I don't do that. I don't even know how that would work." I step off the porch, blinking in the rain.

She almost smiles. "I think that maybe you do."

"I don't," I insist. Then I relent, just a bit. "I never explored it. I don't want it."

She considers this and nods across at me. "Some day. When you have a reason."

I shake my head, and then, as she stares me down, I shrug. "Don't think so."

"I would as soon have done my own killings. You know that," she says.

"Yes, I do know," I say, stepping forward through the knee-high grass that seems to twist around my legs as if working frantically to obstruct my movements. "Love will do that, I know," I say over the wind. "But they're all dead now, and the last one will be in Walpole for many years, if only for murdering the man who worked for him. I can promise you that."

"*Donc il est fini.*"

314

I can't understand, but I get it. "Yeah, exactly. It's finished. So step away from the edge, would you, Agnès?"

"*Aucun plus de meurtre. Aucune plus de planification. Aucune plus de douleur.*"

"Right," I assure her, no idea how I get what she's saying. "All the deaths, all the scheming, plus all the pain. It's over, Agnès. Time to mourn. Let me help with that."

She eyes me, and I think I've got her. I can see her eyes in the light from behind me as the flames start to spread along the underside of the porch roof. "Please," I say. "Come in from the edge, and we can talk about it."

She looks into my eyes and almost smiles. "I will send to you a memoir of all of this. I will hide nothing, I promise. They will promote you, if that is what you want."

"I don't," I say honestly. "What I want is for you to reach out your hand and give it to me." I edge forward, holding out my arm to her, stretching my hand wide.

The sun, such that it is, begins to rise behind her, a vague spread of grey haze throbbing behind the rain. I sense more than see that she begins to lean away, shoulders first.

"Dammit, Agnès!" I say forcefully. "Don't do this!"

"I am not afraid," she assures me. "Do not search for me."

I lunge at her just as she allows herself to fall backwards off the edge. I slide through the grass and then find myself scrambling to put on the brakes, only stopping after I slither over the edge with a hoarse shriek to find myself gripping some ancient wood steps that seem to fritter out only a few yards down the cliff. If I'd seen myself on vid I probably would have caught something comical about it. I crawl back gingerly, and only stand when I'm a good foot from the edge. I can't see her body on the cliff's sand face.

Harry and I tramp the beach for well over an hour, joined by a bunch of Nantucket cops in uniform. The cliff rises like some apocalyptic thing, humbling in its disregard. We come across

Brewster's dinghy and watch as some of the cops clamber around on the *Jane Guy*, then signal to us that there's no sign of Agnès on the boat. We shine our lights into crevices and poke around down some vast manmade tunnel in the beach—an experimental tide return system, we learn later, constructed to retard the beach erosion. There is no possibility that anyone could have squirmed away through that thing. We walk a mile up the rocky sand until we are directly under the massive lighthouse and can stand and watch its rotating light weaken against the grey-white sky. The ocean breaks against the base of the cliff here. Passing beyond will be impossible for quite some time.

She should be dead, her body broken, heavy with sand that it collected in its violent tumble down the cliff just under the Van Ness place. There is no mark we can discern on the face of the cliff. No spot where a body could have hit and then, miraculously, raised itself to walk or swim away. We squint up at the back of the Van Ness shed, sagging down at us, and also the remnants of the cliff stairs, and so we can mark exactly the spot where she disappeared from my sight, between these two items. There is no question about it, Zoey. Agnès—Nightingale—is simply gone.

Eventually we do the unthinkable—we give up. We work with Granger to arrange for Brewster's transfer to Boston, where he will face murder charges even as he recovers from his nonvital flesh wound. Brewster should end up in Walpole for a good long time, but making that happen is not my jurisdiction. We add our names to the report on the fire that partially—nonvitally—destroyed the Van Ness place. I get some preliminary treatment for my nose. Another nonvital injury, although it doesn't feel all that non-any-thing. We accept the offer to hitch a ride back to Boston on the hospital shuttle helicopter. Every moment of that flight sucks. By the time we arrive at New England Medical, I thoroughly hate helicopters.

Harry gets me to my car in Cambridge—they take one look at my badge and then my face, and the gate rises with the charge of zero dollars and zero cents. I'm actually sincerely grateful to the point of near-mistiness. It's the small favors, huh?

I drive home. I clean up. I check my texts and there's one from Malloy: *Rossignol = Nightingale in French lang. So which name do I track?* I say a tiny prayer that he did not send that fun fact to H.P. as well, as he will not share my view that it may show a sliver of hope for Malloy. I turn off the phone and rest a little. Okay, I can't rest so I cry a few emo tears for no reason I can put my finger on. And then I write this journal entry. I can't even think about Agnès Rossignol…Nightingale…Jeanne Moreau's biggest fan.

And look who it is, trudging up the porch stairs and dumping her knives on the kitchen table, ducking to one side for a fruitless peek out into the living room and then doing a double-take at the sight of my bright white nose bandage.

Zoey, cripes. TODAY you decided to cut it baby short and go platinum with streaks? Are you, like, *trying* to give me a heart attack? Somehow I just earned myself a super-sized batch of much needed, much appreciated, much demanded and much returned home-style TLC. And when I say to stop, Zoey? Just keep the TLC coming. Keep that happy stuff coming.

Signing off.

THIRTY-SEVEN

Massachusetts Department of Correction, MCI – Cedar Junction
Division of Human Resources,
Food and Nutritional Services Program
South Walpole, Massachusetts

Dear Prison Food Services Program Manager,

I write in inquiry about employment in your food preparation and services operation, as I note a job posting in the employment opportunity section of your website. As my attached résumé indicates, I have worked in the prison food service industry for one year at this point, and am versed in the areas of cycle menu preparation, sanitation, inventory, tool control, and security, along with the more typical cafeteria work skills not particular to prison food service operations. I am a former long-term home health aide, and as such pride myself on being a clean, steady worker who believes in the virtue of providing domestic services for those in need. I keenly understand the key role that reliable, on-schedule food service plays in maintaining a healthy prison environment. As my current overseer so often observes, "a hungry inmate is a problem inmate, while one who is satisfied with his meals will consider himself treated with dignity—and dignity is the touch-stone of a healthy prison environment." I wholeheartedly agree with these sentiments. They are indeed a compact statement of my work philosophy.

As you will discern from that which precedes, my current position suits me well, but I am a single mother with a son of three months, and as I have family in the Boston area, I would like to relocate so as to allow young Simon to know his relatives as he grows up. Naturally, I am more than happy to provide specific references upon your request.

With every hope of hearing from you,

Jeanne M. Nightingale

ACKNOWLEDGMENTS

A number of people were incredibly generous with their time and creativity as I wrote and rewrote *The Dorchester Five*. My agent, John Silbersack of Trident Media Group, is the consummate literary world professional. My wife Deb spends countless hours working with me on how I might extract my poor characters from the labyrinthine burrows I manage to write them into. The top-notch people at Diversion Books, primarily Publisher Jaime Levine, Production and Art Director Sarah Masterson Hally, and Acquisitions Editor Lia Ottaviano, have all been encouraging, accommodating, practical, and patient during the entire publication process. My sister Nancy G., mother-in-law Kathryn "Mom-Cat" T., and great friend Allison D.—three insightful and articulate readers—all offered valuable advice and encouragement after reading early drafts of *The Dorchester Five*. Finally, I don't possess the facility with language to express my heartfelt thanks and appreciation to Randall Klein, author, editor, and founder of Randall Klein Books. Randall discovered this book years ago and remained dedicated to its achieving its potential and getting published until he made both happen. Randall's sensitivity to tone, plot, and all the subtle nuances that make a novel the best story it can be cannot be learned—it's a gift, and he uses it masterfully.

THE DISTANCE BETWEEN WHAT YOU SEE AND WHAT YOU BELIEVE CAN BE THE DISTANCE BETWEEN LIFE AND DEATH.

On a winter night in Boston, a man falls to his death in front of a subway train. The sole witness, a shaken young woman, explains to the police how the man shoved her aside as he made his way to the tracks. But when her blog turns up on the dead man's computer, the cops begin to look for other connections. Was the man a cyber-stalker, charmed to the point of desperation by the irreverent musings of a noir-obsessed blogger? Or are the connections between subway jumper and innocent bystander more complicated?

This dark and intricate tale of obsession and deception is told in the form of a blog written by an elusive narrator known only by her online name, "l.g. fickel." Deep into the night, every night, fickel blogs about "Mr. Suicide" and the ensuing police investigation with an eerie prescience. She is joined in her blog chats by a loyal group of obsessives, all of whom share with fickel a passion for the dark art of noir. Is fickel's tale that of an innocent woman frantically trying to figure out how her blogging has enmeshed her in a murder spree, or is she a manipulator, playing the part of sexy, hip, young thing as she grinds out her revenge on those she feels have betrayed her?